INTO TWILIGHT

Viceroy's Pride Book One

CALE PLAMANN

ACKNOWLEDGMENTS

First and foremost I need to acknowledge my wife who has tolerated my long nights of typing and gamely tried to read the results even when they were pretty rough. I need to thank my father for loving the dumb stories and home brew roleplaying campaigns I've been concocting since I was a kid and pushing me to make the leap to writing as well as my mother and sister for their constant support.

I need to thank the Brittingham Crew (Brian, Ben, Adam, and Sean) for pushing me into writing my first flawed, choppy, novels and sticking with me ever since.

I also need to thank the discord communities over at The Silver Pen, Bad Cat Hangout and LitRPG Forum for helping me storyboard, workshop, and most importantly keep my sanity throughout the writing process. Including but not limited to (in no particular order): Wolfe Locke, TheDude3445, Bri, Nulls, VeraAnne, Vowron, J. Pal, Traitorman, Origin, 4064, Fae/Kruos, NoDragons, MelasD, Vitaly, Necariin, Khend, Sam, Squirrel, Doom, and Fel.

I also want to acknowledge those who have been supportive and helpful in meatspace- Sarah, Liz, Jack, Eric, and Jerrie. I would also like to thank the support of Princess Charlotte, my cat. Sometimes, the perfect cure for writer's block is a small furry paw on the thigh demanding pets.

I would also like to thank everyone in the one creative writing class I took. Your collective advice was almost as terrible as your purple prose, but you inspired me to actually publish books to prove your dumb opinions wrong, so credit where credit is due.

Also- A big thank you to all of my supporters, but especially to Eli for being there since the beginning, Ari for stepping up to the plate and helping out so much, and Sesharan who has always been there with a kind word.

Finally, but certainly not least, I want to thank the wonderful team at Mountaindale Press. Without their hard work over the course of months and months, none of this book would have been possible.

CHAPTER ONE

Prologue

Viceroy Paltai Amberell stood at the helm of his voidship, a victorious smile plastered across his delicate features. Well, he wasn't a viceroy yet, but he may as well be.

In the inky darkness of space sat a new world, blue and green, a sapphire hanging in the dark ocean of the void. Somehow, despite its strategic location on the border of the Orakh warfront, it had remained undiscovered by any of the civilized races. Teeming with life and ripe for the taking, it sat waiting for the right person to pluck it from the vine.

His seers had identified it as a human world. Their reports told of a massive population of the primitive beings, their numbers almost without end. That population was something the Tellask Empire desperately needed.

The Orakh of this sector had united under a new warlord, Grosk. Or maybe it was Groksk? He could never keep their names straight. It all sounded like meaningless grunting to Paltai.

Regardless of Grosk's name and origin, the Orakh were unified once more, and that meant they were making a push against the Empire's borders. Already, five tributary states and two colonies had fallen. Needless to say, the Imperial Court was not pleased.

They would be pleased with Paltai.

According to the seers, there might even be a hundred million humans on the new world, and the Empire needed warriors more than anything. Humans didn't make the best mages, being too short-lived to actually have any serious accomplishments in magecraft. But, given a little training and proper motivation, they fought adequately.

Obviously, the average human was no match for an elf; they simply didn't live long enough to learn the finer points of warfare. But enough of them could overwhelm even a superior opponent. Quantity being a quality of its own, of the Tellask Empire's non-elven inhabitants, humans made the best soldiers by far .

Some of the more conservative forces in the Empire opposed the heavy usage of humans in the Imperial army, but Paltai disagreed with them. Humans were fine so long as you treated them with a firm hand. They were a shifty and untrustworthy bunch, prone to low cunning and churlish outbursts, but if properly directed, they were valuable tools for the Empire.

Of course, Paltai reflected as the blue sphere grew in the viewport, the conservatives did have something of a point. Almost 70% of the common soldiers in the Imperial Army were human. That was an awful lot of any race to keep under arms at the same time, let alone stubborn humans that all too often needed to be reminded of their place.

It was a boon, however, that the humans were a fractious and warlike lot. Although they didn't enjoy their rightfully inferior position to the elven leadership of the Tellask Empire, they were more likely to vent their displeasure on their fellow humans than an elf.

For some reason, minor shifts in their coloration and language were enough reason for the various tributary states to constantly clamor at each other's throats. No, the problem with human army units wasn't desertion or rebellion. It was ensuring that your unit didn't tear itself apart with infighting.

Paltai strode away from the glass viewport and approached the ship's seeing stone. The *Viceroy's Pride*, as Paltai had renamed it as soon as the seers reported an unclaimed and populated planet, was a bigger voidship. Not quite the size of the great warships of the Imperial and noble fleets, but it was large and well appointed through the considerable effort and expense of his house.

Despite its bulk, the *Viceroy's Pride* only boasted one seeing stone from which the ship's seers could target its spell crystals or view enemy formations from afar. It was a point of pride for Paltai. After all, many lesser vessels didn't even mount a seeing stone, instead having to choose between fumbling aimlessly through the great dark or relying upon reports from allies who did mount a seeing stone.

To power the solitary seeing stone as well as the voidship's engines and armament, the *Viceroy's Pride* was equipped with three mana forges. Usually, a vessel of its size would only require two, one for its engine and defenses as well as one for its weapons and seers, but after calling in some favors, the ship was gutted and almost entirely retrofitted.

It was Paltai's pride and joy, boasting a massive spellcannon capable of punching through a lesser voidship's shields in a single blast and a massive capacitor hooked to the teleportation drive. It could outshoot anything in its weight class and outrun anything else.

As for the seeing stone, it was of such size and power that it required the dedicated mana flow of an entire forge when in use. Personally, Paltai credited the oversized seeing stone with the discovery of the new world.

Already, the seers had focused the stone on the patch of space where the *Pride* would be teleporting in. Per standard first contact procedure, they paused at the outskirts of the solar system and performed reconnaissance via scrying. Immediately after discovering that the new world boasted no magic use what-soever, Paltai gave the order to jump.

The *Pride* housed 300 imperial marines armed with the most affordable enchanted weapons and armor that the Empire could provide. Although disposable in the grand scheme of things, the marines' enchantments and magic users should be sufficient to cow the locals into submission.

If the marines were insufficient, Paltai had the 25 rangers of his house guard, elite elven warriors sworn to House Amberell. Each of them had trained for at least a hundred fifty years before earning such a prestigious post. They moved with a speed and deadly grace that an unenhanced human simply could not match.

The imperial forces would be heavily outnumbered the minute they touched down on the virgin world, but that was hardly a new thing. The Empire had invaded any number of unawakened worlds, and in all past engagements between a mana-less foe and the Empire, the natives' numbers were mean-ingless. It hardly matters if you outnumber your enemy fifty to one if your spell shields simply stop all their attacks.

No, whether the inhabitants knew it or not, this planet was about to become an Imperial colony. The troops would want to collect some trophies, as was their right. Other than that, the goal was to arrive in a suitably intimidating fashion and convince the natives to throw down their arms.

If possible, Paltai wanted to maintain some semblance of the local governments, as ruling a far flung colony was an abso-lute chore without native assistance. But if he had to put some self-important human king to death to prove he was serious, so be it. It wouldn't be the first time.

Finally, the seers relayed their report to Paltai. With ceremo-nial flourish, the coordinates for teleportation were set, and the space mages began the ritual. The lighting in the ship dimmed as magical seals hogged power from the forges, and Paltai took that as his cue to retire to his chambers to prepare himself for the triumphant conquest to come. Nodding to the seers and communication officer who stood on the bridge with him, Paltai returned to his boardroom and opened the chest containing his armor.

Reverently, he placed the armor on his meditation mat. The armor had been passed down in his family for over eleven thousand years. The pauldrons and greaves were made of mythril and etched with tightly-scripted runescripting to increase his strength, agility, and stamina. The breastplate was made of mythril inlaid with mana stones and covered in depictions of his ancestors defeating dragons, demons, and other beings of great power. Perhaps more important than the runescripting itself, the mana stones powered a high-quality spellshield. When activated, the magical field would absorb and repel almost all mundane and magical attacks.

Next, he placed his helmet on the mat next to his breastplate. It was only crafted from silver, a replacement when an unlucky uncle had been beheaded at the battle of Brot'Mattok over one thousand years ago. Even though the silver could not handle the density of runescripting or the same capacity of mana as the mythril original, it was still inlaid with spells that would translate any language, increase his senses, and allow him to slow his perception of time.

Finally, Paltai removed the most important piece of armor from storage, his vambraces. Fitted and created for him personally, they contained his attunement stones and seals. Without them, he was simply a strong and fast soldier. With their assistance, he could bend and create lightning and frost, his two chosen mana affinities.

In all, just the materials had cost five thousand Imperial Drak, enough to equip and pay an entire company of soldiers. Two senior Amberell family enchanters had labored over those materials for almost nine years. It wasn't the most important piece of relic armor in the Amberell family, but then again, Paltai wasn't the Amberell's most important son.

He grinned savagely, examining the equipment lovingly set out before him. With any luck, the events of this day would change that status. Securing a new colony of this size and apparent wealth would do wonders for his social standing.

Paltai began strapping the armor on, carefully double checking every seal, mana stone fitting, and rune pathway. Halfway through the process, he felt the brief moment of disorientation when the *Viceroy's Pride* teleported from deep space to the edge of the planet's atmosphere. It would still take almost an hour for the force mages to lower the ship on telekinetic pads, but they knew their business, and there was no need for Paltai to interrupt his routine to give them unnecessarily duplicative orders.

Forty minutes later, he gazed into the mirror in his chambers. Clad head to toe in the stately, gleaming silver of his mythril armor, Paltai looked every inch the part of an elven warrior. Nodding at his reflection, he placed the helmet over his brow and stared at himself through the crystal eyepiece. As he activated the runes in his helmet, a slight drain pulled on Paltai's internal mana supply. Not much for him, but enough that a non-mage would have been troubled. Now, he truly looked like a noble son of Amberell, stepping forth like from the stories of old to conquer the foes of the Empire and bring honor to his family.

The Amberells needed that honor. The Orakh clawed at their holdings from without, while their enemies within the Empire mocked them and belittled their ineffectiveness. They caused as much damage with whispers and poisoned smiles as the barbarians managed through brute force and bloody conquest.

Of course, if the Emperor had sent more troops, the Amberell could have held the line, but the sabotage and libel of their family's enemies and the need for resources across the Empire's dozen simultaneous warfronts, no troops had come. Instead, the Amberell house guard and their retainers fought, almost always alone.

Sometimes they held, but others they were forced back, and over the last five hundred years, a worrying trend had surfaced.

The Amberells usually won their battles, but they never had the troops needed to reclaim planets from the Orakh. Instead, every loss became a new breeding pit for the infernal monsters. Even now, their house risked losing everything while the vipers of the Imperial Court whispered and belittled them rather than sending assistance.

Paltai took a second to enjoy the time dilation provided by his helmet as he turned to leave his chambers. Perceiving the world as 10% slower didn't sound like a huge advantage, but in battle it could easily be the difference between life and death. His father had often told Paltai that the time runes had saved his life as many times as the spell shield had. It sounded like an exaggeration, as his Father was wont to do, but that did not mean there wasn't some truth to the advice.

Of course, he also had the personal runescripting tattooed into his skin. A series of swirling runes slowly inscribed in his skin over a year while he was in a potion-induced coma. The runes performed two major functions. First, they complimented his armor, letting him move faster, react quicker, and swing his sword harder than should have been possible. Second, they contained a handful of prescripted abilities: an ice cold aura that would chill any opponent within sword range, the ability to fire a handful of ice needles at extreme speed, and a field of thunder that would shock anyone with the temerity to strike him.

A fully-armored and runescripted elven warrior was easily the match for any fifty humans. If that warrior were a noble, with heavily-enchanted equipment and powerful personal runes, that number could just as easily become five hundred. These facts led many commanders to consider their human subordinates disposable.

Five minutes later, he stood before his assembled forces. The twenty-five rangers of the house guard were outfitted in similar, if less spectacular, armor. Veterans of innumerable colonial campaigns, they checked their weapons in silence. Behind them stood the three hundred soldiers of the Imperial Marines.

Mostly human, but with a smattering of amphibious Mispbar and bestial Lythtal, they milled about nervously. Although the imperial marines were allowed to equip themselves, it was rare that one could afford better armor than that provided by the Empire. Instead, they were clad in standard-issue steel chain armor with silver pauldrons that contained their armor's fairly straightforward runescripting. Nothing special, but still a good sight better than any of the demi-elves could afford on their own.

Nodding at the assembled soldiers, Paltai felt that a rousing speech was in order. They seemed hesitant, bogged down by pre-mission jitters. Clearly, they needed an oratory kickstart, something to get their blood flowing. Something to rouse their feelings of patriotism and greed in equal measure.

He smiled, sharp teeth peeking out from under his thin lips. The marines avoided his gaze. Most of the lesser races found elven mouths unsettling, claiming that they reminded them of predators. Good.

Paltai Amberell was a predator, and this planet was prey. Weak, injured, prey, unaware of the doom that perched just above it.

"Men and women of the Empire!" he shouted, his voice amplified by the runes in his helmet. "Today we stand ready to render a great service to our Empire and the house of Amberell!"

The rangers nodded, still silent. They'd already heard speeches before battle dozens of times, and they knew their duty. The marines, on the other hand quieted down, fixing their gaze on Paltai. Pride swelled in his chest. His first solo command, and here he was, about to render the greatest contribution to his family's legacy of anyone in the last half millenia.

"Today we stand before that most sought-after of targets," he continued, his voice swelling to fill the ship's hold. "A world both rich, and poorly defended. There are millions of humans living on this planet. Soon you will have your pick of that wealth, of their most supple men and women. Soon we will have another loyal colony for the Empire, and soldiers from that colony will fight beside you as we protect the Empire from the Orakh hordes."

Fire kindled in their eyes as his words reached them.

"House Amberell will finally have the soldiers needed to clear the captured colonies and reclaim them in the name of the Emperor," he was almost shouting, his right fist raised above his head as he exhorted the soldiers. "We will not have to wait to avenge those who have died on the front. No, soon we will lead the charge ourselves. We will push back the Orakh and fight them in their home systems, far from our friends and families. Today, we take our first step towards making our loved ones safe. Today, we take our first step towards victory!"

The rangers led the marines in a cheer. Paltai suspected that one of the sergeants had ordered the "spontaneous" action, but he didn't really care. Excitement lit their faces and their grips on their weapons shifted. They were no longer worried about what was about to happen, their anxieties and baseless concern about the coming battle forgotten.

They were conquerors, potent beyond the ability of some poor, mana-less natives to resist, and they had the confidence to match.

The *Viceroy's Pride* jolted as it settled into the soft ground of the planet. Paltai idly wondered if he could get away with naming it after himself.

No, it was probably for the best if he was properly filial about the whole matter. He would name it after his father. At least that way, he could shut the demanding man up. A second later, a chime filled the bay and the door to the voidship fell downward, forming a ramp for the troops to exit over.

As was his right, Paltai stepped out from the *Viceroy's Pride* first. Tromping down the metal ramp, he marched out into the harsh light of the new world and took a deep breath before wrinkling his nose. For some reason, the planet smelled like fire and an alchemists' shop, the very air was tainted with chemicals and ash. In front of the ship, gleaming metallic construction jutted up towards the sky.

Before he could take in all of the sights, a delegation approached him. Behind them stood several rows of men in identical uniforms, probably a merchant guild of some sort, as the uniform was made from cloth rather than any sort of metal or leather. Further behind those men sat several large, squat carriages with a large pole jutting from their front.

He dismissed the idiosyncrasy and focused on the man and woman walking toward him. The woman was in the lead, confident and commanding, while the man trailing behind her wore a pensive expression, his entire demeanor submissive and deferential.

She was their commander. It would be her who surrendered this planet to him while the simpering man performed the role of witness and scribe.

"I am Paltai Amberell, and I greet you on this glorious day," Paltai activated his translation rune as he addressed the woman for the first time. "Today is indeed a momentous day as it marks the first day of your incorporation into the Tellask Empire. Rejoice!"

She stared at him in confusion for a second before stepping back and whispering to the man standing next to her. The man shrugged. She whispered to him again, and he said something back. She gestured emphatically at the man while whispering heatedly to him again. He shook his head, a helpless look on his face.

Paltai cocked his head, frustration furrowing his brow. Behind him, the marines stood in formation, their weapons in hand. Something needed to happen soon, before they lost their aggressive edge.

"My name is Jane Conway," she replied, finally stepping away from her companion, "and this is my technical advisor, Daniel Thrush."

The man smiled weakly at Paltai, the submissive grin of a beaten hunting dog.

"I'm not sure that we are interested in joining your Empire at this time," she added with a grandiose flourish of her hand. "but we would be happy to discuss trade and..."

Paltai interrupted her with a lighting bolt from his vambrace. There had been enough talking, and this human clearly did not know her place. An example always needed to be made, and she seemed relatively important. By wasting his time and annoying Paltai, she had volunteered herself.

Her torso exploded as the lightning tore into her, and a sense of euphoria buzzed through Paltai as he absorbed a fraction of her mana. Behind him, the marines screamed a battle cry and charged, their spellshields flaring to life.

The sun glinted off of the towers of glass and metal behind the humans. Truly, this was a glorious day for battle. Their ancestors would see them conquer this hive and return House Amberell to its rightful glory.

A series of explosions thundered, and then Paltai was flying, his spellshield glowing a dangerous red from almost reaching damage capacity. He frowned. That was impossible; it could stand up to anything short of dragonfire.

The humans would need an archmage to land a blow like that, and Paltai had not felt the telltale accumulation of magic that would go with the sort of spellcasting it would take to deal that much damage in one attack.

Then he hit the side of the *Viceroy's Pride*, the force of the blow robbing the wind from his lungs. The shield held, barely, but it clearly couldn't take much more abuse.

He shook his head, staggering to his feet as the telltale red of his spellshield faded to translucency.

Before him, a scene out of hell unfolded. His soldiers' charge had been stopped by a rapid series of explosions from the uniformed humans. Apparently, the rods they were carrying were some sort of ranged weapons, and even with the speed and strength enchantments covering the marines, they were cut down like wheat before a scythe.

The rangers acquitted themselves slightly better, their spells accounting for a handful of lives, but even with their supernatural power and grace, the strange ranged weapons simply fired too quickly. Many of the enemy soldiers were barely even aiming, instead spraying fire in the general direction of the rangers. Spell shields sparkled and failed one after another as elven warriors fell, silenced by the infernal weapons.

Paltai saw red. Everything had been going so well. He was going to be the Viceroy of this awful place, showered in wealth and women. A son of Amberell couldn't let it end like this!

With a bellow, he charged.

Given his speed and the remains of his spell shield, Paltai almost made it to the line of enemy soldiers pointing their rods in his direction before the blows rocked him. The shield failed, a meteor shower of sparks erupting across its surface.

Then, it was like a hammer striking him in the chest. Once, twice, and finally six times in the span of a second. There wasn't any pain, but when he tried to take another step forward, the world spun, and he collapsed.

His breath rasped shallowly in his throat, and the world began to dim. Distantly, he noted that everything was cold, and it had nothing to do with his ice affinity. He was going into shock. Without healing magic, he was as good as dead.

His eyes closed, his battered body unable to keep them open any longer, and the last thing he heard as the world faded to darkness was the words of an enemy soldier, still faithfully translated by his damaged helmet.

"Can you believe this shit, Roy? We finally get to meet honest-to-God space aliens, and they fucking charge us with spears and swords. Spears and goddamn swords."

Their laughter mocked him as he slipped away into the next life.

CHAPTER TWO

Budget Cuts

Music pounded through the sound system of the small lab while Daniel Thrush set up his final experiment of the day. The halls around him had long emptied themselves of foot traffic, seven o'clock on a Friday evening being antithetical to the very core of working for the United States Federal Government.

Dan wouldn't have been able to get away with that even six months ago. Back then, he still had coworkers, schedules, and supervisors. Maybe the lab wasn't exactly teeming with activity, but at least there was always a quiet hum of research.

Then time passed, and they hadn't discovered anything. Massive black budgets disappeared into the research center's hungry maw, month after month. Finally, but thanks to the wonders of a recession and a mystifying lack of results, he had the lab to himself.

After the aliens landed thirteen months ago, the United States Army created the department of xenotechnological research with high hopes. The aliens' technology promised to revolutionize almost every field of science. The talking heads on the news spent weeks tripping over themselves, gushing about how the world was going to change for the better once the extraterrestrial artifacts were understood.

The military, on the other hand, took an altogether darker and more paranoid approach. If aliens found us once, they'd find us again. Whether it was this bunch or another, Earth would need to be ready to fight off another invasion.

Between the civil and military interests, the government poured money into their research. They'd given the team an entire wing of the laboratory and more equipment than they would ever need.

Dan wasn't the original department director, lead researcher, or anything important like that. Instead, he was included primarily because he had been the original contact team's lead engineer and technological liaison, a position solely attributable to him being the only engineer on duty within driving distance on the Sunday when the aliens chose to land.

Originally, the research team was headed by Samantha Weathers, a physicist from MIT. Dan had tried reading some of her theoretical papers, and the woman was an absolute genius. Well, either that or his master's degree in electrical engineering from a state school didn't even begin to make him qualified to comment on cutting-edge research, but he tried to keep a positive attitude about these things.

Unfortunately, despite high hopes and even higher expectations, it seemed like there wasn't that much to discover. Despite their use of swords and shields, the aliens clearly had some sort of advanced technology, but it was completely inscrutable. Using the most advanced instruments available, their team hadn't even been able to isolate the energy the aliens used, let alone how it was transferred or directed.

The aliens themselves were just as much of a mystery. Some of their corpses were definitely human, but others were anything but. Somehow, only humans survived the unmitigated disaster of first contact, but none of the survivors spoke anything even resembling a known language.

At first, after their capture, the handful of survivors tried to convince the team to bring them their helmets via pantomime. Some of the senior scientists raised the prospect that they might be able to converse using translation software in the helmets. Unfortunately, the military was too afraid of the aliens using their incomprehensible technology to call for help. All such requests were summarily denied.

A month passed, and one-by-one, the survivors grew listless and unresponsive before eventually developing fevers and dying. That had been a fun period for the lab workers. The military quarantined the lab, terrified of some sort of alien contagion escaping and infecting the outside world. After three months of being locked in the facility, Dan and the rest of the team had begrudgingly been allowed out, after a whole panel of doctors could find absolutely nothing wrong with them.

The research itself was fascinating, but it didn't yield enough results to keep the government happy. The tall, skinny aliens who did the most damage during the disastrous first contact wore a combination of silver and tungsten armor.

For reasons as alien as the invaders, their armor was covered in designs and some sort of writing, but no one had been able to find out how it worked. It was clearly powered armor of some sort. Recordings of the encounter showed the aliens running at almost 120 miles per hour with reflexes that would put a cocaine-addled leopard to shame.

That was only the most mundane of the aliens' abilities. All of the invaders had been equipped with some sort of forcefield that took at least a couple bullets to crack. They fared noticeably worse against the heavier weapons of the armored vehicles, but hitting the insanely agile aliens was a daunting task for most of the surprised gunners.

Dan shuddered as he remembered the battle, crouching next to Jane Conway's smoking corpse as preternaturally fast warriors blurred around him. If the aliens hadn't been dumb enough to charge across an asphalt parking lot into two companies of infantry supported by a tank and three infantry fighting vehicles, things might have been much rougher for everyone involved.

The department tried every test they could think of, from bombarding the equipment with experimental particles to bathing it in conductive liquids and running an electric current through it. The weapons were given to skilled martial artists and used on live pigs to see if they could elicit a response. Spectrometers were set up and insanely expensive surveillance equipment recorded every second of the entire battery of testing. Dan vividly remembered at one point having to expose a broadsword to a fatal dose of radiation while every more-important scientist came up with an excuse to not attend work that day.

Nevertheless, after seven months, the department of xenotechnological research was left with a pile of artifacts that it couldn't use or explain, a collection of dead bodies, and nothing of use to show for their efforts.

Then the military began cutting down on their funding. At first, it wasn't terribly serious and the liaison officers were apologetic about the cuts, assuring the researchers that the funding would be restored in the next budget cycle. As the department continued to spend money like water with no results, the liaison officers became less polite, and the budget cuts became more drastic.

One by one, the more prestigious researchers were reassigned to other projects or quit until the department only consisted of Doctor Weathers and Dan. He tried to make himself useful, serving as little more than the doctor's glorified research assistant, until two months ago when Doctor Weathers finally left the department altogether, leaving only Dan on staff.

Dan still saw some of the researchers around the complex. About half of them continued working for the military, developing new applications of existing technologies associated with fighting off a potential alien invasion. At times, he wished he could join them. The high-atmosphere fighter jets and robotic exoskeletons seemed a lot more interesting than failing to produce the same results from the same experiment over and over.

It seemed ironic that the one person who never should have been assigned to the project to begin with was the last one left. He still had what remained of the department's formerly generous budget, but it was only a matter of time before a senior officer realized that the project was well and truly dead and finally turned out the lights.

He suspected that the only reason it hadn't happened already was that no one wanted to confront the political ramifications of being the one to stop research into the alien artifacts. If Dan or his former bosses had even come up with a single palatable theory, they would probably still be drowning in funding. Instead, the department developed a reputation as a jinx, a career killer, and no one accepted a reassignment there.

Desperation, energy drinks, and lack of sleep helped Dan develop a theory about the invader's equipment. Namely, that it worked via magic. At this stage of the project, it was as good an explanation as any. Some Ph.D type would probably come up with a fancy name like "extra-dimensional energy confluence," but years of reading science fiction and fantasy had taught Dan to recognize space elves shooting lightning bolts when he saw them.

He knew better than to alert management to his theory without results. For one, they'd probably realize that he was the only one left on the project, and at this point his only real hope was to hide in plain sight. For another, he had some idea how crazy the theory sounded. Without tangible results, he was begging to get shitcanned and mocked.

Music boomed through the empty lab as Dan chuckled to himself, placing cameras around the observation area to catch every angle of the experiment. He could imagine their reactions now. The best and brightest of humanity couldn't figure out the first thing about the alien technology, then some lab assistant starts rambling about swords and sorcery.

No thanks.

He had already done what he could, quietly broaching the theory to Doctor Weathers. They still kept in touch, the research into alien technology one of her few professional failures. She was still interested in the project, but she knew enough to get out before everything went down in flames, a luxury not available to a low-level contract employee like Dan.

At least Doctor Weathers would listen to his theory. After thousands of failures, she was as willing to jump at long shots as Dan. The first thing she said to him, after he brought up the possibility that the alien equipment was magic, was to never let anyone else know his theory without ironclad evidence.

So, there Dan stood, ready to step beyond known science and reason while classic rock pounded in the background. Maybe classical music or jazz would have been more appropriate for such a momentous occasion, but Dan was honest with himself. He needed something to get his blood pumping, to psych him up to take a monumentally risky and stupid step.

He held a handful of the crystals from the alien leader's breastplate. None of the scientists could figure out what they were or what they were made of, but Dan had noticed that, in the months after first contact, they had begun to glow softly.

Every time he handled them, there was a thrill that ran through him, almost like a static charge. Despite this, none of the instruments showed any change to the crystals. As far as modern science was concerned, they were exactly the same as the day he brought them into the lab. Even their newfound glow didn't register on any testing apparatus, an obvious sign that something was amiss.

Really, the crystals were what whispered to him that it was magic. They clearly were infused with some sort of energy that Dan's instruments couldn't detect, and like the artifacts, they had no triggering mechanism.

A desperate part of his brain reasoned that crystals seemed like the sort of thing a sorcerer would use to store power. He was clearly grasping at straws, but magic was the only explanation for the aberrant readings he could come up with whenever he tried to test the alien artifacts, and the mysterious, glowing crystals were his only clue.

At this point, Dan was operating off of movies, books, and roleplaying games from his college days. He was pretty sure the crystals were some sort of magical battery or generator. The alien had used it to fight the army, draining it. Over time, the energy had regenerated. Whatever the power source, the department hadn't been able to replicate it. That seemed like the genesis of their repeated failure. The scientists were like cavemen trying to turn on a computer without electricity.

With a deep breath, he dismissed the part of his mind telling him that he was about to make a mistake, and Dan shoved the cluster of crystals into his mouth. A second later, he washed them down with a mouthful of cola.

He wasn't sure how many rules of lab safety he was breaking right now, but it was too late to turn back. Dan double checked the cameras pointed at himself as well as the various medical diagnostic gear strapped to his body. He wasn't really sure how half of it worked, but he was recording everything, and hopefully someone with more training would be able to sort things out later.

Dan sat down to wait. After a couple of minutes, he began to feel sheepish. The decision to eat the crystals was based one hundred percent off of instinct and intuition. In short, he guessed. As he sat reflecting on his actions, he concluded that he had probably guessed wrong.

In all likelihood, nothing was going to happen. He chuckled to himself as he stretched, careful not to detach any of the diagnostic equipment. Or, he was about to die horribly. All the aliens did grow sick and die, so there certainly was a possibility that he had exposed himself to some sort of disease vector or contagion.

God, he could already see the letter to his mother: "Daniel Thrush died from eating reagents while working on a highly-classified project." At least he would have a chance to disappoint her one last time before he went.

Before he could ponder his plight further, Dan's heart began hammering in his chest. His fingers tingled, pricked by a million invisible needles, but just as he started to mentally investigate the phenomenon, every nerve in his body turned on at once, locking his muscles into a twisted rictus. Molten pain shot through his limbs, forcing his eyes to water.

Strangely, rather than panic, a strange detached sense of euphoria overcame him. A pink fog filled his vision, great cotton candy wisps obscuring his surroundings as he grinned through the twitching and thrashing.

His body was clearly in agony, but it all seemed like it was happening to someone else, like he was on the best painkillers available. Instead, he ignored the pain and focused on a warm sensation in the pit of his stomach. It spread slowly, and inch by agonizing inch, the pain disappeared as his frozen muscles unlocked one-by-one.

Silently, Dan urged the warmth on. Even detached from the pain, each moment was an eternity of torment. Without the warmth and the relief it brought, he probably would have blacked out already. Despite his mental efforts, the warmth traveled through his form at a glacial pace, until eventually his entire body was wrapped up in its comforting embrace. The instant it fully subsumed him, a shudder ran down Dan's back, as if he had just grabbed a live wire. In an instant, the pain stopped. His body felt years lighter, like it had back in high school when he ran cross country, before years of working at a desk and ordering chinese food had slowed him down.

Sitting up, he stretched some of the stiffness out of his aching limbs. Whatever the warmth was, it helped, but it didn't stop his body from screaming at him for being forced to hold the same position for God knows how long. He stood up, wincing as his back popped, and took in his surroundings. The clock on the wall and silent music playlist indicated that he had been out of it for at least three hours. He knew he had lost track of time while he had collapsed, but Dan hadn't realized it had taken anywhere near that long.

He smiled thinly to himself. He supposed he should consider himself lucky it was the same day. Well, at least, he hoped it was the same day. It might very well be eight o'clock in the afternoon on Saturday rather than Friday. It's not like anyone else would come to the lab looking for him and notice his predicament. Glancing down at himself, Dan winced. At some point, he had thrown up all over himself without noticing. That was certainly a delightful surprise after the ordeal he had just been through.

What truly brought a smile to his face, however, was the rainbow of new colors visible to him. Auras of green, blue, gold, and purple surrounded most of the aliens' equipment. Even the air itself seemed more vibrant and alive. Whatever had happened, at a very minimum, he could see the invisible power they used on their equipment. There weren't any promises yet that it would work for him, but at least he no longer felt like a blind man groping for an invisible object in the dark.

He stepped over to the pile of equipment and picked up the tungsten wrist guard that the lead alien had worn, the one it used to murder Jane Conway. The device glowed gold in his new vision, and the minute he picked it up, everything changed. Warmth crackled through his body, flowing down his arm and out of his hand into the alien artifact. In his mind, the essence of the gold aura emerged: its speed, fury, and destructive potential lay restrained and frozen like a caged bolt of lightning. Instinctively, that's what he knew it was: raw electrical energy, waiting and begging to be unleashed.

As soon as Dan thought about freeing the energy, his vision dimmed for a second. A spray of sparks emitted from the hand holding the wrist guard, unfocused and questing for the nearest path to the ground. Almost immediately, a camera he had been using to record his experiment shorted out as the electricity scoured through it. A second later, a wave of exhaustion consumed Dan. His limbs doubled in weight and his eyelids drooped, but the smile never left his face.

He had been right about everything. He was a neophyte, unaware of exactly what the limits were. But the potential to control the power, to shape that raw fury, was there. The aliens used magic, and now so could he. Admittedly, his control was shit, and even a small amount of magic was enough to completely exhaust him, but it was real and it was his. The rest of the details would work themselves out in time, but for now there was only one simple truth that mattered.

He was a goddamn wizard.

CHAPTER THREE

Paying the Bills

"You're not a wizard Dan," Doctor Weathers' voice settled over him like a wet blanket. "If I've learned anything from role-playing games, you're a sorcerer, and a pretty shitty one at that."

"Come on Samantha," he pleaded into his cellphone. "I finally made some headway, and all you have for me is to nitpick whether I'm enough of a real nerd or not?"

"Fine Dan." She sighed through the line. "I didn't mean to make light of what you've done. It sounds incredibly reckless, and more than a little stupid, but now we at least have some idea as to how the invaders' artifacts work. I'd long suspected that there was some sort of biomarker needed to activate their equipment, but the Army wouldn't let us give anything to the survivors to experiment. We might not have a guide as to how things work, but at least now we can finally start taking the first steps towards figuring things out."

"Thanks, I guess," Dan replied, unsure if he should just accept her praise or take issue with her calling his actions stupid. "Now that we have something to work with, are you going to come back? I know that you got that new job as the director of research at the Thoth Foundation, but this is your chance to make history."

"As soon as I let my superiors know that we've made progress," he continued excitedly, "they're going to pour funding back into the department, and we'll be able to do what-ever you need to reverse engineer this stuff. Heck, once we get the ball rolling, we might even be able to get the spaceship from the Air Force impound hanger and take a crack at it, too. From everything I've heard, they're just as stuck as the department was."

"Now Dan," Samantha spoke slowly into the phone, "I'm obviously not advising you to commit treason or withhold infor-mation from your superiors, but I want you to think very hard about what you're saying. Right now, you're the only person who can interact with alien technology. You work for a depart-ment that doesn't officially exist, and the Army has been hungry for advances on alien tech for over a year now. If you were to disappear, only your mother and I would notice, and even then, it would probably take months. You don't have a girlfriend, friends, nearby family, or even any casual connection that would miss you and raise a fuss, unless you're counting a delivery driver."

Doctor Weathers paused for a moment before continuing. "I'm sure you've heard some of the rumors and innuendo about the Army and human testing. They haven't really shied away from it. The army tested radiation exposure on soldiers in the early days of the atomic era, and these days you hear stories about the lax safety standards surrounding experimental combat drugs. If a senior officer thinks that the cost-benefit for you 'dying in a car accident' is in America's favor, they're likely to authorize something drastic."

"Oh shit." He didn't even need to say anything more. He knew all about the Men In Black. In fact, he was pretty sure that he was one.

Well, at least an intern in black.

If he started blabbing about how he had unlocked the secrets of magic and the universe itself, he would disappear into a secure facility, if he was lucky. If he was unlucky, well... he had been present when they vivisected the aliens' corpses, looking for a biomarker that would activate the artifacts. Dan preferred his blood on the inside.

"Yeah Dan, shit," she replied, voice heavy. "Now, it's not all bad news. I can't really tell you what the Thoth Foundation is up to without talking to the chair and making you sign an NDA, but I can say that they are interested in both the invaders and their artifacts."

"I can't confirm that they 'acquired' a couple trinkets on the black market." Dan could almost hear the air quotes as Sam emphasized the word "But I've been able to continue my research from the department without any of the intrusive over-sight. We haven't really gotten anywhere with the alien tech, but I have some things in my lab that would make your hair curl, and most of the fun stuff that actually works was made on Earth."

"What does any of this have to do with me?" Dan asked, more than a little confused and worried. Now that he thought about it, the Thoth Foundation probably counted as a direct competitor to the United States Army, making this phone call somewhere between treason and a fairly explicit violation of his non-disclosure agreement. Either way, he was probably looking at jail time if anyone found out.

"Well, you're a contractor, right?" She asked.

"Yeah." Dan shifted the cellphone to his other ear. The government didn't want to pay him benefits, so he had been stuck as a limited-term contractor with a one-year renewing contract for the last four years. In fact, his current contract was due to run out at the end of the month.

His accelerated research timetable and the motive for his hasty decision to perform the experiment could largely be attributed to his upcoming contract expiration. He wasn't going to get renewed for another year without results, and if the contract didn't get renewed, he was probably going to have to move back in with his mom while he looked for a job. It was truly a future worth risking death via alien plague to avoid.

"Look, Dan, I know you called to try and recruit me," she continued, "but maybe you should just let me return the favor. Even if you didn't have the right degree or any experience in the right fields, you were probably one of the best minds in the department before everyone left."

"The rest of the scientists were stuck on what they thought they knew." Frustration dripped from Doctor Weathers' voice. "But you could think outside the box. Almost everything we know about science needs to be thrown out the window now that we've seen what the invaders could do. They simply weren't willing to turn their backs on decades of possibly incorrect training. Plus, you just cracked open one of the biggest scientific mysteries known to mankind, and whatever energy you have coursing through your blood is the key. I'm going to be honest about that; I mostly just want you for your body."

Dan sputtered, unable to respond as Doctor Weather delivered the last line with a completely deadpan voice. His mind whirled. *Leave the Army?* They weren't paying him much, but they had been his first real job after he got his masters degree. He mostly just didn't want to get arrested for leaking state secrets or wasting government funds.

Still, Dan remembered his last job search. Months of watching his bank account dwindle while hurling resumes and cover letters into the void. Week after week without responses only to jump at e-mails that would invariably thank him for his time while letting him know that he was overqualified for the position.

"Relax, kid," she chuckled. "You're going to have to work out more and be a whole lot more female before I get around to sexually harassing you. I'll talk to the boss, but I'm almost certain he'll approve a job offer for you. I've had standing authority to offer any of my former researchers a job ever since I left, and I suspect that you counted even before your little breakthrough. Plus, I think the boss is going to like you. Just wait out your contract and don't make any waves. The Army will 'go in another direction,' and you'll be free to sign on with Thoth without triggering any of the non-disclosures and non-competes in your contract."

The rest of the month went quickly. Dan learned that the wrist guards of the tall and skinny aliens all contained mechanisms for focusing his new energy, but actually doing anything productive with that energy was another story. He had learned how to use a wrist guard to transform the energy into a new format, but he couldn't control the energy once it left his body. After he gave himself some third degree burns experimenting with a fire focus, Dan decided enough was enough. As curious as he was, he would wait for his new job before experimenting any further. The last thing he needed was to accidentally annihilate himself right when his life was about to turn around.

Then the month ended and things went almost exactly as Doctor Weathers predicted. The Army, through a disinterested captain, assured Dan that "although his work had been exemplary, his services would no longer be needed."

Just like that, four years of Dan's life ended without pomp or fanfare. The Captain assured Dan that the department and all of its artifacts would be turned over to 'top men' for further research and testing, but Dan had seen Indiana Jones. He knew what that meant.

On the first of the next month, the job offer came in the mail. What Doctor Weathers hadn't told him was exactly how much money he would be making.

Apparently the Thoth Foundation was loaded, and they were happy to share a fairly significant chunk of their money with Daniel in exchange for a five-year exclusive contract. He didn't even blink as he signed it.

Even if they were exploiting him, what could he do about it? Try to find a competitor and sell them government secrets or his services? No, that sounded like a good way to end up in the loony bin, prison, or dead. Plus, Samantha had never steered him wrong. If she was willing to vouch for the Thoth Foundation, they at least had to be decent people.

Still, that didn't stop Dan from looking into his new employers. It wasn't like he had anything else to do with his time. Unfortunately, all he could find were dark rumors and speculation. All he could make out for sure was that its founder was a billionaire dozens of times over from an empire of video game and entertainment franchises.

Apparently, he devoted a good portion of that money to technological research and philanthropy. Dan didn't know much about the philanthropy, a lot of it looked like the usual rubbing of shoulders between the rich and politicians, but he was hardly in any position to know. On the other hand, the Thoth Foundation's research was second to none. Almost a tenth of the equipment he used at the lab had a Thoth Foundation patent somewhere in its development.

In the end, he ended up back where he started: unsure as to what he was getting into, weighing the potential salary and Sam's endorsement against a leap into the unknown. Eventually, the promised salary won out. He might be working for an enigmatic billionaire, but there was no denying he was generous with those billions. The number of zeros at the end of Dan's salary went a long way toward silencing his uncertainty.

Five days later, he was leaving his new apartment, having moved from Washington DC to Albany, New York to live closer to the Foundation. After getting lost twice due to his GPS fritzing out, he finally arrived at the Foundation's headquarters.

Rather than a lush, multi-acre campus with golf carts and 'innovation incubation centers,' it was a military compound. Dan had no idea what to expect, but a twelve-foot concrete wall covered in razor wire and studded with cameras wasn't it. He had to give a blood sample to get in, which they compared to the one they had on file. That was mildly distressing. He had never given them a baseline for their file.

Finally, he found himself waiting in a conference room while a well-built man in his early twenties stood in the corner watching him. The young man was wearing a well-tailored and expensive suit that clearly showed the bulge on his hip where he carried a handgun. Dan shifted in his seat slightly, wondering what the hell he had gotten himself into. Even when he had been working for the Army, security had been nowhere near this tight.

After an interminable wait, the door to the conference room opened and Samantha strode in. She was wearing slacks and a button down shirt, all business casual without betraying a hint of their paramilitary surroundings.

Behind her, a spry sixty-year-old man positively bounded into the room. Despite his age, the man still had a full head of mostly grey hair. His brown eyes burned with manic energy, and he couldn't stop smiling as he focused them on Dan. A second later, he was across the room, slapping Dan on the back and engulfing his hand in a firm handshake.

"Thrush, my boy," he said excitedly, a slight southern burr in his voice. "It's good to have you on board. Sam told me about what you've done, and I have to say that it's absolutely top-notch. Everyone but her has been so stodgy about researching the alien tech that we've gotten absolutely nowhere, but with you here, I hope to change that. We're going to do great things together, my boy, great things!"

"Sir..." Dan glanced over at Doctor Weather, who rolled her eyes before taking a seat, "I, uh, don't know who you are. I don't really know what's going on, to be honest. Doctor Weathers just told me that I should accept the offer from the Thoth Foundation when it got sent my way, and that was good enough for me."

"Sorry!" The man was still grinning and shaking Dan's hand excitedly. "Wherever are my manners? The name is Henry Ibis, and I run the Thoth foundation! The goal has always been to take humanity to the next level, find a way to throw off the chains of the mundane.

"The aliens are just the newest avenue!" Henry finally released Dan's hand as he kept rambling excitedly. "We're researching a whole lot of things at the same time. Improved spaceflight, practical consumer cybernetics, robotics, improved virtual reality, and as of right now, alien magic."

"I'm confused," Dan glanced back over at Samantha who ignored his eyes, leaving him to Ibis' mercy. "I could find barely anything on the web about the Thoth Foundation, and everything I could find was from a bunch of crackpots. I don't even know how an operation this expansive is funded. According to the message boards, the rumor is that you're part of the illuminati or something?"

"Those sticks in the mud?" Ibis answered. "No, they're too busy setting trade policy and trying to control the media. No, I made my money off of the human imagination. Immersive virtual reality games, artificially intelligent virtual secretaries, that sort of thing. After a while, though, ripping off Tolkein or making a science fiction video game just isn't enough. I wanted to be there on the bleeding edge. Once humanity took the next step, I wanted to be the one responsible for that step, whatever it may be."

"Wait." Dan tried to slow down the exuberant man. "You're saying that the Illuminati is real? I said that as a joke!"

"Oh they're real all right." Ibis nodded. "We have a couple technology-sharing agreements with them. I might have them beat in software, but there's no way I would be able to match their research in nanites. Plus, they're the ones with all the connections to the government. How would I be able to buy all the artifacts from the alien incursion without their help?"

"What!" Dan and Doctor Weathers interjected simultaneously.

"Now Daniel," Ibis continued with a dramatic wink. "May I call you Dan?"

Dan nodded mutely, his mind traveling a mile a minute. He

didn't have the faintest clue who Henry Ibis was, but whatever was going on was completely above his pay grade. All he knew was that the man was powerful, likely owning more senators than Dan had pairs of socks. Ibis was happy to see him, and that was about all that mattered. Having someone like Ibis mad at you didn't seem conducive to a long life or career.

"So, Dan," Ibis wrapped an arm around Dan's shoulder. "Samantha says that you can use the aliens' magic, but your problems right now are a matter of power and control."

"Yes sir," he replied. "It seems like the magic has to be channeled through a focus of some sort. I think the aliens used their wrist guards. I can channel the energy, and once I do so, it changes from its raw form into something more usable. I've been able to activate wrist guards corresponding to electricity, fire, ice, raw telekinetic force, and gravity so far.

"Unfortunately, I can't really do anything more than convert the energy. When I create electricity, I shock myself and short out electronics around me. When I create fire, I burn myself. That sort of thing. I've tried popping the covers on the wrist guards off, but their insides are covered with incredibly fine carvings that glow whenever I try to channel energy through them. They almost look like microchips, but I don't know the first thing about their architecture, so I was afraid to fiddle with one."

"Good, this is even better than I hoped!" Ibis nodded excitedly. "Now, Dan my boy, I think I know just the thing for your predicament. Tell me, have you played any of my complete immersion VR games?"

"Sorry sir," Dan shook his head. "My mom wouldn't shut up about how they would 'rot my mind,' and the Army barely gave me enough to pay my student loans and make rent. I just didn't have the spare money."

"It's all right," Dan's new boss replied, a flash of disappointment on his face. "One of the major commonalities in all of those games is that the player starts off weak and helpless, but over time they learn skills and abilities that let them triumph over obstacles. A warrior might learn special sword strikes, and a wizard might learn a specific spell, but what all of them need is something to track their status and aid them in learning new abilities."

"Tell me, Dan..." The excitement was back in Ibis' eyes. "What have you heard about using a System?"

CHAPTER FOUR

The System

"Like an operating system?" Dan squinted as he replied. "I jail-broke my phone once in college, if that's the sort of thing you're talking about."

"No, no." Henry shook his head. "Like in a role-playing game or one of those stories where someone goes to another world. The system provides notifications to the player about their progress, achievements, and abilities."

"In that case, no, I really don't have any idea what you're talking about." Dan shrugged. He looked to Samantha for support, only for the woman to shrug back at him.

"Come on," Henry begged them. "Blue text? Popping up in the middle of your vision? Making a dinging noise? Sometimes with a sarcastic personality and makes fun of the user for poor decisions? Is this ringing any bells whatsoever?"

Dan and Dr. Weathers shared another blank look. Even the guard in the conference room looked uncomfortable and lost.

"Well that's what we're going to make." Ibis sulked. "Right now, Daniel is the only one who can even perceive the magic, so any interaction is going to have to be through his eyes. We are going to need our sensors hooked up to his mind and ocular nerves at all times if we want to have any real chance of studying magic in a systematic and scientific way."

"The Thoth Foundation has a suite of medical nanites with a dispersed quasi AI that we're going to inject into Dan," Henry explained. "I've had the software guys working on it ever since Samantha told me about his breakthrough. Right now, it will just monitor and record everything that Dan does or observes, but as we learn more, the plan is to update the AI to be self-learning. With time, it will help Dan analyze his actions in real time and allow him to replicate anything that works. The hope is that we can 'save' Dan's muscle memory and neurological patterns into a macro that he can call up on demand."

"Wait, what do you mean medical nanites?" Dan asked with a frown. "I've been following robotics since I was a kid, and I know for a fact that no one has gotten further than the most theoretical of testing stages on that kind of thing. This is going to be safe, right?"

"Oh it's perfectly, mostly safe, stop being such a baby," Henry retorted. "The nanites are experimental, but we've tested them a couple times with no major side effects. Unfortunately, they aren't really at the levels that science fiction has promised yet, but that doesn't mean they aren't useful. They more or less take over your immune system and supercharge it. They keep you healthy, in shape, end aging, and can instantaneously perform almost any medical test or examination you can think of. A bunch of rich old codgers have been working on them for the last fifteen years to try to live forever."

"Isn't this a little over the top?" Dan asked as he pointedly ignored commenting on Mr. Ibis' age, wealth, and access to the nanites. "Instead of injecting me with some experimental robots that could make me go all 'Borg... Heck, as long as we're going all video game science fiction 'supersoldier,' you can make it sound like a sexy lady and shove me into some body armor. I'm sure it would be a lot more efficient for me to get feedback from her than trying to force our research into the format of ability scores and stat updates."

Henry fell silent, the cheer fleeing his face in a second. Dan opened his mouth to comment when Samantha grabbed his arm.

"Just a second, Mr. Thrush and I have to talk about something I just remembered him mentioning last month," Samantha said loudly and unconvincingly as she pulled Dan from the conference room. As soon as they were in the hallway, she hissed, "Look, you can't bring up that series to the chairman. It's the one science fiction series that outsold *Realm of Legends Online* and *Myths of the Fallen*. Those were his biggest hits, and he takes those sales records very personally."

"Okay, but--" Dan tried to answer, only for Doctor Weathers to cut him off.

"No excuses. You're going to go back in there and tell him that his idea is great, and that you're excited to participate. The chairman might be eccentric, but he's the source of all of the Foundation's money. If we're going to make history here, I need that funding."

"But he's using me as a human guinea pig," Dan whined. "Whatever he's about to do sounds incredibly painful and completely untested. Worse, I'm not sure that it's necessary. There are at least five different ways to monitor me while we experiment with magic that don't involve experimental nonsense that could easily cripple or murder me."

"Dan, this is why I do better with women than you do." She rolled her eyes. "All I hear are complaints and indecision out of you. No one is going to date you until you learn to stand up for yourself. Plus, you gave up your right to gripe about being a guinea pig when you ate a handful of alien tech. Where is that confidence? Where is your excitement to venture forth into the unknown? When I got that call from you, I thought you were finally growing a little bit of a backbone."

She shook her head slowly, clicking her tongue with disappointment at Dan. He opened his mouth to object again only for her to glare at him. He wilted.

"He likes his video games." She shrugged. "He knows that

after he puts the groundwork in developing magic, everyone else is going to copy him. He wants magic to mimic his games and books, and he has the money, so he's going to make magic resemble his games and books. Seriously Dan, it's a lot of money."

Chastened, Dan trudged back into the conference room where Henry was still brooding. Even the security guard, silent until now, was chatting with him in an unsuccessful attempt to cheer the old man up. Dan sighed.

"Doctor Weathers reminded me about how much fun sword and sorcery video games are." Dan winced. He had no talent for lying, but luckily no one cared. "I think you're right, Mr. Ibis. We should do that system thing you talked about. It sounds swell."

"Great, my boy!" Henry immediately lit up. "The tech guys are ready to go right now; let's head over and get started. No reason to delay making history."

Dan's head swam as the chairman practically dragged him through the complex. Doctor Weathers followed closely as they passed through what seemed like a mile of sterile metal hallways. At some point, they picked up a second guard and then a third.

He eyed them nervously. Clearly, they were venturing from a secure area of the compound to a zone that was so restricted that it probably didn't officially exist. Still, the steadily-accumulating stone-faced guards did little to calm his hammering heartbeat.

By the time they reached the research and development part of the building, almost ten armed men and women were part of their convoy. As the chairman gave a fingerprint, verbal password, and retinal scan to pass a security door, he couldn't help but notice that at least half of the security guards were watching him uncomfortably closely.

Inside, they were quickly ushered to a room that resembled a doctor's office, except there were straps on the examination table and locks on the door.

The outside of the door.

Dan stopped walking, only for a hand to land heavily on his shoulder. Samantha leaned in and whispered in his ear.

"It's a lot of money Dan. A lot."

"This doesn't look like it's going to be pleasant," he hesitantly whispered back, eyes darting to the inscrutable medical equipment lining the walls of the room.

"Don't worry about it, Dan," she smiled, a slightly predatory gleam in her eyes. "It's all just a security precaution to stop industrial espionage. As long as you don't plan on stealing anything, there's nothing to worry about."

Twenty minutes later, Dan was strapped to the table and regretting ever trusting Doctor Weathers. Everyone but her, one security guard, and two men in white lab coats had left the room. He was more than a little worried about the fact that everyone but him had put on gas masks. Not quite as worried as he was about one of the anonymous doctors carrying a two-foot-long syringe over to where he was confined. That occupied most of his attention.

"I don't know about this Sam." Dan's eyes didn't leave the gigantic syringe. It gleamed menacingly at him in the room's sterile light.

"Think of it this way, Dan." Sam's voice was muffled by the gas mask. "I'm going to stick this in you, and it's going to make you rich and young forever. Plenty of people would jump at an offer like that."

"Gross," Dan managed a weak smile, his heart thudding in his chest as she moved closer to him.

"Yeah," Sam agreed. "That's what I said to my dissertation advisor, too. Now get ready, this is going to hurt like hell."

He glanced down at his arm as he felt a brief prick on the back of his hand. One of the masked figures had hooked him up to an IV. His vision blurred as he looked back up at Sam. Dan tried to ask her a question, but his mouth felt like it was full of cotton balls. He blinked, but his eyes didn't open again as conscious thought ground to a halt.

Dan opened his eyes in a fog. The room swam around him, and he blinked again against the harsh light. It felt like every hungover Saturday morning from college had combined together and bored a hole into his skull, but at least he could think. He stretched slightly, his muscles sore as hell. Whatever he had been through, he'd be feeling it for the next couple of days.

"Water," he croaked. One of the men in lab coats brought him a paper cup and poured it in his mouth for him. It didn't seem like they were going to let him up anytime soon. It was unclear if this precaution was to protect him from the postoperative weakness or to protect them from him. Before he could follow the line of reasoning any further, a spike of pain drove through his left eye.

His vision blurred for a second, then words appeared in the corner of his sight. They were simple, scrolling blue text that didn't interfere with his vision of the objects behind him. At least that was something; he didn't want whatever had happened to him to distract him and make him drive off the freeway.

Ocular connection established, performing diagnostics.

English Language detected. English preference saved to settings.

Voice activation now enabled.

Thank you <USER> for participating in the Thoth Foundation closed Alpha testing of The System version 0.02. Please perform baseline testing so that starting attributes can be assessed and logged.

The writing remained for about two seconds per line of text before slowly fading from his vision. Dan groaned, then immediately winced from the pain. He definitely wanted the armored suit and sexy AI instead. At least he had actually played that game.

CHAPTER FIVE

Setting the Baseline

Dan gasped for breath as he completed another circuit on the compound's indoor track. Baseline testing appeared to be some sort of euphemism for torture, at least as far as his normally-sedentary body was concerned.

The nanites directed him from one set of exercises to another via notifications in the lower left corner of his vision. At each stop, he would be forced to push himself to the limit.

First, he lifted weights until his chest and biceps burned. Then the System gave him a short period of rest, but almost immediately interrupted Dan's attempts to gather himself. He was allowed to sit, but the nanites directed him to play reaction games, tapping words that corresponded with images as they popped up in his vision as quickly as possible.

Initially, that exercise had been easy. But, as Dan progressed, the images appeared faster and for shorter periods of time. The words they were associated with were surrounded by more decoys and became more tangential to their images. Where a picture of an apple might have corresponded with the word apple, in later waves it would be linked with the words red, sweet and temptation. Eventually, just when Dan was developing a tension headache, the images stopped.

Then, before he could relax properly, a team of attendants had hurried him into a room where softballs were fired at him out of pitching machines. Clearly, it was an exercise to gauge his reflexes, but Dan was afraid his performance had been a bit subpar.

He dodged a decent number of the projectiles, but he still ended the event with both his body and dignity covered in bruises. Later, Dan was locked in a room to solve a series of puzzles and word problems while the temperature slowly increased. By now, he had noticed the pattern, alternating tests of physical activity followed by an exam of focus or mental aptitude.

Unfortunately, after three hours, Dan was just too tired physically and emotionally to make much use of the information. At some point, he had lost track of the testing entirely as everything blurred into a fog of concentration and action.

Then they made him jog. Dan was pretty sure he'd been on the track earlier today, but the morning testing had already faded into almost nothing.

Once upon a time, before alcohol and fast food had betrayed him, Dan had been fit. Not the most athletic person in his area by a long shot, but he was picked in the first five or six people during intramural sporting events at the local gym. Today, his breath echoed raggedly in his ears as he focused all of his will into maintaining the pace suggested by the System. Far from anything impressive, he was hopefully going to finish the two-mile run in right around twenty-two minutes.

It didn't help that a gaggle of physically-fit young men blazed by him every couple minutes. As far as he could tell by their matching workout gear, they were all facility security. Every single one of them was at least six feet tall and looked like they could wrestle an ox. He was pretty sure they were all ex-marines or something.

Not that it mattered. They had already lapped him twice,

and he was pretty sure he could hear them talking and joking as they came by for another pass. Dan could barely breathe. They were in embarrassingly better shape than he had ever been in. Eventually, he completed his final lap. The System activated as he doubled over, breathing heavily.

Baseline performance analyzed. Calculating results.

He wasn't really sure that he was going to get used to the writing appearing in the corner of his vision. Henry sure seemed excited about it, but the entire thing seemed a bit off to Dan. Like he wasn't quite human anymore.

Apparently, that was the point. He had read enough science fiction in his day to know about transhumanism, and everything about the Thoth Foundation gave off that vibe. They didn't tell him everything the Foundation was researching, but the general theme seemed to be about surpassing human limits. Ibis was obsessed with pushing humanity to take the next step it would need to be something greater. At least that's what Dan's employee introduction manual said. The only real surprise in the transhumanist rhetoric was that the Thoth Foundation was decidedly less cyberpunk and more unicorns and dragons than he had expected.

Baseline attributes verified for <USER>

Body 4

Agility 4

Mind 7

Perception 5

Dan walked over to the water fountain, still breathing heavily. The chairman had informed him that an average human would have 5 in all stats. It sounded about right. He wasn't terribly unfit, but he had fallen a fair amount from the days when he worked out regularly.

Years spent working in front of a computer and eating junk food had taken their toll. His mind was sharp, but the rest of him was… decidedly softer. He glanced down briefly at the bit of a gut that had begun to form from a steady diet of delivery. Definitely not sharp, more doughy and round.

Analyzing remaining unknown variables.

Unidentified energy isolated, designated "Mana" per System directive.

Theoretical attribute created governing mana. Designated 'Spirit' per System directive.

Not enough data to establish baseline for Spirit attribute. Spirit set to one until a proper baseline can be established. Please continue with experimentation to establish baseline.

WARNING- insufficient structural integrity detected in <USER> heart valve. Beginning emergency repairs. Please avoid strenuous exercise while repairs are underway. Remedial countermeasures will be deployed if this warning is disregarded.

WARNING- moderate arterial plaque buildup detected in <USER>. Please refrain from eating food with high fat, sugar, or cholesterol content. Remedial countermeasures will be deployed if this warning is disregarded.

Baseline testing complete. Please report to Doctor Weathers for further experimentation.

About ten minutes later, Dan walked into Sam's office only to be immediately kicked out without her even looking up. Apparently, not showering after a day of physical activity was a faux pas. Almost half an hour after that, Dan was back, this time smelling like soap and wearing fresh clothes. This time, Samantha waved him into her office, barely looking up from her computer.

"Glad everything went well, Dan," she said cheerfully, motioning for him to sit. "I'm looking over the test data, and you're going to have to be a little sedate for a week or so. It sounds like the nanites are going to have to rebuild a decent chunk of your heart. That means lean meat, iron supplements, and no strenuous exercise."

"I think I can handle the no strenuous exercise." He frowned, the soreness in his muscles a dull and constant ache. "But I really don't get the rest of what is going on. I mean, I know that science is about repetition. I just didn't really expect the repetition to be this sweaty and painful."

"Dan, you're our only specimen," she shrugged. "We need to keep you fit and healthy because you are more or less priceless. Once we start experimenting in earnest, we have no idea what's going to happen."

"Could you have at least warned me about how much initializing the System would hurt?" Dan quirked an eyebrow at her.

"I thought I did?" Sam threw a quick smile back at him. "Remember? Right after I promised to keep you young and beautiful forever?"

"I'm not sure that's how I remember it," Dan scratched the back of his head sheepishly. "I still think you could have given me more of a heads up. That was pretty last-second."

"After you introduced me to that drunken executive from Meridian Electronics at the cocktail mixer, then mysteriously disappeared? No." Her eyes twinkled. "Look, we were going to have to do it anyway, and there isn't a known procedure to make it not hurt. You know I would have spared you that if I could. I just figured, if the pain was inevitable, you deserved a little bit of a surprise for leaving me to the tender mercies of that drunken ape. I'm pretty sure he propositioned me at least five times before I was able to get away from the party."

"Wait." Dan's brow furrowed, "is that why you made the comment about us needing money to continue our research?"

"I'm glad experimenting with eldritch forces hasn't wiped your memory," she replied with a laugh. "You made a crack to me about how we would need to pursue 'alternative funding sources' and that he would be 'a good networking partner' as you left. Hardly chivalrous of you, leaving a damsel to such a wretched fate."

"Damsel?" Dan smiled and shook his head. "I was mostly afraid he was going to need stitches. The only reason I set you up with him was to get back at you for leaving the coolant cap unscrewed when I was running the alien equipment through the kiln. I ended up covered in the stuff. It took three showers before I even began to feel presentable again."

"In my defense," Sam responded. "It was really funny."

Dan snorted, rolling his eyes as he sank deeper into the

chair, trying his hardest to use the black leather to massage his aching muscles.

"Still, both the nanites and your physical health are important, Dan." Sam settled back in her chair, still wearing a smile on her face. "Even a simple test could trigger an unforeseen reaction in your body. If you're sick or have some sort of malady like your heart valve holding you back, it might be enough to do you in. The nanites in you are going to force you into almost-perfect health, but they're going to need help. Once your heart is repaired, you're going to be jogging, dieting, and working out daily. You're simply too important to humanity to die in a lab mishap."

"Sam," he said, making eye contact with her while she retained her seat. Samantha Weathers was one of the few friends he actually had, and certainly the only one he kept in any sort of touch with. There weren't many other people in his life he could have this kind of conversation with. "Look, I want to be part of this project. Magic is the cutting edge, and I want to be part of exploring how it works. I just don't want to be kept completely in the dark about everything. If nanites are the only way to do it, that's fine, but I just don't like feeling like everything has been decided for me without any input on my part, and *that* I'm not okay with. You of all people should know my problems with that."

"I'm surprised I haven't gotten a call from your mother." Sam's face twisted as if she had bitten into something bitter. "Did you know she called me about your workload at least three times when we both worked for the government? Even though you were an adult and working on a top secret project, she still kept giving me an earful. I had to block her number. Twice. I think she bought a burner phone the second time."

"She means the best, but..." Dan trailed off with a frown. "She thought you were like my ex. That you were going to use your feminine wiles to seduce me away from her and convince me not to come home for Thanksgiving dinner. Really, I had made the decision to try and make it on my own years before we met, but Mom doesn't really respond well to logic."

"I know." She looked up from her computer, a faint smile on her face. "I tried to reason with her myself the first time, and it didn't really go anywhere. Dan, you do know that you can talk to me about this anytime, right? I might not be the best equipped to handle these sorts of things, but I can at least listen and provide a shoulder to lean on."

"Thanks, Sam." Dan smiled slightly. "I think it might be best to focus on the project, though. At least with magic, we have some hopes of making headway."

"Fair enough," Sam chuckled. "The next step is for us to monitor you inside and out while you try to use some of the alien artifacts. In about ten minutes, we'll be heading over to the main observation lab to watch you try and get some of their knick knacks working."

"Sure, that sounds great Sam," he replied wearily. His eyes darted to an open tin of butterscotch candy on her desk. "Now, by way of repayment for you letting me go into the nanite initiation blind, I demand one of your candies as a reward."

His hand darted forward and grabbed one of the candies.

"I wouldn't Dan." She spoke softly, trying to suppress a laugh.

Dan rolled his eyes and popped it into his mouth.

Excess glucose detected.

What in the hell? Dan grumbled to himself. Was the System actually going to be monitoring his diet and giving him crap? He had a doctor for that. Every year, they told him to watch his diet and exercise more, and every year Dan made the same excuses and signed up for a gym membership that he never used. He'd need to find some way of shutting the notifications off, because there was no way in hell he was going to give up on an occasional burger or milkshake. That was not at all what he had signed up for when he agreed to come and work for the Thoth Foundation. Or, at least, it wasn't what he thought he had signed up for. There really were a lot of pages in that employment contract, and he had been a bit dazed after he read the salary figure.

Please refrain from consuming excess glucose, or remedial countermeasures will be deployed.

What in the world were remedial countermeasures? He glanced at Sam. She was grinning at him, shaking her head slowly. He swished the candy around in his mouth. Her smile grew.

"Oh shit!" His eyes widened. "You know I have a sweet tooth; this isn't fair..."

Dan never got a chance to finish the sentence. His body immediately grew warm, like he had a fever. Writing appeared in the lower left corner of his vision

Remedial countermeasure intensity 1 deployed.

Dan's body spasmed, and his vision flashed white. It hurt, but not as much as he had expected it to. Instead, all his muscles seized at once, his spasming jaw cracking the candy in two as he fell to the ground. Several seconds later, the sensation ended. He grimaced. That had been a profoundly unpleasant experience.

"And that was for getting drunk and hitting on my girlfriend at the holiday party," Sam whispered to him with a wink while patting him on the shoulder. "Look, I know things have been a bit lax at the lab since I changed organizations, but you really need to know that randomly putting things in your mouth is terrible lab safety practice."

Please refrain from consuming excess glucose, or remedial countermeasures will be deployed at intensity 2.

"Plus," she shrugged apologetically, "if we're going to fix your diet with negative reinforcement, we need to let you experience it at least once. Sorry about that; your psych profile said it wouldn't work otherwise. You'd just find an excuse to keep sneaking sweets."

He frantically spat out the candy while Samantha looked on with a bemused expression. He staggered to his feet, his pride the only real victim of the entire endeavor. Worst of all, she wasn't wrong. Every diet he had tried before this had been a victim of his own willpower. Briefly, he glared at the offending chunks of candy as they sat on the otherwise pristine floor, taunting him.

"What the hell did I sign up for, Doctor Weathers?" he asked.

"A whole lot of fun, at least for me," she replied, shrugging with a smile.

CHAPTER SIX

The Next Steps

The next handful of months passed in a blur. One of Doctor Weather's earliest successes was in activating the magical effects scripted into the arms and armor of the invaders.

Thankfully, rather than the uncontrolled explosions of mana he was used to, which risked himself and his surroundings, Dan simply had to feed the artifact a trickle of mana, and the enchantment would take from him what it needed to activate. Most importantly, this allowed the research team to use the translation enchantments they discovered in the officers' helmets.

At first, everyone gathered around Dan like children at storytime as he read the contents of the various novels and technical manuals stolen from the aliens, all while wearing a gleaming silver helmet. Then, in frustration, Doctor Weathers announced that Dan's recounting of technical data was "slow and boring."

That was how Dan found out that he didn't have to process what was written for the System in his body to record it. Specifically, Doctor Weathers strapped him into a chair and forced his eyes open as another team member rapidly paged through the books in front of him. Dan wasn't sure how he felt about the "Droog" treatment, as the good doctor called it, but it did the job, rapidly filling the Foundation's database on the aliens.

The rest of the testing was much more arduous. Dan only really had enough mana to attempt activating an alien gauntlet once per hour. Fairly quickly, he was able to discover that each time he used a specific gauntlet, it felt a little more natural to him. He still couldn't really control what he was doing with them, but he was gaining a little bit of intuitive control over their intensity, duration, and range.

The good news was that his reserves replenished fairly quickly. The bad news was that they replenished more quickly while he was exerting himself, which meant even more exercise.

Jogging around the track for what felt like the twentieth time, Dan cursed himself for forgetting about Doctor Weather's savage sense of humor. After she left the Army, the department had been directionless, and all he could remember was her leadership and poise. The woman was brilliant, but inclined to vexing pranks and jokes. Hence, every time he ran out of mana, he was sent back to the gym.

Body has increased by 0.1 to 4.6

After quickly reading the update, Dan chuckled to himself. At least there was a silver lining. The System would periodically update him as his body became quantifiably healthier and stronger. He'd already lost the fast food belly, and he was well on his way towards actual physical fitness. He still wouldn't be any sort of competition for the security team. Every time he shared the track with them, they kept a much faster pace for much longer than Dan, but slow and steady improvement was a lot better than he had managed as a project employee for the Army.

Mana has regenerated to full.

Reading the update, Dan stopped his run and checked his internal timer. About forty minutes. Better than his previous time by about two. He grabbed a bottle of water from his locker and set his sights on the shower. Although the System didn't inherently track his mana, Sam had come up with the idea of setting an alarm once he was "full," preventing him from wasting excess time in the gym when he could be experimenting with a gauntlet.

Dan towelled off. He had a meeting scheduled with Samantha and the chairman to go over the project's preliminary results, and he would prefer to not smell rank for the conference. The shower itself was quick and warm. He'd never admit it to Doctor Weathers, but even the slight increases to his body stat from exercise and dietary changes made him feel remarkably better. Even if the rest of this entire experiment really didn't go anywhere, at least he was coming out the other end healthier than he'd been since high school.

Thirty minutes later, he was in the conference room where he had first met the chairman, wearing fresh clothes. Since the beginning of the project, Henry, Sam, and Dan had met here weekly to go over regular status updates. Each time, the old man had been absolutely filled with excitement. As if summoned by Dan's musing, Henry walked through the doorway, trailed by a security guard with eyes alight.

"Dan, my boy, good news!" he gushed, his southern accent becoming more pronounced with his excitement. "I know we've been running you ragged both literally and figuratively, but our xenology team and Doctor Weathers have advanced our understanding of magic immeasurably in the two and a half months you've been here. I'll let her do the presentation, but we're finally almost ready to switch to beta testing."

"Beta testing?" Dan frowned, his memory immediately focusing upon the unpleasantness of the System's installation. "Does that mean you're going to have to update the System? Are you sure that it's completely necessary? I mean, I'm more than happy to deal with it, if it brings us to the next step in everything, but I would prefer to avoid an update unless it's something good."

"You're the Beta, and you'll be testing." Samantha rolled her eyes. "Just suck it up, Dan, and trust me, this will be good."

"Now!" She coughed theatrically to clear her throat before continuing. "As I was about to say before the chairman stole my thunder and the peanut gallery began complaining, we've cleared the first major hurdle with the System. We now have enough data on mana and the runescript that the aliens use for enchantments that, with a fairly simple update, it will become self-learning."

"Before Dan expresses his concerns about being kept unconscious in a pink pod while the AI uses him as a power source," she uncannily cut him off before he could make the reference, "self-learning is both more and less limited than that. The System doesn't have a true AI, so it will never be able to do more than respond to simple queries. It can't think or act on its own."

"Despite that, the System knows Dan's muscular, skeletal, and nervous system inside and out," Sam continued. "It has been monitoring the way Dan uses his mana. The aliens' writings keep talking about 'mana pathways,' and although we haven't identified exactly where they are in Dan yet, the System has noticed patterns in how the mana is channeled."

"According to the aliens' novice primers, it takes between three years and a decade of our time for a spellcaster to form a proper affinity with an element to the point that they can efficiently channel mana through an attunement stone." Dan paled as Sam clicked a button. A slide of one of the aliens' gauntlets projected onto the wall. "The attunement stones are set into what we have been referring to as the 'magical gauntlets.' Dan's use of an attunement stone will be monitored closely by the System. It's watching what works and what doesn't work. It will discard what doesn't work and upload as a kind of mental muscle memory what does work."

"By the same token, once Dan actually starts to work with an attunement stone he has an affinity for, he will need to shape his mana into a spell." Sam clicked the button again, and the wall of the conference room displayed a picture of a human silhouette with multiple yellow channels running through it.

"The best of the alien mages do this on the fly, but each of them has more than a thousand years of spellcasting experience. Instead, Dan will be creating predetermined effects through the system through trial and error. These will be notated as 'spells,' and he should be able to activate them simply by saying their name or concentrating on them. The System will then replay its recording of what he did to make the spell work in the first place."

"Good!" Henry nodded, a cheshire smile on his face. "You're much further along than I hoped. How are the attempts at duplicating Dan's abilities? As hard of a worker as he is, I'd prefer to have a couple more wizard-candidates running around."

Sam's face soured. She picked up the tablet in front of her and flipped back a couple pages in her report before responding.

"The good news for Dan is that he got tremendously lucky." She clicked the device in her hand, and a series of semi-burned corpses appeared on the wall. "What he did has only succeeded three times in the rather extensive history of the Tellask Empire. Each time, the resulting mage had a tremendous power supply and almost limitless affinities. Unfortunately, eating mana crystals is a great and expensive way to die a painful death via self immolation. We found this out from several of the lab assistants who disregarded our warnings and tried to seize glory by joining Dan in the project without authorization."

"No." She utilized the clicker once more to bring up the Thoth Foundation logo, hiding the previous grisly scene. "The Empire and most rational races usually awaken the mana-sensitive by having a mage of sufficient rank inject mana into them until they are able to activate an affinity. The bad news is that Dan, although full of potential, is far from the required rank. The very bad news is that I'm not really sure we have great options for him to reach that rank on Earth."

"What's this about the Tellask Empire?" Dan asked, only for Henry to cut in.

"No, I'm the boss! Tell me what you mean by us not being able to rank Dan up. Xenology can come next," the chairman demanded, frowning.

"Dan is at the first rank." Samantha flipped a couple pages on her tablet. "Here on Earth, he still has a couple options to improve. He can work on increasing his affinities, which will decrease his mana usage, and he can work on increasing his ability with spell images, improving the spell's strength and his control over it."

"That said," she added with a sigh as she leaned back in her chair. "He needs to encounter and claim more mana in order to actually increase the amount of mana his body can hold. The good news is that his... unorthodox method of becoming a mage has increased his regeneration of mana greatly. The bad news is that claiming mana involves killing a sentient being or mana-infused monster. Most of their mana will fade into the world around them, but a small portion will flow into their murderer and increase that person's total pool."

"We could have Dan kill a bunch of criminals." She shrugged helplessly. "But if they don't have mana themselves, the gains will be minimal. I have no idea what sort of numbers we will need to rank him up once, and from what we can tell, he will have to be at least rank five before he can start awakening people."

"Are you sure we can't rebrand the process of absorbing mana as 'gaining experience'?" Ibis mused, tapping his index finger on the table thoughtfully. "Maybe we can work on the translation. Leveling sounds better than ranking up, too."

Dan barely heard them as Sam put her foot down over the words used by the translation software. He was strangely okay with the idea of violence. Maybe the constant use of the gauntlets had messed with him, or maybe it was all of his time hanging out with soldiers, but he just didn't feel concerned by the prospect.

Intellectually, he knew that this was the point where he should have been wringing his hands, worried about the dangerous route things were taking. Either that, or he should be worried about whether he had the edge needed to take another's life. Instead, he just *knew*. The energy in his chest, the mana, practically begged for him to release it. The idea of having an outlet beyond a stale target excited him.

Shit, maybe he did need to see the Foundation shrink.

He didn't think that a tech nerd like him was supposed to be getting this worked up about the idea of killing someone. Of course, if he talked to someone, they would ground him. Stop him from using the magic. Stop the project entirely. The last thing they'd want was some sort of magically-empowered psychopath running around.

Dan took a deep, shuddering breath. He couldn't let that happen. It wouldn't be fair to him, Doctor Weathers, or to anyone else who had worked so hard. No, he'd just have to watch himself. He had everything under control right now. He could let someone know if things got out of hand.

"The Tellask Empire." Dan blinked. Sam was talking to him, so the least he could do was pay attention rather than worry about nothing. Probably nothing.

She continued, "It's the largest interstellar polity in this arm of the galaxy. It's existed for almost 75,000 years, and as far as we can tell, it's ruled primarily by elves, the tall, skinny elite soldiers from first contact."

"Elves live for thousands of years and don't stop learning in that entire time." She flipped to another page on her tablet. "If you see an elf, and you don't have a full squad at your back, you should run."

"Young elves are only slightly stronger than humans," Sam lectured on. "But they usually don't leave their home worlds until they reach at least six hundred. By that point, taking one down will be a problem. We're just lucky that almost all interstellar technology has stagnated. All of the major players focused on magic as soon as they got it, and almost no one has anything more impressive than a black powder six shooter, and even that is considered the secret signature weapon of the dwarves."

"Politically," she continued, "the Tellask Empire is ruled by multiple noble houses, each of which control a region of space. They are responsible for repelling threats in their region and supporting the Empire as a whole in times of need. Our region is controlled by House Amberell."

"Now, it's not uncommon for a House or the Empire as a whole to have a tributary state." She flipped through a couple of pages on her tablet. "A tributary state is a planet that provides soldiers and taxes to the Empire, but otherwise gets to run its own business. Our region has several tributary states, but the bad news is that the Tellask aren't who we need to be worried about. That is the Orakh, a bloodthirsty race held together by a warlord who lays waste to planet after planet. They're pushing House Amberell pretty hard in our region, and even if we don't end up in contact with the Tellask for a while, it's only a matter of time before the Orakh stumble upon us, and we very much do not want that."

"Are the Orakh green?" The chairman asked excitedly. "Big and musclebound? Maybe prone to organizing in clans? Shamans, that sort of thing?"

"Yes..." Samantha frowned slightly. "How did you know? That wasn't in the briefing."

"This is perfect!" Henry shouted, clapping his hands. "Space elves, space dwarves, and now space orcs. We even need to have Dan earn XP so that he can level up enough to use more powerful spells. This is what the System was made for!"

"For your cardiologist's sake, I hesitate to continue," Sam drawled, rolling her eyes. "But I do think you're going to be even more excited about this part."

"We've managed to come up with a solution to the problem of Dan's 'level'." She practically glared at Ibis as she buried the final word in sarcasm. "Dan is going to need to attune himself to space magic. We've salvaged a teleportation pad from the alien voidship, and with a proper attunement and enough power, he'll be able to use it."

"We should be able to scrounge up just enough mana to teleport Dan to an awakened Tellask tributary world." Sam sighed, bracing herself for Ibis' reaction. "There, he can fight monsters, save maidens, and gain power. All of that fun stuff. Eventually, once he surpasses Rank 5, which will probably take some time, he can return home, and we can look into awakening Earth. With our technology supplemented by magic, we can probably hold off the Orakh and establish ourselves as a power in our own right."

The chairman was too busy twitching in excitement to follow up on Samantha's delivery. Dan was pretty sure Sam had been joking when she made the crack about the chairman's cardiologist, but now he wasn't so certain. Regardless, the chairman didn't seem up to carrying on the conversation at the moment, so Dan filled in.

"All right, Doctor Weathers, what's the next step?" he asked hesitantly.

"Dan..." She smiled at him. "You told me to warn you first, but this is going to hurt."

"Is there any alternative?" he asked, frowning as she shook her head. "Fine then, Sam. Hurt me."

"Dan," she replied, her grin all teeth, "I thought you'd never ask. System, authorization Samantha J Weathers Fourteen B Seven Hash L Three. Initialize beta update for User."

Dan's vision went white, and his body was wracked with pain.

Firmware update beginning 1%
Please do not turn off the System. This will take a while.
You may lose consciousness and reawaken several times
Goddamnit, Sam.

CHAPTER SEVEN

Training and Waiting

After the update, it took almost a year for Dan to reach a level of skill that made Samantha and Henry comfortable with sending him through the portal.

Dan appreciated their concern for his safety, but he was starting to get antsy. Every spare minute he wasn't raising an affinity or practicing a spell, Dan was either working out or training a skill Henry thought necessary under the supervision of a nationally-renowned expert. It was more than enough to drive him slightly stir crazy. Through a combination of hard work and the Thoth Foundation's seemingly-limitless resources, he had gained all of these skills. Now, he just wanted an opportunity to use them.

His attributes reflected the effort, both on his part and on the part of the nutritionists and personal trainers hired to help him. Specifically, his Body grew to 6, his Perception grew to 6, and his Agility grew to 7. Gone was his awkward gait and beer belly. Dan still didn't look like a professional athlete. After all, even the best routine can't overcome decidedly average genetics, but he was definitely in better shape than most twenty-year-olds.

Unfortunately, his physical trainer warned him that he'd

about hit his limit. A lot of physique was hard work, but past a certain point, it could only maintain what he'd earned. Body 6 wasn't enough to compete in the Olympics, but with any luck, it'd keep him healthy and alive.

His skills were another point of pride. Henry insisted that he train in swordsmanship, brawling, archery, and general wilderness survival. For almost two months, the chairman tried to force Dan to learn how to fight with two weapons, but he just wasn't good enough with his left hand to make it work.

Eventually, after much grumbling, Henry relented, and Dan truly began to excel. He quickly found that he enjoyed the exertion and freedom of sword fighting. Hand-to-hand fighting was also fun, with his instructors teaching him a combination of Krav Maga and Aikido, but he just didn't get the same exhilaration he did from swinging a sword. That said, either option felt more productive than constantly running in a circle or lifting heavy objects as a medium for breaking a sweat.

Dan was pleasantly surprised to find that the self-learning aspect of the System applied to skills as well. It quickly developed a baseline for his height and build and began subtly nudging him toward proper form. Without thinking, he would keep his elbow in while striking or keep his arms up in a guard while kicking. Where the System really shined was in assisting him in learning more complex moves. He only needed to perform a hold, strike, or parry perfectly once before it simply became his default. Even Dan's balance improved markedly as the System took over many of the finer points of muscular coordination.

Really, the System was a marvel. It wouldn't let him do anything he couldn't accomplish normally, but it helped him learn at an accelerated pace and assured consistent execution of forms he had already mastered.

Magic was its crowning glory. Affinities were simply a frustrating matter of mana and practice, but spells would have been almost impossible without its influence. Six months ago, he had gained enough electric affinity to actually begin experimenting with spells, and it was an absolute nightmare. The number of variables he needed to hold in his head while channeling the raw, untamed mana was daunting beyond belief. Even the simplest of effects was like performing calculus while juggling on one leg during a blizzard.

Dan couldn't even count the number of times that he lost control of some aspect of his electrical affinity and shocked himself. The time he lost focus on the voltage and let it spike? Shock. The time he didn't define the flow of the current as he introduced electricity? Shock. The time he accidentally started the amperage a little too high? Well not a shock, but it instantly arced and shorted out his cellphone.

It was like any action really, except humans didn't have years of evolution to aid them in the form of their subconscious. You didn't think about all of the calculations that went into something as simple as catching a ball. Discerning its speed, rate of drop, and trajectory as well as commanding your arms to move at the right speed to be in the right spot for you to order your hands to cradle and catch the ball are all second nature. Magic was like that, except humans didn't even have the subconscious instincts to move their mana properly. The System couldn't bridge all of these gaps, but it at least made the process just challenging, rather than almost impossible.

Later, Dan found out that even elves didn't try to create all spells from raw, elementally-attuned mana. Instead, most attunement stones were inserted in gauntlets with runescript inscribed on them that would do the heavy lifting for a portion of the spell. As an example, the lightning stone used by the elven commander was attached to circuitry that just required him to determine a direction and an amount of energy to be expended, and it would generate a stroke of lightning. Evidently, this is what he had used to kill Jane in front of Dan. Unfortunately, it was a powerful ability. Even by expending all of his mana, Dan could only fire a jolt of electricity about two feet.

When he had been disappointed by the effect, Samantha

just rolled her eyes and explained lightning to him. Air was a bad conductor. Like, a really bad conductor. It took a lot of power to arc electricity through the air, so the fact that the spell could deliver anything above a mild static shock at two feet was incredibly impressive.

Instead, she convinced him to focus his lightning magic on touches and strikes, at least until he gained some more power. It was a bit anticlimactic after months of imagining his new life as the second coming of the god of thunder to only come away with two spells: *Shocking Fist* and *Spark Field*. *Shocking Fist* simply allowed him to deliver a taser-like shock when he touched or punched someone. *Spark Field* allowed Dan to infuse a handful of dirt or dust with a strong negative or positive charge before throwing it. The charged dust would then mildly and repeatedly shock anything it encountered until the charge was expended. Not exactly a damaging ability, but one that Dan developed in secret over the course of two weeks, mostly to use on Doctor Weathers during one of her smug moments. It was surprising and distracting, something that might come in useful at some point, even if it couldn't directly cause harm.

As much as he enjoyed playing with electricity, most of his time and mana over the year was spent on increasing his affinity with space magic. The teleportation pad required a significant amount of energy, and given Dan's rather pathetic mana levels, that meant increasing the efficiency of that mana to the point where he could activate the pad, even for a second.

He did learn one incredibly useful spell that Henry named *Spatial Shield*. *Spatial Shield* deflected attacks. It wasn't enough to completely protect Dan, but it could turn a solid hit into a glancing blow, and more than one sparring strike that should have hit him had been turned into a near miss. He could only keep the spell going for about ten seconds before he ran out of mana entirely, but before long he got the hang of activating the spell in the split second before an attack would hit him.

He smiled to himself. Finally, it was all paying off. Dan sat in the conference room where he had first met Director Ibis and where he had spent so many hours reviewing the results of his training over the past year, and he waited. Leaning up against the wall sat a backpack stuffed with camping supplies and food as well as the equipment he had trained with: a simple recurve shortbow, quiver, and longsword.

Dan wore the armor he planned on using on the other side, a suit of stainless steel chainmail with a silver helmet that some of the simple translation runescripts had been transferred to. The scientists had prioritized translation for obvious reasons, but they were hopeful that they would be able to replicate the enhancement and protection runes within the next year or two. There had been a few setbacks with writing the runes. Even when identically recreated, the new runes didn't accept mana. In short, Dan looked like he was ready to head off to a renaissance fair... which, upon reflection, he concluded was more or less the goal. After his final debriefing, he would be stepping onto the teleportation pad and become the first Earthling to set foot on an extrasolar body.

As for magic, the Foundation's scientists had done a fair amount of research into the attunement stones. Apparently, they could be made from any crystal so long as you inscribed the correct runes on them. The only requirement for using them was that they remained in contact with his body.

Of course, this led to Samantha having a handful of rose quartz attunement stones implanted surgically in the bones of his forearms. Mercifully, they put him under for the operation.

Even though he had only really worked on his lightning and space affinities, Sam convinced him to include fire, metal, gravity, and force stones as well. He wouldn't be able to use them without substantial experimentation, but everyone expected him to be on the other side for at least a year or two. Giving him room to expand was essential.

"Status" he said aloud. He didn't need to speak to activate the System anymore. Simply subvocalizing, shaping the word with his mouth without actually speaking, was sufficient to activate it. He just preferred actually saying the words. It all seemed a little more real and grounded that way.

<USER> Status
Rank 1

Body 6
Agility 7
Mind 7
Perception 6
Spirit 1

Skills
Swords 4, Brawling 3, Archery 2

Affinity
Space 9, Lightning 5, Fire 1, Gravity 1

Spells
Shocking Fist 4, Spark Field 2, Spatial Shield 5

The door opened to let the chairman and Doctor Weathers into the conference room. For once, Samantha was serious, but the chairman was as exuberant as ever. They sat down, and she pulled out her tablet, ready to give Dan his final briefing.

"So, how are you feeling?" She asked as she tapped away at the tablet, "Any nerves, or are you ready to leap forth into the unknown?"

"Honestly?" Dan replied with a shrug, "I'm pretty excited. It might be dangerous, but I'm finally going to have a chance to put everything I've been learning into action. Maybe I'd be more worried if I hadn't been stuck training for a year, but I'm starting to get bored. I just don't really get the point of having mystic powers if I can't use them to smite someone."

She grinned at him. "Well, at least your mood has improved."

"We've identified your target." She tapped her tablet, and a picture of a gas giant appeared on the conference room wall. "One of the moons orbiting what we think is a gas giant in Alpha Centauri. Unfortunately, we don't have a whole lot of information about the target. The books we got from the alien spaceship were mostly focused on theory, politics, and popular culture. The place we're sending you barely rated a mention, but there were only two targets within the teleport pad's theoretical range, and the other is infested with Orakh. The moon we are sending you to is known as "Twilight" in the elvish tongue. It's a human tributary state. It's close enough that we can get you there. That's about all we know."

"Nothing on the locals?" Dan questioned. "Flora, fauna, currency, anything like that?"

"No one cared enough to write it down," Doctor Weathers replied with a shrug. "It's in the Empire, so its mana is awakened, and you will be able to fight and claim mana. That's about everything we know. We're hopeful that the translation runes in your helmet will allow you to gain more information when you're there, but that's about all we have on the situation we're going to drop you into."

"What about the teleportation?" Dan followed up, a slight frown creeping onto his face. "Do we have any idea where it's going to drop me? What happens when I hit Rank five? How am I supposed to get home?"

"Level five!" Dan and Samantha looked up briefly as the chairman called out to them from across the room.

Sam rolled her eyes before turning back to Dan and fussing over the straps and fit of his armor.

"The teleportation should drop you within fifty miles of an active beacon in one of their cities." She tapped at her tablet before looking up. "If you were more powerful, you could drop yourself directly on the beacon, but I suspect this is a blessing in disguise.

"I'm not sure you could integrate immediately upon teleporting in." Sam chuckled wryly. "I've seen you trying to tell lies, and there's a reason you haven't unlocked an acting skill through the System. Teleporting outside city limits might not be ideal for the purpose of avoiding monsters, but the goal is for you to kill them, anyway. I guess you're just going to start the process sooner rather than later."

"As for returning..." She tapped the side of her head. "Teleportation is mostly done via complex calculations related to stellar landmarks. Your System is programmed with the return route, but we aren't going to let you consciously activate it. That way even if someone tortures you, they won't find the way to Earth. There's only one route home; step onto the pad and activate it."

"I'd prefer to avoid being tortured," Dan retorted, smiling slightly.

"That's what they all say at first." Sam rolled her eyes. "Now, unless there are any further questions, I think I've covered everything we know. Namely, nothing other than the name and general stellar location of the place we are sending you. So, uh... good luck, I guess?"

"Are you sure I can't have a gun?" Dan asked. "I've gotten pretty good with a sword, but I have to be honest. An 'in case of emergency' pistol would go a long way toward easing my concerns."

"Absolutely not!" Ibis shook his head resolutely. "It would absolutely ruin the ambiance. Who ever heard of a world traveler just shooting monsters? The hero is a swordsman, and that's final!"

Sam ignored the excited old man. "I'm sorry, Dan, modern technology is too much of a risk. If you get captured, that's awful, but the Tellask won't have a full picture of Earth's capabilities. A pistol or a computer would be too much of a risk, especially if they torture you into talking about how they work."

"So, I'm on my own," Dan replied, the full impact of what he was about to do finally beginning to settle in.

"I'm afraid so," Sam agreed. "I wish we had another

option, but this is our best chance to keep Earth free and safe. Just play it safe, and you'll come home both a wizard and hero."

"Play it safe?" Ibis squinted at Sam, his incredulous voice completely at odds with the grim tone of the room.

"Doctor Weathers, can I have a minute with Mr. Thrush?" After a couple seconds of silence, the chairman spoke to Sam. "I'd like to wish him luck in private before we send him into the great unknown."

Samantha nodded and stood up. She walked around the table and hugged Dan. Even though she insisted on making his life hell from time to time, that's what friends did. He could see it in her eyes. She was worried about everything, even if she couldn't just come out and say it. She smiled tightly and exited the room, leaving Dan alone with the chairman. After almost a minute of silence, the older man broke it.

"Dan, I know that you are ready to do this," Henry's voice was serious, his eyes unwavering. "You've trained for a year with the best that Earth has to offer, and you're as ready as you will ever be. What you're doing is important, a tremendous boon to the planet as a whole. If you don't succeed, I don't know how we'll be able to hold off the Orakh. Our technology is superior, but man for man, we simply won't be able to match them without magic, and they have multiple planets. They will have more soldiers than us. We *need* Earth awakened. We need the hope that magic has to offer us!

"But," Henry took a deep breath, a strange gleam lighting his eyes, "there are some things that are more important. You are doing your duty to humanity, but you need to do your duty as a man. We are sending you to another world with spectacular powers that the locals won't be able to understand or match. As a red-blooded man, you must do us all proud!"

He reached across the table and grabbed Dan's hand, holding it in an iron grip that belied his age. "You need to conquer an alien girl, preferably an elf. You're going to a world of magic, wonder, and easily-impressed locals. It's part of the narrative. It's essential to your duty as a human man."

Dan agreed noncommittally, more than slightly disturbed by the zeal in chairman Ibis' voice. He really wasn't sure what the man was talking about, but the conversation was making him more than a little uncomfortable.

"I'm too old, my boy." A strange fire burned in Ibis' eyes. "Years of whiskey and hard living have taken their toll on me. Even when a girl catches my fancy, it's more a matter of science and chemicals than flesh and will for me, but you? You're still young, Dan!"

This was about *girls*? He struggled to keep the disgust from his face. The chairman was sending him to fight aliens, the risk of torture hanging over his head like the Sword of Damocles, and the old man was trying to relive his youth?

"I really don't know if I'll have time," Dan responded, trying to placate the excited old man. "I'll be stuck in constant life and death struggles trying to gain enough mana to return."

Hopefully that would put an end to things. He was bad enough at dating one girl. Even if the option presented itself, Dan knew better than to bite off more than he could chew.

Henry grabbed Dan's wrist, refusing to let him leave. "My boy, you can't let this opportunity pass you by. You have dark hair, a weak personality, and you're heading to a new world. I bet you'll have a buffet of women dragging you to a beach or a hot spring within a week of your arrival."

He demurred, mumbling something that the manic old man could loosely interpret as agreement. The chairman walked him to the teleportation pad, whispering progressively more outlandish tips and hints regarding the local woman to an increasingly-alarmed Dan.

The pad looked like a ten-foot-by-ten-foot stone pedestal wreathed in runescript with a three-foot-tall stone pillar sticking up from its center. Around it, scientists bustled as they connected mana batteries and scavenged from the invader's equipment he had painstakingly charged point-by-point over the last month.

The entire array looked like something whipped up by a

mad scientist, glowing gems connected by silver wiring to metal plates covered in strange sigils, all around a humming obelisk. To complete the slapdash appearance, a laptop was connected via a USB cable to a crystal in the pillar, a complex map of the galaxy rotating on its screen.

Dan took a deep breath and walked to the center of the pad. Glancing around, he took in the sights of Earth one last time before putting his hand on the pad and willing his mana into it.

The world went white.

At least this time it didn't hurt.

CHAPTER EIGHT

Beyond

Dan fell to his knees on something spongy and slightly damp as his vision wavered. The world around him swam as he fought through the vertigo. It took a couple seconds before he could actually make out his surroundings, but slowly the blurriness worked its way back into focus. It was evening, dark but not quite night, and he was in a swamp of some sort. Dan gazed up into the sky to get his bearings and did a double take.

Gone was the sun, a moon, or any sort of familiar markers. In fact, Dan couldn't spot Alpha Centauri A no matter where he looked. Instead, almost the entire sky was filled with a tan gas giant, hovering just out of reach and illuminating the planet softly with reflected light. He bounced on his toes. It might have been the springy moss analogue he was standing on, but Dan was pretty sure he jumped higher than he should have. He didn't exactly have precision equipment, but his gut said that the gravity was a noticeable amount lower than Earth standard.

Dan shivered. The air was brisk but not exactly cold. He'd have to keep moving, find warmer clothes, or start a fire, or things would get uncomfortable. Dan began trekking through the mossy swamp, careful to avoid the brackish water. He chuckled to himself. That would be a fitting end for Daniel Thrush, explorer and adventurer. Dying of hypothermia the first night on an alien world. It certainly felt like it would fit with the trajectory of his luck and life to date.

A certain part of his brain couldn't help but reflect on the icy and bleak expanse and compare it to chairman Ibis' fever dreams. There were many ways to describe Dan's surroundings, but "hot springs" certainly wasn't one of them.

A growl echoed behind him. Dan turned around and saw a flash of green eyes in the murky light. A rust-colored bear, almost three feet at the shoulder, crouched on an island of the moss. A monster, immediately upon arrival! There was his luck at work.

The bear seemed a bit small to him, but he had hunted black bears on the family land in Michigan with his Dad before. They weren't much bigger than the thing before him, but it certainly wasn't a great idea to tangle with them. He amended his morose thoughts. *Daniel Thrush, first extrasolar explorer, eaten by a tiny bear.*

Dan unsheathed his sword, keeping his eyes trained on the bear. It moved slowly towards him, eyes unblinking. He chuckled slightly. That wasn't a great sign. Most black bears on Earth avoided people, concluding that humans were more trouble than they were worth. This thing didn't look at him like he was a threat. It looked at him the same way he looked at the mess hall's steamed dumplings after a long run. He wasn't a problem; he was prey.

It charged him, scrambling toward him across the uncertain surface of the springy moss. Almost six feet from him, it leapt into the air, and Dan sensed a ripple of mana that reminded him of weight and gravity. Great, it could use magic. Ten minutes into his grand space adventure, and he ran into a tiny, hungry, magical bear.

Dan threw himself to the side, grabbing his sword in both hands and swinging it at the flying bear. It twisted in the air and swung a paw at his shoulder. Despite the low gravity, he realized in an instant that he wasn't going to be able to completely dodge the incoming claw. The monster was just too fast for his trained, but decidedly mundane reflexes. Instead, he muttered "Spatial Shield" and felt the System pull mana from him for a split second. In that moment, the thrill and the adrenaline from the magic use poured through him.

The bear's paw seemed to impact on a soap bubble of magic that briefly popped into existence around Dan before its claws slipped off the surface and swung past him. His sword, on the other hand, dug deep into the bear's ribs, cutting through its thick fur and eliciting a spray of blood. A smile flashed across Dan's face. This is what he had trained for. That split second of adrenaline and terror was what it was all about. Then, he landed in the foul swamp water with a splash.

He tried to pull himself to his feet, but it was hard to find enough purchase on the now-slippery moss, and in that moment the bear was back upon him. This time, Dan was stuck on his back, flailing wildly. There wouldn't be any dodging. It snapped its jaws towards his throat, trying to end the fight in one stroke now that he was off balance. Panic flowed down his spine as he swung his free arm ineffectually to try and knock the incoming snout away from him. At the last second, inspiration struck him and Dan mumbled "Shocking Fist."

Again, mana flowed out of his core, and the adrenaline-laced thrill shuddered through his body. Only two spells into the fight, and he was already beginning to feel the emptiness and hunger of mana depletion. He would have to finish things soon.

His hand hit the side of the bear's head, and it rocked back with an audible *crack* and flash of light as the electricity discharged. Stunned, the creature didn't react as Dan grabbed his sword with both hands and stabbed up into the creature's underbelly. The blade skittered off of its thick ribs before it slipped between them. In a panic, Dan ripped the blade sideways, lengthening the wound.

The pain snapped the creature out of its stupor, and it swung a claw at Dan. It was practically on top of him. No amount of artifice or magic was going to stop him from taking the blow. Instead, he turned his armored left shoulder into the blow and let its force knock him clear of the bear.

He wasn't sure if it had broken anything, but it sure hurt like hell before the System clamped down on the nerves and shut down the pain. He tried to open and close the hand, but it didn't respond. Whether his inability was due to serious structural damage or the System's influence to keep him from being distracted by the pain, he didn't know. It'd be a problem to deal with later.

He pulled his knife from his belt with his remaining hand. The bear didn't look hungry or predatory anymore. Instead, blood matted its fur and the hilt of the longsword glittered from its stomach. Its breath clouded the chilly air with a wet rattle. He had definitely stabbed a lung in their earlier exchange.

With a hole in a lung, the bear was on its last legs. Or, it was an alien and had more than one pair of lungs, in which case Dan was completely and irrevocably boned. That said, the last year had taught him the importance of positive thinking.

He darted forward, his left arm flopping bonelessly behind him, probably exacerbating the damage caused by the bear's claws. He stopped short, his boots digging into the spongy moss of the swamp as he let a sluggish swing sail past him before he lunged forward once again. The bear's eyes tracked him, but they were clouded. Even with his arm disabled, Dan had dealt more damage to the monster than it had to him.

"Shocking Fist!" he shouted as he brought his right elbow around into the side of its head. Again, there was the rush of adrenaline and heat as his mana flowed into his elbow and discharged, its flash lighting the night. The bear's eyes lost any semblance of focus and its body shuddered as the electricity flowed through it. This time, Dan took advantage of the creature being stunned by the blow and drove the knife into its eye.

He jumped back in time to avoid its death throes, breathing heavily. It lunged in his direction, flailing wildly, but stopped short. It collapsed into the mud and moss, and slowly the green light left its remaining eye.

Then, Dan felt it. The bear had been awakened. Its mana transferred into him. The feeling was indescribable. It was like having sex for the first time while eating the best meal of his life and skydiving, but somehow better. His entire body shuddered in euphoria as sparks of pure creative energy jolted back and forth inside him.

He dropped to his knees, his left arm forgotten. He could almost see the stream of energy flowing from the bear's corpse into him. He felt the mana sate a hunger that he hadn't even known existed, and he vowed to himself that, no matter what the cost, he *would* get more of this. Dan needed to feel this again.

Eventually, a rasping sound woke him from his magical, euphoria-induced stupor. Dan blinked and chuckled to himself as he realized that the sound was him breathing heavily. In the corner of his vision, an innocent notification burned in blue:

Mana influx detected. Recalculating Spirit.

Spirit is now 2.

He smiled. It would take a while, but he was starting. Sam had theorized that the next rank would require a Spirit of 10, but he had time. It was just a matter of finding more monsters to kill. Hopefully, the next fight wouldn't be such a desperate life-or-death struggle. What he really needed at this stage was something more to the tune of magic chipmunks or bunnies. Bears were a bit much.

Injuries detected. Infection detected.

System needs material to make repairs, it is suggested that <USER> find a source of protein immediately.

He sighed. Definitely magical bunnies and chipmunks.

CHAPTER NINE

Camping

Dan sighed as he sat next to the fire. It had taken him almost two hours to collect and dry enough moss to actually attempt to make the fire with just one arm, but the warmth was essential. The strange planet didn't have a traditional 'night' like Earth, instead the gas giant hung in the sky, bathing the swamp in its dim reflected light.

He stretched the kinks from his back and arms. Despite the fire, he was still getting tired, and it was still cold. Plus, he needed something to cook the bear meat. Well, cooking was a stretch. Dan stared mournfully at the slightly-blacked meat hissing on a short wooden spit in the fire. Searing it until it hopefully wouldn't make him sick sounded a bit more correct.

He bit into the haunch, trying to ignore the way the sizzling meat burned his remaining hand. It was gamey and under-seasoned, but to Dan's nutrient-starved body, it was the best meal ever. He could almost feel the nanites grabbing the protein from his stomach and using it to reconstruct his mangled shoulder.

Since the System was originally based on nanites designed

to keep billionaires alive forever, it was hardly surprising that they came with a regenerative function. Really, outside of aiding Dan's muscle memory and providing analysis as a sort of internal personal computer, the only thing the System did was keep him healthy, given enough raw materials. It wouldn't heal a gaping wound overnight, but it would be able to handle the heavy bruising and cracked shoulder from the bear.

Now that the fight was over, the adrenaline drained from Dan's body. He could fight better than most people, and he was in good shape, but if he was going to fight monsters, he needed more magic. Spatial Shield and Shocking Fist had given him the extra edge he needed, but they still weren't terribly impressive. Really, any magic that involved punching a bear in the face needed some heavy reworking.

Feeling began to return to his shoulder along with an itchy burning sensation as the nanites restored neural connections. The System was an absolute godsend for recovering from bruises, aches, and hairline fractures, but Dan couldn't help but wish that there was a way to turn off the annoying phantom sensations.

"Set alarm, 120 minutes, wake me early if an intruder is detected," Dan said aloud as he arranged his sleeping bag on the moss. It was likely going to be a wet and uncomfortable two hours, but if he had to spend that time conscious, waiting for his shoulder to fix itself, he would probably go crazy. Plus, he needed a nap before he started hiking again. He had no idea what lurked in the gloom outside of the circle of light cast by his fire, but if his first five minutes on the planet were anything to go by, he would need to be sharp if he wanted to survive.

Acknowledged. Alarm will sound in 119 minutes.

Reading the System reply, Dan curled up next to the fire and did his best to ignore his shoulder. After about ten minutes of fitful rest, he finally dozed off. He dreamt of a starless night sky. Shapes moved in the dark, always just out of reach. Just as one of the figures reached for him, the alarm went off silently, shocking him awake.

He checked the time, frowning as he noticed that only an hour and a half had passed. He flexed his left arm, stiff and a little weak but otherwise functional. Surveying his surroundings, Dan picked up his sword. In the distance, a shape was running toward him across the swamp, screaming something. Behind it, other shapes swooped toward it in the dim light.

Whoever it was, the System must have heard it and woken him early. He cracked his neck and began stringing his short-bow. Whoever was running toward him was still a couple thousand feet out, and travel was slow over the swamp, especially when the runner had to occasionally stop to dodge the flying shapes.

Dan wasn't nearly as good with the bow as he was the sword, but with any luck he could at least wing one of the dark shapes. Silently, he cursed the omnipresent gloom. His vision was nowhere near good enough in the darkness. He finished stringing the bow when the figure was about 600 feet away. Dan nocked an arrow and strained his senses.

"Eoli myarh dis, fassun dis taun derre tear," a feminine voice shouted.

Dan rolled his eyes. Of course she would speak another language. That's why the one enchantment he actually had with him was a translation rune. He ran some mana into his helmet, static fizzling faintly before it projected her voice directly into his mind by the magic.

"Shit, shit, shit!" she was yelling as one of the monsters swooped towards her. "At the fire, there are nightgliders after me. I request sanctuary! I'm with the adventurer's guild and I'll pay guild rate!"

For a second, Dan considered the request. Her eyes seemed to shine in the dark as he made contact with them. The static filled his hearing once again, and his face felt warm. He blinked it away.

Good enough for him. Whatever a nightglider was, it sounded like a source of mana, and he would need to talk to someone local sooner or later. He might as well do it out in the middle of nowhere where he wouldn't be arrested for an accidental faux pas.

He loosed the nocked arrow at one of the swooping shapes. It swooped to the side rather than toward the running figure, and he missed. Dan rapidly began filling the air with arrows, only taking the barest second to aim. Although he didn't hit any of the shapes, the attacks served their purpose and they kept the flying shapes from attacking. After a harrowing stretch of time, the running woman made it to him unscathed. Dan barely looked at her as he dropped the bow and drew his sword, a handful of iron filings in his left hand ready to be infused with magic.

Almost immediately, one of the shapes dove toward him. Dan muttered "Spark Field" and shuddered as the mana flowed from him. He threw the filings into the nightglider's flight path. Sure enough, the creature ignited into a nimbus of crackling blue light as it passed through the cloud of iron filings. Dan knew from experience that the electric field created by Spark Field mostly served as a distraction, but to an unsuspecting target like the diving bat in front of him, it would hopefully serve as enough of a surprise to make the creature drop its guard.

Bats. Dan hated bats, and this was a gigantic freaking bat. The nightglider had an almost ten-foot wingspan, but rather than the snub nose of a normal bat, it had the jaws and face of a wolf. Specifically, a wolf that was snarling at him and lunging for his throat before the electric charges from the iron filings brought a surprised yelp from its throat.

Rather than the weaving and dodging descent he had seen from the other gliders, this one tumbled straight towards him. Dan cleaved its wing off, his sword snapping through the bone frame of its wing then ripping the leathery membrane like tissue paper.

Another two of the gliders descended, trying to rake him with their claws, while the remaining bat flapped past overhead. At the last second, he activated Spatial Shield, causing their claws to skitter off the soap bubble of distorted space. He used the moment of confusion, when one of the swooping night-gliders thought it had hit him, to stab upward, punching the point of his sword through its fragile torso.

The remaining gliders circled overhead. Dan spared a second to glance at the woman standing near him, a short sword in her hand, staring defiance at the circling shapes above. Then, one of the gliders unleashed a high pitched screech. Dan's vision grew blurry and his knees wobbled before the balance assist from the System kicked in. Next to him, the woman fell over to her hands and knees, a look of fear on her face.

One of them dove at Dan. He activated Shocking Fist with a quick vocalization, the thrill of mana coursing through his body. As it approached, he held his sword at guard and prepared himself to grab the bat with his electrically-charged left hand. Its claws clattered off of his sword as he barely blocked it.

In his mind's eye, Dan saw himself grabbing the creature's leg, the electricity immobilizing it as he pulled it to the ground and finished it with a smooth stroke of his sword. Instead, his hand closed on nothing, the magic discharging in a flash of light and a puff of ozone.

The two remaining nightgliders circled the fire once in the air, all the while making chirping noises to each other. Then, as one, they turned and flew away. Dan watched them go, then shuddered as mana flowed into him. Next to him, the woman had regained her feet and was using a one-foot-long short sword to finish off the injured gliders. It was intoxicating. His body felt lighter, and electricity seemed to run through his veins. An easy smile plastered itself onto his face. He could get used to this.

The woman coughed to get his attention. She was about five foot seven, heavily tanned, and dressed in dark leathers. She shifted slightly, eyeing Dan up in turn. Across her chest was a bandolier of knives, and at her side rode the sheath for the foot-long short sword she was wiping monster blood from. She sheathed the sword. On her back was an empty quiver, although he couldn't see any sort of bow. Given her headlong sprint across the swamp, it was very possible she had lost it at some point.

"Thanks for the assist, friend," she said cheerfully, her eyes still warily trained on his sword. "I got separated from my party when the nightgliders attacked us. We really should have been more prepared, but I was scouting ahead, and no one else was really looking at the sky. I spotted them in time, but part of the pack broke off and chased me off before my party could meet up with me."

"Not a problem," Dan replied as he sheathed his sword as well. "I was just laying down and trying to take a nap when your shouting woke me up. You're the first non-monster I've seen in this swamp, so that was a bit of a surprise."

She shrugged. "I know. We're pretty far from the main hunting grounds, and there really isn't much out here but grezdu moss and non-profitable monsters.

We were on a mission to gather some rare herbs from the swamp. I was against it, personally, everything out here is either an advanced rank or a pack hunter." She flashed a bright smile at Dan. "Given that we have no idea where the herbs are, we were almost certainly going to be stuck out here searching for a while. With only five of us, the odds weren't good that we were all coming back, given the difficulty of the monsters in the area.

"But..." She rolled her eyes as she crossed her arms. "Ishlar was greedy, and he thought we could handle it. We were only out of town for a day, and we've already been ambushed and separated. There's no way they're going to find anything without me, so the only question is whether they come looking for me, or if they turn around and return to town."

Dan tried to process the torrent of information she was feeding him. Really, he had next to no idea what she was talking about. He could infer some of it. Advanced rank likely referred to monsters that were above first rank as an example. The rest may as well be Greek to him. He just didn't have the context to put half of what she was saying in the right place. Internally, he shrugged.

He paused for a second, uncertain as to how to proceed. He needed more information, but at the same time everything about his origins needed to stay a secret. Dan pursed his lips. He didn't even know this woman's name, and he needed to make a decision as to whether to trust her with part of his story. Distantly, he heard static. Her eyes seemed to devour his gaze as he weighed his options. Fuck it. He would have to make a gamble sometime, it might as well be now.

"I'm going to be honest here," he tried to look as trustworthy as possible. "I just teleported in, but I have no idea where I am. I think I was supposed to arrive near a beacon, but instead I showed up in the middle of this swamp.

"I barely understand what you're talking about." He chuckled uncertainly. "But I would appreciate being pointed in the direction of a town and some sort of occupation where I can make enough money to afford to feed myself.

"I've tried cooking bear," he continued, motioning half-heartedly to the poorly-seared haunch of his first encounter. "But I clearly have no idea what I'm doing, and I would prefer something edible if at all possible."

"Ew." She wrinkled her nose at the charred bear meat. "Blood bears taste awful, even if you cook them properly. Still, they're rank two beasts, and it's impressive that you were able to bring one down. I'd be happy to guide you to the nearest town after you pulled me out of that tight spot back there. If nothing else, there should be a spot for you in the guild if you can solo a blood bear."

She paused, hesitantly eyeing Dan up and down. After a couple seconds of her chewing her lip in awkward silence, she seemed to come to some sort of decision.

"I noticed that you took down one of the nightgliders back there with magic," she stated slowly. "Is it possible that you're a mage of some sort? I haven't seen any runescript on you other than your helmet, but if you can manage combat spells, I can probably help get you placed into a team right away."

He frowned. Dan didn't know the social norms of the planet, but it didn't seem likely that strangers who met under possibly hostile circumstances would share the details of their combat abilities. Everything was going a bit too fast for him to process, but he still got a vague feeling of wrongness. Still, there was something about her eyes that drew him in, told him to trust her.

"I might know some magic," Dan relented, shifting awkwardly under her scrutiny. Girls usually didn't look at him this closely unless they were Doctor Weathers. Even then, it was only as a friend. "I don't feel terribly comfortable talking about it with a complete stranger, even if you are planning on helping me. Hell, I don't even know your name."

"Well that's easy," she replied, smiling back at him. "My name's Nora Strasshill and I'm a Ranger. Now we aren't strangers, and you can tell me all about your magic as we head back to town before it gets dark."

Dan began to frown as he formulated his reply. Static sounded in the distance. That had been happening a lot. He'd have to talk to Sam when he got back to Earth about the way the System interacted with the translation rune of the helmet.

"What do you mean, before it gets dark?" He motioned to his dim surroundings. "It seems pretty dark out to me."

"If you're off planet, you wouldn't know." She shrugged, already hopping out onto a tuft of moss in the swamp a couple feet from his camp, "the days here are about forty hours. When Tanloff gets between the planet and the sun, we have about four hours of actual darkness rather than this murky half-light. You don't want to be out at night.

"Unless you have a set of sanctuary runes, it's a death sentence." She turned and smiled back at him from the lump of grass she was standing on. "Ishlar was probably the only one for miles that has sanctuary runes. Without them, you're at the mercy of things from the bowels of the planet that would absolutely make your skin crawl. Even inside a sanctuary, it's not a treat to spend the night outside of a city with those things just prowling outside the light of the runes."

"Wait," Dan tried to interject. "What does that.."

Alarm. 120 minutes have passed. Alarm.

The System jolted his body, and Dan swore quietly to himself. He turned to stop her, but Nora jumped onto another island of moss and began working her way across the swamp. Despite all of her assurances, he didn't really feel like he had learned anything. Her nimble form hopped over another brackish puddle. He sighed to himself and hurried to catch up.

CHAPTER TEN

Getting Established

Dan followed Nora for about an hour in silence through the swamp. Occasionally, they spotted a creature of some sort, but Nora's low light vision was good enough that they were able to avoid them. Inside, he couldn't help but wonder how he would be able to match up to some of the more imposing creatures they avoided. The giant thin-legged spider that vaguely resembled a daddy long legs in particular piqued his curiosity. He managed to suppress that curiosity as he followed Nora. Finally, the mossy swamp gave way to a grassy plains.

"It should be safe to talk now," she said, still setting a brisk pace. "Now that we're out of the swamp, there shouldn't be anything too threatening until nightfall. The last thing we needed while we raced Tanloff was to get stuck in a fight with a blood bear or a mire strider."

"Why did you ask about magic anyway?" Dan asked. "I know it's not super common, but I would assume you have mages of your own."

"We do," she replied with a helpless shrug without turning to look at him. "But most of them consider themselves too important to join the adventurer's guild. Mages around here are elves or older humans.

"Elves don't work with humans unless they're the ones employing us." Nora hopped nimbly across an empty expanse of water as she spoke. "Even then, working with an elf isn't something I would recommend. They tend to have a rather troubling definition of 'acceptable losses' where we're concerned.

Her voice dripped with disdain. "Human mages tend to be pompous and usually only know a few spells. They adventure with guild members from time to time, but they usually have really strict contracts that require bodyguards."

"Most of the humans with any real talent skip town to join the Imperial Army." Nora stopped for a second to glance at Dan as he struggled to keep up with her. "You might be putting your life on the line, but there you'll at least get proper magical training and runescripted armor. The mages on Twilight that are worth a damn are all ex-imperial soldiers. They don't need to gather mana or prove anything, so they tend not to work as adventurers. When they do go to a hunting ground, they usually do it together."

"You look like an ex-imperial," she glanced back at Dan, "but your armor isn't quite there. The helmet is runescripted, but the rest of it is just well-crafted. I don't think they would be caught dead in armor as weak as that. Still, you took the night-glider's 'sonic screech' skill like a champ, and you were able to cast your own spells quickly and to good effect. That's what I would expect out of an imperial.

"In short," Nora shrugged. "You might be a deserter, or you might be a merc, but the one thing you aren't is from around here."

"I'm not imperial," Dan replied as he jogged after her. "Just a traveler with a couple spells under his belt."

"Very mysterious." She nodded sagely. "I'm sure it spreads all of the village girls' knees. Just the right amount of brooding with a hint of danger."

Dan didn't reply, mostly because he was blushing, and he didn't want Nora to be able to hear it. She had been unduly perceptive so far, and he really didn't trust his voice. He was pretty sure she was just making fun of him, but none of the women in his life had accused him of picking up on social cues. Who knew, maybe she *was* flirting with him. They kept jogging for another five or so minutes before she spoke again.

"But really, mysterious traveling swamp mage. What is your name? I don't know what etiquette is like wherever you're from, but I've already told you mine. It just seems easier to have something to call you. Also, if you're going to make something up, try and keep it normal-sounding. I'm not going to be able to call you 'Nemesis, the Hand of Darkness' or something stupid like that without cracking up."

"Sorry about that." Dan blushed again. "My name is Daniel Thrush, but I usually go by Dan; is that good enough for you?"

"Good enough for now," she replied. "We'll be getting to Morganville shortly. Just let me do the talking. We get travelers from time to time, but usually you're sent by a high enough leveled space mage that you arrive right next to the beacon."

"Wait..." She glanced over her shoulder at Dan, squinting through the gloom. "You aren't a wanted criminal or something, are you? Your teleportation has all the hallmarks of an amateurish hack job. Probably something that a low-ranked and desperate human would pull off. Sounds like someone running from the Imperial Army or a House Guard to me."

Dan's eyes widened slightly. She had hit it on the nose there. His teleportation had been shitty because he was weak, and any real member-state in the Tellask Empire would have access to properly-trained space mages. He had to admit that the skillset he had displayed to date screamed criminal, thief, or deserter. His mind spun frantically as he tried to come up with a believable excuse on the spot. He couldn't believe that they hadn't planned for this back at the Foundation. A real failure to plan ahead there. God, what did he even know about lying? Mix in a pinch of truth, try not to make it too outlandish. Shit. This is why he preferred lab to field work.

"Uh, I don't think I'm a criminal," he began slowly, voice hesitant. "I was training to be a bodyguard, maybe join the Imperial Army, but then a ship crashed down near my town. Where I'm from, there's very limited access to monsters, so people who rank up are either rich or murderers. I figured that this was my chance to get somewhere else, kill some monsters, and gain some ranks. Maybe I wasn't allowed to use the teleportation pad without permission? I suppose that might make me some brand of criminal."

"Oh that's fine." She winked at him. "I just wanted to make sure you weren't a runescript thief or a serial killer after my mana or something. We're a tributary state out here, not actually part of the Empire. No one is going to care too much about which House's serf you were, so long as you're willing to work."

"Amberell," he supplied, naming the one elven house he actually knew the name of. "I was training to work for House Amberell."

"Tough break." She winced. "The Orakh are pushing them pretty hard, and human soldiers under them don't have all that great of a survival rate. A lot of the local levies end up working for them and not coming back. Made the soldiering profession unpopular as of late, but on the other hand, The Orakh are on our doorstep. Still, the last I heard, House Amberell was using us for spell fodder. I'm all for fighting the Orakh, but I would prefer to actually have a chance at coming home at the end of the day."

They jogged in silence until Morganville's walls loomed in front of them. By that point, Dan was sucking down harsh breaths. He might be in better shape, but jogging 3-4 miles across rough terrain while wearing a backpack and armor wasn't his idea of fun. Of course, it was still better than being stuck outside the walls whenever this 'nightfall' happened. Nora hadn't been very specific about the creatures that came out at night, but Dan was content to avoid them for now.

Again, he was more in the mood for magical bunnies and chipmunks.

The gates to the town were open, and Nora went ahead to talk to one of the guards posted on duty. The other one stared him down, as if daring Dan to commit some sort of crime. He focused his energy on catching his breath and looking innocent.

A minute or two later, a cheerful Nora waved him over and they walked into the town together. Dan didn't know what to expect from a magical medieval town, but Morganville impressed him. Every hundred or so feet, mana-infused crystals gave off enough light that he no longer had to squint. The shops were made of evenly-cut stone bricks and most of them had a fresh coat of paint or lime. There were even some planters with flowers in them outside the more affluent-looking stores. Just inside the gate stood a stable where horses and more exotic mounts were quartered while their owners explored the town. The town itself was bustling, but not crowded. Dan had to watch where he was going, but as long as he was aware of his surroundings, he didn't run a great risk of running into any of the residents.

While Dan remained intent on gazing about like a country bumpkin and making a spectacle of himself, Nora took him by the elbow and began guiding him through the streets. Fairly rapidly, the quality of the buildings faded. They still looked well-maintained, but she had clearly moved him to a more middle class quarter of the town. As they walked, a couple of the locals glanced at them, but quickly looked away. Dan blushed slightly. They certainly looked like they were on a date, something he hadn't had any luck with since college. Come to think of it, remembering his ex-girlfriend, he wasn't sure "luck" was the right term for his success back then.

Finally, they stopped outside of a two-story stone building. A sign, translated courtesy of Dan's helmet, said simply 'Morganville Adventurer's Guild' above a well-drawn crossed sword and bow. She made to step inside, then stopped. She looked back at Dan and frowned, chewing on her lower lip while she stared at him, deep in thought.

"Daniel," she said slowly. "Do you have a class rune?"

He stared back at her blankly.

"Shit," she said. "The good news is, that means you won't be recognizable as an outcast or a deserter, but the bad news is that it will make you weak."

"Wait!" Her eyes widened. "You're casting spells without a class rune? You killed a blood bear without a class rune? What have they been feeding you on your homeworld, concentrated strength potions?"

"It might help," he replied slowly, reluctant to betray his ignorance, "if you told me what a class rune is? I was just drilled in using a sword and casting spells. No one really explained things any further than that with me."

"Ok," she answered, shooting him a look out of the corner of her eye. "Almost everyone who fights for a living has a class rune. They're expensive, but not crazy expensive, at least for a basic rune. Most importantly, they let a human use their mana without having to actually cast spells. They take the form of a runic tattoo on your body. Depending upon the strength of the person who gives you your class, the power of your class varies greatly. Power takes several forms. It can be the number of abilities your class grants, the efficiency with which it lets you use your mana, or the ability to improve your physical abilities or senses. As an example, fighter and brute are two of the more common classes. They let their user channel mana to improve their strength and stamina. Fighter has a couple slots to add on skills, such as the ability to project a weak mana shield or to increase their own mass, making them harder to tackle or grapple.

"I'm a ranger," she turned and stared directly at Dan. "Technically, it's an uncommon class, but we're pretty common on Twilight given the light conditions. We get minor improvements to our hand-eye coordination, but my senses and low light vision are almost triple an ordinary human's. Pretty much every adventurer team has at least one of us, to avoid some of the nastier monsters out there. Really, the only people who fight without classes are elves. They can manipulate mana directly, and it makes them much more powerful than a classed human. It just takes them hundreds of years to manage. We can still look into getting a class for you, but we will be telling everyone that you are classed as a mage. If I were you, I wouldn't go around advertising that you can cast spells without a class rune. It would attract the wrong sort of attention. Amberell attention."

"Got it." Dan nodded, sweating slightly despite the chill. "I'm a mage, but I'm shy about my tattoo, so I don't show it to anyone."

"There we go," she replied, most of her suspicious glare gone. "I knew you could use that big mage brain for something useful. Now, let's go inside and get you registered. We can probably put a new team together pretty quickly if I advertise you as a thunder mage. Then, we can get some paying work and talk things over in more depth."

Nora pushed the door open and walked into the building. The ground floor was a bar complete with the smell of stale beer, unwashed warrior, and the acidic tang of vomit covered in scented sawdust. Next to the bar stood a kiosk where a pleasant, middle-aged woman sat bored, above her head a sign stating blandly "administration." Nora walked Dan over to the stand and stepped forward, a bright smile on her face.

"Opal!" Nora said cheerfully. "Just the wonderful person I want to see this fine night."

"Ms. Strasshill," the middle aged woman replied, nodding curtly. "I just gave Ishlar the herb job out in the swamp. You know the rules; your party will have to forfeit the downpayment and pay the penalty before you can get another job. Unless, of course, you have ten pounds of bloodvine and moon root hidden somewhere on you."

"Unfortunately, I am no longer a member of Ishlar's party," Nora replied, her voice dripping with faux sorrow. "Ishlar left me to die out on the swamp and didn't put together a rescue sortie, voiding my contract with him. I am a free agent, and one that was saved from Ishlar's negligence by this strapping gentleman right here. Alas, he hasn't joined the guild yet, so I am here to sponsor him."

"Sure," Opal said evenly, never taking her eyes off of Nora. "Nothing in the rules says you can't sponsor a newbie while under contract. What's his name and class?"

"Dan Bird," Nora answered with a flourish. "Thunder mage."

"Wait," Dan butted in frantically, eyes glued to Opal's pen as she began writing down his information. "My name is Dan Thrush. It must be the translation runes. A thrush is a type of bird; my last name isn't Bird."

"You do realize that you just said 'a bird is a type of bird,' right?" Nora asked with a grin.

Dan groaned. Apparently the translation runes weren't all powerful. They didn't have an analogue for thrush, so they improvised. He had never really cared one way or another about his last name, it was just a name after all, but Dan Bird just sounded… stupid.

"Dan Bird, thunder mage," Opal finished her writing, much to Dan's dismay. "Rank one, I presume?"

Dan nodded, sighing as Opal's pen scribbled something further. He supposed that he could try to make a game of it, Dan Bird could be the superman to Dan Thrush's Clark Kent. Maybe.

The door slammed open, disrupting Dan's moping. In walked a six-foot-three-inch man. Every inch of him that wasn't covered in gleaming steel plates was covered in bulging muscles. The man shined in an almost unhealthy way. Dan was tempted to ask Nora if Twilight had vaseline, because he was pretty sure that the man in the doorway had used it on his biceps. Before he could say anything snide, the man began shoving his way through the bar towards Dan. Vaguely, he could make out two individuals following him, but it was hard to focus on anything else when three hundred pounds of pro wrestler and armor was approaching this rapidly.

"Nora Strasshill!" The man exclaimed, pointing at the annoyed ranger. "What are you doing here? Your contract says you were supposed to guide the party towards any designated mineral or plant deposits. You never met back up with us after you ran off. We came back here to cancel the mission and pay the penalty, all because you couldn't do a simple job!"

"Hello Ishlar." She glared at the gigantic man. "Nice to see you again after you left me to my death out in the swamp. I don't suppose you even bothered to send anyone to help when I was being chased by four nightgliders?"

CHAPTER ELEVEN

Making New Friends

"How could we find you without a ranger, Nora?" Ishlar asked, muscles glistening in the bar's firelight. "You abandoned us on the moors all alone. We were lucky to be able to fight our way back to Morganville at all. Now that we have you, we can thank the stars above and finish that contract. I know I wasn't excited about paying the cancellation penalty."

"I saw you turn away when I called for help, Ishlar," Nora's voice was frosty as she stared down the much larger man. Dan tried his best to blend into the wood paneling next to an unamused Opal. "I screamed and tried to get back to you, but you banded together and activated the sanctuary runescript, trapping me outside. What was I supposed to do but run away when my choices were only fleeing or death? No, my contract with you is void. I won't accept any further pay from you, and I won't work any further missions with you. If I wanted to be treated as expendable, I would work for your elven friends."

"What magical reagents did you eat to get this confidence?" Ishlar growled through gritted teeth. "My patrons have been nothing but good to us, and you signed a binding contract. One that I plan on holding you to. You've been paid very well, and you will continue to be well-paid, but I won't have you speaking ill of our sponsors just because they're elves."

"Do you really want to know why I have the courage to finally talk back after a year and a half of your dumb schemes and close calls?" Nora asked, her eyes burning. "Here is your answer."

She grabbed Dan from where he had been lurking in the corner and pulled him into the light. For a brief second, he panicked, eyes glancing everywhere around the bar as he suddenly became the center of attention. Ishlar looked him in the eyes and snorted. A fair assessment in Dan's opinion, the man could probably kill him by flexing.

"Who in the Emperor's name is this?" Ishlar glared at Dan. "Are you really that much of a trollop that you just ran out and found a random swordsman the minute you became angry with me? You're an oath-breaker, and your only assistance is a warrior who has just taken his class. You'll never work a serious job again in this town, if I have my say."

"He's a combat mage, Ishlar," Nora sneered at him. Dan groaned internally as the situation spun wildly out of control.

"If he can cast magic, let's see him do it in the arena," Ishlar shouted at Nora. "I'm sure he told you about all of his spells to get you to spread your legs, but I'll believe that this twig of a man is a caster when I see it. Even if he isn't, at least I can work out my frustration on this failed mission by beating him black and blue. Once he fails publicly, everyone will see you for the fraud you are."

"Five gold sovereigns that Bird wins," Nora replied, a predatory gleam in her eyes.

Rather than reply verbally, the huge man spat in his hand and offered the expansive mitt to Nora, who promptly did the same and shook it. Dan looked from her to Ishlar. He wasn't entirely sure how this had happened, but it sure seemed like he was about to be in a fight with the gigantic man. Admittedly, he seemed like a bit of a boor, but Dan wasn't entirely sure how he had gone from zero enmity to bloodsport, but here he was. It sounded like Nora had a bit of a grudge against the other man, but Dan was a bit confused as to why he would be the one fighting the mountain of muscle, rather than her.

As Ishlar and his cronies stormed out, he noticed that a decent number of the bar's patrons were paying their bills and getting up as well. Evidently most of them wanted to see the upcoming fight, probably to watch him get pulled apart like barbequed pork. Before Nora could leave, his hand darted out and grabbed her by the shoulder.

"What the hell was that?" he asked the grinning woman. "All I know about this Ishlar guy is that he looks like he was born with a freeweight in his hand, and now I'm fighting him. Why and how am I supposed to beat this guy?"

"His class is Brute," she replied in a whisper. "All of his mana is focused on strength, but he can barely use that sword. I was impressed with his strength when I signed on with him too, but after a couple battles I realized that he's basically an amateur that the elves handed power to. I saw you against the nightgliders; you aren't going to have a problem with him. Plus, the sovereigns will be the nest egg we need to hire some party members and take a more profitable mission. I just egged him on until his manly pride was hurt, and he basically offered us free money. Now, you just need to go out there and earn it."

"If the money is free, why am I the one earning it?" Dan questioned, but Nora just shot him a wink and sauntered away. With a sigh, he slung his backpack over his shoulder and followed her.

Before long, a small crowd was following them as Nora guided them to a stone cylinder. He followed her inside. It was an impressive building with almost ten rows of stands surrounding a raised wooden platform covered in sand. Nearby, a small stone tower rose about five feet above the platform housing an announcer, a fifty-something short, greying man. As they walked in, his magically-enhanced voice echoed through the arena.

"--And here comes our challenger, the man, the mage, the bird!"

Dan winced. He needed a cooler moniker. Maybe the raptor, the bear, or the scorpion. Really, anything but the bird. It was hard to intimidate local thugs and bullies when everyone kept calling you "the bird."

"We have no idea where he comes from or what his abilities are," the announcer's voice boomed out. "All we know is that he's run afoul of our very own Ishlar, the Human Bull. As most of you know, Ishlar has a strength-based class and a very respectable ten and three record in the arena. Only time will see if he can use that strength to send the bird flying from the ring."

Dan glared at Nora while she studiously avoided his gaze. Ten and three record? How the hell was that free money from an amateur handed strength? In frustration, he noted that Nora had made her way to the arena's bookie to put down a bet, while the crowd pushed him out onto the sand-covered platform. Immediately those gathered in the stands started booing.

"Now, we all know the rules here," the announcer shouted once more. "Bladed weapons will be replaced with lead training weapons. The battle goes on until one party loses consciousness for more than three seconds or yields. Are there any questions?"

Dan looked down blankly as someone thrust a heavy training sword into his hand. He took a quick practice swing with it. Its balance was shit. As he turned to say something to the referee next to him, the announcer cut him off.

"Everyone is armed, and now bets are final. Let the match of honor between Ishlar the Human Bull and The Bird begin."

Ishlar bellowed and ran right at him, both hands gripping a heavy club. At least Nora was right about him being untrained. The man didn't have a hint of grace or martial arts training to him. On the other hand, given his size and the ease with which he moved the lead club, he probably didn't need it. If the larger man grabbed him or hit him with that club, it was game over for sure. Dan might be in much better shape than a year ago, but there wasn't any way he was going to tangle with Ishlar up close and come out the winner.

Instead he muttered 'Shocking Fist' and 'Spatial Shield' in close succession and ducked to the side. The mana flowed out of Dan's core, and the buzz of combat filled him. Ishlar didn't look like as big of a threat anymore. His mana, clumped in his bulging muscles, looked clumsy. Dan couldn't help but wonder what it would feel like to taste the man's mana. To finish him here and let it flow through him. The club swished over his head, and Dan didn't have the luxury of checking whether the miss was due to his reflexes or magic. Instead, he slapped the larger man's thigh with his free hand causing a flash of light as the electricity discharged into him.

Ishlar's leg spasmed, and he fell to one knee. In a smooth motion, Dan stepped past him and whipped his heavy sword into the back of the kneeling man's head. Apparently all of those muscles protected him from concussions, because the larger man only fell to his hands and knees. Dan stepped forward, stomping on Ishlar's hand with his boot, and brought the sword down again on the back of his head. This time, there was a crack.

The mana inside Ishlar smoothed and relaxed. The man no longer gave off an aura of strength and menace. He collapsed face-first to the sand of the arena floor, unmoving. The crowd cheered. Dan could almost taste Ishlar's mana. It was like a cloud full of butterflies, fluttering just out of his reach. He raised the training sword again.

"Hold!" a voice next to him whispered urgently as a hand grasped his wrist.

Dan blinked. It was Nora. Some of the soft-focus haze of the fight faded from him at the look of concern in her eyes. He looked down. Ishlar was clearly unconscious at his feet. He had almost killed an unconscious man in front of the crowded arena. Luckily, most of them were carried away in his unexpected victory. Maybe Nora had been right. Ishlar had been strong, but he barely knew how to fight. As Dan ran the battle over in his head, he realized that he still probably would have beaten the man without magic. It just would have taken longer.

Still, he thought about that final moment when the urge to kill had filled him, and shuddered. Something was going on, and it was more than just wanting to put his training into use. Killing monsters was different, it was more or less what he had trained for, but this was different. Ishlar was an asshole, but he was a person.

CHAPTER TWELVE

Assembling a Party

Nora quickly ushered him out of the Arena. It was a blessing, he supposed, that the crowd was so rowdy after his quick victory that no one noticed them slipping out. Quickly, she brought him to a nearby restaurant and pulled him inside. She motioned to the waiter before sitting him down and glancing at Dan with concern.

"What in the blazes was that?" There was a smile on her face, but worry colored her voice. "I know Ishlar is an asshole, but you had him down. Do you not have spars where you come from, or is every fight to the death?"

"I… I don't really know," Dan replied, shaken. "The adrenaline rush from the battle just didn't fade, and then suddenly I could almost taste his mana. I couldn't think about anything else, other than how much I needed his mana. I just knew how easy it would be to crush his head like a grape, and I couldn't stop myself.

"Thank you." He gazed up at her, a hint of fear clenching his stomach. "That's never happened before, but I don't know what I would have become if you hadn't stopped me. I don't have a problem with killing people, but murdering an incapacitated opponent isn't something that I want to be comfortable with."

She nodded, deep in thought.

Dan shuddered thinking the way his mana sang while he used it. Every moment of casting took on a more sinister tone. For the longest time, he had thought that it was simply the adrenaline rush of combat, but it was time to face the possibility that it was something else. Even now, magic and combat held a seductive allure to him. He wasn't sure what exactly was going on, but he would need to be careful. Dan snorted. As if that would even be possible. His mission was to develop his magic and kill enough monsters to rank up. He wasn't sure how careful worked as an element of that equation.

"Well, don't do it again," she said with finality. "The good news is that you were pretty impressive out there. Ishlar isn't anywhere near a top-tier warrior, but he's a local bully with a bit of renown. You handled him quickly and efficiently. If we're going to take on the more lucrative missions, we will need at least another two party members. I'm a known commodity, but you just did a great job advertising yourself. If we put out word that we're forming a new party, we'll probably be able to get a couple applicants pretty quickly."

"What kind of adventurers are we looking for?" Dan leaned back in the poorly-crafted wooden chair. "I have no idea what classes are even out there."

"We have a mage and a ranger." She shrugged easily. "That leaves mostly combatants. There are a number of qualifying classes: duelists, fighters, warriors, crusaders, and berserkers come to mind immediately. That said, around here you aren't going to see too many fancy classes. If we can get two to three fighters, I'd be happy, but we can settle for warriors. I'm not too favorably inclined to thug or brute classes unless they're high-level."

Both of them nodded as the waiter came back and plunked a bowl of soup down in front of each of them. He hadn't realized how hungry he was until the steaming wooden bowl was set down in front of him. Through an unspoken agreement, neither spoke while they ate. The soup was surprisingly good, if a bit brothy. Dan wasn't entirely sure he wanted to know what the balls of meat floating in it were composed of, but they were well-seasoned. He wished that he had some bread to go with the soup, but at the end of the meal, he was more than satisfied.

"I just realized that I don't have any money," Dan began slowly, only for Nora to interrupt him.

"You're paying after a fashion, anyway." She gave him a quick, mischievous grin. "I earned five golden sovereigns from Ishlar and another ten betting on you. I think it's only fair to give you five of them. I staked the claim, so I'll keep the other ten. A girl's got needs, after all."

Theatrically, she dropped a small sack that hit the table with a satisfying clunk. Dan picked up the bag, a smile flashing over his face as he felt its heft. He didn't have any idea what a sovereign could get him, but the coins were heavy and gold. Even if they weren't much in the grand scheme of things, there was something satisfying about having a heavy bag full of gold.

"Good," she leaned back in her chair with a harsh scraping sound as it skittered across the stone floor. "That should be enough money to get you some better gear. If you aren't going to have a combat class, you should look into getting some rune-scripted armor. I don't think you're going to find anything impressive or efficient around here, but you're already pretty strong and agile. A little bit of a magical boost could be all you need to fill in as a front line fighter in a pinch."

Dan nodded at her slowly. The Foundation was aware that the armor the imperial marines wore was covered in runescript. They hadn't been able to decipher all of its meaning, but they had exhibited physical characteristics firmly in the comic book range. Dan might be fit for a normal human, but he certainly would need something a little extra if he planned on fighting superheroes.

"This place has an inn attached to it," she continued. "You should rent a room from Jeffrey here, and I'll come back tomorrow. I'm going to see if I can recruit a couple fighters for us. It might be a bit ambitious, but I think we can give the Mashress silver mine a try. The thing is lousy with monsters, but if we can fight our way through them, silver is a pretty straightforward product to sell."

"Won't the mine's owner have an issue with us just wandering in there and collecting silver?" Dan asked with a frown.

"Where is he going to find miners willing to work in close proximity to monsters?" She shrugged quizzically. "No, he's happy to have adventurers come through. The monsters tend to dig the ore out of the walls, and we pick it up. The contract requires us to sell it only to him at 50% of its market rate, but we don't have to put anything down. Of course, the mine is considered to be a challenging contract in this area. He lets anyone try that wants to, but a good portion of the teams come back empty-handed or missing members. I'd never be willing to risk the mines with Ishlar, but if we can get a good enough team, there's good money to be made. Plus, plenty of high rank monsters for you to rank up on. If we do the mine run a couple of times, we might even get you ranked up."

Ranked up. Dan liked the sound of that. He agreed with her plan then paid the innkeeper. The rate was one silver sheaf for the night and ten copper bits for dinner and breakfast. Apparently there were twenty silver sheaves to a golden sovereign and fifty copper bits to the sheaf. Hopefully, Jeffrey didn't short him. For all he knew, the actual values were three times that. At least the bed was comfortable and the food was warm the next morning.

Nora walked in while he was eating breakfast. Her face was covered with smiles, the perfect contrast to the two large, well-muscled frowning women who followed her in. She sauntered over to Dan's table and grabbed the fork from his hands. A mouthful of Dan's eggs later, she was sitting down across from him.

"Daniel," she stated cheerfully. "I would like to introduce

you to your two newest employees, Emily and Andrea Cragson. They're both classed as fighters and well-acquainted with the arena, where they have more than respectable records. In short, I think we're ready to give the mine a try."

"Wait." Dan frowned, forkful of eggs halfway to his mouth. "What do you mean by employees?"

"Well it's obvious that I'm the charismatic face of the party," she replied with a winsome smile. "But our real selling point is that we have a combat mage. Therefore, you are the party leader, and I am the charming and intelligent advisor with all of the real power. A very simple equation, really."

"It sounds needlessly convoluted to me," Dan said, slowly putting his fork down on the table. "I still don't understand why Emily and Andrea are employees rather than members of the party. Also, can you tell me why they're frowning at me; it's getting unsettling."

Nora glanced back over her shoulder at the two tall women. They were both standing about ten feet behind her and glaring at Dan. She turned back to him and grinned.

"Well the sisters may have heard rumors about your insatiable proclivities." She snickered slightly. "I didn't start the rumors, but Ishlar apparently won't shut up about how you've bedded every maiden in town. Frankly, I think it's hilarious. Despite out-massing you by about fifty pounds, I believe they think you're going to try to forcibly bed them. Please try, by the way; I have money on the outcome."

"I guess that explains the staring." Dan sighed. "You still haven't explained why they're my employees or what that means."

"Obviously, it means you or an agent operating on your behalf..." Nora pointed at herself, "...signed an employment contract with them. In short, you have to pay their wages for the missions we go on, one sovereign per mission plus 10% of the loot each, but they aren't entitled to any say in the missions selected or the strategy employed on said mission. Also, part of their frowning might be that they didn't realize that they were signing on for the silver mine. Oh well, they probably should have thought of that before signing on with an unknown thrillseeker of ill-repute such as you."

Dan fixed her with a baleful gaze. Slowly and meaningfully, he ate another forkful of eggs.

CHAPTER THIRTEEN

Delving (I)

After breakfast, Nora led Dan to the town's marketplace. There, he quickly found that although five sovereigns was a decent amount of money, being an adventurer was very expensive. Traveling out after dark meant that he, as the party leader, had to buy a set of sanctuary runes. That set him back almost three sovereigns immediately and probably had a lot to do with why he was the party leader, even if Nora was doing most of the party leading. Then, he found out that preserved food was expensive. Not break-the-bank expensive, but a day's worth of food that might usually cost 10-15 bits ran him a whole silver sheaf if he wanted something that could last for a couple days.

Next time, he vowed to himself, he would come back with a backpack full of power bars and avoid the price gougers that preyed upon adventurers. Two weeks of food later, he barely had anything left for equipment.

Finally, he settled on a set of bracers with 'power' runes on them. They cost him his final sovereign, leaving him with some pocket change and the hope that he would earn enough money to pay the Cragson sisters, but he couldn't argue with their effectiveness. The bracers hogged mana, and they only really improved Dan's arm strength, but they added a noticeable amount of extra force to his blows. He wasn't going to be competing with Ishlar anytime soon, but he actually hit like an athlete now, rather than just a guy who was in pretty good shape.

Nora wanted to leave immediately after they were done shopping, but Dan was able to convince her to let him get used to the bracers. Of the Cragson sisters, only Emily was willing to spar with him, but even then, she was a bit hesitant. Apparently, they had both noticed his lack of restraint at the end of the battle in the arena. It was a bit hard to focus on the fight with Andrea trying to burn a hole in his back while he fought her sister, but he quickly grew to appreciate Emily's strength and flexibility.

She didn't have the same overwhelming physical strength that Ishlar did, but she stood almost six and a half feet tall, and even with the bracers, she overpowered Dan on most blows. Dan, on the other hand, had a slight edge on her in agility and sword skill. Quickly, the match devolved into a game of cat and mouse where he would circle her just outside of her superior range before darting in and trying to score a hit without getting walloped by her greatsword.

After a half hour of Nora grumbling about them wasting daylight and Andrea staring daggers at the fight, Emily and Dan called a break. Emily still wasn't exactly thrilled to have been tricked into doing a run on the silver mine, but she didn't seem quite as stiff around Dan anymore. He wasn't sure he could blame her as he had also been tricked into the silver mine mission, but Nora was quite insistent that it had been his plan. She had signed off on it as his registered agent, after all.

The hike itself to the mine was fairly unremarkable. The land around Morganville was mostly plains with occasional irrigation ditches feeding orchards and grain fields. Periodically, they saw small herds of large, shaggy, bison-like mammals that Nora informed him were called 'aurochs.' Apparently, they filled the role of sheep and cows, providing Morganville with wool, pack animals, meat, and dairy products. Although docile, Nora warned him to stay away from them during the breeding season. According to her, the bulls got very territorial and had a tendency to attack any traveler that crossed their path.

Five hours into the hike, the plains began to transition into hills, and Dan got to see his first daylight. Specifically, Alpha Centauri A appeared around the curve of Tanloff and they got a couple hours of full light before it dipped behind the horizon. According to Nora, the day-night cycle was two hours of daylight, roughly twenty-five hours of twilight, another two hours of daylight, four hours of twilight, two hours of night, and another four hours of twilight before things began again. Internally, Dan couldn't help but wonder what the planet's suicide rate was. Four hours of daylight, thirty-four hours of gloom, and then two hours of night? He was already a little worried about his mental health from the arena. He really didn't need to add mega seasonal depression to his list of concerns.

Finally, just as the star slipped below the horizon restoring the planet's customary murkiness, they arrived at the Mashress Silver Mine. A small, walled compound sat around the mouth of the mine. Worryingly, its defenses faced in all directions, including the mine itself. The compound consisted of an inn, a small general store, a barracks for the local guard, and an administrative office for the mine itself.

Nora quickly went into the compound to alert the administrator that they were ready to enter the mine, and to get the soldiers to open the reinforced gate that kept the mineshaft shut. Belatedly, Dan realized that he probably should have gone in with her. She'd already volunteered him once, and he'd prefer to avoid that becoming a habit.

She came back out, chatting casually with a soldier who promptly began cranking the winch to open the mine's gate. Five minutes later, the gate was open far enough to go in. Nora led the way inside and promptly pointed out the brazier where they would have to burn the small chunk of rhys wood that she had been given to alert the guards when they wanted to leave the mine. The rhys wood wasn't native to the region, and would emit a dark purple smoke which would rise through a cleverly-designed flue and disperse outside the mine. Frankly, Dan was more than a little unsettled with the significant amount of effort that seemed to go into keeping whatever was in the mine from leaving. The doors were bad enough, but the security measures regarding the rhys wood spoke of worryingly-intelligent foes. In his experience, that usually wasn't a good combination. Behind him, Andrea gripped her maul, and Emily drew her sword.

Nora ranged ahead without a care in the world, occasionally checking a map when they came to twists and turns in the mine. The further they went, the more Dan realized how truly lost they were without Nora. Perhaps unconsciously, Andrea stayed closer to the rest of the party while holding the torch. Outside of its light, the mine took on a menacing tone. Dan strained his ears, certain that he heard occasional whispers and skittering.

Suddenly, Nora came to a stop with everyone halting abruptly behind her in an uncomfortable series of bumps and jangling metal. The party clustered around the opening to another tunnel as she looked at the map once more. Dan glanced around the tunnel and frowned. The stone walls around them were rough, unhewn, and covered in condensation. At some point, they had left tunnels worked by humans and strayed into a cave complex of some sort. Once again, he hoped that Nora was half of the scout and pathfinder she claimed to be. If not, and they got lost in these caverns, the fourteen days worth of food in his backpack might not be nearly enough.

"Good news, everyone!" Nora announced as she rolled the map up. "We've reached a side branch that hasn't been explored by a previous expedition. That means that we have no idea what the danger level is, but that there will probably be fresh treasure down there for us to loot."

"What do you mean, we won't know the danger level?" Andrea asked darkly, glancing into the rather ominous opening.

"Well I would imagine we'll be fighting mostly second-rank monsters." Nora shrugged. "But no one has gone down this tunnel and reported back. That might mean this tunnel has opened recently, or it might mean that anyone who has gone down it has died terribly. Either way, it's our best chance to do anything other than pick over the refuse from previous parties."

"But we're all rank one," Andrea stated. It wasn't a question. "We might be able to take down a rank two monster, but if that's all we're fighting, this is probably going to be over fairly quickly."

Nora smiled. "Not true! Plus, I have complete faith in you." Without warning, she ran past Dan, grinning like a madwoman. He stared at her, bemused, only for the hair on the back of his neck to stick up as a low growl echoed from the tunnel.

He turned back to the cave entrance, drawing his sword and straining his eyes. A faint, hulking shape filled the entrance. The thing shifted slightly, growling again. Behind Dan, the sisters shifted slightly and metal scraped. He cursed to himself as whatever it was sized them up, and wished that he could do the same, but it was just outside the circle of light cast by Andrea's torch.

That changed as it charged forward without warning, swinging a stone club at Dan's head. Whatever the thing was, it was almost eight feet tall and dark as pitch. It had four limbs, but Dan couldn't quite tell if they were legs or arms. As it swung the club, it supported its large, furry bulk on three of them while the fourth gripped the weapon. Its face was dominated by large, ivory tusks that almost hid its beady eyes.

Dan ducked under the club, not even bothering to use Spatial Shield. A single blow from that club would probably be fatal, but the opening swing had been haphazard and poorly aimed. He darted forward and stabbed his blade into its flank, drawing a small drop of blood. The beast didn't even seem to notice, instead charging past him toward Andrea. His eyes widened in the dark.

"Andrea drop the torch!" he shouted. "It's homing in on the torch!"

She threw the offending stick of wood and burning tar, and the monster's gaze tracked it. While it was distracted, an arrow from Nora erupted into the shoulder of its club arm. Emily stepped in, swinging her greatsword in a horizontal sweep at chest level. The blade struck the corded muscle of its forward leg arms and cut into it. This time, the creature noticed the wounds.

The entire tunnel shook as it bellowed. One of its rear leg arms grasped blindly for Dan as he circled behind it. It was moving forward again, seemingly lunging for Emily. He activated the runescript in his bracers, his mana pool draining noticeably as he sidestepped the hand and stabbed his sword deep into the other leg of the creature. Out of the corner of his eye he caught the other arm reaching for him. He tried unsuccessfully to withdraw his blade. Feeling his weakened mana pool, he grimaced and activated Spatial Shield as he abandoned his sword to jump back. The hand missed, bouncing off the outside of the shield as he backpedaled frantically.

On the other side of the monster, an impact thudded, and Emily grunted. All he could do was pray she was all right and draw his dagger. He glanced down at the pitiful weapon. If a stainless steel longsword wasn't enough to stop this thing, what hope did he have with only eight inches of metal? Helplessly, he took a couple steps back before breaking into a sprint and jumping onto the creature's back. The dagger went in and out like a sewing needle, barely drawing blood. He was hurting it, but the creature didn't seem to care, instead focusing on the larger weapons of the sisters and the angry whir of Nora's bow.

Frustrated, Dan clung on as the creature bucked like an angry bull, one hand full of its dark, wiry fur, the other gripping the blood-slicked hilt of his dagger. The monster was likely too big to harm with Shocking Grasp; he would just generate a localized muscle spasm with the level of shock he was capable of. Spark Field would be worse than a joke against this thing, and without his sword, his physical attacks were basically useless. Hell, with his sword, he had only managed to do real damage to it once. His gaze flitted to the torch. It really hadn't liked fire. Maybe that was something he could work with. Either that, or he had gone completely crazy.

Ignoring the consequences, he thought back to his experiments with the fire affinity stone. He hadn't earned any spells yet, but he could still access the most basic effects. Converting raw mana into elemental mana. Not terribly useful for most affinities, but even undirected fire was still fire. Ignoring the part of his mind that screamed that he was making a mistake, Dan channeled mana into the fire affinity stone buried in his arm. For a second nothing happened as the creature hit Andrea with an open palm, throwing her across the chamber. Then, fire poured out of his free hand and blasted into the creature's back.

For one glorious second, everything went perfectly, and Dan grinned like an absolute idiot as the flames poured into its exposed back. Then, the oily fur burst into flame, and the creature went mad.

Flames licked at him from every direction, charring his skin and stealing the air from his lungs. Frantically, he released his grip on the creature's back and pushed off, dropping ever so slowly to the ground to avoid the billowing inferno.

The fall stunned him. Maybe he misjudged the height, or maybe he fell at a funny angle. Regardless, his legs didn't catch him, and Dan tumbled to the cavern floor, cracking his head on the hard stone. His face slammed forward in the helmet from the impact. A distant part of his mind wondered if he had landed hard enough to dent the back of the metal armor.

With a flash of pain, his forehead bounced off the nose guard of the helmet. A blooming, sticky dampness on his face warned Dan that the guard had slashed open the skin of his face. His vision blurred, and everything took on a dreamlike quality as the flaming behemoth rampaged around the tunnel. Luckily, one of its first casualties had been its eyes, or the enraged monster would have almost certainly killed a party member or two.

Dan blinked, and for some reason the creature was on the other end of the tunnel, still burning, chasing Emily. He blinked and the burning monster was much closer, but someone was dragging him from the fight by the collar of his armor while swearing inventively. He blinked again and the monster was right on top of him, only to be distracted by an arrow erupting from its neck. Dan tried to sit himself up woozily, only to feel an intense wave of nausea flow through him. He leaned back and blinked again.

This time, the warmth of mana flowed into him, but it just kept going. If the nightgliders were a candle, and the blood bear was a torch, this was a raging bonfire. The warmth coursed up and down his body, causing pleasant tingling to erupt in its wake. Dan smiled as he basked in the afterglow of the mana.

Mana influx detected. Recalculating Spirit.

Spirit is now 4.

WARNING: <USER> has gained 2 points of Spirit at once. Irregularities detected. Please exercise caution in the future.

WARNING: <USER> is concussed. Please consume protein and liquids as soon as possible, so that System may effectuate repairs.

CHAPTER FOURTEEN

Delving (II)

Nora stood next to the smoldering corpse of the creature that the party had just slain. Emily was binding her wounds while Andrea arranged wood for a fire. She looked down at Daniel's still form and sighed. She poked him with her foot, looking for a reaction. Finding none and convincing herself that he was truly unconscious, she released the flow of mana to her charm skill with a sigh. On her back, the runescript for her class tattoo cooled noticeably as her mana stopped running through it.

Honestly, she wasn't even sure she needed the charm skill with Daniel. Technically, her class used mind affinity to allow her to manipulate other sentient beings into being positively disposed towards her, but Dan just seemed to go with the flow regardless. It was almost frustrating how much effort she had gone to, only for it to all appear unnecessary in the end.

From the moment she had seen him using thunder magic to fight the blood bear, to when she had purposefully aimed Ishlar's party toward the nightglider nest, to when she had run off to be 'saved' by him with her charm running at full power... She couldn't help but shake the feeling that it would have been just as effective to simply walk up to him and offer to buy him a drink. He was just so reasonable and affable about everything that artifice and subterfuge just seemed like a pointless waste.

Regardless, her enigmatic companion really only seemed capable of deepening the mysteries surrounding him. Although he wasn't terribly powerful as a mage, he was much too young for the amount of magic that he wielded. On top of that, so much of what he had normalized was profoundly alien. He managed to use magic without a class tattoo, which should be impossible for anyone with less than a century worth of practice.

He didn't seem to understand how rare it was for a mage to fight with weapons while wearing armor, when most found physical fitness and combat beneath them. Now, it turned out that he could also use fire magic. She hadn't even found an attunement stone on him for the thunder, and now the fire.

Admittedly, it was poorly-cast and mana-inefficient fire, but at a minimum he was a classless dual affinity caster. She snorted. Triple affinity. She had forgotten that he kept using minor space magic to avoid attacks. There was no way he had happened upon a crashed ship and figured out how to use the teleporter on his own. His claims of being some sort of serf being trained for the imperial army were equally hollow. Even elven arrogance would wane around a human this talented. She didn't doubt that they would train him, but he would have been an elite, given access to the greatest arms and supplements that his sponsor could afford.

No, he was a liar, but an incredibly naive one. She had originally assumed that he was a spy of some sort, which seemed fairly logical given his ability set. But if he was a spy, he was awful at it. He made up a terrible and transparent story, and couldn't stop himself from wringing his hands the entire time he told it. She didn't even need the Detect Falsehood skill to tell that he was lying, but it was almost worse that he didn't even notice that she was using it. After spending a day or so with him, she had come to the bizarre conclusion that he honestly didn't know the first thing about Twilight or its politics.

He was still lying about something, but he wasn't a spy from the Kingdom of Dubarr. The Alliance of Free Cities had seen any number of spies after they declared independence, and Nora had made a good deal of coin spotting them for the authorities. Usually, they were fairly easy to pick out. Some still had the accent, but most couldn't help but ask "casual" questions about local politics and defenses as soon as they were distracted by her batting her eyelashes. Daniel, on the other hand, just seemed content to follow her lead. She didn't even really want to do a run on the Mashress Silver Mine; she just thought that pushing the issue would make him more likely to show his true colors.

No matter, even if he was just a talented mage with some sort of past he wanted to hide from, the Alliance of Free Cities was the right place for him. The Alliance was a bit lawless, but if you wanted to avoid the great powers on Twilight, it was probably the place to be. Of course, if any of the great powers actually wanted to crush the Alliance, it would've been a foregone conclusion.

Instead, the Alliance continued to exist because it cost too much money and effort to invade or co-opt. Rather than take over directly, the great powers used it as a sort of neutral middle ground where their representatives could interact. They mostly only acted through sponsorships, offering themselves up as patrons for individuals like Ishlar within the Alliance and using them to try and gain enough influence to force out their rivals.

To date, the Alliance had successfully played a dangerous balancing act, not allowing any one power to gain enough influence to allow an easy takeover. It would take some time and effort to develop Daniel, but he could be a powerful asset to keeping the word "free" in the Alliance of Free Cities.

"Andrea, what's taking so long?" She asked the tall woman, stepping away from their recent kill. "Daniel has a head wound, and I want to make sure that he doesn't die from hypothermia or something stupid like that, after he saved us from whatever this thing is." Nora motioned offhandedly at the heavily-burnt beast.

"I'll get right on it," Andrea replied, fishing a flint striker from her travel pack. Within a couple seconds, the tinder ignited, and the tunnel was lit by a low, but hearty flame. All of them stared at it for a couple seconds before Andrea looked at Daniel and took a deep breath.

The three of them sat in silence, weapons at the ready as they eyed up the darkness. Packs of monsters weren't terribly common. More often than not, anything big enough to be a threat was territorial and would drive competition away. Still, they'd just made a lot of noise and it didn't hurt to be cautious.

"Look, I'll say it for Emily and me," she said, voice a little shaky. "What exactly is going on with him? What exactly is the story with this Dan guy? At first I thought the lightning flashes from the arena were some sort of class specific ability, but that was straight up magecraft. He's low rank, that's for sure, but he shouldn't be able to cast like that at his age, especially with two affinities. I don't think I've ever seen a caster under forty-five, and that guy was only really capable of creating magical torchlight."

"Nora," she continued, "we took this job because of your reputation. There was something off about him from the very beginning, and we assumed he would turn out to be a spy or something of the sort. You told us to trust you, and we do. I just need to know what we're dealing with here."

"Honestly?" Nora looked the other woman in the eyes, "I don't know. He claims that he teleported in from another planet where he had been trained by an elven house, but I'm not sure I buy it. He just doesn't seem to understand how abnormal his abilities are. If no one tells him that mages don't fight with a sword and armor, I suspect it'll take him months to figure out."

"How did he learn to fight like that?" Emily interrupted, wincing slightly as she placed the last bandage over a bloody gash on her side. "He isn't the most skilled swordsman I've ever seen, but I don't know the style he's using. I mean, it's clear that he isn't self-taught; everything he's doing seems to be part of some sort of orthodox collection of moves, but I figured I'd at least have an idea as to what school he trained with. Instead, he's a gigantic question mark."

"I do know that he has the potential to be powerful," Nora replied. "He's hiding something, but he's simply too talented to be wasted in a backwater like this. If he wants to hide here for a little while, that's fine. It would certainly be better for us to work with him and earn some mana and coin, rather than get in his way. He's weak now, but if he's given a chance, he could turn into something new and powerful."

"I don't know if the Alliance is a backwater," Andrea chided Nora. "We're actually pretty close to most of the great powers. Plus, even if we are a backwater, the Alliance is the one paying our bills. Being polite and cordial toward the hand with the purse is just good business sense. No need to antagonize some council member for no reason by pointing out geopolitical truth. That isn't the sort of thing that wins them voters."

"I wasn't talking about the Alliance, Andrea," Nora answered, eyes not leaving Daniel's unconscious form. "I'm talking about Twilight as a whole. I don't know what someone with the body of a fighter and three affinities is doing in a tributary state. Void ships visit us what, maybe once a year, once every other year? The Empire barely even admits that we exist. We're really only a source of fairly common raw materials and Imperial soldiers. Even the great powers that rule over Twilight are almost nothing in the grand scheme of things. A contingent of the Amberell House Guard could do a surgical strike and wipe out the ruling families of any nation on the entire planet, and there's nothing anyone here could do about it."

"The Orakh are nearby." Emily shrugged. "Maybe he's someone sent by the elves as an advance scout. I wouldn't be surprised if a local house tries to consolidate us under their banner, so that they can fortify the planet and use us as cannon fodder to fight off the horde."

"That does bear watching," Andrea responded, nodding

thoughtfully. "I wouldn't mind fighting the Orakh, but if that has to happen, I want to do it on my own, not as a disposable meat shield for some two-thousand-year-old noble. None of us might survive if the horde invades, but we could at least fight them as citizens of Twilight, rather than as a cog in some stratagem that is designed to weaken the horde as a whole, probably at the expense of our lives."

"I agree." Nora pursed her lips. "I don't think he's from the Kingdom of Dubarr, and they're the greatest threat right now, but it is certainly possible that he's an elven plant. His magical aptitude and strange fighting style scream of their influence. If he represents offworld forces, it might be for the best if he doesn't make it back to them to report. I think we could do without some Imperial lordling showing up on our doorstep and declaring himself our ruler."

The three women sat in the flickering light of the fire and thought. Daniel represented a potential ally, but he could also be a risk to all of them. If he were an elven agent or a deserter, he could easily bring the Empire to the Alliance of Free Cities. One Imperial officer on Twilight could easily upset the strange balance that kept the cities free from the competing powers.

"Let's wait and see," Nora finally said, eyes locked on the dancing flames. "If he is simply here to find wealth and power, there is enough of that to go around in the mines. If he's here as a spy or an agent, there are plenty of hungry monsters in the mines, too. Not everyone who ventures into the darkness comes back out. No one would bother to look for him, and even if they did, carrion doesn't last long near this many monsters."

The other two women nodded in agreement but didn't speak. Silently, Emily pulled out a pot and began making them some stew for dinner. The other two watched her cook and waited for Daniel to awaken.

CHAPTER FIFTEEN

Delving (III)

Dan awoke with blurry vision and a splitting headache. Luckily, the worst of his injuries had more or less healed themselves, but even the nanites of the System struggled with head wounds. He sat up and tried to blink away the vertigo. About six feet from him, the rest of the party sat around a campfire where they were roasting a shank of the creature. Hunger warred with physical weakness for a couple seconds before Dan pulled himself to his feet and took a couple wobbly steps towards the fire. Yep, definitely a concussion.

"Ah, the dreamer awakens," Nora stated, waving to him with a grin that matched the fire's warmth. "Come on and get some dinner. It may surprise you, given the primitive accommodations, but with a little seasoning and some proper cooking, the meat tastes terrible. Still, it's free and it's protein. We're going to need some energy to keep exploring."

"The meat will help." The world wobbled as Dan tried to nod. "But I took a bit of a hit to the head there. It might take a little bit before I'm ready to fight, and I would prefer it to be against something much smaller than whatever the hell that thing was. I don't really have much control over fire, and I can really only use it to start myself and something near me on fire. Not really the most useful expenditure of mana."

"Is there any way that you can polish that up?" Nora asked with a glint in her eye. "We wouldn't need you to jump on the back of the next monster if you could throw fireballs."

"I could work on it?" Dan replied with a weak shrug. "I have some affinity with fire, but I can't say that it's an area of focus. Practicing with fire had a nasty tendency to leave me covered in burns and soot, so I tried to stick to affinities that were less likely to physically harm me."

"Don't you just have a class skill you can use?" Emily asked, taking a bite from the greasy, charred meat. "It might take some practice to be any good with it, but you can always work on it while we cut our way through this place."

"I actually don't..." he began, only for Nora to cut him off.

"Maybe you should just practice on the monster's corpse," she suggested pointedly, warning him into silence with a pointed look. "Subterranean monsters are often weak against light and fire. You should've alerted me to your affinity, so that we could have figured something out before we left."

"You do realize that you basically kidnapped me, right?" Dan asked as he wandered over to the corpse, shank of meat in hand. "I mean, you tricked me into a fight, and then woke me up the next morning to tell me that I had to go on a mission of some sort. We never even talked about what I could or couldn't do."

"Well, Dan," she questioned sweetly as he tried to focus on creating just a small amount of fire out of his free hand. "What can you do?"

There was a flicker in the darkness as his mana ignited, but it quickly guttered out as he lost control of the stream of mana feeding the flame. He frowned and pushed again, and this time the fire remained, lighting up the misshapen and burned corpse of the beast. It danced about an inch above his palm for ten seconds before he accidentally fed it too much mana, causing it to flare and die. He tried again, creating the flame and walking the delicate line of ensuring that it received enough mana to stay lit while avoiding oversaturating it. As he stared at the soft red flame hovering over his hand, Dan thought back to his chemistry. Fire consisted of a fragile mix of combustible gases, oxygen, and heat. If he added too much of any category, the flame would either smother itself or burn all available fuel in an instant.

He focused on the magic flowing through his attunement stone. After a second, the gases and heat produced by the ignition of his mana warmed him. Almost immediately, he became lost in the sensation, and the flame burned out of control, singing his hand before disappearing. Frowning, he shook his hand to dull the pain and tried again. He could almost feel the System kicking in and dealing with the heavy lifting of moderating the flow of energy. Struggling, Dan maintained the small red flame for almost a minute before he was distracted by the System.

Detecting new skill. Tentative name Create Flame assigned. Would you like to designate Create Flame as a skill?

The flame wavered, on the verge of him losing control. Instead of relying on the system, Dan created a jet of oxygen and combustible gas, pushing them both forward through the flame. This time, a burst of flame erupted from his open hand, fully illuminating the chamber as it traveled almost five feet before it faded. He frowned and looked at his hand; the heat from the blast had burned him, too.

"No," he whispered, dismissing the System prompt. He needed something more than a flame to light a candle. He needed to fire the combustible gas through the flame with enough speed that it only truly started burning away from him. He needed the speed of the combustible gas to carry it into a target while it was still burning. What he needed was a flamethrower.

In the back of his mind, a voice shouted at him. This same process had taken days of experimentation and burns back on Earth, but he didn't have that luxury. He needed something flashy, and he needed it now. Desperation might not be the best kind of inspiration, but it was all he had in stock.

He recreated the dim red flame with a thought. Then, he created the mental image of hydrogen gas and imagined throwing it as fast as possible through the open flame. This time, the fire first appeared almost a foot and a half ahead of him and shot forward almost fifteen feet before it dispersed into nothingness. This time he nodded in satisfaction, the slight wobble of the vertigo lost in the rush of elation over achieving his goal.

Dan could still feel the fire through his attunement stone. It was still something cold and weak, little more than an explosion given direction. It would do for now, but deep down, he hungered for more. To let his mana run wild and create a pure flame with no effort wasted to guide or shape it. Something with the heat that could burn through all adversity, that could melt the very bedrock of the world itself. He smiled to himself.

Detecting increase in Fire Affinity. Fire Affinity is now 2.

Detecting new skill. Tentative name Flame Jet assigned. Would you like to designate Flame Jet as a skill?

"Yes," Dan said quietly. His whole body tingled for a second as the self learning nanites of the System updated themselves. An unpleasant feeling, but still much better than the unending waves of pain he was used to when Samantha updated the System. He turned back to the party sitting around the fire, a strange lethargy settling over him. Even with double his previous mana pool, those experiments had almost run him dry. He'd need to work on his fire affinity if he wanted to be able to use it in combat.

"That is what I do," Dan said with a bit more authority than he felt. "I learn quickly. If I practice Flame Jet enough, I should be able to use it a lot more freely."

"Did you just teach yourself a skill in a half hour?" Andrea asked, her previous wariness having given way to surprise. "I just watched you go from being unable to maintain a basic flame to firing a beam of fire, didn't I?"

"Yes," Dan shrugged. "It's still a weak ability and it hogs mana every time I activate it, but the more I work on it, the stronger and cheaper it will become. I really should have developed my fire affinity more. Electricity is tantalizing, but it just takes too much energy to get it to arc properly. I'm sure it will be powerful later, but right now I need some firepower, and 'Flame Jet' seems to fulfill that need."

"I suppose different classes have their strengths," Nora said through gritted teeth, staring at Dan. "Now, are we ready to head out, or do you still need to rest your head? As far as I can tell, the stone you landed on is dented and you are fine, so I don't possibly see why we would need to delay ourselves."

Dan felt the slight wobble of vertigo and winced. He had been so excited by the idea of creating a flame skill that he had forgotten about Nora's rather explicit warnings not to let anyone know that he was casting without a class. She didn't exactly seem happy with his demonstration, so he avoided complaining about his still-throbbing head and the lethargy of his mana exhaustion. It just seemed like a better strategy to hope that he didn't get jumped by some sort of bug-eyed terror before his mana regenerated than to brave the storm of annoying her any further.

The next hour or so of exploration went smoothly. Although Nora noted a couple creatures, most of them scuttled away rather than approach the four-person party. Dan was a little disappointed that he wouldn't have a chance to test out his new skill, but no one other than Nora could see well enough in the dark to get anywhere near the monsters as they ran away, so pursuit didn't seem like the best idea. He wasn't disappointed, however, with the silver they found. Silver ore might be a better term for it, but many of the creatures dwelling in the caves would dig in the walls for the stuff. Already, they had collected almost 15 pounds of silver-laden stone. Not quite enough to pay off the Cragson sisters' contract for the expedition, but they were only a couple hours into the cave.

"I still can't figure out why they dig this stuff out," Dan

spoke as he hefted a fist-sized chunk of ore. "I get humans coveting it. It doesn't corrode and it's relatively rare, giving it value. I just don't understand why a breed of monster, let alone all monsters we've run into, would mine for the stuff."

"It's a magical catalyst," Nora replied from just outside of the circle of light cast by Andrea's torch. "Silver conducts mana better than anything but gold or mythril. That's why you see so many magical weapons and armor made from silver or silver alloys. It's not the strength of the metal, that's for sure. Steel or copper will do in a pinch, but products made from them break down fairly quickly and are generally considered inferior. Rune-scripters are rarer than silver, so it's strange for you to see a magical tool crafted from anything less powerful than silver."

"As for the monsters..." A shuffle of fabric from the darkness indicated a dismissive gesture from Nora. "Biologists believe that it helps them with their mana in a similar way. We do know that magical creatures tend to rank up faster if given access to silver, even if it doesn't have any mana of its own. No one has bothered to look much deeper into it than that. We know that they love the stuff to the point where you can bait traps with it, but beyond that, who cares? They'll mine it for us; we just need to kill them and take it from them before they can actually ingest it."

"I suppose," Dan pursed his lips as he replied. He might not be the scientist that Doctor Weathers was, but he was still inquisitive by nature. Simply accepting a dead end and ignoring it because there was no immediate profit just didn't sit right with him. Still, he didn't even know where to start on pursuing that piece of knowledge. What could he do, monitor what deadly captured monsters did with silver to see why they mined it?

"Shh!" Nora interrupted his thoughts as she put one hand up, indicating that the party stop. "Quick, put out the torch; I think we've found a nest of some sort."

Dan peered ahead, but he couldn't really make anything out. He did hear an occasional clicking that might be associated with something walking across the stone floor, but even with the torch, he was relatively helpless in the cave. Then, the torch went out, plunging the entire chamber into absolute darkness. He shifted uncomfortably, images of the creature that greeted their journey into the cave sneaking up on the party playing through his head.

"Ants," Nora whispered. "Big ants. It looks like they're carrying some silver into the nest. Probably for their young. The good and bad news is that ants have a lot of young. There are almost certainly hundreds if not thousands of ants in that nest. On the other hand, there is almost certainly an insane amount of silver in there."

CHAPTER SIXTEEN

Ants! (I)

Dan silently cursed himself as he sneaked closer to the collapsed wall that served as the entrance to the ant hive. Nora had said that the ants were big, but he didn't ask any questions. At some point, he found himself agreeing to strike the first blow against the hive before falling back to where the rest of the party was hiding in a more defensible position. At least the area around the hive was illuminated by bioluminescent lichen. Dan couldn't even imagine trying to handle this sort of scouting mission in the dark.

He stared angrily at the horse-sized ant as it stood next to the collapsed wall. He wasn't sure what he had been expecting when Nora said that there would be "hundreds to thousands of big ants." Maybe ants the size of a cat or a golden retriever. Something challenging but manageable. He wasn't really sure where the girl got her optimism from, but he certainly didn't share it. God, even its mandibles were as big as his sword.

In his head, Sam mocked him again for his indecision and cowardice. Every time he came upon a situation with risk or pain, he always looked for excuses or worried himself into inaction. The only time he had really leapt into the unknown and taken a risk was when he swallowed the mana crystals, and that had unlocked a whole suite of new possibilities for him.

Sure, that ant could probably dismember him if he wasn't careful, but it also represented possibilities. Nora seemed convinced that there would be more silver ore in the mine, and the ant was sure to have mana. The mana in Dan's core bubbled in response to his thoughts. Unbidden, a phantom of the euphoria he felt when absorbing mana rumbled through his body.

He gritted his teeth. That was the plan: focus on the good he would get out of this. The ant hive wasn't just a danger zone filled with chitin-covered monsters. It was a fountain of mana for him to absorb and grow stronger. Dan licked his lips briefly. He was crouched in an alcove only ten feet from the ant standing guard. Before he could think about what he was doing, he extended his left hand toward the ant and whispered 'Flame Jet.'

The streamer of red flame reached out and struck the unsuspecting ant in the thorax. Immediately, it began chittering angrily, swinging its mandibled head back and forth, searching for its assailant. Granting its wish, Dan stepped out into the open and unleashed another Flame Jet, blinding the ant temporarily with the burning flash of light. Already, the hollowness brought on by mana deprivation wore on him. Dan ignored it, instead stepping forward and swinging his sword at the ant.

With a clatter and spray of sparks, the ant deflected the blow into the air, leaving little more than a deep scratch on the ant's armored face. Dan grimaced and sprinted for the fall back position before the ant completely recovered from his spell. The next attempt would have to focus on a joint or other crack in the ant's armor. It didn't seem like brute force was going to get through its thick chitin.

Behind him, an incensed chittering echoed along with the rapid clicking of the ant's legs as they impacted the stone floor of the tunnel. Well, at least Dan's actions had earned the ant's attention. Possibly too much attention. He probably should have realized that a large creature with six legs would be able to outpace him fairly rapidly. Firing an unaimed Flame Jet behind him to distract it, Dan was rewarded by a loud thud as the partially-blinded ant crashed into an obstacle of some sort. It was unlikely that the collision severely hurt it, but it served Dan's purpose and bought him enough time to round the corner where Andrea, Emily, and Nora were hiding.

It rounded the corner after him, only to meet Emily's greatsword. With a flash, one of the ant's legs fell twitching to the ground, and it slewed to the side, off-balance with only five legs. Andrea stepped forward and brought her maul down on its thorax. Although the blow didn't immediately finish the ant, an audible breaking sounded.

He could easily make out a web of cracks on the creature's back as the force of the blow slammed it into the ground. Almost without thinking, he stepped forward and shoved his hand into the shattered hole in the ant's chitin and unleashed a Flame Jet. Briefly, their side chamber flashed with light. The ant let out a deep, thrumming wail as the spell boiled its insides.

For a second, everyone held their position with bated breath as they eyed the prone and writhing ant. Then, Dan stumbled backward as the flow of mana from the dead creature washed over him. His eyes fluttered and closed as unrefined pleasure wrapped him in a warm blanket. For a brief moment, he didn't care about the risks of their raid on the mine or the danger that Earth was. All that existed was the mana flowing freely into him.

The flow of magic cut off, and his eyes opened. Dan shivered in the pervasive chill of the cave as he squinted his eyes against the dark. The rest of the party stood around the felled ant. It didn't look like any of them had noticed his moment of weakness. Idly, Nora reached out with a booted foot and prodded the creature.

"Could you have found another way, Dan?" she asked

unhappily. "You know I have enhanced senses from my class, and now this entire place smells awful."

"Sorry Ms. Nora," he replied, rolling his eyes. "I should have put more thought into how to fight the armored death beast that we had temporarily incapacitated. I'm sure it would have stayed in the same spot if we asked nicely while we tried to figure out a way to kill it."

"There's no need to get smart." Nora glared at him while she plugged her nose with her free hand. "This seriously smells like you burnt garbage that someone left out in the sun for a week. Next time, just put a sword through the weak spot on its armor and don't assault my poor nose."

"Are we done bickering yet?" Emily interjected as she sheathed her sword. "If we're going to raid the hive, we've eliminated its guard and now is the time to do so. If we're going to slink away into the night, now is the time to do so as well, before the hive notices its guard is missing. Either way, we need to act quickly, because I don't think we want to fight more than a handful of these things at once."

Dan nodded grudgingly. Her point was sound. They had a narrow window to sneak into the hive and try to escape with some silver. Arguing over how bad the half-melted ant smelled wasn't a productive pursuit, even if it did smell positively rancid to his unenhanced senses.

"Fine, I've mostly recovered my mana, anyway," Dan replied, trying to keep any hint of a sulking tone from his voice.

"Didn't you just cast that flame spell twice?" Andrea asked, her brow furrowed. "I don't know what your reserves look like or how much that spell uses, but that seems awfully fast. I mean, I don't want to sit around here smelling burning armpit any longer than we have to, but I also don't want us to rush into combat with a mana-depleted mage."

"I'm not completely back to normal." Dan shrugged. "But there was a bit of a run here. I've always found that physical exertion helps me recover mana. Plus, it'll be at least a couple minutes before we run into anything new. Plenty of time for me to top off completely."

In the gloom, he made out all three of the women shooting him startled looks. He winced internally. *Shit.* Sam had said that his method of awakening had greatly increased his rate of mana regeneration, but he just didn't have any frame of reference. Apparently, being ready to fight again ten to fifteen minutes after he used magic was a bit attention-grabbing. He'd just been so excited at the prospect of fighting and siphoning mana again that he hadn't even thought of the repercussions for revealing his abilities. In the future, he'd have to find a way to hide his regeneration or otherwise downplay it.

"Come on, the ants aren't going to kill themselves!" He exclaimed quickly, a hint of panic in his voice as he began power walking back towards the hive. After a second or two, the rest of the party followed him. Internally, he kept swearing at himself. Nora believed his stories so far, but if he kept showing unbelievable abilities, she was sure to suspect him eventually.

Sneaking into the hive itself was surprisingly easy now that the guard was gone. The ants were big enough that the tunnels they carved easily accommodated even Andrea and Emily. Occasionally, Nora would grab the back of his armor, and they would duck into a side tunnel to avoid working ants. As they searched chamber by chamber, looking for a collection of ore, tension began to build. It was only a matter of time before their luck would run out, but despite that, they just couldn't find anything of value. Every doorway seemed to lead to nothing more than a room full of eggs, food, or a half-completed passageway.

Then, they turned a corner and found themselves a mere five feet from another ant. Both sides stood in silence for a moment before bursting into action. An arrow bounced off of the ant's thick chitin as Dan unleashed a Flame Jet into its mandibles in an attempt to buy time for Emily and Andrea to draw their weapons.

Detecting increase in Fire Affinity. Fire Affinity is now 3.

Flame Jet is now 2.

Dan blinked away the notifications. While the increases in efficiency would certainly help, he knew from experience that low-level skills and affinities would grow much quicker than his more developed ones.

Then, the ant clumsily lunged forward and he hopped back to dodge it, having no real faith in his ability to parry the ant's mandibles with a sword. Unfortunately, Nora was standing right behind him with her bow, and Dan crashed directly into her, bringing both of them to the ground in a tangle of interconnected limbs as her nocked arrow flew off into the dark. Before the ant could capitalize on their misfortune, Andrea stepped past them and took the creature in the side of its head with a horizontal swing. Blinded by the flames from Dan's spell searing its soft eyes, it didn't even dodge. The maul cracked the fire-weakened chitin of the ant's head, staggering it.

Dan tried to stand up, only to run into Nora once again as she had the same idea. He fell backward, and the stone wall behind him knocked the wind out of him through the chain of his armor. He grimaced in sympathy as she took a similar spill, but with armor much less fit to handle the impact.

Andrea swung her maul again, and this time the ant's head cracked like a melon. Dan bit his lip and hissed in pleasure as the mana poured into him. The pain in his back faded into a distant memory as ripples of euphoria flooded through him. This time, they ended much more quickly. He grunted in dissatisfaction. It was probably because he landed the killing blow last time, rather than distracting it while Andrea finished it off. Mentally, he made a note to try and land the final blow on the next monster. After all, the more mana he absorbed, the closer he was to helping Earth. He shuddered once more as an aftershock from the pleasure washed through him.

Mana influx detected. Recalculating Spirit.

Spirit is now 5.

"I knew you liked me, Dan, but that was a bit much!" Nora exclaimed cheerfully as she pulled herself to her feet. "Usually when I end up in a sweaty pile of limbs with a guy I just met, I make him buy me dinner first."

He shook his head to dismiss the System notifications, ignoring the slightest hint of vertigo from his earlier concussion. As he opened his mouth to respond, Nora kept speaking.

"I guess that just means you owe me dinner, then!" She nodded authoritatively. "We should also work on your situational awareness. You're an alright fighter, but it's pretty clear you've never really fought as a team before. It's one thing for you to run into me, but I really want us to nip this problem in the bud before you accidentally set one of us on fire."

Dan scowled slightly as Emily and Andrea began nodding empathetically in agreement. He had some control over the Flame Jets now, but ultimately the spell involved accelerating combustible gases through a flame to ignite them. Accuracy was more of a direction he pointed it in than anything pinpoint. In short, they might be right, but that didn't mean they had to be so enthusiastic about it.

"Fine, once we get back to the surface, I'll..." his dry response was cut off by the clatter of hundreds of legs rushing towards them from both directions. Deep in his lungs, the angry, low-pitched hum throbbed as soundwaves too low to register pulsed through the air.

"Shit!" Emily spat on the ground. "I think we just woke up the entire hive. I vote that we keep Daniel in front until he runs out of mana. I really don't want to end up blackened and crispy if I can help it."

Simultaneously, the rest of the party stepped back, leaving an entire tunnel to him. Dan glared balefully back at them, trying to ignore their good-natured chuckling while he drew his sword. It was time to see how useful an extra point in spirit, fire, and Flame Jet actually were.

CHAPTER SEVENTEEN

Ants! (II)

The party made it to a partially-dug chamber about fifty feet away before the hive's guardians found them. The first ant around the corner was maybe knee-high, skittering under Dan's surprised sword thrust only for Emily's greatsword to bisect it almost immediately. Then another dog-sized ant ran into the room. Dan raised an eyebrow and made eye contact with Nora, who just shrugged.

"Either we're the monsters and fighting babies, or they have a worker caste," Nora stated as she unleashed an arrow into the tiny ant, killing it instantly. "My current bet is that it's a worker. It doesn't make sense for all the ants to be gigantic and have jaws that can shear through a tree trunk. Some of them have to be smaller."

Before Dan could reply, a swarm of the dog-sized ants poured into the room. Dan lunged forward and skewered one with his sword, it's much thinner chitin barely slowing the piercing point of the weapon. He withdrew the blade and kicked away another ant that drew too close to him before bringing his sword down on it. This time, the slashing edge of the sword slammed into the thorax of the ant with much less effect. It still cracked the rather adorable chittering creature's armor open, but the chitin slowed the blade enough that it mostly just left a gash wreathed in a web of cracks. He withdrew his weapon and stabbed downward in one quick motion, ending the ant.

Got it, use the point of the blade. The chitin was hard enough to severely dampen the effectiveness of the cutting blade, even on the smaller ants. At the entryway, Emily and Andrea were clearing the small ants back with wide strokes from their weapons while Nora picked off the few creatures that slipped in under their guard.

Each dead ant brought another heady rush of energy as mana poured into him. At first, Dan tried to keep track of how many of the creatures he killed, but before long, the pleasant pink tingles traveling up and down his spine began to blur and merge.

They were holding the swarm back for now, it was only a matter of time before the sisters tired or a couple too many ants slipped through and the party was surrounded. The mandibles on the smaller ants were nowhere near the size of their larger cousins, but Dan had no desire to test the resiliency of his leather boots against them.

"Close your eyes in three!" Dan shouted as he stepped forward, just out of the range of the sisters' backswings, and unleashed a Flame Jet into the oncoming ants. The first hint of emptiness hollowed within him as the mana was pulled from his body, but the flash of light elicited a satisfying cacophony of chittering from the hallway as it stunned the various insects that had become accustomed to the gloomy environment. His sword darted into the stunned and injured swarm once, then twice, each time mortally wounding an ant already wounded by the fire.

"What the hell was that?" Andrea yelled back, blinking her eyes as she staggered a step or two. She almost dropped her hammer as she put a hand over her face. Evidently, she had been staring right at the ants when the jet had gone off.

Dan strode forward and took her spot next to the door as she tried to regain her vision. His sword thrust out, punching through the chitin on another semi-blind smaller ant. In the future, they'd have to work on teamwork. Right now, his magic was only really useful to distract and disable foes, and if the rest of his team couldn't take advantage of the openings he was producing, it would almost be better for him to stick to simple swordplay. Luckily, Emily and Nora had shielded their eyes in time, and both tore into the crowd of stunned and unprotected ants with ease.

Without warning, the stream of ants stopped. Dan was breathing a little heavily, but other than that, the previous attack hadn't even caused him to break a sweat. After a second or three of silence, two waist-high ants stormed through the door, vice-like blunted mandibles held wide. Dan thrust at one of the two and made a sour face as his sword's point only sunk a couple of inches into the ant. From its chattered response, it clearly wasn't happy, but the strike was far from the instant kills he had been inflicting against their smaller brethren.

He stepped back as the wounded ant lunged at him, making room for another mid-sized insect to scurry into the room. It seemed like the previous struggle exhausted the hive's supply of the smaller and easier-to-handle ants. Dan took note of this worrying development as he slashed his sword at the oncoming ant's head. It didn't even dodge as the sword struck it with all the elegance and effectiveness of a shovel, stunning the monster but doing little actual damage as its chitin turned the blow. Nearby, one of Nora's arrows bounced off the newly-arriving ant's armored thorax.

He cursed to himself. Emily and Andrea had the strength and crushing power to fight the annoying vermin, but Nora and him were finesse fighters. Although the chitin didn't have the thickness or durability of plate armor, it was distressingly durable, nonetheless. What they really needed was spears or crossbows, something with enough reach to keep the clacking mandibles away and still pierce the resilient chitin. If he made it out of this mess, he'd mention his concerns to Sam. The Foundation had focused his training all too much on fighting human enemies leaving him in the weeds when struggling with more exotic foes. It all made a kind of sense he supposed, no one on Earth knew what mana infused monsters would look or act like, so no one even began to know how to train him. The peril of being a trailblazer he supposed.

The ant he was fighting shook off its surprise and skittered toward him once again. Rather than give ground, Dan stepped to the side and swung his sword at the creature's legs which sheared off with a satisfying snap. The little beasties might be fairly heavily-armored, but at a minimum, he could take their legs off one-by-one, then cook them. It might not be quick or efficient, but he'd be damned if anything but a full-sized warrior ant did him in. Anything less just wouldn't be dignified.

His ant hit the ground and let out another low, thrumming moan. Dan ignored it and brought his sword down in a stabbing motion, wounding it. From the corner of his eye, he saw another two of the mid-sized ants entering the room. Out of time, he grunted and fed a wisp of mana into his bracers as he stabbed downward once more. This time, the blade sunk deep into the crippled ant's head. With one last shudder, it stopped moving, and Dan withdrew his sword just as the swell of mana hit him.

Dan's body must have hit some sort of limit, unable to keep the energy flowing into him in check. That specific ant wasn't anything special, just one more violent package of chitin and mandibles, but its death transformed the gentle pleasant trickle of mana into a tsunami of light and white noise.

The room grew bright and fuzzy, almost like one of the camera filters his college buddies back on Earth kept trying to get him to use. A smile split across his face as he looked down at his hand. Everything about him felt lighter, sharper. His movements became effortless, like he was a swallow flowing through the clouds, flitting from current to current. Briefly, he wondered why the littlest ants didn't syphon mana to him, but then he realized that he didn't care. The mid-sized ants had mana, so that was what he was going to kill.

Without really thinking, he ran up to another ant and triggered Shocking Fist as he slapped it upside the head, barely avoiding its snapping mandibles. With a flash, the electricity grounded itself through the creature's brain, rendering it temporarily insensible. He fed mana into his bracers and used the extra strength to bring the blade down in a double-fisted overhand blow, striking the weak point in its armor where the head attached to the thorax, decapitating the creature. More mana pulsed into him, and the world became brighter.

He sighted another ant and shifted to a one-handed grip, firing a Flame Jet into its charging form. Its antenna ignited almost immediately, but the sudden burst of heat wasn't able to do much more than blind and hurt the insect. It hardly mattered; Dan smashed the beast to the ground with his sword and planted a foot on its back before stabbing downward with the aid of his bracers. It took two stabs before the creature stopped moving. He shuddered as a lightning bolt of pleasure traveled down his spine.

His clouded eyes snapped up as he looked for another foe. Somewhere in the back of his mind, Dan knew that what he was doing was wrong. Even with the increases to his mana pool, it was a limited commodity, and it seemed like there were a whole lot of ants in the hive. He should be saving his resources, relying on good, old-fashioned stabbing wherever possible. He just couldn't, though. The excitement and adrenaline was too much. He needed to finish the ants off as quickly as possible. Maybe it was to test himself, maybe it was to protect his friends, and maybe it was to keep chasing the euphoric thrill of the raw mana coursing into him. He didn't really know, nor did he care.

Instead, he ducked under the guard of a full grown warrior ant and discharged a Shocking Fist into it. He didn't know when a warrior had entered the room, but he took advantage of the moment of distraction created by partially electrocuting the insect to swing himself up onto its back. In a fugue, he dropped his sword. It was too long and unwieldy, so he let it clatter to the floor. Instead, he jabbed the point of his dagger into the spot at the back of its neck where the plates of its facial armor ended and the flexible muscles of its neck began. Wedging the blade under the armor plates, he levered them up, exposing a gap in the chitin. Beneath him, the ant began to buck in an attempt to throw him off. Dan giggled like a maniac as he put his free hand up against the crack and activated Flame Jet.

The facial armor bulged slightly from the overpressure created by the detonating gases, but the creature dropped to the floor almost immediately, its legs twitching slightly. Dan staggered towards his sword, lost in a pink-colored cloud. Every nerve in his body purred to him.

Even his usually-uncomfortable chain shirt felt like a velvet caress. Mindlessly, he picked up the sword and stabbed it into a nearby warrior. Andrea was fighting the creature and screaming at Dan. He didn't really care. He stabbed again and again, finally finding the weak spot where the thorax and the abdomen connected and wounding it in a spray of ichor.

The ant turned on him, ignoring Andrea. Dan giggled and fired a Flame Jet straight into its face. Somewhere in the back of his mind, he acknowledged that he was almost out of mana. That didn't matter to him, nor the newly-blinded ant. Its mandibles closed on his sword blade, ripping the weapon from his hand. He reached for his dagger, only to stare dumbly at his empty hand.

That's right, the weapon was already melted to the other warrior. He shrugged and turned back to the ant, only for it to rush into him and knock Dan to the ground. On his back, he watched the underside of the warrior skitter past him, chased by Andrea, who shot him a dirty look. After a couple seconds of searching through the chaos, he found his sword. Dead ants littered the chamber, making it hard for both humans and their cousins to move freely. Yet, still more came.

He fired another Flame Jet into a crowd of mid-sized ants, feeling a mana deprivation headache beginning to war with the cloud of pleasure he was hiding in. He staggered over to a disoriented ant and brought his sword down on it with both hands, knocking it to the ground. He swung again and again, almost insensible as his sword skittered off the ant's chitin. Finally, the blade found its neck, and he was rewarded with another burst of mana.

Then the pink fog consumed him entirely. He vaguely remembered laughing like a maniac as he cast more spells and swung his sword wildly. At one point, he faded back in to find himself on top of a warrior ant with an ichor-stained rock in his hands, tears streaming down his face, and its head a bloody ruin. At some point, he remembered Emily grimly running out of the hive with him slung over her shoulder as he screamed nonsense obscenities at the pursuing ants and Emily. It almost sounded like he was begging her to put him back down so he could dive back into the fray.

Dan blinked his eyes open and immediately regretted it. His mouth felt like it was stuffed with cotton balls, and his head throbbed in agony to an invisible beat. He shivered. His entire body felt cold and weak, like he was recovering from a really bad bout of the flu. Suddenly, he leaned over and heaved, vomiting up the previous day's dinner.

"Just another Friday morning in college," he mumbled to himself, stopping his hand before it could wipe the puke from his face. He really only had one good outfit and he didn't want to get bile all over its sleeve.

"Well, good morning again," Nora interjected brightly, sending another spike of pain through Dan's sensitive skull. "You really need to stop making a habit of passing out as part of battles. Also, if you could let us know the next time you go into some sort of insane berserk frenzy, we would really appreciate it."

"Sorry 'bout that." He rolled up into a sitting position, trying to suppress another wave of nausea. They were still in a tunnel, but Andrea and Emily had started another fire. Both of them were eyeing him warily, although he couldn't tell if that was more related to the berserk frenzy or him throwing up everywhere.

"System, display status," he muttered, trying to gain some sort of sense of what he had gained from the battle.

<USER> Status
Rank 1

Body 6
Agility 7
Mind 7
Perception 6
Spirit 8

Skills
Swords 6, Brawling 3, Archery 2

Affinity
Space 9, Lightning 6, Fire 5, Gravity 1

Spells
Shocking Fist 5, Spark Field 2, Spatial Shield 5, Flame Jet 4

God, he didn't even remember enough to know what actually went up. It looked like Spirit and Flame Jet had gone up for sure. He'd have to check the System log once he had a minute where his head didn't feel like it was about to erupt.

"So, Dan," Nora stated brightly as she walked over to his hunched form. "Should I start with the good news or the bad news?"

"What?" he replied blearily, barely able to focus on her.

"The good news is that we were able to find the hive treasury on our way out," she continued, a thousand-watt smile still glued to her face. "We have officially struck it rich! Congratulations on your first wildly-successful run as the party leader. The bad news is that those mid-sized ants were definitely the workers. That first wave you killed were actually babies, which does make you a monster and a baby-killer, per our earlier conversation."

CHAPTER EIGHTEEN

Back to Town

"Why am I the baby killer?" Dan asked Nora bemusedly. "You three killed more of the tiny ants than I did."

"You're the party leader." Emily smiled with a shrug. "All our actions reflect on you. Ultimately, we are your responsibility. I certainly plan on using that to clear up some outstanding bar tabs when we get back to Morganville."

"We've just completed a lucrative mission," he replied, exhausted. "You're each getting a sovereign plus commission. Shouldn't that be more than enough to pay off your tab?"

"You've grossly underestimated how much she can drink." Andrea rolled her eyes. "We haven't been able to upgrade our gear in months because we're always in debt to some barkeep or another. If it isn't a bill for her drinking her daily bottle of rotgut, it was a bill for her getting into a bar fight and wrecking the place. I've seen her swinging a bottle in one hand and a broken chair in another well before the day laborers had returned for dinner."

"You're just a stick in the mud, Andrea." Emily stuck her tongue out. "You won't let me cut loose at all unless we're out adventuring. It's nothing but whining about collateral damage, costs, and risks. Half the reason I took a class was so I could have an excuse to engage in some good, old-fashioned, mana-empowered mayhem."

"That's it?" Dan cocked his head as he glanced at Emily. "Not the promise of riches, not to restore your family's lost honor, not some impossible quest for revenge? You just want an excuse to get a little drunk and wreck up the place?"

"Is that really so bad?" She asked as she shrugged sheepishly. "We had a fairly conservative childhood, and Papa wouldn't even let me ride a horse. I guess I'm just repressed or something. Andrea says I should probably see a therapist, but that seems like a lot less fun than throwing some asshole off of a balcony."

"She actually threw the last therapist I hired off of a balcony," Andrea interjected sourly. "I've more or less decided she's a lost cause, and at this point, it's more a matter of minimizing the damage she causes, rather than making any real effort to actually stop her."

"What about you, Nora?" Emily asked cheerfully. "What drove you to take up a class and head out into the wilds?"

The ranger glanced up at the rest of the party from her perch next to the fire. Her face scrunched for a second before falling into pensive thought. Dan took advantage of the moment of silence to massage his temples. He wasn't sure what caused his current condition, but he was more than sick of it. The worst of it was that, due to the local technology level, he couldn't even take an aspirin for the splitting headache.

"Power, mostly," Nora finally replied. "In this world, the powerful feast while the mundane starve. I grew up in a slum. Despite years of taxes being paid on time, the local lord cut corners and refused to pay full price for our town's sanctuary runes. One night, they failed. We were hunted like animals by the monsters until night broke. I was only a girl when it happened. I survived by hiding in a wine cellar, rocking back and forth while waiting for the screams to stop."

"Jesus," Dan said bitterly. "That's a whole lot to work

through. I don't know about Emily. Maybe Nora is the one who needs therapy."

"Oh, it's not that bad," Nora stood up from the fire and took a couple of steps into the cave's darkness. "It's a harsh world, and there are countless stories just like mine. The rich cut corners and the poor suffer. It's a tale as old as the mountains. The only proper way to break the cycle is to become powerful enough that no noble would dare step on you, lest you break their royal foot. That means money, and that means stealing mana for our classes from monsters. Now, are we going to start singing songs around the campfire, or are we going to head back to Morganville?"

Dan glanced at Andrea and Emily. Andrea shrugged and slung Emily back over her shoulder. He returned the shrug before taking up his own pack. Nora might have taken the conversation in a dark direction, but she had a point. There really wasn't much of a purpose in lurking about the mine. They had all the silver that they could carry. It was time to sell what they had earned and invest it in better gear.

"Wait!" Emily shouted after them as they set out into the cave. "I thought we had the option of singing songs around the campfire? That sounded like fun to me."

Both Dan and Andrea made a point of ignoring her as they walked away. It was a long hike back to town, and neither of them were terribly excited to deal with Emily's antics the entire way. The only saving grace was that Nora's mood had soured to the point that her usually-irreverent attitude had disappeared. Dan wasn't sure he could take both of them at once with his splitting headache.

They exited the mine without incident, quietly selling the silver ore in their packs to the servants of the mine's owner. After paying the twins and Nora, Dan received another six sovereigns. Good pay for a day or so worth of work, or so Nora said. Then, with fresh coins jingling in their pockets, they began the long walk back to Morganville. The journey was fairly uneventful with the handful of monsters Nora sighted running away before the party could get close to them.

Finally, they stopped an hour or so outside of town as the sky began to darken. Tanloff completely eclipsed the sun, heralding what the locals referred to as night. With practiced hands, Nora began placing the sanctuary runes in a circle around the party's campsite. Before long, they were all illuminated by the indigo glow of the protective runes.

Unconsciously, Dan let out a breath of relief. The runes were brand new and hadn't yet been tested. Deep down, he couldn't help but have some anxiety that he had spent half of his sovereigns on a fake or damaged product. No one had told him what exactly came out during the brief night, but everyone seemed to agree that whatever it was could threaten even high-rank members of elite classes. All but the most foolhardy of adventurers would rely on the runes to keep them safe.

As far as Dan could tell, the runes could only be used every twenty to thirty hours, but for a brief, four-hour window, they would create an impenetrable barrier that nothing could pass. Once the runes were up, be they the weaker, portable runes used to protect a campsite, or the larger more permanent runes carved into the walls of the cities and towns, they stayed up. Anyone trapped outside a city stayed trapped outside. Without portable runes of one's own, even being late to return from a simple errand outside the walls could be a death sentence.

Once the protective purple glow of the runes illuminated the campsite, Andrea quickly set up a fire and began cooking their dinner of stew while Emily polished her blade. As the camp fell into fairly routine behaviors, Dan found a rock near the edge of the runic barrier and sat down to look up into the sky.

It would be his first proper night, after all, and he was at least a little interested in the process. Already, the reflected light of Tanloff was mostly obscured, with only a sliver of the gas giant still visible as it passed between Twilight and Alpha Centauri. He looked up suddenly as a rock clattered under

Nora's shoes next to him. She took a seat on another rock nearby.

They both sat for a time, uncomfortable on the cold stone, watching the sky darken further. Dan shifted slightly to work a crick out of his back. Nora perked up at his sudden movement, then settled back into pensive silence once she realized he wasn't going to speak. Finally, she broke the silence.

"It really is something, isn't it?" she asked, gazing up at the rapidly-depleting gas giant in the dark sky. "I've only talked to a couple other travelers, but apparently most worlds don't have something like this. One of them said it's because we're tidally-locked, constantly facing Tanloff. According to him, there's another side of the planet with much longer days and nights because it's either directly facing the star or completely dark. Apparently, the days over there are incredibly hot, and the nights are bitterly cold. He even told me that the night spirits probably originated over there because they can hunt for ten to fifteen hours straight, due to the much longer nights."

"Do you know if any of that is true?" Dan didn't even look at her, still staring up into the sky, trying to take in every moment of the strange phenomena.

"It is," a different, masculine voice answered him. Dan whipped his head down to see Ishlar standing just outside of the camp's sanctuary runes. The large man appeared to be completely healed, but his gaze was heavy with barely-suppressed anger as he stared at Dan and his party. Behind Ishlar stood another three people wearing armor with weapons in their hands. At least those individuals had the good sense to nervously glance at the sky as night approached.

"Nora," Ishlar continued. "You broke a contract with me, then took money from me in a crooked bet. I'm here to take back what's mine. You have some time before your runes run out, but when they do, there isn't a town guard here to save you."

"Ishlar," she acknowledged evenly. "I didn't break the contract, you did. I was a free agent the minute you left me to my death, and we both know the bet wasn't crooked. You get excited, and you get in over your head; it's what always happens. Your patron might let you get away with blaming everyone else for your lapses in judgement, but it was my life you risked. I'm not going to die on some excursion because a personal vendetta of yours caused you to take an unnecessary risk."

"That's where you're wrong, Nora," the large man replied through gritted teeth. "You are going to die because of a personal vendetta. I know you just went to the silver mine. You're either weak from the fighting or heavy with gold. As soon as your runes go down, I'm going to take that gold and your head. It's what I'm owed, after all of the public humiliation you've put me through. I just wanted to offer you a couple hours to make peace with your fate."

"Ishlar!" one of the men behind him called out. "She's going to try to keep you talking until night falls and let the spirits do her work for her. We need to set up sanctuary before they come out, or she'll win without having to draw a single arrow."

Ishlar glowered at the campsite before relenting and stalking back to his own party. Only a couple hundred yards from them, their own purple runes sprang up, to the visible relief of Ishlar's party. Dan chuckled to himself as he realized that they must have been setting up their own runes while Ishlar came over to taunt them.

"Davis was always a little too smart for his own good." Nora spat on the ground, glaring at the rival campsite. "Ishlar has always been an easy-to-manipulate idiot, but Davis is usually nearby to keep him honest. He was too worked up when we challenged him to the arena for Davis to intervene, but usually he's always lurking nearby to prevent Ishlar's pride and arrogance from getting the better of him."

"Honestly," she sighed, "I don't even really understand why he follows that oaf. Ishlar's patron is powerful, but he doesn't have a terrible amount of influence in Morganville. Really, he's even a better fighter than Ishlar. For all of the brute strength he lacks, he's much harder to bait with feints. If Ishlar can't overpower someone in one rush, which admittedly isn't terribly common, the idiot is almost always at a loss as to how to proceed. Davis, on the other hand, will stand back and carve you up."

Then, a mournful howling echoed across the rocky plains of Twilight just as the last of the light faded from the sky. The only illumination came from the fires and twin set of sanctuary runes, almost like lanterns in the absolute darkness. Outside their circle of light came the hiss of movement as something large, unseen, and predatory shifted. Suddenly, Dan understood everyone's nerves and concerns. For his first time outside the runes of a town, night had fallen.

CHAPTER NINETEEN

A Night Outdoors

Nora shivered as the gaunt howled in the distance. Nights meant that the terrors of Twilight's deep places stalked the surface, but she hated the gaunts. Stalkers would hunt you through the wastes, and behemoths would simply crush you, but gaunts preyed upon your psyche. They weren't an enemy that you could defeat with steel or skills. Well, if one got close enough, you could probably stab them, but usually they wouldn't even let you see them. Unlike more traditional enemies, they would stay just out of sight, letting their baleful aura sap away at their victims until little more than a shell was left. Only then would they show their skeletal, horse-like forms.

When her town's sanctuary runes had failed, stalkers and behemoths accounted for the deaths of most of her friends and family, but the gaunts were what stuck with Nora. She had been trapped in a basement for hours, and the aura of a gaunt cared nothing for the walls and floor she was hiding behind. Each minute was an eternity as the gaunts' magic bared her inner-most self and found it wanting.

The aura had a way of making you think that you were nothing, that you had always been nothing, and that it would never change. It replayed all of your flaws on a loop while emphasizing humanity and your own cosmic insignificance. She shuddered. According to the other night survivors that she met later, she was lucky to have survived. Most who were exposed to the aura of a gaunt for more than an hour simply killed themselves, but even those who survived did so as shells.

Maybe it was because she was young and had a resilient mind when exposed, or maybe it was because she was stronger than other people, but from the minute Nora stepped out of the basement after night broke, she knew that she wasn't going to be a statistic. Whatever it took, she was going to be strong enough to stop it from happening again. Whether that meant making sure that the rich and powerful didn't cut corners at the cost of poor folks' lives, or getting powerful enough to actually protect the less fortunate, she wasn't entirely sure. What she did know was that protecting people would require ranks.

That was about fifteen years ago, and here she was. A recently-minted second rank. Finally, a veteran after her little sojourn into the mines. It might make her a big deal in a smaller town like Morganville, but in a real city, it wasn't worth much more than a respectful nod.

Even the Mayor, Morgan, was rumored to only be a fourth rank.

Nora snorted. Morgan might call herself a mayor, but it's not like anyone had voted for her. Instead, the woman showed up one day with enough muscle at her back to crush anyone opposing her. As if that wasn't enough, people like Nora were drafted as scouts to help identify 'potential allies' as well as 'subversive elements.'

As much as Nora wanted to escape the system, second rank was far from where she'd need to be to escape Morgan's influence. No, for now, her dreams of being a masked avenger righting wrongs and protecting the weak would have to be put on hold until she gained a couple ranks.

At least with Daniel, that was a possibility. She still couldn't put her finger on whether he was the real deal, dangerously naive, or some sort of spy, but she couldn't deny that he knew how to accumulate mana. Whatever that frenzy he went into in the ant hive was, it certainly warranted watching, but it was effective. He had killed almost thirty of the ants on his own, and he probably would have gotten even more if Andrea hadn't clubbed him over the back of the head so that they could drag him out of the hive along with the silver. Associating with him was both physically and politically risky, but in a couple days, she had gained more mana than she had in the previous five years of adventuring.

She sighed and paced the perimeter of the runes. Deep inside, something was trying to hold her back. To tell her that she was still that insignificant little girl hiding in the basement of a ruined town. That even if she fought and clawed her entire life, she would only be able to make a local difference. If she was lucky, she might be able to found a town like Morganville. Maybe keep a few thousand people safe for a few decades. It was certainly better than nothing, but in the grand scheme of things, it was a grain of sand on a beach. It wouldn't stop hundreds of people from dying in poverty on Twilight and across the entire Tellask Empire every day.

One day, the plan was to actually go into the dungeons to seek out revenge. It was probably just the dream of an angry little girl, but the cracks in Twilight's surface that housed the monsters before night fell were a lucrative prospect. Not many adventurers returned, which was unsurprising considering they were fighting stalkers, behemoths, and gaunts in their own homes without the protection of sanctuary runes, but the ones who did came back rich. The bones of the planet were riddled with enough mana, mythril, and gold to transform any survivor into a powerhouse. More than that, she would actually be able to strike back against the invisible demons that weighed her down. She would finally be something more than prey, a hunter in her own right, taking the fight to the implacable monsters that took her family from her.

A shape moved in the dark, barely visible through the

purple light of the runic barrier. Nora stopped walking and stared into the night. Suddenly, a shadow passed between Ishlar's campsite and her. She squinted her eyes and triggered a flow of mana towards the runic mark in the shape of a cat's eye on her class tattoo. A second later, the skill kicked in, and her night vision improved greatly. The inky darkness transformed into an eerie black and white tableau. There, sitting fifteen feet from her, was a gaunt.

It sat back on its bony haunches and simply watched her with empty eye sockets. Nora sucked in a breath and stepped back from the barrier. Its gaze followed her. The ribs on its sides moved rhythmically, barely concealing the shining, rotten flesh beneath them.

The sages weren't sure whether gaunts were truly alive or not. They resembled undead both in their appearance and ability, but they had at least some of the most basic vestiges of life. Their lungs inhaled, they ate, and their hearts pumped a thick dark ichor through their veins. Still, their heads had no flesh whatsoever, instead resembling a horse skull with horns and the fangs and sharp teeth of a carnivore. Their bodies were made of rotting flesh inside an exoskeleton of bone, and they seemed to feed off of the negative feelings they created almost as much as the flesh of their victims.

The sanctuary runes muted the impact of its aura, but having its attention focused on their campsite still wasn't good. It wasn't unknown for travelers to come upon bodies with self-inflicted wounds inside intact runes. Given enough time, it would wear all of them down to the point where they couldn't go on. It was just a race between night ending and the party's willpower cracking to the point where suicide seemed a better option. Even now, Nora's mood lagged as self-doubt creeped in. Perversely, she couldn't even tell if it was her own anxiety or something induced by the gaunt staring at her.

"I just realized something." Behind her, Daniel was talking to the sisters. "For all the exploration and the growth we've gone through, I don't even have the faintest idea how to get home. It was all well and good to hop over here with the help of a tele-portation array, but I don't even know the first thing about getting back, even if I had the power to do it."

Shit. Already the aura was impacting the rest of the party. Internally, Nora warred over whether she should tell them. On one hand, they had a right to know that a denizen of the night had fixed its sightless gaze on them. On the other hand, there was nothing they could do about it until the runes went down, and letting them know would only give it another lever with which to pry into their minds. Indecision paralyzed her, but in the back of her mind, a voice whispered that even the indeci-sion might be a product of the gaunt's power.

"So Dan," she butted in with forced cheer as she tried to distract herself and the party. "Since you're our party leader, it might be for the best if you let us know what your affinities are. So far you've revealed fire, thunder, and space, but I just want to make sure there aren't any more hiding out there. It's all well and good for you to play up the 'mysterious stranger' angle in town when preying upon the local girls, but if we're going to work together, I think it would be helpful for us to actually know what you can do."

"Aren't all of you local girls?" he responded quickly, eyeing Andrea and Emily meaningfully. "Why can't I use my man of mystery bit to prey on all of you?"

Instantly, Andrea grabbed Emily by the shoulder, and both of them stumbled backward, eyes glued to Daniel. Distrust bloomed on the large woman's face as her hand gripped the handle of her maul. A giggle bubbled up inside Nora as Daniel threw his hands into the air in frustration.

"Are you fucking kidding me?" he asked, rhetorically. "It was a joke. I have enough problems without getting wrapped up with you guys."

"What is that supposed to mean?" Emily questioned defen-sively. "Is this just a matter of you not finding us attractive enough for your predations? Do you think pursuing us would just create problems? Is that the only reason why you haven't come after us?"

Nora doubled over laughing, the gloom from the gaunt almost palpably ejected from their gathering. There was something about two six-foot-and-change women, covered in muscles, huddled together and staring fearfully at Daniel. He wasn't unfit or unattractive, but it was simply hard to find him menacing. He might be able to defeat one of the sisters in a fight, but that would be a matter of agility and range. Either of them could snap him in half like a twig if they actually got their hands on him.

"Jesus tapdancing..." Daniel shook his head and forcibly stopped himself. "No," he muttered, too quietly for the sisters to hear. "You lose if you engage; you know better than this."

"Tell us, Dan," Nora couldn't help but prod at the uncomfortable man. "What about Emily and Andrea make them unfit for your interest? Perhaps you're simply afraid that the weapon you wield will be insufficient to wound them?"

Daniel shot her a dirty look then kept muttering to himself. Outside the circle, the gaunt stood up and walked closer. The chill of its aura warred against their party's fire and conversation. She avoided looking at it, but somehow she knew it was still staring at her, seeking to pull her back into the night with it.

Daniel turned to Nora, ignoring her mirth. "To answer your original question. I have affinities in fire, metal, gravity, force, lightning, and space. I've only really worked on lightning, fire, space, and gravity, but I do have the attunement stones on hand for the other two. It's just always been a matter of time and resources. Until I rank up, it will be hard for me to devote enough mana to attuning myself to the remaining two, and I always thought it would be best to focus on the spells that would provide me with immediate benefit. I'm sure metal and force will be useful down the line, but I suspect that low-level applications of them would annoy foes more than anything."

"Six affinities?" Nora quirked an eyebrow at Daniel. "Are you sure you aren't a princeling of some sort who has escaped his minders? I don't think I've heard of a human having more than three affinities, and even amongst elves, it's supposed to be rare."

She shrugged dismissively. "Or so they tell us. I honestly don't know what to believe about the elves, other than that they're powerful. I really don't know if they're over or under-stating their magic. I just know working with them is usually a losing prospect."

"I don't know anyone who has come out ahead after they've entered a contract with an elf." Emily nodded in agreement as she extricated herself from Andrea. "Even when the agreement seems like a win-win on the surface, elves usually find a way to push for every last drop of advantage out of a bargain. With humans, most of us see the value in maintaining a friendly rela-tionship with a business or trade partner, but the elves see us as disposable. As far as I can tell, they just think that we're going to succumb to disease or old age in the blink of an eye, so they don't even see the point of maintaining a friendly relationship with us."

"I suppose a sixty-year lifespan is pretty much meaningless to someone who expects to live five to six millenia," Emily continued. "We're like dogs to elves, just less cute. By the time they form an emotional connection, we just up and die."

"Just better to avoid them." Andrea spat on the ground. "They can have their power and their schemes out in space. We won't antagonize them; it's not worth the trouble. They're powerful enough to back up any slight, but you just don't come out ahead if you try to work with them. It's why no one but the desperate really worked with Ishlar."

"Nora worked for him." Daniel nodded in her direction. "Does that mean she was desperate?"

"I'm sure she had her reasons," Andrea responded before Nora could defend herself. "But, after a fashion, yes. His patron is an elf. The patronage has made Ishlar a force in a town like Morganville, but ultimately it will come with a cost. None of us really know when he will have to pay the price, but no one wants to be caught in the collateral damage when it comes due."

"He just seems like a bully to me," Daniel shrugged, glancing out towards the purple beacon of Ishlar's camp. "He's strong, but he doesn't really even know how to fight. I guess he would be useful fighting against unskilled, but physically-talented monsters, but anything with a hint of agility would rip him apart."

"You're forgetting how dumb he is," Nora chimed in. "He's all right as an adventurer, but his biggest asset is his patron's political support. As much as the authorities in Morganville would like to shut him down, doing so would anger his patron. Despite that, he's out here picking a fight with someone who already brought him down once. If he doesn't make it back to town, oh well. It's a dangerous world out here, and he did spend a night outside. Sometimes things just happen at night."

A predatory grin slipped across her face. She might not know what she would be doing in two years or a decade, but in the short term, her course was clear. Ishlar was an annoying asshole who made life more difficult for everyone in Morganville. Cosmically, it might not matter, but a Twilight without him was a better world, and in a couple of hours he would be nothing but mana in their systems and carrion. In the darkness, the gaunt stood and ambled away. She didn't know whether her emotional strength had driven it off, or if it had grown bored, but either way, it was a small victory against the night she could cling to.

CHAPTER TWENTY

Rematch (I)

A sliver of reflected light from the gas giant Tanloff signalled the end of the night. Dan briefly took off his helmet and ran his hand through his matted hair. He really needed a shower and access to a laundromat of some sort. The helmet was a godsend; without the translation runes, he would have been completely lost, but the thing really didn't breathe. Any time he ended up sweating, the foam lining the helmet would trap the liquid in a dark, warm environment against his skin. Given the amount of exercise he had gotten across various sword fights, let alone his experiments playing with fire, the helmet charitably smelled like something between a public gymnasium and a dumpster.

He slipped the helmet back over his head and wrinkled his nose. He suspected Nora's advanced senses were getting all they could from him. It was a blessing she was polite enough to not say anything. Yet. Knowing her, she was probably biding her time to spring some sort of critical comment on him.

Above him, Tanloff became more and more visible in the sky. It would only be a matter of minutes before their sanctuary runes expired, then they would have a choice. They could either try to hurry back to Morganville and outrun Ishlar and his team, or they could wait for their runes to run out. Running might avoid the conflict, but at the same time, they wouldn't be able to move fast enough to avoid Ishlar and scout ahead. There was a very real possibility they would run into some sort of monster in the wilds that could delay them long enough to land them in a three-way battle between the monster and Ishlar. Maybe it was the last year or so of Doctor Weathers giving Dan crap for always playing it safe, but he was sick of running. Still, it wasn't entirely his decision.

"So," he said, checking the straps on his armor to ensure that nothing would slip off at the last minute. "I would prefer to not let Ishlar chase us back into town like some sort of beaten dog, but I might be missing something. What's everyone else's vote?"

Nora snorted. "He's an idiot with a lot of money and he is positively handing us self defense as an excuse. Even if he wasn't coming for us, given my history with that ass, I'd probably be willing to go bandit to bring him down, so long as I didn't think that there were going to be any witnesses. If you think that the haul from the silver mine is a lot, wait until we take his patron's sovereigns from him."

"I'm pretty sure our contract doesn't give us a vote," Emily glanced at Andrea before shrugging. "Even without your magic, I'm pretty sure that we could take him. Everyone knows that running across the wastes is an awful idea. That's why teams hire rangers. I'm not about to discard the first rule of adventuring and run headlong into some sort of cosmic horror just because some pissant wants a fight. If he wants to take what's ours, he can earn it."

"That's what I was thinking," Dan nodded, cracking his neck. "Plus, I wouldn't mind having a second set of sanctuary runes, just in case we run into an issue. After having experienced a night out here, I believe I can firmly say I'd prefer to not be exposed to whatever the hell was prowling out there, if at all possible."

The party checked their equipment and packed their camp gear. Then, one-by-one, they stood, waiting in pensive silence for the runes to run out of energy. There was no real room for strategy. Both sides were equally balanced, and there weren't really any features to the landscape to exploit.

No, this fight wasn't going to be a tactical masterpiece. Dan wasn't going to wrack his brain out-thinking and out-positioning. As soon as both sets of runes ran out of power, a scrum was going to break out, and Dan was going to use his increased magical aptitude to replicate his performance in the arena. Simple as that.

The second the runes stopped powering the shield, Nora quickly gathered them from the circle around the campsite and together they walked over to Ishlar's site. As they approached, Ishlar and his companions stood from where they had been lounging on a series of primitive sleeping bags around their campfire. Ishlar walked to the edge of the runes and grinned at them, his face taking on a sickly hue from the purple light of the barrier.

"Back for a rematch, Bird?" The giant man spat on the ground. "At least you're not a coward, I suppose. There won't be any practice weapons or arena rules to save you this time. This time I'm gonna kill you."

Daniel frowned slightly. "Okay, I know we're doing melodramatic speeches and everything, but are we both remembering the same fight? I took you down in under ten seconds. If it wasn't for the arena rules, we wouldn't be having this conversation, because scavengers would be picking over your bones, and I would already have your mana. I'm only here because you made it obvious that you were going to make trouble for me, and I'd rather face any trouble head on rather than wait for you to come after me with a knife when I'm trying to take a nap. If you don't want to fight, I'm happy to walk away."

"I had you before they called that match on a technicality!" Ishlar picked up a large, dull grey club that looked worryingly like tungsten. "If the referee hadn't stepped in, you would have been finished. Instead, Nora all but stole my sovereigns, and I aim to have them back along with a little mana from you as interest."

The club worried Dan slightly. Tungsten was incredibly mana-conductive and referred to as mythril by the citizens of the Tellask Empire. In addition to being heavy and durable, skilled runescripters could put powerful enchantments into objects made of Tungsten. Gold and, to a lesser extent, silver filled the same role, but both were much cheaper and easier to work. The fact that Ishlar had a tungsten club, let alone the fact that he was able to heft and brandish it so easily, weren't good signs. It was possible that a good portion of the man's combat prowess relied upon the heavily-enchanted club. In that case, the fight in the arena with training weapons really wasn't a good measure of the man's ability. Still, that didn't mean that he had to let the senseless bragging stand without comment.

"Is the technicality that I knocked you out cold?" Dan asked, drawing his blade and inspecting the edge. "I'm not really sure you can call that a technicality. I will say, though, if you could weaponize your ego, I don't think I've met a warrior who could stand against you. Unfortunately for you, we're stuck fighting in the real world where you will have to actually rely upon your own strength and skill, rather than your inflated opinion of yourself."

Ishlar opened his mouth to respond but no sound came out. His eyes blazed with fury while a vein pulsed visibly on his forehead. *Well*, Dan thought to himself. *You've successfully baited the musclebound psychopath. If he wasn't going to attack you before, he certainly will now. Now the real question is how to avoid being smashed into paste by that enchanted club long enough to finish him off.*

With a flicker of purple light, the humming of the sanctuary runes stopped. Immediately, Ishlar was surrounded by a shell of mana as he activated a spell shield. The enraged man held his club up in the air, golden runes igniting up and down its sides. Pressure settled on Dan's shoulders as his feet sank into the rocky soil.

In his forearm, the gravity attunement stone began vibrating slightly under the influence of his opponent's ability. With some difficulty, Dan shifted his feet into a defensive stance, his sword heavy as he raised it into a textbook guard position. His smile faded as he transferred weight from foot to foot, struggling under the extra pull of gravity weighing him down. That was new.

"Let's see how you fare, now that I get to use all of my toys," Ishlar snarled at him, experimentally swinging the club. "You seemed really keen on dancing back and forth the last time we fought. Let's see how that works now that I've used a gravity blanket on you."

Without responding verbally, Dan shot a Flame Jet at Ishlar's face. It was too much to hope that the lance of burning gases would penetrate the spell shield, but in the dim light that came after night broke, it was more than enough to surprise the larger man into taking a step back. Dan took that opportunity to charge him and bounce a sword off of Ishlar's spell shield. It barely rippled as it dispersed the kinetic force from his slash.

He frowned. That wasn't supposed to happen. His peripheral vision caught sight of the rest of the party dueling Ishlar's companions. Both sides had even numbers, and it looked like they were fighting careful, defensive battles. No help was coming, for either of them, until someone slipped up.

Ishlar responded with a horizontal double-handed swing of his club. Whatever magic was flowing through it made Ishlar fast, inhumanly so. Dan swung his sword up, trying to deflect it over his head with the help of a spatial shield. He connected, but it felt like striking a brick wall. With a little magical help and a whole lot of ducking, the blow sailed over his head, but Dan's hands were already a little numb. Just one exchange, and he had almost lost his grip on the sword. Mentally, he made a note to avoid any further direct clashes with the club. When the brute swung that thing, it had enough momentum to end him. He was either going to dodge it or be turned into strawberry jam.

As the club swung past him, Dan noticed a brief fluctuation

of mana and gravity just as Ishlar began recovering from the swing. Luckily, he was too shaken from the previous exchange to attack the larger man while he was overbalanced, because Ishlar managed to pull the club back into a guard position with surprising speed.

"Well, you've lasted one swing longer than I expected," Ishlar boomed, a cruel grin on his face. "Spinebreaker here is a gift from my patron. Apparently, I have a rare affinity in gravity. It's a waste of time for me to use magic directly. I don't have years to waste losing my eyesight pouring over old grimoires when there's money to be earned and women to be bedded, but once he gave me a proper focus, my power skyrocketed. Everyone looks down on clubs. Says they're only good for hitting people, but they're too awkward to block with. But I can almost double Spinebreaker's weight when I swing and halve it when I need to move quickly. It took some getting used to, but I've been able to crush my share of assholes like you that have underestimated me."

Dan kept his eyes on the club. Even without the shield, it would be a problem. It was fast, hit like a train, and Ishlar could use it for both offense and defense. With the shield, he was having a hard time seeing a path forward in the fight.

As humanity had learned from the aborted invasion, depending upon the quality of a spell shield, they could usually absorb ten to fifty shots from a rifle. If he was going to have to replicate that level of kinetic force while dodging a supersonic bar of tungsten, he wasn't likely to have all that good of a day.

Ishlar swung again, this time one-handed. Dan fired another Flame Jet at him, activating the larger man's spell shield as he tried to sidestep the diagonal blow. The distraction allowed him to escape, but as he prepared to counter attack, Ishlar's free hand smashed into Dan's face like a wrecking ball. He got a small amount of satisfaction out of instinctively triggering Shocking Fist, using his nose as a medium, but the sickening crunch that followed erased any warm feelings.

Dan's vision narrowed and swam as he staggered backward.

His face was partially numb from his previous spell, but the way blood flowed freely didn't make him hopeful for the status of his nose. From somewhere, the roar of a jet engine or a freight train drowned out his surroundings. A gust of wind blew his short-cropped, matted hair to and fro. He blinked rapidly, trying to clear his vision. In the back of his mind, a voice screamed at him that something was wrong. He glanced at his free hand, drops of blood from his nose rhythmically stained it. He shook his head again, trying to clear it. Ishlar should have used his moment of distraction to finish him off by now; something must have happened. He stared up at the larger man and cocked his head, suddenly aware that some of the background noise was a voice.

"-tennek dar gasoon!" Ishlar's left arm hung limply at his side as he screamed nonsense at Dan, red-faced. "Stak lask dar perrote!"

Dan blinked again, the combination of the nanites and the cold post-night air mostly clearing his vision. He ran his bloody hand through his hair. *Shit.* His helmet, translation function now permanently deactivated from the force of Ishlar's punch, lay bent and warped several feet to his right.

CHAPTER TWENTY-ONE

Rematch (II)

Dan stood there, glancing dumbly from his battered helmet to where Ishlar stood, giving an incomprehensible angry monologue. It was a small blessing that Ishlar was an idiot. Anyone else would have followed up on his disorientation with a fatal blow. God knows his trainer back at the Thoth foundation would have capitalized on a moment of weakness like that. She certainly hadn't been shy about letting him wake up in the medical bay when he made mistakes.

Unknown language detected. Initializing translation sub-routine.

Please expose yourself to more of this language to expand your vocabulary and syntax.

Well, at least Sam hadn't left him completely high and dry. He wasn't exactly sure that he wanted to be learning a new language, even with science-fiction-level assistance during the middle of a fight, but it was a lot better than the old-fashioned way. At least this way, he might be able to convince someone that his last name was Thrush rather than Bird.

God, Ishlar was still talking. The rest of the fights continued around them, but the man positively would not shut up. Deep inside himself, Dan vowed that he couldn't lose to this idiot. He had used magic to fight giant ants, bats, and other monstrosities. His body had something like fifteen million dollars worth of medical equipment in it. He had lived through the disastrous first contact with the elves of the Tellask Empire. Hell, he had beaten odds so high that they still weren't able to calculate them by surviving ingesting a mana crystal.

All stories have an end, but his wasn't going to be here, to an idiot that most resembled the assholes who gave him crap in highschool when he didn't make the football team. If he was going to die on Twilight, it was going to be to an actual honest-to-God magical monster. Not someone who was pumped full of the magical equivalent of steroids while using their daddy's toys to push him around.

A flicker of rage ignited in his chest. He was better than Ishlar. He had beaten the man in the arena on an even footing, and now Ishlar wanted another crack at Dan. Fine. This time, there wouldn't be a referee to stop him from dealing a killing blow. He had already earned the man's mana once. It was just a matter of doing it again.

Ishlar just stood there, ranting, trusting in his spell shield to keep him safe. He was right, after a fashion. Dan didn't have anything that could quickly punch through the kinetic shield, but that didn't mean he was helpless. With a deep, steadying breath, Dan muttered "Flame Jet" to activate the ability.

Ishlar yelped in surprise and stepped to the side as the line of fire washed over him, only to catch another Flame Jet. Even if the shield protected him, not all shields were created equal.

A cheap spellshield, the kind used by the rank and file soldiers in the invasion on Earth, would solely protect against basic kinetic attacks such as arrows, swords, and bullets. Only a high-level spell shield would have environmental protection runes built into it.

Even if Dan couldn't lay a hand on the bigger man, that wouldn't stop him from cooking him alive. Ishlar screamed something, probably about Dan's honor or parentage, even if he could understand the idiot, it wouldn't have mattered. He was beyond caring about the nonsense boasts and jibes Ishlar constantly spewed.

The huge man lunged toward Dan, leading with a club swing aimed at his head. Dan fired another Flame Jet into Ishlar's face, temporarily blinding the man, then threw himself at Ishlar's knees. For once, the extra gravity created by Ishlar's skill helped more than hindered Dan. Rather than trying to fight the skill by jumping to the side or dancing backwards, he moved with it, letting the magic pull him towards the ground and under the now-blind swing.

Dan's breath left his body as Ishlar's shin caught him in the ribs. Even through the stainless steel chain, the impact rocked into him. Luckily, the blow tripped Ishlar and sent the man flying face-first into the rocky soil. Once again, the spell shield glowed, absorbing the kinetic force of the impact, but this time the glow wasn't quite as bright. Apparently, catching almost three hundred pounds of muscle plummeting face-first into a rock was a bit much for the runes crafting the shield. Good to know. Dan unleashed another Flame Jet into Ishlar's sprawling prone form. The dull ache of mana exhaustion began to war with the twinge in his side where he had been kicked.

Hoping that his ribs were just cracked, Dan gritted his teeth against the pain in his side and swung down at Ishlar as the other man tried to stand up. After two blows deflected off of the increasingly-dull spell shield, Dan smiled at the sweating man and fired another Flame Jet into him before backpedaling. Ishlar swung Spinebreaker half-heartedly, easily missing. As Dan waited for his vision to return to normal after the most recent Flame Jet, the other man's breath rasped.

"Vornook dar gasoon." Sweat was pouring down Ishlar's now-lobster-red body as the other man fought to breathe. "Salaat ben selaar tannik, elok tir boslap." He pointed at Dan with the club, arm trembling.

Dan rolled his eyes and shot yet another Flame Jet at the man. Behind his eyes, the headache began to build, but he had no option other than to keep the pressure on Ishlar. Right now, his only advantage over the bigger man was his agility and stamina. Giving him a moment to catch his breath could spell disaster. Dan strongly suspected that Ishlar would be able to recover from low-grade heat exhaustion faster than Dan could recover mana for the relatively-inefficient Flame Jets.

Ishlar stepped towards him and stumbled slightly. He stopped to swipe at his brow with his only partially-responsive left hand. Dan glared at his blood smearing that hand and now Ishlar's face. His nose was definitely broken. As if reminded by the visual cue, his entire face throbbed. Silently, Dan gave thanks to the nanites minimizing the pain responses from the wound. Fighting someone with this much better gear was hard enough even without being blinded by pain.

He fired another Flame Jet at the man, gritting his teeth against the painful emptiness of mana exhaustion. He closed the distance as best he could under the weight of Ishlar's gravity skill. Somewhere, the rest of the party was still fighting, but they were almost a dream. All Dan could see was Ishlar's reeling form. He slashed out with his sword and bounced yet again off the weakening edge of the spell shield. Ishlar blinked at him through a mixture of sweat and Dan's own blood, bringing back the club for a one-handed swing. Even through the shield radiating heat poured off of Ishlar. He didn't hesitate. Dan fired another Flame Jet at point blank range into the man's side. He winced slightly as the heat from the deflected flame scorched him as well.

The light and heat caused the blow to falter just enough for Dan to step into and duck under it. Gone was Ishlar's mana-enhanced speed and grace from the beginning of the battle. Instead, the man looked tired and defeated. Grinning at him through a mask of his own blood, Dan reached up and grabbed the spell shield around the hand holding Spinebreaker and triggered Shocking Fist. Only a small amount of electricity arced through the inch or two of air between the shield and Ishlar's wrist, but it was enough. The hand spasmed, and Spinebreaker fell to the ground.

Ishlar stared at his hand as if betrayed, and the constant pressure from the increased gravity abated. Dan's head was pounding from the broken nose and his mana expenditure, but he stepped back and kicked the club away. At least he tried to. The thing was heavy as hell. Ignoring his newly-injured foot and the pain in his side, Dan swung his sword again. This time, the spell shield shattered in a cascade of shimmering light. Ishlar glanced up at him. His gaze was blank. Dan's sword slid between the man's ribs with ease.

He withdrew the bloody blade and stepped back. The mountain of a man still stood before him, gasping for breath as blood flowed out of his side. He didn't even seem to notice that he was wounded. Dan frowned and gripped his sword with both hands before swinging again. This time, he slashed open Ishlar's chest, cutting through at least two ribs before catching on a third. Ishlar took a hesitant step towards him, eyes still blank. Dan stepped back again and squared himself before swinging. The blade hit Ishlar's knee and bisected the man's right leg. He fell to the ground, air escaping in deep, gurgling breaths.

For a second, Dan hesitated, eyes locked on Ishlar's moaning and thrashing body. The man stared up at him, all bravado gone from his face as he bled out.

Killing a man was different than killing an animal. With the bear and the ants, it had been almost like a game. There might be consequences if they got the better of you, but there were no ethical questions. Stab here, fire a spell there, and you receive a reward of mana. With another human, that illusion was shattered. He had just murdered a man. True, it was in self-defense. Ishlar had sought him out, and wouldn't have let Dan leave without a fatal fight, but there was no question what had just happened.

Then the mana hit, and the questions stopped. Dan had been almost dry when his duel ended, and the river of energy almost took his breath away. Compared to the glass of water he received for killing an ant, or the water bottle for the blood bear, Ishlar was a waterfall. Dan's eyes twitched beneath their lids as wave after wave of euphoria consumed him. He sank down to his knees, insensible as blood continued to flow freely from his face. The pain and the movement didn't even register for him as neon pleasure coursed through his veins.

Unnoticed in the corner of his vision, the System began spewing updates.

Detecting increase in Fire Affinity. Fire Affinity is now 6.

Mana influx detected. Recalculating Spirit.
Spirit is now 10.

Fluctuation in Rank detected.
Recalculating.

Rank is now 2
Detecting abnormalities in <USER>'s mana.
Entering diagnostic mode.

Results inconclusive
Please contact System administration at your earliest convenience. The Thoth Foundation is not liable for any mutations, dismemberment, or sudden untimely deaths that may occur if <USER> fails to contact System administration.

Thank you for your cooperation <USER>

Dan drooled slightly and twitched.

CHAPTER TWENTY-TWO

Ranking Up

Dan opened his eyes. He didn't really remember when he closed them, but this passing out at the end of battles was beginning to be a problem. It was probably time to ask Nora if she knew of any method to take the edge off when absorbing mana. Looking around for her, he tried to shut down the nagging voice whispering to him that maybe he shouldn't dull the mana when he was absorbing it.

It made excuse after excuse: he needed the full flow of the mana to stay on edge. Dulling the mana could reduce the amount he absorbed. There might be secrets hidden in the mana just waiting for him to discover them. But deep down, Dan knew it was all crap. Really, a part of him just wanted more of that electric pleasure. It wanted that moment when colors were brighter and the world seemed more solid and real.

He shook his head and stood up, only to float a foot or two as lack of gravity let his momentum carry him. Dan frowned and glanced more closely at his surroundings as he floated back toward the ground. Well, ground was a stretch. He was standing on a pink cloud, and as far as he could see, his surroundings were nothing but a serene landscape of other pink clouds lit by a diffused light that seemed to come from everywhere. After a brief check, he confirmed that Nora, Emily, and Andrea were nowhere in sight. Neither was anything else from the surface of Twilight.

E))&)! Pl%^/ #%^^&?*

The System's normally inobtrusive writing suddenly lit up the sky with incomprehensible symbols and hashes. Dan's mouth tightened into a severe line. That wasn't good. Briefly, his mind went over the previous battle and what could've happened. Worryingly, he kept coming back to the possibility that the amount of mana unleashed by Ishlar's death had over-whelmed his nervous system.

Things had been awfully touch and go there for a while, and Sam had been clear before he left that no research had been done on the mana absorption process. Dan wasn't exactly keen on the idea of his skin turning green or growing another thumb or something, but there had to be at least a relatively safe way of doing things.

Maybe it was just finally time to come clean to Nora. It would be hard to admit that he had been deceiving her, but there was something about her that made him want to confide in her. It could be her general aura of affability, or it might be the way that she had helped him through every hiccup to date, but talking to her about his mission just seemed like the next step. Something about the unending plain of pink clouds reminded him that this wasn't a game. Even if the nanites gave him a huge advantage, he was still playing for keeps. If he was going to gamble his life to gain superhuman powers, he needed to stop flying blind.

She knew what was going on in this world, and she didn't seem overly hung up on him being from another planet. The torrent of new experiences had been novel at first, but he desperately needed the help of someone local who could actu-ally ground him. He was doing his best to adjust to the magical civilization that the Foundation had temporarily transplanted him into, but at the end of the day, he really didn't even know what was possible or impossible. He just needed to get over his paranoia that she had some sort of hidden agenda and his general sense of pride and ask her for help.

REM communication shunt functioning

The words again occupied the center of the ethereal landscape. At least this time, they spelled out something comprehensible.

<USER>'s mana has become destabilized. Attempts to stabilize mana via nanite intervention have failed. <USER> has entered a comatose state. Attempts to wake <USER> from coma have failed.

NOTE: Failure to contact Thoth Foundation System administration before attempting to modify <USER>'s mana has voided System warranty. Please speak to a System sales representative about renewing your warranty.

The System is not responsible for death, mutation, dismemberment, or sudden catastrophic reality failures while <USER> remains outside of warranty.

Thank you for continuing to use the System.

Great. The notice didn't even include a tech support number for a call center where he could wait on hold for the next two hours. Dan massaged his likely-imaginary temples. At least that made a little sense of his situation. He was in some sort of dreamscape while his body lay undefended and inert in the middle of pitched combat. Absolutely swell.

"System," he queried the empty air, "can you respond to vocal prompts?"

For a second, nothing happened. Then the writing appeared in the center of his vision once again.

The System is designed to respond to vocal input as well as a limited range of subvocal, nonverbal, and subconscious input.

WARNING: <USER> has not been fully mapped for subconscious input. Communication may be slow or inexact if <USER> continues to attempt subconscious interactions with the System.

Dan sighed. Of course everything he was doing was subconscious. It was easy to forget when whatever was left of his mind created a comforting figment of him standing in a cloudscape, but his real body was laying insensible in the real world. Luckily, the System could still understand him after a fashion, but it didn't look like complex topics were an option.

"System," he spoke slowly, "you've mentioned that my mana has become destabilized. Can you tell me what's happened?"

Again, there was a pause. Then an image of a human body appeared in front of Dan, floating in the air. Staring at it for a second, he quickly noticed the accuracy of the diagram. As far as he could tell, it mapped the musculature, skeleton, and circulatory system of a human body he strongly suspected was his.

Optimal mana configuration is a self-replenishing sphere located next to <USER>'s heart.

On the diagram, a silver ball pulsed in the figure's chest. It might have been his imagination or the placebo effect, but Dan could swear a resonance in his chest throbbed in time with the model.

Spirit sphere has reached maximum mana capacity, but excess mana has been absorbed. Currently <USER> has excess mana in their body with no storage or outlet.

On the diagram, silver light appeared in the figure's veins. This time Dan definitely felt something. Specifically pain. A whole lot of pain. Everywhere the image showed the silver light, it was like his nerves had been doused in lava. On the model, individual motes of silver burned through his veins and spread into the rest of his body. The free mana was burning him like acid, hollowing him out.

Almost immediately, he remembered the agony after he swallowed the mana crystal. This is why people who swallowed mana crystals died. Unless the mana was contained in a sphere, it was poison that would destroy your body. He would need to recreate the miracle that allowed him to survive his first ill-advised adventure with mana. He could only hope his unfortunate experience gaining his first sphere would let him succeed again where so many others had failed.

Instinctively, he reached toward the diagram and *pulled* on the mana in his veins. For a second his pain-addled mind thought that his actions were in vain. Then slowly, like a brick dragged through treacle, the mana began to move. The pain from before doubled. The extremities of Dan's subconscious self-projection began to blur and fade. He wasn't sure what exactly that meant, or what happened when his self-image faded entirely, but he wasn't exactly keen to find out.

Luckily for him, a year dealing with Samantha Weathers, amateur dominatrix, had prepared him for this. Dan focused every ounce of his being on the mana in his veins as it moved with glacial slowness back through his body and toward his chest. A detached part of him reflected that the process reminded him of his junior project in college, when he had worked for an environmental engineering firm dredging silt from river beds so that larger ships could take goods down the rivers. The project had been soothing, involving months of monitoring equipment on boats as they slowly drifted down the river, dragging large scoops that dug deep into the dirt.

He seized that image and clung to it as the nerve-fraying pain sought to shatter him. In his mind's eye, hundreds of the dredges moved slowly through his body, gathering up every free drop of mana. Already his fingers had blurred and become indistinct to the point where they resembled a flesh-colored fin. He ignored them. That was a problem for a future time. Instead, he continued pulling, using his willpower to power the imaginary dredges trawling through his body.

He lost track of time. Like his blurry hands and feet, it wasn't a factor that he could control. Every moment was a constant battle against the omnipresent pain, but as seconds flowed into minutes, a second sphere began to take shape. It was faint and unstable, but already the pain was slowly abating. It was still at a level that made him suspect he had soiled himself in the real world, but he could feel himself turning the corner.

Dan grabbed onto that moment of hope and let it fuel his will. The dredges running through his body increased their speed, again wracking his body with pain, but well over half of the free mana was in the second sphere. He spared a brief moment to glance at his arms and grimaced. His hands were gone entirely, and his forearms were ethereal and ghost-like. Maybe time was a concern after all. Still, all he could do was his best. He had his task; anything else was a distraction.

Second spirit sphere detected, beginning stabilization

He almost gasped with relief as half of the pressure on his body faded. It was still agony pulling the mana particle by particle from his body and dragging the unwilling energy to the sphere, but at least he didn't have to expend any energy actually maintaining the sphere itself. Bit by bit, he pushed the free mana in his system back into the sphere.

In the back of his mind, a voice whispered to him that it would be easier to give up. That his arms and legs didn't hurt anymore. That if he just gave up, he could not hurt anymore. There would just be a brief burst of pain, then nothing. He couldn't deny that on some level, succumbing to the void appealed to him, but there was just too much at stake. Even if he was willing to let himself die, humanity couldn't let that happen. The Tellask and the Orakh were coming, and Earth deserved more than to be crushed under the technologically-inferior heels of space racists. This pain was nothing compared to what everyone he knew would face if he let them down.

Finally, he turned the corner. The new sphere glowed dimly in his chest. No longer inert, it began sucking on its own, pulling the last of the free mana into itself. His entire body was awash, like he'd been dipped in a cool spring. For one brief moment, nothing hurt. Then everything went black.

Dan opened his eyes. His head hurt like hell, and the dampness of drying blood covered his face and the front of his chest. Next to him, Nora was shaking his shoulder and shouting something, but for some reason it seemed like she was so terribly far away. His entire body hurt. Not as bad as when he had been consolidating the spirit sphere, but it was a constant, ugly pain. God, was he tired. He reached up and touched Nora's cheek with a bloody hand. He tried to say that everything was ok, but he wasn't actually sure that he said anything.

Congratulations on stabilizing your mana and reaching Rank 2 <USER>. Further options will be available to you depending upon your achievements.

He closed his eyes again. He could deal with that tomorrow.

CHAPTER TWENTY-THREE

Morning's Harsh Light

Dan opened his eyes only to almost immediately close them. Honest-to-God daylight pounded down on him and his headache really didn't appreciate it. After waiting a couple seconds, he reopened his eyes. Unfortunately, Alpha Centauri was still there, peeking around the corner of Tanloff. He debated closing his eyes again and trying to sleep off the brief day, but ultimately decided against it. As far as he could remember, they were stuck in the wastelands, and he didn't know how the rest of the party had fared in the aftermath of the battle with Ishlar and his cronies.

With a struggle, he pushed the fur blanket that passed for a medieval sleeping bag off of himself and sat up. His headache cranked up its intensity, but at least now Dan had a decent view of his surroundings. They were still in the wasteland, and at some point the rest of the party had arranged their bedding in a circle. Andrea was untouched, but Emily now sported a large blood-stained bandage on her left bicep. Nora didn't seem to be sporting any real injuries, but she had bags under her eyes and seemed to stare somewhat blankly off into space until she noticed that he was awake.

"Gran doseen bilst!" she shouted excitedly, hurrying over to him. Even her words and actions seemed dull and tired. She put her hand on his shoulder before beginning to speak further. "Stran dar rastoon, jassel ban stallas."

"I'm sorry, but I lost my helmet," he replied, miming putting something on his head. "I don't understand what you're saying."

Even speaking a couple sentences hurt. It probably had something to do with the nanites not having enough raw material to completely fix his broken nose, but he couldn't help but worry that it at least had something to do with aftereffects from the process of ranking up. He sure didn't remember his arms and legs aching nearly this much before he went under.

She cocked her head and began speaking to him again. Once again it came out as a stream of gibberish. Dan sighed as he tried to recall the basics of learning a new language. He had learned Spanish in highschool, but he hadn't ever been terribly good at it. His mom had gotten him some "how to learn French" audiobooks back when she was in the middle of one of her attempts to culture him, but he hadn't gotten more than a couple minutes into them. He barely even knew the nuances of English syntax and grammar. Rather, he just said what sounded right and hoped that he didn't end up sounding like some sort of back-woods hooligan. In short, he didn't even know where to begin with learning a new language.

Syntax and basic sentence structure analyzed

Beginning analysis of vocabulary, currently at 2%.

Dan stood up, ignoring generalized ache in his body and the pounding in his skull. At least he had the System to assist him. It didn't seem like an immediate solution, but it was still better than him accidentally asking someone why they were wearing a cat or insulting their mother's duck or something of that sort. He reached for his flask, hoping for some water to wash the blood from his face and neck, only to frown when he couldn't find it. At a minimum, he was going to need food and water so the System could fix his body up. It looked like it was time for him to rely upon his much-maligned charades skills. It wasn't his fault that everyone at the last holiday party thought that his rendition of a car, a bicycle, and Sean Connery all looked like "an epileptic fit."

"Do we have any food or something to drink," he enunciated slowly while miming bringing a spoon to his mouth.

Nora cocked her head at him and blushed. Emily burst out laughing, slapping her knee with her good hand. Dan swore to himself. Maybe he should have taken those community theater classes his Mom had tried to get him into. His charades skills were officially zero for two.

———

Nora certainly hoped that it was Dan's head wound that had encouraged him to request a crude sex act on him. If not, she was more than willing to encourage the process along. That sort of "joke" had been a large part of the reason why Ishlar needed to die. Well, that and being a likely agent of a hostile foreign power. The Alliance of Free cities tried to stay out of the eyes of all major powers, and if that meant an agent or spy occasionally disappearing, well, Twilight was a dangerous place. Even if someone put two and two together and realized that adventurers from the major powers had a suspiciously hard time in the lands of the Alliance, they still had plausible deniability. Just like the Alliance couldn't seize spies from a neighbor on suspicion that they were gathering information, those powers couldn't complain too loudly when their assets had frequent "accidents." It was all part of the bloody game the rulers played to maintain the balance of power and keep the peace.

Daniel started speaking again, motioning towards his mouth and making a chewing motion. At least that was fairly straightforward. She opened her pack and handed him a shank of dried and salted monster meat. The stuff didn't taste all that good, but it kept well. Now that Ishlar's reserves had been added to their own, the party had more than enough of the somewhat-unpleasant jerky.

She glanced at the pile of rocks where Andrea had made a cairn for Ishlar and his companions. Nora had never taken the other woman for the religious or superstitious type, but as soon as the final member of Ishlar's party had fallen, she insisted on giving them a proper, if scant, burial. Some people insisted that the unburied bodies of those who died outside of the sanctuary runes would lead to ghosts or spirits, but Nora had never believed. There were enough very real problems with the world without focusing on the unverified and mystical. Between ordinary monsters and the stalkers, gaunts, and behemoths that prowled the night, every story of a spirit sighting had a logical explanation.

Sure, zombies were real, but they were simply the result of a parasite passed through blood and other bodily fluids taking over the nervous system of a dead body. As for the rest? Those were stories told around a campfire and encouraged by the various churches to try to shore up their power. After all, if everyone has the potential to gain enough mana to fight monsters, what need would the average person have for the divine? It was perfectly logical and cynical that the priests would invent a new foe that ignored magic and steel. Supposedly, only holy relics and faith could repel spirits and ghosts. At least, that's what the priests said while passing around the collection tin.

"Pfak dt ff water?" Daniel croaked out at her, smiling hopefully as he mimed bringing a glass to his mouth.

"This time, it might be water that he wants," Emily chuckled. Standing next to her, the prudish Andrea scowled.

"Even if his translation runes are broken, he still shouldn't have mimicked such a crude gesture," she interjected, blushing again as she glared at Daniel. "Whatever he wanted, there surely was a better hand motion for him to use."

"Unless, he really did want Nora to--" Emily tried to speak over her sister, only to be shushed once again.

"Despite what we were told, Dan isn't some sort of monster." Andrea's glare transferred to Emily. "He might not have the first clue what he's doing, and he might have a bit of a bloodlust issue, but he's been a perfect gentleman to all of us for the entirety of the mission."

"I don't know, he's kinda cute in a skinny and disheveled sort of way," Emily shrugged. "I just figured that Nora had dibs with the way they've been going back and forth. I mean, he'd have to buy me a couple drinks first, but we have a dangerous job. You've gotta blow off steam somehow."

"Emily, you're absolutely disgusting." Andrea shook her head while Nora turned bright red. "We haven't even known the man for a week, and already you're making a pass at him. At least get to know him and his family first. I'm not ready to be an aunt yet."

"Oh I don't know about dating him," Emily grinned, pointedly ignoring everyone else's discomfort. "I'm just saying that after a couple drinks, sometimes things happen up against the wall behind the bar. Just a couple of adults having fun."

"No bar, no alcohol," Dan was speaking again. Strangely enough his mouth kept moving long after he stopped speaking. Rather than his voice, a strangely neutral and toneless voice spoke for him. "Need water, not copulate."

"Shit!" This time Emily ended up blushing. "I thought you didn't speak the language, what in the blazes is going on?"

"Use skill to translate." His voice was still toneless, despite his rather animated face and hands. "I learn as you speak. Slow, but it works. Please need water. No need copulate. Body hurts; not good idea."

Everyone stood frozen staring at Daniel as he made another motion of drinking from a cup of water. It was impossible for him to have learned the language. Yet, here he was. Then, she realized the conversation he had intruded upon and blushed further.

"Well," Emily said slowly, stretching the kinks out of her back. "Now that I've accidentally crudely propositioned my boss, I'm going to find a river and walk into it. It's been good working with all of you. Make sure my gravestone is tasteful. Maybe something about my boundless strength and honor. Preferably no reference to this."

For the first time in a while, Andrea started laughing. Daniel frantically made another water-drinking motion. Nora shook her head, eyes unfocused. This couldn't be happening. Everything was supposed to be under control, but this was chaos. If Daniel heard Emily, he might think that she had feelings for him and...

Her thoughts fizzled a bit. It wasn't like she had any feelings for him. Really, the main reason she was spending time with him was that he was suspicious, and he had potential. Either way, it was her duty to use her charm skill to gain information on him and to see if he could be brought over to the Alliance.

She shook her head to clear her thoughts and handed him her water flask. As he drank greedily from it, she reflected on the fact that he had even partially learned the language so quickly. Although it would be for the best if he didn't understand Emily, no one should have been able to even learn the basics of the language that quickly. She concentrated on ramping up the power of her skill. Daniel had his share of secrets, and she was going to figure out what they were if it was the end of her.

CHAPTER TWENTY-FOUR

Mistranslations and Explanations

Analysis of vocabulary currently at 50%

Please continue exposure to local speakers to increase comprehension

Dan reflected that he was further along than expected. Despite his original misgivings about being loaded with millions of dollars worth of Thoth Foundation hardware that had the potential to tase him at any time, he couldn't argue that the little suckers were industrious. Of course, they were much more useful than off-brand translation software. He put a hand on his now decidedly-unbroken nose, face itching a little as dried blood rubbed off. Before he left Earth, Sam had told him that, given enough proteins and the right sets of vitamins, he'd recover from almost anything, and he had tested that proposition.

Setting down Nora's water flask, he stood up. Already, the aches and pains from his rank up were starting to fade as the nanites worked their magic. Inside his chest, the second sphere of mana thrummed quietly with barely-contained energy. Maybe the previous year deadened him to the sensation of the first sphere, but his body just felt different. It was more than a question of the amount of mana available to him; something more fundamental had changed. Never one for a huge amount of introspection, Dan opted to take a shortcut.

"System," he whispered, ignoring the rest of the party's poorly-translated, distracting back and forth. "Display status."

<USER> Status
Rank 2

Body 6
Agility 7
Mind 7
Perception 6
Spirit 11

Skills
Swords 6, Brawling 3, Archery 2

Affinity
Space 9, Lightning 6, Fire 6, Gravity 1

Spells
Shocking Fist 5, Spark Field 2, Spatial Shield 5, Flame Jet 4

"System," he continued, forehead furrowing. "Before everything went pink, my Spirit was at 10. Why did it raise again?"

Each sphere can contain up to ten Spirit. <USER> could not absorb the remaining point of mana until another sphere was condensed. It would not be suggested to attempt to condense more than one point of Spirit at a time. In the event that <USER> tries to condense more than one point of Spirit, odds are greater than 90% that <USER> will perish.

"That's grim," he muttered. "Do we have any idea what the second sphere does? I know it's making me feel good right now, but after that near death experience I suspect anything would be a relief."

Both spheres appear to have the same rate of mana regeneration.

Although <USER>'s total mana capacity has not raised significantly, mana regeneration appears to have doubled.

Dan raised an eyebrow. Doubled mana regeneration was hardly insignificant. According to the Tellask records, his rather painful and unusual method for awakening his magical potential already should've given him a fairly robust amount of regeneration. Of course, they didn't really have any 'normal' magic users to compare the effect against, so everything was a matter of speculation, but even with his fairly modest affinity levels, that level of regeneration should allow him to vastly improve his magical repertoire. Right now, his spells could create interesting phenomena, but more than anything, they served as distractions. Shocking Fist could cause a target's muscles to convulse and induce temporary paralysis, and Flame Jet hurt people, but more than anything it just surprised or blinded them. Either spell could be hard countered by a prepared foe.

"Are we ready to get going?" he asked. The rest of the party was arguing about something, but after the rank up, Dan hardly gave a crap. He needed to get back to town and find a real bed as soon as possible. "I think Emily said something about going to a bar? I could really use a drink."

He really wasn't sure what she had meant by reproducing the walls of the bar, but he certainly needed a drink. The System was still a bit new at translations, and he was pretty sure that it was feeding both sides clunky and inaccurate wordings, but at this point it was all he had. Maybe she meant that they would be drunkenly looking at the mosaics and graffiti outside the bar.

"No bar." Emily shook her head, cheeks completely red. "Plan to walk to river. End embarrass. No alcohol, only more embarrass."

Whatever that meant. Hopefully she'd have fun swimming in her downtime. He was just sick of sleeping outdoors under the stars and not showering. Well, mostly sleeping under a looming gas giant in some sort of dim, eternal half light. The point of not showering still stood. Even with the helmet gone, he smelled pretty vile, and he was pretty sure being soaked in his own dried blood really wasn't helping the situation.

"Fine, no bars." Dan shrugged as he picked up his travel pack and slung it over his shoulder. "I really want to get back to town though. I've had more than enough sleeping on rocks."

The walk back was fairly straightforward. Nora and Emily spent most of the time refusing to talk or make eye contact with him, but for some reason Andrea of all people kept laughing until she teared up. There was probably some sort of explanation for why everyone's roles had reversed, but Dan figured that it could wait until the System could translate their conversations with more accuracy than simple caveman grunts. Instead, he spent the walk experimenting with his new mana recovery. The System wasn't lying about the increased speed. He didn't try anything too complicated, instead using the attunement stones in his arms to convert the pure mana from the spheres in his chest into its elemental form.

Unfortunately, all of his affinities had reached a fairly high level, so the benefits of holding and releasing the elemental mana were limited. It seemed like the first couple levels of an affinity would be fairly straightforward, but after that, he would really have to grind away at them in order to level up. Luckily, his increased mana capacity and regeneration made that an actual possibility. Without them, well... he didn't doubt the background information that had indicated that humans were passable mages at best. It simply would take decades to amass enough affinity to be useful, unless someone ranked up multiple times.

Finally, his thoughts were interrupted as Morganville appeared on the horizon. Once again, as they approached, Nora broke off from the party to talk to the guards while Dan admired the town's walls. After a brief exchange of coins, whether an admission fee or a bribe, Dan had no idea, they entered the town once again. The party separated just past the gate with some broken promises to meet up at the adventurer's guild the next day. Or maybe they were supposed to go on an adventure the next day. One of the two.

Dan pocketed his share of the loot and walked towards the inn he had stayed in the last time he was in Morganville. The innkeeper, Jeffrey, greeted him with a nod while cleaning a mug when he walked in the door.

"Jeffrey," he asked tiredly. "I don't suppose you have a room, bath, and food available. I've had a rough couple of days."

"You speak bad," Jeffrey cocked his head as he replied. "You not speak this bad when you here last."

God damnit this was getting old. Dan was torn between trying to track down a new helmet with translation runes and taking his lumps, letting the System learn the local language. Ultimately, he was almost half done with the vocabulary. It seemed like a waste to just use a helmet again after all of the hassle he had already put up with.

"I don't speak the language," Dan massaged his temples while he answered. "The helmet I was wearing last time translated for me. It got broken in a fight, so now I'm stuck trying to make myself understood without it."

"My cousin sell new one." Jeffrey smiled and set down the glass. "He merchant, sells clothes and armor. He set you up with good price."

"Thank you, but no," Dan shook his head ruefully. "I have a habit for getting hit in the face. If I buy another helmet from you, I'll probably just lose it again. For now, I just need a room, a bath and some food. I might want to talk to your cousin tomorrow about upgrading my armor. The stuff I'm wearing right now is well-made, but there isn't any runescripting on it, and that seems like a bit of an oversight."

"Good!" Jeffrey's face was beaming. "Same price as last time, and I introduce to Markus tomorrow. He give fair price. Very fair."

Somehow, Dan doubted that Jeffrey's cousin would give him a "very fair" or even a "fair" price. The look on the innkeeper's face was positively predatory. Like so many other things, he pushed those concerns off until tomorrow, instead focusing on the bath. It was heavenly. The water wasn't terribly warm, and the soap was one step short of lye, but he didn't care. After some judicious abuse of Flame Jet to keep the water at an acceptable temperature, and a good long soak, he went to his room.

By Earth standards, the bed wasn't soft. In fact, it was fairly lumpy, and he was pretty sure that the locals hadn't invented springs, let alone a box spring. Instead, it was more of a futon thrown on top of straw, but after sleeping in a cave and on a pile of rocks in the wastes, it was divine. As he lay on the bed, staring up at the white plaster of the inn's ceiling, he began fiddling with his mana. He didn't know how much downtime he would have, but more than anything, he needed a ranged spell that could actually deal some damage. He mentally went through his affinities and tried to find something that jumped out at him, but more and more, he kept coming back to Shocking Fist.

He was an electrical engineer before all of this insanity happened to him. Admittedly, most of his training was more focused on micro amperages, but if he was going to get a super power, he was going to go full Thor. It might take a while before he could generate the sort of amperage he'd need to arc electricity properly, but really most low-level forces available to him weren't much more than party tricks anyway. Even if the System helped him to learn at an unprecedented rate, learning true combat magic was a bit of a long-term prospect.

Dan brought his fingers together and ran his mana through the electrical attunement stone. Slowly, he built up the positive and negative charges between his index finger and thumb until a spark arced between them. It'd probably take at least a month or so, even with the longer days on Twilight, before he'd actually be able to generate a proper arc. Still, being able to launch lightning bolts from the back row of a team seemed to have much greater survival prospects than fighting from the front. This was especially true given how big and heavily-muscled most of the melee fighters he'd run into were. Ishlar, Andrea, and Emily all reminded him of the security staff back at the Thoth Foundation. Some differences were genetic. No matter how much he trained, he wouldn't be built like them. He wasn't overweight or uncoordinated anymore, but he was beginning to reach the limits of what a fairly-average guy could physically do, even with a robust training regimen.

Speaking of which, Dan thought to himself. The first couple of days on Twilight had been too hectic for him to put anything together like a training plan. Now that he decided to focus his energies on electricity, it would only make sense for him to exhaust his mana for the night trying to strengthen his affinity, or maybe put together some of the variables of a full-blown spell. It didn't make sense for him to run himself dry on mana while they were out adventuring. After all, you never really knew when some sort of monster would leap out and try to eat your face, but in the relative safety of Morganville, he could begin to practice in earnest.

Before long, Dan was dozing off. The room smelled of ozone from his constant attempts to create a proper lighting bolt. He had been able to create and stabilize an arc between his hands when held a shoulder's length apart for almost five seconds, but outside of looking impressive, he couldn't really find a proper use for the ability. Still, it was enough of an accomplishment for the evening that it earned him a System notification.

Detecting increase in Lightning Affinity. Lightning Affinity is now 7.

Sync completed with <USER>'s subconscious, <USER> can now use the System without vocalization as the System will be reading <USER>'s thoughts in real time. Please state 'privacy policy' if <USER> would like to review the System's privacy policy regarding personal thoughts and financial tendencies.

Dan frowned at the second notification. That was probably a result of his efforts during the rank up, but he wasn't sure how he felt about the System literally reading his mind.

"Privacy Policy," he enunciated clearly into the empty room, still frowning.

NOTICE: This feature is not yet implemented. Please contact a System administrator for further information.

"Contact System Administrator," he spoke again slowly. It was worth a shot.

Attempting to contact System Administrator. Wifi not detected. Satellites connection not detected. Infrared connection not detected. Terminating contact.

Dan sighed in exasperation. He didn't know what he expected. It wasn't like he was on Earth. Maybe he hoped that there would be a subroutine with more information, or at least something that could explain half of what was going on with the multitude of tiny robots living in his body. Suddenly, his brooding was interrupted by a dinging sound.

Your satisfaction is important to us. Please state "Survey" to fill out a survey regarding the customer service and helpfulness of the System Admin-istrator.

Figures. Dan rolled over in the slightly lumpy bed. He was pretty sure the contract he had signed with the Thoth Founda-tion allowed them to download his brain anyway. It's not like he was disloyal or anything. Hell, he genuinely liked Henry. He didn't really have much to hide except the more shameful parts of the male experience, usually reserved for a restroom in incognito mode. If the Foundation wanted more information on that, they could be his guest. With a slight smile on his face, Dan went to sleep.

CHAPTER TWENTY-FIVE

Friendships?

The next morning, as Dan decided to stubbornly refer to the period when he woke up, despite Alpha Centauri not being visible in the sky, he awoke refreshed for the first time in a while. After a breakfast of meat porridge where the origin of the meat remained a blissful mystery, Dan dodged out of the inn before Jeffrey could invite his cousin over. The stainless steel of his chainmail was probably more robust than anything he was likely to find on Twilight, but after using the runescripted gauntlets, he wanted more magical tools if possible.

Even if most of the monsters he encountered were stronger and faster than him naturally, he could always make up the difference with a little bit of magical performance enhancement. Ishlar was an idiot, but Dan couldn't help but remember how much more difficult it was to fight against him once he had proper gear. The oaf was an absolute pushover in the first fight, but the minute he activated his spell shield and started swinging Spinebreaker around, he graduated to a fairly serious threat.

At the very minimum, Dan wanted a general upgrade to his gear. Compared to Spinebreaker, his sword was little more than a sharp piece of metal. His year of training didn't mean that much in the face of increased gravity that upset the delicate balance of all of his movements. Come to think of it, he did have a gravity affinity that he was barely using. Maybe he should study the runes on the club to see if he could replicate the Gravity Blanket ability that Ishlar used. It didn't seem terribly complex, which would make it a decent starter spell for the affinity. Unfortunately, it took a tremendous amount of energy to produce gravitational forces at the moment. It would still be a long time before he could do anything truly useful with gravity other than impede or annoy people, but Dan was beginning to suspect that long-term investments and gradual improvement were just how magic worked.

Still, after the fight they had money and equipment. The sisters were holding onto the club, testing it out to see if Andrea wanted it as their combined share of the loot, and Nora had most of the team's earnings, almost twenty sovereigns. More than enough for a simple enchantment or two to help round out his arsenal.

Of course, he'd have to ask Nora what would help the most. Maybe a pauldron with a spellshield inscribed on it or some sort of armor that would help him replicate a skill or effect. Preferably healing. The nanites would bring him back from any non-fatal wound, but it wasn't quick or painless.

On the other hand, it might be best to save his money until he could afford truly high-end gear. After all, it would be a huge waste of money to buy a bunch of low-end gear, only to struggle with reselling it once he outgrew its usefulness.

Dan opened the door to the Adventurer's Guild and stepped inside. Instantly, he was inundated with the chattering of voices and the stale scent of cheap beer. At least the constant speaking would help the System learn the vocabulary. He glanced around the bar portion of the guild. Apparently, things were fairly sedate the last time he was here. Everywhere, huge, muscle-bound men and women ate, drank, and joked raucously. At least two tables had arm wrestling contests, and one of the back walls was involved in an impromptu hatchet throwing contest.

In short, compared to the rest of the vikings in the bar, Dan couldn't help but feel absolutely tiny.

Spotting Andrea and Emily in the corner, he stepped over to their table. Andrea was sipping water out of a ceramic mug, but Emily was face down on the table, her tunic covered in beer. It was clear from the occasional groans of pain that the woman was still alive, but suffering from a severe headache. Dan recognized a monster hangover from his ill-spent college years, so with a brief nod directed at Emily, he sat down next to Andrea.

"I thought she wasn't going to be drinking." He gestured at Emily's moaning form as the woman put both of her hands over her head.

"She drinks after every mission." Andrea took a sip from her water. "It's a tradition. You are speaking much better. Do you have mind magic?

"Something like that." Dan shrugged. "The more I listen to other people speak the language without a translation helmet on, the more I understand. If we keep chatting, I should be able to speak normally before too long."

"A useful ability," Andrea stated agreeably. "Nora says you are from afar? A skill to quickly learn how to speak would be worth much to a diplomat or an explorer. If you can share the ability, you would be a rich man."

"Unfortunately, it was more something done to me than something I can do," Dan replied ruefully, glancing around for someone to sell him an ale. He really didn't want to wade through the crowd of boisterous adventurers to get a beer, but he did want a drink.

"A class skill, then?" Andrea asked, absently darting a hand out to steady Emily before she could slip off of the table and onto the floor.

"I guess," Dan said noncommittally. "We don't really have classes where I come from. I have something else that helps me adapt and learn instead. How do classes work on Twilight, anyway? Nora mentioned them, but we had to get going before she got a chance to explain them further."

"No class?" Andrea raised an eyebrow. "Well, you're a strange sort in general, so I suppose I shouldn't be surprised. Really, the only beings I know that don't use classes are elves, but that's only because they live for thousands of years. A class is a magically-enhanced tattoo, usually attuned to a certain type of mana, that helps you use the mana you earn from killing monsters. Depending upon the skill of the person who gives you the class, it will have a number of skills in it at each rank. In Morganville, you aren't going to find anyone capable of giving you a class with skills past rank 3, and most of the adventurers around here only have classes that go to rank 1."

She took another sip from her water mug before continuing, ignoring the groaning Emily. "You can usually continue to rank up once or twice after you reach the limit of your class, but everyone has heard rumors of people ignoring their class' rank limit and spontaneously combusting. It might be an urban legend, but I'm not inclined to give it a try. Unfortunately, the only real option is to get an advanced class, and that usually means signing on with an army or a noble house. Advanced classes are a kind of addition to the class tattoo that allows you to specialize your skills further. I don't know if they're worth the five to ten years of indentured service that comes with getting them, but it's better than getting burned inside out by mana."

"Wait," Dan frowned, "so if you want to continue earning mana past rank 3, you have to enlist in the army?"

"Basically." Andrea shrugged. "That's only if you have an original class that can go up to rank 3. Emily and I only have rank 2 classes. After that escapade in the mine, we're probably going to have to start looking for advanced classes sooner or later as well. Of course, there are still a decent number of options. The Alliance of Free Cities has all right class options, and it pays its soldiers fairly well. The Imperial Marines are risky, but from what I've heard, you can get a class going all the way up to rank 10. The surrounding kingdoms have better class options, but they put more restrictions on their soldiers. If you're feeling really adventurous, there are always mercenary or criminal groups. They don't have that great of class options available, but the pay is much better, so long as you don't mind engaging in fairly questionable work."

"It sounds like most of the class system is designed to control the more powerful citizens?" Dan asked. "What do skills look like, anyway? Do they make a big difference? Wouldn't it be possible to just keep going without getting a class and becoming indebted to some sort of power?"

"I really don't know how you'd compete without a class and skills." Andrea glanced at him with slightly narrowed eyes. "Without skills, you're just a regular human. Emily and I both have skills to make us stronger and faster. I have a skill that lets me strike someone harder than normal with a blow. Most mages have skills that let them cast specific spells. From what I hear, it's still hard work to regulate the amount of mana and the effects of the spell, but their class makes it so they only have to deal with four or five variables in their head, rather than hundreds."

"To be perfectly clear," Andrea set down her glass of water, eyes focused on Dan. "The elves and our scholars all agree that humans can't learn magic without a class. They say that it's too hard for us to be able to handle the complexity of even the most basic magic spell in our heads. The fact that you don't have a class, and yet you are clearly inventing and casting spells is both perplexing and troubling. You have the potential to upset the natural order of things, which is probably good in the long run, but I just hope you don't do it near my sister and I. We just want to become good, run-of-the-mill adventurers without getting drawn into some sort of web of intrigue and magic."

Dan scratched his chin awkwardly. Stubble was already starting to grow in. Unless he wanted to embarrass himself further with a patchwork, scraggly beard, he would need to get a razor at some point to shave. He exhaled thankfully as Nora sat down and rescued him from the awkward silence and Andrea's gaze.

"What'd I miss?" She asked cheerfully, chuckling slightly as she took in Emily's groaning form.

"Daniel revealed that he doesn't have a class, and that he doesn't even know what classes are," Andrea replied, taking another sip from her mug. "A revelation that I plan on promptly forgetting, as it seems likely to cause trouble."

"Dan!" Nora turned her brilliant smile on him. "You really are capable of so much. I knew you were special when I ran into you in the swamp, but I really didn't have any idea that you would be this extraordinary. What else can you do? It can be a secret between you, me, Andrea, and Emily's hungover corpse."

Warmth coursed through Dan as he squirmed in her gaze. There was something about Nora that spoke to him. She reminded him of his ex-girlfriend on their good days, combined with his Mother before she became disappointed in the lack of grandchildren and steady work. She was a warm cup of cocoa on a cold day. That perfect pair of sweatpants and a beer after a double shift at work. She was comfortable in a way that he hadn't expected in a strange and dangerous new...

Subconscious interference detected. Analyzing.

Mind magic detected. <USER> is suffering from a compulsion. Purging now.

The warmth disappeared. Dan blinked. Nora was still smiling at him, but the smile seemed predatory. Dan shivered. Her interest was something much more than casual, and definitely not in a fun or sexy way. Despite himself, Dan almost chuckled. Maybe she did have something in common with his ex-girlfriend, after all.

CHAPTER TWENTY-SIX

Hasty Decisions

"So, Nora." Dan's voice shook a little more than he would like. "Did you know that I recently gained the ability to resist mind magic and mental interference?"

Immediately, her trademark mischievous expression flashed to guilt followed by practiced feigned innocence. If Dan hadn't been watching for it, he likely wouldn't have noticed anything, but now that his paranoia was aroused, it was as plain as day. Really, he should have noticed it days ago. Nora was friendly and helpful, but his mission was much too important to risk it for a pretty smile and some kind words.

Worse, she was clearly trying to mine him for information. A cold tingle ran down his spine. Dan had no idea who she was working for, but anyone who tried to compile information on strangers without any reason or prompting was probably some brand of nefarious.

"That's an interesting ability," she replied, her expression betraying nothing. "Mind magic isn't terribly common outside of translation magic, but an extra layer of defense is always useful."

"Even more useful is the ability to detect when it's being

used against you," Dan agreed, his eyes fixed on her. "Mind magic usually doesn't give itself away the way that fireballs and lightning bolts do. Sometimes practitioners can get a little cocky. They use it in public and just assume no one will notice."

The smile froze on Nora's face. Andrea slowly set down her mug of water and glanced back and forth between them.

"Nora." a hint of pain was in Dan's voice. "I thought we were friends. Then again, you already knew that, didn't you? You've been using some sort of skill to lower my guard, to make me trust you. How long have you been using it?"

"My class has a charm ability," she whispered, unable to meet his gaze. "It makes the target friendlier, more agreeable to the user's suggestions, less likely to second guess the user."

"I asked how long you were using it." Dan repeated himself, his voice dangerously calm.

"From the moment we met." her lower lip quivered, attempting a more mundane version of her skill. "When we were out on the swamp, I wasn't sure that you would help me with the gliders. I started using the skill to ensure that I would survive being abandoned by my party, and I never really found a good time to stop using it. Every time I would think about just trying to be normal friends with you, I would get so worried about how you would react. That maybe you only liked me because of the magic, and not because of me."

Subconscious interference detected. Analyzing.

Mind magic detected. <USER> is suffering from a compulsion type <Pity>. Purging now.

"Can you at least cut it out for long enough that we can talk like adults?" Dan slammed a hand on the table, causing Emily to groan and shift. "Even now, you're trying to influence me magically rather than actually explaining yourself. How do you expect me to believe anything you have to say?"

"Dan," she began, her eyes tearing up.

"Look," he cut her off. "You've been using magic to soften me up, and you've been prying into how I can do the things I do. I'm not going to let you guilt me into feeling bad about being upset about this. I just need to know why, and then I'm going to need some time to think. I'm going to have to sort out what I think is real and what's a rosy picture painted by your mana. I hope you can understand how much of an invasion of trust this all is."

Dan paused and cocked his head. "Let me amend that. 'I hope you can understand' is way too light. You need to understand. Maybe everyone around here uses mind magic on each other, but where I'm from, that's not something friends do. Right now, I need to know that you're not some sort of con woman, and that I'm not some sort of mark, and I need you to explain it to me without using your magic to smooth over the rough edges."

"You've been using magic on Daniel?" Andrea spoke softly, barely above the din of the guildhall. "Have you been using that skill on Emily and me as well? Now that I'm thinking back, we normally wouldn't have agreed to go on such a risky mission as the silver mine without more information. I remember being upset, but normally it would go much further than that. I don't risk myself like that unless there is no other choice."

"I'm sorry to all of you." Nora was openly crying now. "I was just afraid that you wouldn't like me or help me if I didn't use the skill. I keep the skill on at most times. It doesn't really make you do anything you wouldn't do anyway, but it just makes you see me in a better light. I would never use an actual mind control skill on you, but that isn't what I did. The charm skill… it just helps."

Dan struggled to stay strong in front of her guilt trip. "Nora, you didn't tell me why you were asking all of those questions about me. Are you working for someone? Why do you need to know about my skill growth and development?"

"I can't answer that, Dan." She gazed at him plaintively, tears streaming down her face. "There are important people in the area who need to know if the Empire is making a move on Twilight. You clearly aren't just another person. You fight like an elf, but you're a human. We all know the struggle with the

Orakh isn't going well, but no one wants the Tellask to annex Twilight and force us into their Empire. We'd just be cannon fodder. I need to let people know if you're the first step toward the Empire trying to force us to the front of that war. I may not look like it, but I'm a patriot. I'm not going to let my people get slaughtered in a war where we don't have any real chance."

"I'm not with the Empire, Nora," he replied, running a hand through his hair as he closed his eyes. "I have some secrets, but I'm not Imperial. Of course, I don't like it when my 'friends' use magic to weaken my will so they can spy on me. I'm going for a walk. I might be back. I might not. I have a lot to think about."

He stood up and turned to leave the guild hall, only to find his way blocked by two large men. Both of them were just shy of seven feet tall and built like bulls. Something inside of him could sense that they weren't first rank, and immediately began clamoring for him to take their mana. The din in the hall quieted down. All eyes were on Dan and the two giant bruisers blocking his way. He closed his eyes and took a deep, shuddering breath as he tried to calm the boiling anger and homicidal urges.

"Dan," Nora beseeched him from the table. "I really don't want to do this, but there are important people who need to know about you. It would really be better for everyone if you could do all of this voluntarily. If you're not from some sort of destabilizing force, no one is going to care. Everyone out here has a couple secrets. Half of the people here have committed something that would be considered a crime in another kingdom. We don't care about that sort of thing."

"What if I don't come voluntarily?" Dan didn't take his eyes off of the two large men. One of them smiled, and the other reached for a rather large sword at his side.

"Stop acting like an idiot!" Nora was getting close to shouting. "You're coming one way or another, but this doesn't have to be a bad thing! The people I work for aren't that bad. If you take a simple oath of fealty, everything should be fine, so long as you agree to do jobs for them. Please Dan, this really doesn't have to be a bad thing! You get used to it after a while."

"She's right, Dan," Andrea put her hand on his shoulder. "No one makes it that far in this world without a master. My sister and I needed advanced classes. Nora's employers gave us an offer that we couldn't really turn down. They aren't bad people, Dan. You have a lot of potential, but right now you aren't nearly strong enough to defend yourself. If you can convince them that you have value, they'll protect you and train you. If you strike out on your own, someone else with money and power will see you as a threat, and they will have retainers powerful enough to rip you in half with their bare hands. Don't charge off on your own; this is all for the best."

"So the entire time in the mine..." Dan spoke slowly, his eyes still on the individuals standing in front of him. "That entire time when you were 'afraid' of me, what was all of that?"

"Acting," Andrea replied evenly. "I might not have Nora's skill, but as a girl, I always wanted to be in the theater. Life got in the way, and I ended up fighting monsters. Nora needed a team to evaluate how much of a threat you might be, and I have to say she's right. You have the potential to be an archmage. Given enough mana and a decade, you could be the most powerful human on Twilight. That's commendable, but it's never going to happen unless you have someone working with you. There are plenty of other claimants to the same title who'd be happy to smother you in the cradle."

"We're trying to help, Dan," Nora was practically begging him.

Dan closed his eyes. He didn't need enemies, but he couldn't answer the kind of questions that Nora's unnamed employers would want to ask. Even if they didn't chain him down, the Tellask couldn't find out about Earth. He wasn't a hero by nature, but at this point, he really didn't have much of an option. Even if he died in this shitty bar, it would be better than being manipulated into giving up information on Earth. *Fuck it.* He'd made it through most of his life with few friends other than his mother constantly telling him what to do. Time to just carry that over into a new world.

"Fine," he said smiling, putting a hand on the shoulder of each of the bruisers. He fought to keep the smile on his face as he saw a flash of smug satisfaction in each of their eyes. Then he activated Shocking Fist.

Even with two spheres, activating it from each hand and the shoulder that Andrea was touching strained his focus. With a brief crackle and a hiss of moisture flash evaporating, both of the men in front of him collapsed, muscles spasming as their eyes rolled up into their skulls. Dan only had a second before the bar erupted into chaos, so he spent it well, throwing a handful of filaments into the air with his left hand and activating Spark Field while he launched a Flame Jet with his right.

Bar patrons screamed and shielded their eyes from the sudden light as the line of fire hit the ceiling and partially blew back. The temperature in the room immediately jumped a notch. Then people began screaming, due to the Spark Field. Dan rarely used the skill due to it being decidedly non-lethal, but shocked and distracted everyone it touched, giving him a window to sprint toward the exit.

His predictions held true, and the bar erupted into absolute chaos. At least a couple of the patrons lunged for him, but they were largely drunk or distracted by his spells. Seconds later, he was in the street, smelling vaguely of smoke and stale beer. Bidding a silent goodbye to Morganville, he sprinted for the nearest city wall.

Luckily, he had brought his travel pack with him, not entirely trusting Jeffrey at the Inn. He had a couple days worth of food, a firestarter, his bedroll, some pocket change, and the sanctuary runes.

Nora had the rest. She'd always insisted on holding the valuables. He'd never thought anything of it or the rest of her behavior in the moment. From the way she'd led him around by his nose, to making decisions on his behalf and forcing him to either confront her or accept them... As much as he'd like to blame it entirely on her ability, it was a pattern for Dan.

He'd lived his life as a doormat, but the System was a chance to change that. He chuckled. Two simple goals. Save Earth and break the toxic habits that had held him back. Becoming powerful enough that no one could easily ignore him was an added side benefit.

As for the money and gear he had left in his headlong flight? It made his chest ache, but he would just have to consider it Nora's severance package. He doubted that the offer of "meeting her employers peacefully" was still on the table.

CHAPTER TWENTY-SEVEN

Escape

Eyeing Morganville's walls, Dan mentally added "learn a gravity spell" to his to-do list. The walls themselves were made of a single sheet of greyish white stone that seemed to grow up from the very ground itself. Without any cracks to wedge a hand or foot into, there was about zero chance of him climbing over the wall without magic or a rope. Luckily, they were designed to keep monsters and bandits out, not disaffected villagers in. Watchtowers liberally spotted the walls, and each one had a door at ground level and presumably a spiral staircase or ladder inside. He could still jump the wall, but doing so meant sprinting through a guard post.

Listening to the clamor behind him, Dan smiled wryly. Nora, Andrea, and their "friends" were definitely still pursuing him. There really wasn't any chance of him making it through the gate, and if he waited long enough, they'd find him even here. He'd picked a fairly remote section of the walls in a poorer section of town, but he had a strong suspicion that Nora's employers were already arranging a search of the entire village.

"No sense waiting, then," he mumbled to himself before

sprinting toward the nearest watchtower. As a pleasant side effect of being in a poor section of town, whatever ordinances or social norms usually prevented people from building their residences up against Morganville's walls went unenforced. In short, he only had to cross about thirty feet between the shack he was hiding behind to reach the front door of the tower. One kick later, the unbarred door slammed inward, revealing a small waiting area where three surprised guards were playing some sort of card game.

Dan didn't give them a chance to react, instead throwing a handful of metal filings and activating Spark Field. One of these days, he would get around to upgrading the spell to make it more than a distraction, but with the surprised guards, it served its purpose. The air around the coffee table they were playing on shimmered with electrical charge as Dan tore past them and took the steps of the tower's staircase two at a time. Below him, the guards screamed and swore as they tried to escape from the distracting and annoying shocks from the spell.

Almost fifteen seconds later, Dan reached the wall level of the tower. The staircase continued up, but this room was a small armory with archways opening up to the battlements going in either direction. Already, the guards thundered toward the steps below him. He quickly glanced around the guard post before grabbing a length of rope from where it hung next to a hammer and some other tools. Figuring that he had pushed his luck with the pursuing guards about as far as it was likely to go, Dan ran out onto the wall and immediately wrapped the length of rope around a battlement.

A poorly-aimed arrow clattered off of the stone next to him, forcing Dan to look up. On top of the tower were two guards with shortbows. Gritting his teeth, he activated Spatial Shield and kept it on. Even with his greatly-enhanced mana supply, it greedily drained his reserves, but he had no desire to test the effectiveness of his chainmail against those bows. Almost immediately, his conservative impulses were confirmed as an arrow sailed into the barrier and curved. It still hit him in the side and cut skin through the chain, but it would have been a critical blow without the help of the spell.

Spurred on by the arrows, he finished the simple knot, hoping that the Thoth Foundation's brief refresher of his years in the boy scouts would be enough for the knot to hold. Grabbing onto the rope, he threw himself over the edge just as the first guards from the ground floor reached the top of the wall. Kicking off the wall with his back to the ground, Dan tried to lower himself as quickly as possible. Another arrow sailed past him, a victim of the bad angles formed by him hugging the wall, as well as the spatial shield spell. Above, yelling echoed off the walls, and the rope vibrated in his hands as someone tried to cut it with a knife. Just before he reached the ground, the rope gave way, and Dan fell the final three to four feet and landed on his back.

Ignoring the pain in his side from the arrow and the dull ache in his back, Dan hauled himself to his feet and ran. Behind him, a horn sounded, and he redoubled his speed as arrows fell around him. About three hundred feet from the wall, he cut the mana to Spatial Shield. Already, his head ached from the strain of maintaining the spell. He hoped that the range was too much for the archers to precisely target him, but he wasn't going to stop and turn around to judge the accuracy of his prediction.

Dan slowed his sprint to a more maintainable jog. He didn't know if Nora and her employers would be coming after him, but there was no question she knew her way around Twilight's wastes much better than him. Instead, his only real option was to look for another location where her organization wouldn't have much interest, be that another town or simply holing up in a mountain like a hermit or a bandit. Unfortunately, he didn't even know where a nearby town would be.

Nora had handled all navigation. He swore under his breath. Yet another way she kept him dependent on her.

He thought back on the previous couple of days and cursed to himself. He could blame Nora's magic, but the truth was that he had fallen back into bad habits. From childhood on, his father had been a distant but friendly character, but his mother controlled his life. She picked his highschool, she picked his extracurriculars, she vetoed his friends that were "bad characters."

Any time he tried to oppose her, it lead to hours of screaming and guilt trips. How much she had sacrificed to give him everything he had, how she just wanted the best for him. Before long, it became easier for him to give in, rather than fight. He knew that his relationship with her was toxic and codependent, but it wasn't like he could simply cut his mother out of his life.

Well, he had tried. In college, he dated Annabelle, and his mother hated her. She was beautiful, she was witty, and she wasted no time explaining to Dan how his mother was stunting him. After a screaming match over Christmas dinner, his mother had given him an ultimatum. Break up with Annabelle, or find his own way to pay for college. With Annabelle's help, he had filed for grants and applied for loans. Even with everything that happened later, one of the happiest moments of his life was when he had been able to tell his mother what she could do with her financial aid.

Unfortunately, he just traded one set of handcuffs for another. As soon as he stopped talking with his mother, Annabelle more or less took over her role. He was told which of his friends were unacceptable, and which of his classes he needed to drop. More and more, he stopped hanging out with his group of friends and ended up spending time with Annabelle's clique. Then, after almost two years of dating, he found her in bed with his former best friend.

It had torn him apart, but the worst thing was that she didn't even try to fight him. She just laughed at the lost look on his face and told him, "Your lack of confidence and indecision are exactly why this has been going on for the past six months." At that point, Dan had turned to his mother for emotional support. All it took was admitting through gritted teeth that she had always been right about the trollop, and he was back in her good graces... So long as he was a dutiful son and did everything she asked.

At some point, he had realized that his life was completely out of control. He was a follower, bouncing from one strong personality to another and going with the flow. He had gone to grad school and signed on as a contractor with the army far away from home to try and make something of himself, gain some independence. It worked after a fashion, but here he was again.

It would be so easy for him to blame outside forces. Nora used magic on him. He didn't understand the new world, so he used her as a guide. He needed help to fight monsters and gain magic. All of them had a grain of truth, but deep down Dan knew the real problem was him. Emotionally, he was a wounded animal, and he drew in predators. Nora, Annabelle, and his mom were all the same person. Going to another town wouldn't change the outcome until he could learn to actually stick up for himself.

Almost two miles from Morganville, he stopped running, heaving for breath. If he was going to find confidence, he might as well do it fighting magic-fueled monsters in the middle of nowhere.

Honestly, it wasn't the worst idea ever. The nanites would protect him from poisons and disease. He could eat the monsters he killed, counting on the System to help him digest the alien meat. So long as the sanctuary runes held out, and he didn't mind living a little rough, Dan could live outdoors indefinitely.

More importantly, constant encounters with monsters would serve as a perfect whetstone for him. Dan could simply spend a month or so fighting monsters and honing his skills, far away from the confusion and social pitfalls of civilization.

The formula was simple. If he killed enough monsters, he'd earn the mana he needed to gain a rank. If he practiced magic enough, he'd learn a new spell. The creatures he encountered would all want to kill and eat him, and if he wanted to survive, he'd simply have to beat them to the punch.

As easy as it would be to sulk away with his tail between his legs, Dan refused to treat his exile from civilization as anything more than a temporary setback. So long as he could remain undiscovered, the monster and mana-rich mountains far outside of Morganville were more opportunity than punishment. More than anything, they were a prime chance for him to gain the confidence he'd need to avoid being someone's doormat ever again.

CHAPTER TWENTY-EIGHT

Exile

Dan tried to stretch the stiffness out of his neck while walking the trapline. It had been two weeks worth of Twilight's extended days since he fled Morganville, and he was absolutely sick of sleeping on rocks. True, he had found a cave, more of a crevice really, but a bedroll of fur only did so much. Every time he woke up, it was the same series of aches and muscle strains until the nanites got around to healing the minor pains inflicted by a night of restless sleep. Even when the soreness was officially healed, Dan could still swear that he felt some stiffness and lack of mobility.

So far, he had fallen into an easy routine. Maintain the trapline of pits and snares made from corded plant fiber and scout for monsters. Return to his cave and practice magic. Repeat. Only once or twice did he have to deviate from that routine when he saw parties of adventurers. He didn't know if they were ordinary groups on quests or scouts out looking for him, but after Nora's betrayal, he wasn't going to risk it. Luckily, the cave was located in an isolated valley nestled in the foothills before a truly imposing set of mountains. So long as he kept his activities largely in the valley, no one was going to see his activities unless they actually climbed one of the specific hills ringing the valley.

The limited mobility did hamper his growth. He only occasionally ran into monsters, and usually only monsters of a lower rank. At this point, he barely even felt the rush from taking their mana. Really, if he hadn't trained in woodcraft at the Thoth Foundation, he probably would have been in a lot of trouble. Right now, he was mostly feeding himself from the trapline, and he was thankful that, even on a new world, game trails still looked more or less the same. The snares mostly caught creatures he referred to as "jackalopes" because they resembled rabbits covered in horns and spines, while the pit traps caught larger game such as the faux-pigs and white deer. Of course, Dan didn't actually know the names for any of the things he was eating, they just more or less looked like their Earth equivalents.

It wasn't all bad, though. The extra time to focus on magic had already paid dividends. He gained three levels of gravity affinity as well as two new spells. The first, "Lightning Stroke," generated an arc of electricity that could travel about fifteen feet. It could stun like Shocking Fist, but unlike the rest of his spells, it actually dealt a fair amount of damage by using the electricity to superheat a fist-sized chunk of whatever it struck. Dan's experiments had left the rock wall outside of his cave pitted with small holes and cracks. It might not be enough to directly kill an opponent, but for the first time, he could actually deal serious damage at range without having to awkwardly change from his sword to his short bow. The spell's only real downside was that each casting ate up a significant portion of his mana. Air was still an excellent insulator, and he hadn't been able to find a way to increase the efficiency by which electricity passed through it. Instead, he simply fell back on brute force, directing enough electrical mana to overcome that resistance.

The second spell was another utility spell, but one that helped every aspect a small amount. Called "Gravitational Easing," it only took a trickle of mana, but it reduced Dan's weight and the weight of everything he carried by about 10%. It wasn't really enough to have a major effect, but in the handful of battles that he had fought with monsters since fleeing Morganville, it noticeably improved his speed and maneuverability. Even better, it allowed him to patrol and climb the walls of his valley with much less strain.

At the moment, the weight reduction was a godsend. Between sleeping on hard rocks and spending the entire night staring at the ceiling of his cave while *something* prowled just outside the sanctuary runes, Dan wasn't exactly well-rested or in good cheer. He sighed. Maybe he'd be in a better mood if the valley was actually anything to look at, but the trees on Twilight were tiny and a drab, grayish black.

Apparently whatever chlorophyll analogue they used just didn't have any sort of coloration, and the thick, rocky soil prevented them from growing all that large. He would leave it up to the taxonomists to determine whether the six-to-seven-foot plants were tiny trees or large bushes, but the only thing he could conclude was that having a bunch of leaves around at head level was intensely annoying.

After confirming that the third snare had nothing in it, Dan changed course and headed towards the small river running through the center of the valley. Once again, he lamented being stuck here alone. The first couple of days hadn't been terrible. He had a goal in his mind of training his magic, making himself stronger, and returning to Morganville with a level of power that would make even Nora's employers take him seriously.

Then, as time passed, he got more and more stir crazy. He only had so much mana to train with, and when it ran out, boredom began to overtake him. The entire situation wasn't helped by the large tracks and claw marks he kept finding outside of his campsite after each night. Dan was pretty sure something was hunting him, and without a local guide, he had no idea how dangerous it might actually be.

It really was a shame that Nora turned out to be some sort

of cross between a spy and a press gang. Having someone to talk to while he tried to stage his very own training montage would have certainly made everything easier. He sighed as he pushed some gray leaves out of his face. Sometimes, right when he was on the edge of snapping, he could almost hear her voice as the wind rustled through the valley.

Tracks her voice seemed to float towards him from the river.

God, he really needed to figure out some way to get some social interaction into his life. If things kept up at this rate, he'd end up talking to a volleyball.

No... end at water. He could barely hear her over the rustling of the leaves.

Dan frowned. This wasn't how things usually went when he heard things. Usually, there was some sort of speech about how things would get better, and that she would listen to him in the future. Then, her voice would change into Annabelle's or his mother's. He was also beginning to suspect that the System's nanites weren't completely filtering out some sort of hallucinogen in his diet. Those jackalopes mostly ate mushrooms. It would make sense.

He laid down and crawled the last two hundred or so feet to where the plants ended and the river began, wincing as the rocky ground bit into his hands and knees. Peering through the grey bushes, he saw Nora standing next to Andrea and the two thugs he had disabled in the adventurer's guild.

"Could he be living somewhere in this valley?" One of the men asked. "We've already lost and found his trail three times. I'm not even sure we're following the right guy at this point."

"The tracks approach the river, and then they stop." Nora shrugged as she replied. "They're at least ten days old. I'm mostly proud that I was able to follow them at all across this sort of terrain. He might be here, and he might not. He had enough of a head start across the wasteland that, without a scent tracker, there was almost no chance of us finding him."

"Nora," the man who had spoken previously turned to her. "I know you were in a party for a little while with him, but it goes without saying that if you side with him, I will skin you. I was willing to follow your recommendations and try to get him to join the guard until he attacked us. No one attacks Morgan's guards and gets away with it. If one of the surrounding kingdoms found out, we would be a laughingstock."

"I know my job, Geoff," Nora replied, crossing her arms. "I still don't know how he figured out that I was using the charm skill on him. I've wracked my brain, but I have no idea why he bolted. Frankly, that just makes me more inclined to try to get him to join up. The Alliance of Free Cities has a decent number of heavy hitters, but no one with the weight to actually stand toe to toe with an archmage or an Imperial Knight. Right now, we're surviving off of political savvy and luck. Daniel Bird has enough potential to turn that around. It would be criminal of us to waste it just because he wounded your ego."

"This isn't about ego," Geoff sputtered. "He's a destabilizing element. If anyone finds out that we're harboring a human who can cast spells like an elf, everyone will band together to attack us. Blazes, even the Tellask themselves might intervene. You've seen how much damage a couple of their retired army sergeants can do. Can you imagine a full contingent of house soldiers or a couple of knights?"

"Drop it, Geoff," Andrea stated evenly, her eyes on the water of the small river. "If Daniel resists, we kill him. That's always been the job. If he doesn't resist, we take him alive. He's full of tricks, as we all found out, and I would prefer to not lose my head because he surprised me. Morgan can decide what to do with him when we bring him to her."

"He took me by surprise!" Geoff was definitely sulking now. "He's tiny. In a stand-up fight, I would cut him in half."

"Since when do magi get into stand-up fights with melee types?" Andrea snorted. "He's small, but that makes him fast. All he has to do is tag you and activate that ability, and you're on the ground again. Maybe this time, he doesn't bother running away and instead he puts a knife in your throat."

"He can't touch me if I use my Bulwark skill," Geoff

bragged, glaring at Andrea. "It's not as good as some fancy spell shield, but no one under rank 4 is going to be able to get through that while my mana lasts."

"He might not be able to touch you," the other man chimed in for the first time. "But you won't be able to move. The skill will help out the rest of the party, but you're hardly going to be able to win a duel while immobile and unable to swing your sword."

"Well fuck you, too, Brandon..." Geoff began, only for Nora to cut him off with a hissing sound.

"Put it back in your pants boys," she whispered, gaze flicking around the river. "My hunter's sense skill just triggered. We're being watched, and next to a river, that could be anything. There are a lot of nasty predators stalking the water sources in the wastes, and I'd prefer not to end up as one of their dinners."

She drew an arrow from her quiver and nocked it as the rest of the party prepared itself for combat with practiced ease. Andrea's maul was immediately at the ready, but Geoff's two-handed sword and Brandon's axe and shield were just behind it. All of them took a step back from the edge of the river and took up defensive positions around Nora as she continued to scan for the threat.

Her eyes widened as a flash of light from Dan's chainmail betrayed his position. She raised the bow in a smooth motion and unleashed the arrow directly at him.

CHAPTER TWENTY-NINE

Mad Scramble

Dan activated Spatial Shield in the split second before the arrow hit him. The magic bent the shaft of the arrow away from him, but Nora was a skilled archer. Instead of hitting him in the forehead, the arrow slashed open a deep cut on his left bicep. He gritted his teeth against the pain as he jumped to his feet. Already Brandon and Geoff were wading through the waist-deep river toward him while Andrea stood back, guarding Nora. He flexed his left arm to ensure that the arrow had done no serious damage, then triggered a Lightning Stroke into the river between the two men.

Diffused by the water, it didn't do any real damage, but the electricity caused both men to collapse in the water. This time, the second Lighnting Stroke burned through their entire bodies, rather than just their legs. Dan frantically hoped it would be enough as he ducked back behind one of the unnaturally-short trees and an arrow sailed past him. Already, a mana depletion headache was setting in, and he could do the math. Even if the two men were knocked out by the lightning, he was still outnumbered two to one. At full mana, he could beat either Andrea or Nora, but fighting both would be a tall order. Plus, he was pretty sure they had ranked up since they had last sparred before their adventure in the mine. That meant they likely had new class abilities. As much as he might want to get revenge on them for stringing him along and betraying him, this wasn't a fight that he should stick around for.

"Dan, it doesn't have to be like this!" Nora shouted to him across the river. "The Alliance of Free Cities is as good of a patron as you're going to find. You're not going to survive on Twilight without a master of some sort, so you might as well join up with us! You'll just need to swear an oath to Morgan and ensure that you're not a spy for a hostile power, and we can just make all of this go away! Please, Dan."

His memory immediately flashed to the dozens of other times his mother or Anabelle had said 'please, Dan' to him. Asking him to drop out of boy scouts and focus on the cello. Telling him to stop hanging out with his friends from the dorms in college because they drank too much and were a "bad influence" on him. Demanding that he sell his video game console so he could focus on his relationship and career. Each time, it was a minor concession phrased as an obvious decision that was in his own interest, and each time he gave in, until one day he looked back on himself and didn't even recognize who he was anymore. Daniel Thrush was nothing more than a piece of clay molded by the stronger personalities in his life.

Hell, even Doctor Weathers bossed him around. At least with her, it was more a matter of picking on him while telling him to stand up for himself. Funnily enough, she was the only person actually trying to get him to improve himself. Admittedly, she'd gained a fair amount professionally from working with Dan, but at the same time, it felt different.

She took his colossal stroke of luck and gave him a path to turn himself into some sort of magical superman, but at least she realized that he would have to do it himself. Sure, he needed some prodding here and there, but without some self-agency and confidence, even if he was perfectly fit, he would just end up being a tool in someone else's hands. Just like what Nora was trying to do to him.

Subconscious interference detected. Analyzing.

Mind magic detected. <USER> has broken the effects of a compulsion. No need for further action.

"Nora," he shouted back, his back pressed against a tree for cover. "I literally do not know who you work for or who the powers in this area are. I want absolutely nothing to do with a local political struggle. I'm just here to gain experience and go home. I can't swear an oath to serve and protect someone if my plan is to leave in a year. It just wouldn't be fair to anyone."

He glanced around the corner of the tree to see her reaction, and immediately whipped his head back as another arrow whirred past. It certainly wasn't aimed to wound. That was the second arrow fired at his face, and if he had learned anything in his year or so of combat training, it was that you should keep your face arrow and blade free.

"What the fuck was that, Nora," Geoff sputtered between hacking coughs. "I thought he wasn't supposed to have any ranged attacks except that fire blast thing. That's the only reason we engaged him from the water, so we would have cover from the fire. If I find out you've been holding out on us..."

"You'll skin me," Nora replied from the bank. "I got it the first four times you threatened it. If I were you, I'd get moving. You're still standing in the middle of a river while we fight a thunder mage. It just doesn't seem like the best thought out of plans."

Taking Nora's inadvertent advice, Dan peeked around his tree and unleashed another Lightning Stroke at Geoff. The man stood in the middle of the small river, his hands on his knees as he coughed out the water he had inhaled while under the surface. Dan noted that the man's sword was nowhere to be seen, hopefully washed downstream.

Geoff's eyes widened noticeably as the mana accumulated in Dan's free hand for the fraction of a second before the spell triggered. A sphere of energy sprang into being around the man as he frantically tried to divert the attack.

The electricity slammed into the bubble and curved down into the water. Whatever the man had used, it functioned like an advanced spell shield. A second later, it flickered out of existence and Geoff stood in the river once again, startled but unharmed. Dan took the man's survival and his building headache as his cue to leave and began sprinting through the forest back toward his cave. With any luck, the blacks and greys of the foliage would conceal his equally-drab armor, and he would get a bit of a head start as he tried to escape the search party.

"I am going to fucking skin that prick!" Geoff screamed from behind him. "This is the second time he's shocked me rather than fight me like a man! Where in the blazes is his honor?"

Mentally, Dan rolled his eyes. Since when was he supposed to honorably fight someone who outnumbered him four to one and had spied on him for the entirety of his time on the planet? No, if he trusted any of his traps to evade Nora's keen vision, he would already be leading them towards a pit trap. The goal of the day wasn't honor; it was survival.

He made it to the cave before them and grabbed his pack. He didn't have any idea where to go, but his only real chance was to travel further into the mountains in an attempt to lose them. He quickly ran to one of the valley walls with a slightly more shallow incline and pushed Gravitational Easing to the maximum as he began climbing. He made it almost half way up before an arrow embedded in his travel pack. Cursing slightly, he activated Spatial Shield.

Keeping both spells on at once strained his ability to focus to the limit, and even then it was only a matter of time before his mana ran out. Although impressive during the fight, using Lightning Stroke three times had eaten deeply into his reserves. Still, he was almost over the edge of the valley wall, and his spatial magic had already saved him from an arrow in the calf or thigh at least twice as Nora shot at him from below.

Finally, he heaved himself over the edge and took a couple seconds to catch his breath, adrenaline coursing through his veins. They might not be able to climb the wall as well as him, especially while defending against potential magical ambushes, but he didn't have as much of a head start as he would like. Nora knew the wastes of Twilight too well, so long as he went anywhere she was familiar with.

That left the mountains. He seemed to recall that most of the mountains on Twilight contained higher rank monsters and potentially dungeons. No one had really explained what dungeons were to him, but Nora had been fairly fearful. At this point, his only real option was to throw himself into danger and hope that Nora and her party would refuse to follow him.

The next two hours were tense, but anticlimactic. He turned off all of his abilities but Gravitational Easing and jogged up foothills towards the nearby mountains as he recharged his mana. Before too long, Nora's party appeared over the valley lip behind him and gave chase. Maybe it was Dan's fitness and magic, or maybe the other party was just cautious for traps, but he was able to maintain a good half mile to mile of distance between them.

Finally, Tanloff's light began to dim as the eclipse began. Both parties kept running as the light became dimmer as they played a game of chicken. If either stopped to set down their sanctuary runes, the other would be able to achieve its objective of either catching up or escaping. As things grew darker, the sparse vegetation of the foothills appeared more and more sinister. Dan glanced up. Only a sliver of Tanloff's reflected light was still visible. It was only a matter of minutes before night fell, and the sanctuary runes needed to be active.

Dan spared a look back at the pursuing party. He had trouble making out fine details, but they looked equally nervous.

"Fuck it," he muttered to himself, pursing his lips before stopping and opening up his travel pack. Hopefully, the other side would honor the truce and set up their own runes. After all, if everyone got eaten by unspeakable horrors, no one would win.

For a second, luck was with him. As soon as Nora's group saw him stop and open his backpack, they stopped as well. The frantic chase could continue when the planet itself was no longer an existential threat. Dan began removing the rune plaques and placing them one by one in a circle around himself. Then, his luck failed him. As he pulled out the second to last rune plaque, there was some difficulty. When he finally removed it from the plaque, he saw the problem and began swearing to himself. One of Nora's arrowheads was lodged in the rune, disrupting it and leaving it inoperable. That one arrow to his travel pack while he was climbing the valley wall had ruined everything.

He stood there, holding the wrecked rune and staring back at Nora's camp. Already, it glowed purple as their sanctuary runes flickered with eldritch energy. He would have no such protection. With one rune damaged, the entirety of his sanctuary runes were nothing more than fancy and expensive calligraphy.

Somehow, in her camp, Nora turned and met his eyes. Despite the distance, her skills let her see the broken rune in his hand. She clapped a hand over her mouth before shouting across the distance at him.

"I'm so sorry, Dan!" her voice took on an ethereal quality as night fell. "It was never supposed to be like this. You have to believe me, I only wanted the best for you!"

His breath caught in his throat. It might all be another ruse, an attempt to play on his sympathy one last time, but he doubted it. For once, she sounded sincere.

"You could have said something, Nora," he shouted back bitterly. "You could have let me run. I just wanted to be left alone!"

"We all want things we can't have." He could barely make

out her wistful smile in the distance before she turned away from him.

Dan sighed. He supposed he could take some comfort in the fact that she felt bad for him as he was ripped apart by some unspeakable monstrosity that crawled up from the bowels of the planet. He quietly put the runes back into the travel pack. Maybe, if he survived the night, he could repair them at some point. A big if.

Then, Tanloff's light disappeared from the horizon, and the howling started.

CHAPTER THIRTY

Nightfall Reprise

As soon as Dan's travelpack was full, he got moving. The stars were barely enough to light his way, but even if he made it through the night, he didn't want to be stuck, wounded and exhausted, a little more than a half mile from Nora and her party. If he was going to risk it all, he might as well open up some distance between the groups. At a minimum, he was going to keep jogging until he found a more defensible location. He had only stopped in the open scrubland of the foothills because he was counting on the runes to keep him safe. If he actually had to fight, Dan would vastly prefer to have a wall of some sort at his back. Getting flanked in the dark didn't exactly sound like his idea of fun.

"Four hours," he whispered to himself as the mournful howling chased him across the inky landscape. Night only lasted four hours, then things would return to normal.

Dan's thoughts paused for a second. Really, he only had Nora's word for it that traveling at night was impossible. Sure, he had seen claw marks on the walls outside of his cave, and *something* made blood-chilling howling noises every night, but there was no assurance that the night was completely impassable.

There were monsters everywhere outside of settlements, but most weren't a proper threat to a prepared adventuring party. For all he knew, the rumors about how dangerous the night was were nothing more than folk tales designed by the powers that be to keep citizens inside town walls where they could be controlled. Nora certainly hadn't shown herself trustworthy on other fronts; it wouldn't be too surprising if her fear of traveling alone at night was yet another excuse to control him.

At least, so he hoped. He'd seen and heard things at night, just beyond the purple barrier of the sanctuary stones. Nothing definite, but enough that dread and bile filled the back of his throat as he ran.

For a period, Dan jogged on through the night with only the stars to guide him. Since coming to Twilight, the constant murk had improved his night vision immeasurably. Still, it was hard to make things out just by starlight, especially while moving quickly. Dan glanced up to the stars above him for a brief second. Under any other circumstances, this would be beautiful. Nothing but the icy night air and a brilliant garland of lights without any smog or reflected city light to obscure them.

Then, a silent, dark shape passed overhead, blotting out the stars directly above him. The hair on the back of his neck stood up for a second as ice water poured down his spine. Whatever it was, it blocked out a lot of the night sky. That meant one of two things. It was huge, or it was far too close. Unwilling to risk it, Dan threw himself to the side, and was rewarded with a muffled thump as a huge, opaque shape landed where he had just stood.

With a squint against the darkness, Dan realized it was huge. This wasn't a fight that he could win in the dark, and apparently his assailant could either leap or fly. This was one problem he wouldn't be able to run away from. Apparently, Nora told him the truth at least once. Going out at night without sanctuary runes was incredibly dangerous. *Great.*

Dan fired a Flame Jet at it and was rewarded with an

unearthly screech. Finally, he got a good look at what he was fighting. It was a wolf. A gigantic winged wolf. About seven feet tall at the shoulders and almost fifteen feet in length, it put any predator from Earth that he could think of to shame in size alone. That didn't take into account the three-and-a-half-foot-long curved blades adorning the end of each paw. In short, it was officially bad news.

The good news was that its dark, matted fur was apparently flammable, and the Flame Jet had started its coat smoldering. Even better, it had gigantic eyes, about a foot in diameter and mostly pupil. The creature was clearly adapted to seeing in the dark, and the brief flash of light temporarily blinded and disorientated it. The bad news was that the attack had done minimal damage at best, and the thing was pissed.

It let out a blood-curdling screeching howl and swatted a giant, bladed paw at him. Dan fired another Flame Jet as he backpedaled, igniting a small portion of the fur on its paw. Given the paws' impossible speed and multiple foot-long claws, he wasn't inclined to try the thing out in any sort of test of strength. He had made that mistake before, and this time, he didn't have a party to rescue him when it inevitably threw him across the landscape. Worse, even if he traded injuries with this thing, it was only a half hour or so into the night. He wasn't sure if any of the night's denizens tracked by smell, but he wasn't keen on the idea of running around injured and covered in blood for another three hours and simply hoping that something else didn't come for him.

It opened its mouth and snarled at him. Dan gagged slightly as the stench of rotting meat wafted over him. Then it lunged at him. He activated Spatial Shield, but almost instantly a strange pressure laced the edge of the spell, then it gave way with a pop. His face broke into a betrayed look of surprise as the spell dissipated into a series of briefly shimmering streamers of blue mana. Time itself seemed to slow as they glimmered and faded into the night air, illuminating the blade-like rancid teeth as they closed in on him. Its jaws clamped down on his left arm as he frantically brought it up to protect his torso.

For a brief moment of clarity, he could feel each fang as they punched through the woven chain of his armor and into the bone of his shoulder as little more than abrupt pressure. Then the pain started. It felt like his bicep and shoulder were dipped in magma. His shoulder was clearly broken, the meat around it little more than hamburger. Almost without thinking, he immediately triggered a Lightning Stroke from his mangled arm down the monster's throat.

At least that triggered a reaction. Its eyes widened as, for the first time, Dan's spell landed on unprotected flesh rather than the matted fur and leather of its coat. It convulsed and spat him out.

Dan staggered back and fell down to one knee before trying to unsuccessfully lift his injured arm to unleash another spell. The tortured limb screamed in agony at him, but it didn't respond, hanging limp and lifeless at his side. Eyes watering, Dan dropped his sword and fired a Flame Jet at point blank range into the creature's eyes.

This time he earned another unearthly screech as the brief flash of heat seared the unprotected and light-sensitive retinas. It almost seemed to forget about him as it thrashed back and forth making unearthly sounds of pain. He tried to get to his feet, only to be floored once again by a wave of pain from his left shoulder.

Critical damage to <USER>'s left arm detected. <USER> is temporarily operating at -2 to both Body and Agility.

Infectious agents detected in <USER>'s left arm.

Please seek out calcium and protein so repairs can be effectuated. <USER> is directed to avoid strenuous activity until repairs to <USER>'s structure can be completed. Please note that failure to follow directions can void <USER>'s warranty.

Disabling pain connection to left arm.

Dan gasped in relief as the unhelpful System notifications ended, and he lost all feeling in his left arm. He was still bleeding out, but at least he could function. He stood, arm flopping at his side. The creature was still thrashing about, mindlessly preventing Dan from approaching. Even without meaning to, it could easily end him. Each swing of its head, paws, or wings was more than enough to break ribs and puncture internal organs, even through his chainmail. Whatever this thing was, it was both fast and strong. Really, no one should be fighting this with anything short of an armored personnel carrier, but here he was in the dark with it. It might not be paying attention to him now, but he had pissed it off. Running might work, but this was his best chance to actually finish it off.

A month ago, he would have run for sure. This was his chance to get out of a bad situation, even if running involved some risks. Now, he knew it was the fear talking, the part of himself that would put off until tomorrow a problem he should deal with today. Something inside told Dan that this creature wouldn't simply let this slight go. Whatever it was, it was clearly near the top of the food chain. Everything about it screamed apex predator toying with its prey: the way it attacked him casually, the way it settled for a bite to his arm when it could have ended the fight by going for his torso, and the fact that, once he injured it, it simply ignored him. Even with the injuries he had inflicted, it didn't consider him to be a true threat. Instead, he had pissed it off, and if he didn't take this chance, it would find him, and it would end him.

Plus, now that the pain in his arm was forgotten, Dan couldn't help but think of how much mana was in the creature. Anything that size moving that fast must be worth a lot. He clenched his right hand. He needed to get enough power to defeat Nora and her group. He needed enough power to operate freely on Twilight without fearing whoever employed her. He needed enough mana to go back to Earth and help it prepare for the coming storm. He... Dan shuddered as he remembered the warmth of mana flowing into him. He licked his lips. How much did it have? A minute's worth of mana flow? Two?

With a deep breath, he fired a Lightning Stroke, then another into it, then grabbed his sword. His head hurt from the sudden drop in his mana, but he charged anyway, taking advantage of the creature's sudden convulsions. He stabbed down with as much strength as he could muster with only his right arm into a patch of the monster's fur that smoldered from one of his bolts of lightning. The blade cut an inch deep before it caught on the thick leather of its hide.

He was so close. There would only be one chance at this. Dan triggered a Flame Jet from the hand still holding the sword's hilt and activated his bracers. Immediately, pain enveloped his hand as the sword's pommel heated up from the burst of flames. The fire followed the sword's blade and rushed into the monster's side. With the stench of charred flesh, either his or the monster's, Dan couldn't exactly tell, the blade punched through its hide.

It screamed again and jerked upward, pumping its wings as it tried to escape. Dan's shoulder dislocated as he refused to release his grip. Frankly, at this point, he wasn't sure if he could, given that his hand was a charred claw wrapped around the sword's hilt. Then, the sword ripped downward through the beast's stomach. Dan fell on his back, the wind knocked out of him. Despite the pain in his hand and back, he chuckled to himself. There was no way he was strong enough to cut through the monster's tough skin on his own. Only with the aid of its strength as it attempted to escape was he actually able to deal any sort of real damage.

Almost absently, he glanced up at the still-smoldering form of the creature as it struggled to fly away with the gaping hole in its stomach. As if in a dream, he raised his still-functioning arm and and triggered Lightning Stroke, brain fuzzing slightly as some of the backblast from trying to cast the spell while holding a sword flowed through him. Somehow, the bolt flew true and struck the creature. It convulsed, its wings missing a beat.

It tried to catch itself in the air, but it was too wounded. The monster plowed into the ground, a broken heap to match Dan himself. A low laughter filled his lungs. For almost a minute, he lay in the dark on his back, laughing maniacally as the adrenaline and endorphins faded. Then the mana hit him, and he was buffeted by walls of pink light. Pleasure tingled through his body as he lost track of time.

Whatever the hell that was, he had survived. It was bigger than him, stronger than him, and a whole hell of a lot more deadly than him, but he had survived.

Mana influx detected. Recalculating Spirit.

Spirit is now 13.

Lightning Stroke is now 3

"Thanks System," he croaked, still staring up into the night sky, hoping to not see the stars blot out once more. "If you could look into fixing my arms enough that I could stand up without blacking out, that would be pretty great."

"It figures," a masculine voice responded from the dark. "I come down here to save some poor soul trapped out at night, watch him bring down a stalker, and he's talking to himself. Still, after all of this time, I'll settle for someone crazy to talk to."

Dan tried to pull himself up into a defensive position, but even his right arm failed him. He hissed in agony and collapsed onto his back once more. A figure clad in a brown cloak walked in front of him and looked down at Dan with golden eyes.

"And a human at that," the man continued, quizzically. "I don't feel the chains of a class on you, boy, but with the abilities you've just displayed, there's no way that should be possible."

"Come on." The man waved a hand, and an unseen force wrapped around Dan's waist and pulled him to his feet. "Where there is one stalker, there will soon be three. The night has plenty of fight left in it, and we have a lot to talk about."

CHAPTER THIRTY-ONE

Helpless

Dan took a tottering step away from the hooded man and almost fell once again. The man sighed and waved his arm, revealing a glimpse of dull silver wrapped around the hand concealed in his robes. The invisible grip wrapped around Dan's waist tightened, preventing him from slouching over. It didn't hurt, and on a certain level, he appreciated the way it helped him take some pressure off of the injured portions of his body, but it served as a reminder that he wasn't escaping from this situation.

Even if he did, where would Dan go? The night was far from over, and with zero functional arms, barely able to stand, he wasn't in a position to fight off anything more menacing than a toddler. In the distance, something howled and was answered almost immediately by another howl, this one far closer. A shiver ran down his spine.

The hooded figure began to lose patience. "Human, comparing my power to yours is like comparing the stars in the sky to a handful of embers, but even I would prefer not to face an entire pack of stalkers enraged over losing one of their numbers. It is time to move as best your damaged body can carry you."

Another hand motion and flash of silver, and the invisible force nudged him. Not enough to knock him over or harm him, but enough to make the point. The man turned around and began walking away, trusting Dan to follow him. Dan glanced into the darkness behind him once before turning back to the mysterious departing form. He could follow the man or die. Maybe he would get an explanation once they got wherever the man was going, but all he had to look forward to out here was the lower intestines of some nightmare beast. With a sigh, he trudged after him.

After almost twenty minutes of travel with only a brief pause for his guide to fire some sort of spear of force into the darkness to drive off a monster that Dan hadn't even realized was tailing them, they reached the man's abode. It glowed silver in the darkness and resembled a wide, two-story mansion. He didn't recognize the frescos and artwork carved into the home's pillars, which was hardly a surprise, but Dan knew quality when he saw it. Whoever this man was, that artwork cost serious money.

Without a further word, Dan's rescuer strode into the building and turned to wait for him. He gritted his teeth against the dull ache that filled his entire body and followed. The System had shut off most of his damaged nerve endings, but that didn't stop the rest of his body from complaining about the general damage and blood loss. As soon as he stepped past the row of pillars that lined the outside of the building, the man put his hand onto one of them.

This time, a tungsten vambrace showed clearly on the man's wrist. Whoever he was, he could afford mythril, and he used the same sort of spellcasting aids that the elves did. A second later, a bubble of force appeared around the entire mansion, locking out the night. Whatever the man had done, it didn't have the acrid purple light of the sanctuary runes. Instead, it created a soap bubble of energy around them.

Finally, the man turned to Dan and motioned for him to follow as he stepped into the mansion itself. Somehow, the interior was even more opulent than the outside. Almost every surface was made of marble with frescos of semi-precious gems depicting various battles adorning the atrium. Silently, Dan followed the man until they reached what looked like a cross between a kitchen and a pantry. An oven stood on one wall of the room while the other was lined with steel bins. Inside the bins were the frost-covered limbs of various monsters. Somehow, despite standing only fifteen feet away from the stack of frozen remains, Dan didn't even feel a hint of cold.

"I apologize for the haste and the state of my larder," the man said absently, walking over to a cabinet and searching through various vials of liquid. "Normally, I would greet a guest with a feast and entertainment, but for the past couple years, I have been living far from civilization. The only food I can offer is from the bodies of the monsters that patrol these mountains, and I haven't even seen a servant or musician in the past year. I suppose you will have to accept my limited hospitality."

The man found the vial he was looking for and turned around to face Dan. "Here, I'm going to pour a minor healing potion in your mouth. I don't have a source to get more, so I hate to waste these, but you look unable to feed and care for yourself. I would rather waste a potion than deal with that bother, so congratulations."

The man approached and tipped the vial back, pouring the thick sludge down Dan's throat. It tasted bad. Like, rotting garbage bad. Then, his throat grew warm and his mana reacted to whatever he had drunk.

Unknown substance detected. Analyzing.

Substance is rich in nutrients and mana. No other foreign contaminants detected.

<USER>'s body is attempting to repair itself. Assisting.

Tingling shot up and down his right arm and his back. He suspected that the same process was taking place in his savaged left arm, but the System still hadn't turned those nerves back on. Given the occasional glimpses he had gotten of the deep wounds in the arm and shoulder, Dan was okay with that. At least the System had stopped the bleeding, but even with proper resources, it was going to take a couple days for the industrious nanites to get him back up and running.

"Now." The figure pulled back his hood, revealing his fine features, gold eyes, and pointed ears. "My name is Daeson Amberell, and I am very curious about you, Mister...?"

"Thrush," Dan supplied. "Daniel Thrush."

HIs mind was racing. Amberell wasn't just a name in the Tellask Empire. It was a major noble house. Even a random elf was a threat, but an Amberell? A slip up here had the potential to doom Earth.

In all likelihood, the elves were already on their way to check up on the missing voidship, but providing definitive proof that Earth could defend itself against a casual attack was not in the game plan. One thing was clear from the Tellask historical records, that sort of evidence had a tendency to wound the Empire's pride, and that had a tendency to make the follow-up attack anything but casual.

"Mr. Thrush." Dacson smilcd. He had the sharp, needle-like teeth of a consummate carnivore. "Only a handful of humans can interact with mana directly to the point that they can actually cast spells, and all of those are old men. House Amberell created the class system for its human thralls out of a paternal sense of obligation. Worlds such as Twilight are dangerous, and we were hardly going to waste resources staying here and keeping humanity safe.

"That said," Daeson continued, "not all of us agreed with the system's restrictions. True, a class lets a human use their mana without actually knowing how to cast spells, but ultimately, it restricts your race. Without being able to actu-ally cast spells, your species will never be anything other than cannon fodder and common labor for the Elves. Some of my race find that not only acceptable but desirable. Personally, I must confess that, before the Orakh incursions,

I didn't really give the plight of your species much thought."

Daeson shrugged, "You live such short lives. I would prefer those lives not to be wretched existences, but to a certain extent, all beings suffer. Then the Orakh came, and the Empire started scooping entire tributary kingdoms up and forcing them to the front lines. Even Elven shock troops with millennia of training struggled to hold back the Orakh Hordes. How could we expect human warriors barely thirty years of age, to actually hold them back? You didn't. It was massacre after massacre while the Elven elite used your sacrifices to buy time."

"I didn't think an Elf would be so straightforward about it." Dan smiled wryly as he replied. "I think most of us expect to get a lecture about the nobility of our sacrifice."

"Your sacrifice would be noble if it wasn't a pointless waste," Daeson answered with a snort. "The classes let humans gain power in a short period of time, but they are designed to stop you from ever being a threat to the stability of the Tellask Empire. True, they let you become stronger or move faster, and sometimes they can replicate actual magic in a limited fashion, but a proper spellcaster of the same rank outclasses them in every possible way. My kind insist that the classes are the limit of human power, and even the laws of the Empire itself ensure that individuals with class tattoos will never receive the same rights as an actual magi. You, though..."

Daeson stepped around Dan, glancing him up and down. "You are what I was looking for when I came to this godforsaken planet. You cast spells like a child, inefficient and limited, but you cast them. You've ranked up without the help of a class. You are a diamond in the rough with the potential to actually prove the worth of your species. With you, we can change things. Prove to my rivals that humanity should be given succor and trained into a force to fight the Orakh, rather than spent cheaply to buy time."

Dan shifted uncomfortably. Daeson's gaze was that of a hungry man looking at a feast. He couldn't help but notice that

Daeson had only let him get a handful of words in during the entirety of the monologue. For all of his compliments and attempts to assure Dan that he was important, to the elf, he was an interesting lab specimen and nothing more.

"So, Mr. Thrush." Daeson strode back into his vision, smiling once again. "What do you say to the proposition that you become my disciple? I'll whip you into proper shape in ten to twenty years, then we can prove to the others at the academy that, as always, I was right and they were wrong."

CHAPTER THIRTY-TWO

Tutelage

"Sure," Dan said to Daeson, feeling a little sick to his stomach as he forced a smile onto his face. Even if he were uninjured, he doubted that he would be able to get away from the elf. Plus, he wasn't completely wrong. Dan really did need some training and polishing. Everything he had accomplished so far had been by the seat of his pants. Even without looking at his presently-destroyed body, he was very lucky to have made it as far as he had. A misstep or two at any point would've ended with him in an unmarked grave or enslaved.

Of course, Dan reflected to himself, enslaved was still on the table. Daeson didn't strike him as the worst sort, but he recognized his type from graduate school. Professors and researchers who only cared about their research. Anything that didn't advance them towards their hypotheses, sometimes including facts that disproved that hypothesis, would simply be discarded.

Right now, Daeson saw him as a valuable piece of research and nothing more. So long as Dan continued to learn and "prove" that humans had the potential to fight alongside elves against the Orakh, he was liable to be treated well. Luckily, with the help of the System, it shouldn't be all that difficult. Of course, there was no real need to let the elf know about the System. In fact, Dan had a sneaking suspicion that informing Daeson about the System would lead to the elf trying to cut him open and remove it.

"Great," Daeson smiled and motioned for Dan to follow him once again. "The healing potion will need some time to work, and I'm sure you would like to get some rest after your little excursion. Let me lead you to your room."

He followed Daeson as the elf led him to a fairly large room with a bed and a dresser. Gingerly, Dan laid down a beaten-up travel pack as the elf excused himself from the room. He sighed as he looked at the pack. He had only been on Twilight for two to three weeks and already he needed a replacement. Even his armor was slashed up pretty badly by the stalker and stiff with Dan's blood.

Thankfully, his right hand had repaired itself enough that Dan was able to slowly strip himself one-handed and wash his upper body in a silver basin of water that he assumed was provided for that purpose. Dan was tired enough that he really didn't care if there was some other cultural or ritualistic signifi-cance to the water. Once he was somewhat clean, albeit still smelling fairly awful from the sweaty, long-distance chase, Dan slowly lowered himself into the bed. Almost immediately, he fell asleep.

The next morning, he stood up and was rewarded with a sharp burst of pain from his left arm. He winced and inspected the wound in the silver-framed mirror sitting next to the basin. As far as he could tell, the System had handled the infection, but large gashes still remained. It was clear that they were heal-ing. He couldn't see bone any longer, but even with the help of the nanites and potion, it would still be at least a couple days. He held up his right hand and sighed in relief. A night had been all it took to shed the burnt and charred skin. It looked out of place and overly pink compared to the rest of his moderate tan, but he was able to make a fist without pain, so he would take that as a win.

Dan stepped out into the corridor and cocked his head quizzically. He really had no idea how to find Daeson. He barely even had an idea as to how to get back to the kitchen, let alone the front door of the mansion. A second later, his confusion was cut short by the elf walking up the hallway.

Now that Dan actually had a proper chance to look at Daeson, he saw that the elf was about an inch taller than him, making him six foot one. Daeson had finely-boned features and gold hair to complement his golden eyes. Everything about his appearance oozed boyish charm, balance, and symmetry. In short, if it wasn't for the sharp, predatory teeth that he was currently smiling at Dan with, he looked like he could make a living in a boy band.

"Daniel!" the elf beamed at him. "I'm glad you are up and about. I've taken the liberty of putting alarms in your room to alert me every time you awaken. Humans require so much more sleep than elves, so this way I can continue working when you go to bed, then meet up with you when you rise without losing any unnecessary time."

"Thank you for the consideration," Dan replied, internally wincing. Already the elf was tracking his every move. Hardly surprising, but definitely not an ideal turn of events.

Daeson glanced down at Dan's more or less healed right hand. "I am glad to see you so intact. "It means we are already prepared to begin my research today. No, our research." The elf smiled, his sharp teeth making him look like a particularly self-satisfied alligator.

"By research, do you mean training?" Dan questioned, trailing off as he glanced uncertainly at Daeson.

"Of course, Daniel!" Daeson nodded, once again waving for him to follow and turning without checking for a response. "The fools at the academy barely recognize xenology as a valid field. What little grant money gets doled out all goes right to the Lythtal selective breeding programs.

"It's true that everyone can see the value in a seven-foot-tall wolf-man that can stand toe-to-toe with an Orakh warrior, but we are still centuries away from that research bearing any fruit. Plus, the Lythtal can't even use mana. At best, we will be able to put them in heavy armor and use them as infantry, but they don't have the power to turn the course of the war on their own. Frankly, all of the research I've seen shows that breeding them to be larger and stronger makes them more aggressive. When I tried to tell my colleagues that the last thing the Empire needs is a slave revolt, they all shouted me down. Whispered behind my back that I was simply jealous because their research was bearing fruit."

Dan stopped abruptly as Daeson halted in front of a room. The elf whirled around, his pupils slightly dilated as he stared intently at Dan with mania-filled eyes.

Daeson spoke quickly, barely registering his existence. "Daniel, you are the human development test case we need to focus the Empire's energies on. More importantly, you can save my name. They stripped me of library access and lecturing privileges. If I didn't have tenure, I would have been removed from the faculty entirely. Shallow, jealous politicians, all of them. If I am to put them in their place, it cannot be through half measures."

"I really don't understand what you're talking about," Dan responded uncertainly.

"If humans are going to make an impact on the war with the Orakh," Daeson replied, finally focusing on Dan, "you will need to fight at least as well as an elven youth. Unfortunately, that means we are going to need to make up hundreds of years of magical and martial training in a few scant decades. The only way we can do that is to increase the intensity of your training. You will be risking your life frequently, and your only breaks will be sleep. If you can survive with your mind intact, I am sure that I can carve you into something… truly special."

"That doesn't sound that much different than what I've been doing on my own to date." Dan shrugged. "How do we get started?"

"Behind this door is my gymnasium," Daeson answered

with a toothy smile. "Today, you demonstrate what you can do, and I will begin your magical training. Given your rather severe injuries, I won't expect you to run the obstacle course today, but starting tomorrow, you will be expected to make a single run in under three and a third minutes before we can begin magic training. After all, your body is the shell that holds your magical potential. If the shell grows thin and weak, it will shatter during your next rank up and create a terrible mess. Given that the servants have left, I really don't want to have to clean up a botched rank up on my own. Burnt viscera was never my thing."

Dan sighed and followed Daeson into the room. It was huge, two stories tall and thirty by sixty feet wide. Almost half of the room was occupied by a track that ran through a series of rotating wooden beams. Periodically, there were gaps where an individual would have to jump across a clearing or use their upper body to navigate a series of pegs or bars to cross the gap. Clearly, this was the obstacle course. Dan could already feel those wooden poles slamming into him. He sighed. Daeson wasn't lying; this wasn't going to be pleasant.

The elf led him over to another corner of the gymnasium. There, a mannequin stood alone in front of a wall made of a dark matte material. The ground and wall were scored with scratches and small divots. Daeson clapped his hand down on Dan's good shoulder.

"Now," the elf filled the complete silence of the gymnasium. "I've already seen that you have a thunder and fire affinity. Are there any other affinities I need to know about?"

"I also have a spatial, force, metal, and gravity affinity," Dan replied. If he was going to rely on Daeson for training, he might as well get training in everything. "I haven't really developed the metal and force affinities, but they're there."

"Good, good!" Daeson shouted, manic glee in his eyes. "Six affinities! If we can pull this off, I'll wipe the smug smiles off their faces for good. You have the makings of an arch magi; it's just a matter of putting in some effort."

Dan sighed as Daeson cackled to himself and looked past him. The elf had saved his life, and he certainly was capable, but Dan couldn't help but feel that living out in Twilight's wastes on his own for this long couldn't be emotionally healthy. Regardless, the die was cast, and Dan was stuck with an incredibly powerful being of questionable mental stability for the foreseeable future.

CHAPTER THIRTY-THREE

Training Montage

The next two months of Dan's life quickly fell into a routine. He would sleep for about five hours, then wake up and run the obstacle course until he met whatever arbitrary time Daeson thought was appropriate.

Occasionally, the elf would change the course, lengthening the jumps, increasing the speed of the poles or forcing him to climb walls were common additions. Then, after the physical warmup, Dan would practice spellcasting with Daeson until he ran out of mana, at which point he would do cardio until his mana recovered.

After about ten hours, Daeson and him would share another meal, then he would practice for another five hours before going to bed. At first, shifting from a forty-hour day back to a twenty-hour "day" was a bit disorienting, but in those months, Dan never left the mansion, and the mana lighting synced to the new schedule.

At first, he worried about Nora, and what the woman was doing back in Morganville, whether she would keep combing the desolate landscape of Twilight for him, or if he had simply been left for dead, but Daeson's practice schedule didn't leave much time for introspection. If Dan wasn't exercising physically or recovering from one of his brutal workouts, the elf would force him to study spellcraft.

Spellcasting practice took two different forms. Most days, Daeson would sit with Dan and explain the theory behind spell-casting for a period before observing him casting his spells. Dan knew he shouldn't be surprised at the sophistication of the Tellask Empire's magical theory and education. After all the Empire had been starfaring before Earth even invented agricul-ture, but it was still jarring each time someone who had never even seen indoor plumbing, let alone an airplane, rapped him across the knuckles for being ignorant. After he got over his shock, Dan quickly realized Daeson was right. It was partially how the System worked, but to date, all of his spells were instinctive. He would imagine an effect and hope that his expe-rience would make things work out.

Daeson taught him how to cast spells more efficiently by having him slow down and shape mana in a much more mindful and purposeful fashion. Each time he would force Dan to isolate and focus on a specific aspect of the spell. At first, it was the amperage of Lightning Stroke and Shocking Fist. Then, Daeson made him analyze the specific electrical pulses that made up those spells to see if he could speed or slow the rate at which the spell operated.

Later, he made him focus on the specific makeup of the flammable gases generated in Flame Jet. Ultimately, Daeson made Dan realize that, although the spell was flashy and fun, it would never amount to much more. The speed that the gases needed to move at as they passed through the ignition flame to avoid burning the caster was simply too fast to expose a target for any real period of time. It was hot and bright, but the heat ended too quickly to do much against anything but eyes or other sensitive targets. The speed of the blast even made it difficult to start moderately flammable targets on fire.

Luckily, Daeson had a solution. Almost all high-level magic involved the fusion of multiple types of mana with certain utility fields, such as force and space. Daeson was overjoyed that Dan had a force affinity, as the elf specialized in force magic and immediately made him start working on the affinity. Even though Daeson couldn't use fire magic himself, the elf was able to explain how force magic could be used to contain a ball of burning gas and plasma.

This led to a new spell, Fireball, which allowed Dan to launch a grapefruit-sized ball, which would explode at a specific range, toward a target. As an added effect, Fireball allowed him to keep the flammable gases under extreme pressure, giving the explosion a concussive effect that tended to knock Daeson's target mannequin off of its feet. For some reason, despite Dan's best efforts to name the spell 'Firebolt' the System kept returning an error, stating "Director's Override: spell meets definition of spell 'Fireball'. <USER> must name spell 'Fireball'." It didn't really make much sense to Dan, but it seemed like a very Henry Ibis thing to do, so he just let the old man pick the spell's name from afar.

In order to learn Fireball, Dan also learned his first force spell, which quickly became very useful. He dubbed it "Force Bubble" and it consisted of a melon-sized ball of energy that deflected most attacks. It was nowhere near as good as a full spell shield, but being able to quickly make a small shield was much better than nothing. Already, he was able to use it to soften the blows of the wooden poles on the obstacle course.

At first, Dan was afraid that Daeson would get angry at him for cheating, but the elf just grunted and pointed out that his magic was a part of him. So long as Dan didn't damage the course, he was free to use whatever spells he wanted. After that epiphany, the combination of Force Bubble and Gravitational Easing made running the course much easier, which only led to Daeson immediately increasing the difficulty once more.

In fact, Daeson actively mocked him for not using his spells earlier. According to the elf, simply being able to cast a spell was only half of the struggle. The real challenge was being able to incorporate magic into combat or stressful situations.

Unfortunately, that only led to Daeson upping the difficulty of Dan's daily routine by drinking wine and blasting him with low-level spells while he tried to improve his times on the obstacle course.

The other form of spellcasting practice wasn't nearly as useful. On the days when Daeson imbibed too much wine, the elf would simply tell him to "practice his affinities," then make some comment about how "proper affinities are the foundation of a mage" before retiring to his corner to nurse a hangover and mutter about how his colleagues had wronged him. Having attended public school, Dan was very familiar with unscheduled movie days when a teacher or professor would show up to class ten minutes late with a five o'clock shadow and smelling like a distillery. He simply didn't comment and engaged in his quiet self-study time without bothering the elf.

After about sixty-five of Twilight's longer days, Daeson approached Dan smelling like the bottom of a brandy bottle. The elf's eyes were lidded and his gait had more than a couple stumbles interspersed in it. Dan had been halfway through a normal force affinity self study session, and he glanced up nervously at the elf. Daeson swayed slightly before bringing an amphora of red liquid to his mouth and taking another pull.

"Daniel," he slurred, his sharp teeth stained red with an expensive vintage. "There's something queer about you."

Dan yelped in pain as he lost control of the mana flow to his force attunement stone, causing a wave of force to expand uncontrollably and knock him on his back. Brushing himself off, he sat up and glanced back at the elf.

"I don't know what you're talking about, Daeson." He shrugged and stammered nervously. "I'm just trying to do what you tell me."

"That's the thing." Daeson leaned up against a nearby wall. "Some of what I'm teaching you, you learn too fast. Your insights into that fire spell you've made were genius-level work. Other things, you're so far behind. You don't have a class, which is good, but you don't have any sort of runescript on your body.

No matter how good you are at casting spells, it's not going to matter when you are that weak and slow."

"Runescript?" Dan asked, cocking his head. "Like the stuff that's on magic weapons and armor?"

Daeson threw up his hands, sloshing some of the wine onto the shoulder of his tunic. "There you go again! Everyone should know what runescript does, even if they don't have the power to activate it. It's like a class tattoo that you can run mana into to give yourself physical boosts. It's an awful hassle to find someone who can inscribe the stuff, as it has to be custom made for the recipient. But without it, the sapient races are just too slow and weak to fight half of the galaxy's denizens. Except the Orakh. They can fight just fine with their bastardized half-magic."

"None of the humans I've talked to used runescript." Dan frowned.

"Of course not," Daeson shook his head, his tone as if he were chiding a child. "It takes years to learn how to inscribe runescript, and it takes years to properly attune it to someone else's body. If you don't do it right, you increase the strength or speed of one specific part of the person, which often leads to messy results. Arms swinging swords so fast they go flying off, hearts pumping so much blood that it results in massive hemorrhaging, skin so thick that the person can't move their limbs, that sort of thing."

"Sometimes, Daniel," Daeson stopped and took another pull. "Sometimes I wonder where a genius like you came from. You have more potential than any noble scion I've ever met, but every time I talk to you, its like you were raised under a rock."

Dan grew very still as Daeson strayed onto a dangerous line of questioning.

The drunken elf shrugged messily. "Still, it's probably not something I actually want to know the answer to. You're probably from some rival house's private laboratory, broken free and trying to make something of himself. If I ask too many questions, I'll probably find out that you aren't a baseline human, and it would invalidate this experiment, and we can't have that."

The elf drunkenly chuckled as he gave Dan an overexaggerated wink. Dan exhaled in a whoosh of relief.

"Good news though, Daniel." Daeson reached clumsily into a pouch he kept on his hip and fished around for a good two minutes before he pulled out a slightly-glowing needle. "You're in the presence of a runecrafter of some notoriety. We can fix you up and get rid of all of those human imperfections. I'll make you strong enough, fast enough, and tough enough to fight an Orakh. Then, once we prove to those idiots at the Academy that I'm right, we'll put you out to stud. Even if you aren't a standard human, we just need to get your genes out there, and we can make use of them."

"What do you mean by notoriety?" Dan eyed the needle warily. "Usually people say that they're famous rather than notorious when they're bragging. Also, by way of clarification, what do you mean by putting me out to stud? I thought the point was to train me for combat?"

"Notorious." Daeson rolled his eyes as he took a halting step towards Dan. "It's just like being famous, except you melted a couple younglings. It was their fault, really; they kept squirming when I tried to craft the runes into them. If they sat still, it never would have been an issue, but no. They had to go and tarnish my reputation like that. Damn selfish wretches."

"And what about this 'stud' thing?" Dan's eyes were now locked on the needle.

The elf gave him a leering smile. "Well, Daniel, you're simply too exceptional to waste on the front lines. We need your genes to breed the next level of human warriors. Once I prove my point to the Chancellor, we'll find a nice place for you to retire, and I'll get you a steady stream of human women. Soon, you'll have thousands of sons and daughters for us to train for the war effort. With a couple potions of virility, you'll have contributed more to the war effort than any human ever. You'll be a positive hero of the Empire."

CHAPTER THIRTY-FOUR

Gilded Cage

"Is it possible to teach me runescript?" Dan didn't take his gaze off of Daeson's wobbly hand that loosely held the needle. "Either that, or we do whatever you need to do when you're actually sober?"

"Pfah," Daeson sloshed the amphora of wine while he laughed. "You think this is drunk? You should have seen the faculty luncheons. Servants as far as the eye can see and tables weighted down with delicacies. I would drink the finest of wines from sundown until noon the next day, all while those fools would pamper and compliment me. Even better than the other faculty were the graduate students."

Daeson's voice rose in pitch to mimic a woman's timbre. "Professor Amberell, you simply must tell us more about your theories on the role of steam vent placement in dwarven architecture and its reflection in cultural norms! Perhaps we can come to your office for a more personal lesson."

The elf stopped speaking to take another drink from one of his omnipresent amphoras of wine. When he glanced up at Dan, tears brightened the corner of his golden eyes. Dan couldn't help but notice that Daeson still held the runic tattoo needle.

"I wrote a book on that, you know." Daeson's voice was quieter, subdued. "It was the talk of high society. The various houses were inviting me to speak at their gatherings. As much money as I could want, but more than that, I had prestige. People of power bent their ears to listen to me, and I had my choice of any number of pretty young things." His voice took on a bitter note. "Then the Orakh came. Suddenly, trade deals with the dwarves didn't matter as much, and all anyone could talk about was the war. Then, I suggested that we use humans on the front lines, and it all came tumbling down."

Daeson paused to take another drink, only to find the wine vessel empty. He sat down next to where Dan remained frozen in a meditative pose and wrapped the arm that held the rune-scripting needle around Dan's shoulders. The elf positively stank of wine. This clearly wasn't his first bottle of the evening.

"You don't know what it's like, Daniel." Daeson was almost whispering now. "To go from a respected academic, the top authority in a lucrative but suitably-obscure field to an absolute laughingstock. I lost everything. Friends stopped returning correspondences, students stopped signing up for my classes. Worst of all, I stopped getting appointed to prestigious committees. I went from chairing the tenure committee to non-academic misconduct."

"At that point, you might as well bar me from any committee whatsoever." The elf spat on the ground, the reddish saliva standing out against the dull gray of the gymnasium floor. "I went from deciding who had tenure to settling disputes between custodians and students. Just like the class system, it was all a calculated insult. Take my proposal of training humans to be elites and pervert it by forcing them to walk a path that capped their potential early. Just steal my idea and bastardize it."

"Daeson,. are you all right?" Dan asked slowly. "It sounds to me like I want runescripting, but I don't think you're in a good spot emotionally right now. Do you need me to get you a glass of water and help you to your room?"

"No," Daeson shook his head, fixing his dull eyes on Dan. "We have to do it now. The Academy forbids runescripting humans; they fear what you might become. We have to do it while I have the courage to act. That's why I drank the wine. It'd be a waste of a 681 Balsanno if we don't, and that would be a true crime. Even if my hands aren't the most steady and the script comes out imperfect, that is a risk that we will have to take."

"Is there any rule against teaching runescripting to humans?" Dan replied while gingerly removing the elf's arm from his shoulders. "I would much rather spend some time learning how to do it, rather than risk being reduced to goop."

Daeson stared at him blankly for a couple seconds before smiling. The wine had stained his teeth and lips completely red, giving his usually predatory smile a positively cannibalistic look.

"Good," the elf hiccuped while talking. "That's a capital idea, Daniel. When they passed the rules, the regulatory body figured that no one would bother to waste time on educating a human on runescripting. It would be like lecturing a donkey on the intricacies of a string quartet. That said, you have a knack for learning things you shouldn't be able to learn."

"Ha!" Dan was knocked forward by Daeson's exuberant slap on his back. "This is even better. I can imagine their faces when I show up with a genuine runescripting and magic-using human. Then they'll have to admit there is something to my theories, and I can finally end this farce of a research expedition on this awful planet."

The elf stood on wobbly legs and staggered towards the exit of the gymnasium, stopping at the door. Briefly, Daeson leaned against the doorframe before turning to Dan.

"Daniel," Daeson was slurring now, barely able to get the words out. "I need to rest briefly. I feel a bit indisposed at the moment. When I wake up, we will add runescripting to your lessons. Teaching a human runescripting, a positively inspired idea on my part!"

Daeson staggered from the room, and Dan exhaled. Standing up, he worked the stiffness out of his back and neck. Daeson insisted that he practice his affinities while in the lotus position. Something about it aligning his mana with the energy of the world. It all sounded like mumbo jumbo to him.

That was the problem in learning magical theory from someone like Daeson. The Empire had a twenty-thousand-year legacy in magical research, but at the same time, they hadn't figured out steam power, internal combustion, or electricity. As far as he could tell, the scientific method wasn't widely recognized in the Tellask Empire. Instead, their academics would see something, make up an explanation for it, then defend that explanation to the point of bloodshed. Over the millenia, they had managed to figure out a good number of things that worked, simply via trial and error, but Dan couldn't help but doubt much of the information he had been given.

Still, with the help of the System, two months of Daeson's teachings had revealed more about the nature of magic than he had figured out in a year on his own. He still wasn't sure how he had survived as long as he had without realizing that his body had a phantom circulatory system that allowed the spheres of energy to pump mana through his body. Not only did it let his body store even more mana in the "veins" as the mana spheres served as the heart pushing the mana, but it made mana present throughout most of his body.

This meant two important things. First, he could more easily and quickly cast spells from extremities other than his hands. No longer did he suffer from a half-second delay as mana transferred from his spheres to wherever he was casting from. Second, when he ranked up, it would be much easier to simply draw the free mana in his body into the phantom channels. Apparently, the inability to visualize these channels and circulate mana was a large part of the why many unawakened worlds never discovered magic. Even if someone had mana injected into their system, without a guide to move that magic into the channels, it would ravage their bodies, poisoning and destroying them.

Dan shrugged as he walked over to a nearby towel and wiped off the sweat and wine staining his shirt. Despite how useful studying with Daeson was, the elf was getting worse. He was willing to brave a little longer to learn runescripting, but neither he nor Earth had the time for him to wait around forever studying at the feet of some reclusive master. Dan suspected that presenting him to this Academy would be a disaster for him.

Maybe Daeson would win some acclaim, but Dan doubted that the Tellask Empire would actually be thrilled to discover that humans could rival elves for dominance. In graduate school, he'd been involved in enough faculty meetings involving old men screaming at each other over who only partially-credited whom in an academic paper from ten years ago to know that infighting could get vicious. The odds that a rival of Daeson's would simply have him killed were astronomical.

No, he needed to learn what he could from the elf before he had a complete emotional breakdown, then get out. The real problem was figuring out how to do that. Over the past two months, Dan had seen hints of the elf's power, and he wasn't thrilled by his prospects. Daeson was much more limited in his attunements, only using ice, force, and from time to time, light. That said, he was a master using force, and the amount of mana at his disposal was frankly ridiculous. Dan suspected that he was at least rank ten or eleven.

As Dan walked to his bedroom, ending practice for the day, he shook his head. Daeson wasn't someone he could beat in a stand-up fight. Maybe he could flee the elf, but he suspected that it wouldn't end well. He strongly suspected that Daeson could sense him through walls, and Dan didn't really want to test the distance on whatever mana sense the insane archmage was using.

Dan laid down and looked at the ceiling. It was all a

problem for tomorrow. Eventually, he would have to escape the insane elf, but for now he wasn't in immediate danger, and he was still learning. Maybe he'd make his break for it the next time the elf tried to drunkenly enroll him in an experiment that would risk his life. Dan shuddered. Hopefully before that.

The next morning, Dan ate breakfast alone, ran the obstacle course, then settled down to wait at the gymnasium for Daeson to make his appearance. Finally, the elf worked off enough of his hangover to show up, eyes bloodshot and barely open. With a wave of his hand, Daeson dimmed the gymnasium lights and set a sketchbook down in front of Dan. Dan opened the book and flipped through a series of intricate, flowing drawings.

"Don't let anyone know I let you look at that," Daeson whispered, closing his eyes. "That's the primer the Amberell runescripting masters taught me from. The first step is to memorize the form of the rune, and that is where this book comes into play. The second..."

Daeson hissed and stopped speaking for a moment before drinking from a glass of water. "As I was saying, the second is to memorize the order and boldness of the lines. If you draw a single stroke out of order or too dark it will imbalance the entire rune, and it could lead to instability. If you're using enough mana, that instability could be explosive. As such, all runescripting practice will take place in the spell-testing bunker." Daeson motioned toward the blackened area of the gymnasium with the mannequin.

"How will I be learning the order?" Dan asked, still paging through the book. "I can memorize each of the runes, but each one looks like it has something like sixty to three hundred strokes."

"Don't interrupt me," Daeson muttered impatiently. "That said, you're right. Even simple runes require one hundred pen strokes to finish. You will simply have to watch me craft the rune and try your best to copy my pen. It will be slow and arduous, but that is simply the way of things."

"Now, where was I?" Daeson muttered to himself. "Right,

ink. The third step is creating the ink used to draw the rune. It needs to be something mana conductive, preferably gold or mythril. Silver will do in a pinch, but I don't want to hear about an apprentice of mine dirtying their pen with copper. Now, each rune requires you to mix certain proportions of monster essence with the powdered mana-conductive base. This usually means monster blood, but it can sometimes mean the extract of certain organs or ground up claws.

"Usually there is a symbolic connection between the monster used and the effect of the rune. A speed rune will often require a fast or agile monster, while a strength rune will call for brutish and powerful monster. Unfortunately, monster essence fades fairly quickly unless it's stored properly, and the runes must usually be crafted within a day of the ink being created. As for the proportions, you will learn them the same way you learn the order of the strokes: by watching me craft the runes until you can make the ink yourself. Each master has their own formulas, and you must not share the ink formulas I teach with anyone. They are secrets of House Amberell, and if I were you, I would avoid drawing their ire upon your head.

"The final step is the easiest but the most dangerous," Daeson continued while removing a small gold bar and two vials of blood. "The runescripter must invest mana of the correct affinity into the rune. Too little and the ink will clump, and the inscription will fall off after a day or two. Too much, and the ink will dry up, destroying the rune. Far too much, and the rune will simply blow up in your face. I would prefer if you don't do that anywhere near me.

Daeson laid down a silver plate and pulled out his metallic pen. "Now, I will demonstrate with a simple rune for pain reduction as I need its effects dearly. The ink for this rune is simple: one part powdered gold, one part blood of the verdant bog snake, famous for its regeneration, and one part the ichor of an undead." The elf's hands blurred as he performed dozens of intricate actions while his voice droned on.

Eventually, a flash of purple light illuminated the silver

plate, and Daeson let out a sigh before placing it on his fore-head. Almost immediately, the tension left his shoulders and a smile tugged at the corner of his lips.

Skill learned: Runecrafting

Rune learned: Pain Reduction

Dan smiled back at Daeson.

CHAPTER THIRTY-FIVE

Downtime

"That isn't how you craft the shock absorption rune," Daeson called out from the doorway, causing Dan to jump, wrecking the intricate whorls and lines of the inscription he'd been trying to carve into a piece of scrap silver.

"Are you sure?" Dan asked with a sigh, putting down the now-useless piece of metal. "I can swear I got the angles of the interior scripting just right."

"You did," Daeson agreed, striding into the room, a bottle of wine and two glasses in hand. "Your hand slipped when you were crafting the exterior connectors. The rune was fine, but if you tried to run any mana through the input, the entire thing would short out and probably burn down half of the lab."

"That sounds painful," Dan remarked, carefully pushing the possibly-explosive rune away from himself. "Thanks for the heads up."

Daeson nodded, filling both glasses with wine and setting one in front of Dan. He looked back at the elf in confusion.

"It's my birthday, and I'm feeling sentimental," the elf huffed, taking a sip of the ruby vintage. "Now drink up; that wine is older and more valuable than you."

Dan raised the glass to his mouth, frantically wondering what game Daeson was playing. The nanites would handle any poison, but he wouldn't know that. Dan would be fine, but the real question was how Daeson would react when his ploy didn't work.

The wine spilled across Dan's tongue, not quite as sweet and a little drier than he'd like, but overall a lot better than what he usually bought from the local corner store.

"Taste that!" Daeson swirled his glass before bringing it to his lips once more. "That's a hint of capprola root. It really brings out the body in the red snow grapes."

"We both know I only understood about every fourth word of that." Dan shrugged before taking another nip of the drink. "It tastes good, for what it's worth."

"Good?" Daeson snorted. "There was a time when virgins would strip naked just to sniff the cork of an Amberell Ice Red. It took us almost two thousand years of magic and selective breeding to develop a strain of sub-arctic grapes to take advantage of the unique mineral melange of Astooth. After that, it was another thousand years to perfect the mix of grape skin to juice, to ensure the right amount of tannins. Literally, civilizations have risen and fallen in the time it took to develop that glass of wine in your hands, and all you can say is that it's good?"

The elf took another drink of the wine, closing his eyes to enjoy the dark red liquid as it coated his tongue. "You're a barbarian, Daniel." He shook his head, a half smile on his face as he basked in the drink's flavor bouquet.

"What can I say?" Dan shrugged. "It's good."

"That bottle is priceless." Daeson shook his head, pouring himself another glass. "Astooth has fallen to the Orakh some two hundred years ago, their advance as relentless as it is boorish."

"I thought the Tellask were beating the Orakh?" Dan frowned, setting his wineglass on the table.

"Oh, we win most of the battles." Daeson waved a hand

flippantly. "Grand stories of heroism, each warrior standing tall atop a small mountain of green bodies. Very heroic and noble."

Daeson gestured at Dan with his glass. "What they don't say is that the Orakh just need biological material, water, and time to grow an army. If you kill five hundred of the things and leave a planet, they just eat their dead and give birth to another four hundred and fifty. You can wear them out eventually; it just takes decades of warfare and hundreds of thousands of deaths, and for what?"

He sloshed the cup, almost spilling it, but recovering just in time with the help of his finely-tuned reflexes to catch the precious liquid in his glass once more.

"By the time we recapture the planet, it will be denuded." Daeson set the glass down, a mournful expression on his face. "Stripped bare of all life in order to power the Orakh war machine. We stop their incursions, but without support from the rest of the Empire, we'll never be able to take back a single world overrun by the Orakh. Like poor Ashtooth. Three thousand years of careful work turned into a couple hundred ravening grunts."

"What about here?" Dan asked. "Do you think we're safe on Twilight? I know we're close to the front, but no one really talks about it."

"Fuck no." Daeson chuckled, then blinked, a half smile rising on his face. "Pardon me, the wine must be hitting me harder than I thought. But to answer your question, no. We are not safe from the Orakh here. The planet has no Amberell support, let alone units from the Tellask Empire. By the void, it isn't even unified. A single Orakh incursion craft would be enough to take over the entire place in six months."

"Why don't you leave?" Dan asked, curious despite himself.

"Stubbornness?" The elf replied, swirling his wine in its glass before taking another sip. "I suppose I could return to the Empire, but I'm not welcome anywhere I'd want to be. That just leaves the rest of the frontier.

"It'd be one uncivilized hellhole or another." Daeson sighed, shrugging at Dan. "At least on Twilight, the entire planet is run by warring city states. They don't even have their act together enough to realize I'm here. It certainly has cut down on requests for assistance." He chuckled, forcing a wry smile from Dan. "But there really aren't any other options."

Daeson took another sip of the wine. "My great nephew once removed, Paltai, was on a scouting mission in this area. I was sort of hoping he'd find some frontier world worth hiding out on while I completed my research. He even reported back that he'd found a planet teeming with humans that he was going to try and conquer."

Dan stiffened, the name triggering a brief memory of the invasion of Earth. He forced out a breath, hoping that Daeson was drunk enough to overcome his normally keen senses.

"The damn fool kid never sent a follow up message." The elf set his empty glass back down on the table, looking at it mournfully before stealing a glance at his still half-full bottle. "He probably bit off more than he could chew and got himself killed. I guess we'll have to wait until the follow up subjugation expedition sets out to find out."

"Subjugation?" Dan asked, his earlier attempts at nonchalance shattering with a crack of his voice. "Does that mean what I think it does?"

"A voidship setting up a teleportation gate to bring in Imperial and Amberell troops until we overrun whatever killed Paltai?" Daeson inquired rhetorically.

"Why would they bother with some sort of punitive expedition when the Orakh could arrive at any moment?" Dan leaned back in his chair, the half-finished glass of wine in front of him forgotten.

"The planet could be a threat," Daeson recorked the wine bottle with an audible sigh before continuing. "There could be an Orakh infestation, just waiting to build its population up enough to build and crew an incursion ship. If all else fails, it's a stain on the Empire's honor. A world full of savages resisting the Empire doesn't sit well with the Imperial Court."

"Will the expedition begin soon?" Dan asked hesitantly.

"Who knows." The elf leaned unsteadily forward, snagging the cup of wine from Dan and pulling it back to his side of the table. "The Empire moves when it's good and ready. It's possible that the ships have already been dispatched, but it's more likely that they are still in their planning stages. It could be years to a decade before they find the planet Paltai was visiting. Happy birthday to me." Daeson winked at Dan before downing the wine from the stolen cup.

"Happy birthday to you," Dan agreed, struggling to contain the rush of worry filling him. He needed to return to Earth, and soon.

"That's what I like about humans." Daeson smiled, placing the two empty wine glasses next to each other. "You're like dogs, but you can talk back. It really helps cut down on the loneliness of being trapped in a barren wasteland."

"Thanks?" Dan replied, struggling to find a suitable answer.

"No, thank you." Daeson stood up, grabbing the glasses and the bottle as he walked to the room's exit. "Keep up the good work, Daniel, and thank you for being a sport about my spots of mopiness."

Dan watched him go, a mixed expression on his face. Despite himself, and as awful his elven jailor could be, he felt some pride at Daeson's words. Of course, that didn't change the fact that he needed to escape as soon as possible. Now, more than ever, Earth needed him.

CHAPTER THIRTY-SIX

Runescripting Apprentice

The next six months of Dan's time with Daeson passed with a frustrating regularity. He continued his normal routine, but with the addition of runescripting practice. Once or twice a week, Daeson would demonstrate a new rune for Dan, which he would usually learn immediately with the help of the System.

Actually drawing the runes, on the other hand, was a bit more of an issue. Even with a perfect memory of Daeson's work, it was still incredibly difficult for Dan to exactly replicate the order and width of the pen strokes needed to craft each rune. Between rune demonstrations, Dan would practice his craftsmanship on scraps of silver.

Daeson informed Dan that these scraps of silver were known as spellshards, runescripted enchantments embedded in surfaces too weak to contain the power of the effect they generated. After one use, the runescript would overheat and melt off the surface it was embedded on. Although permanent enchantments could be inscribed in silver, the amount of mana that an enchantment could carry was directly related to the rarity and cost of the materials used in inscribing it. Copper would self-destruct after the simplest of cantrips was cast through it. Silver could bear minor permanent enchantments or more serious spellshards. Gold and mythril could both handle almost the same power of enchantment, but clearly mythril was much more suited to combat.

Apparently, low level magi often used spellshards or something like them to empower their spell arsenals, given how much time and effort went into actually learning and memorizing a spell. A spellshard might only be used once, but it could let a magi create any effect that they had the right affinity for. As Dan learned during another wine-fueled lesson from Daeson, spellshards were also the reason why the class system used by the rest of humans on Twilight was so limiting. Ultimately, classes taught humans to rely on skills that were runescripted into them. The minute they tried to run too much mana through a skill, it would melt like a spellshard, almost-certainly killing the caster.

Now, this wouldn't be as big of a concern if the classes were well-crafted, but most of them were "hack jobs at best" per Daeson's drunken mutterings. Runescripting on a human body could either be a custom job or mass produced. A custom set of runescripting embedded in a person's body would generally grow with them, using the body's natural mana conductivity to supplement the ink. The downside was that it took a tremendous amount of time and skill to make a custom set.

The crafter needed constant feedback from the person that they were inscribing the runescript on, either verbally or through a spell monitoring their body. The process had a tendency to overtax the system of its recipients, and without constant medical care, it was easy to accidentally murder the person you were supposed to be enchanting.

Given the time and pain involved, most who could afford the spells were put into a magical stasis and monitored by servants. Even those fanatical about self-perfection and training weren't exactly keen to spend months to years of agony slowly adapting to the enchantments.

Even worse, usually, the runes needed to be adjusted after

the recipient ranked up the first and second time, to ensure that they were growing properly with the user. The average custom inscription took almost two years to inscribe and fine tune enough where the user could rely upon it. Mass-produced rune inscriptions like armor and classes had an upper limit defined by the quality of the materials used and the skill of the crafter.

"Wait!" Dan cut Daeson short as the elf lectured him while sipping from a bottle of wine. "Are you telling me that every adventurer on Twilight functionally has a time bomb inscribed onto their skin?"

"More or less." Daeson shrugged, glancing at the inscription Dan had made for a force amplification rune. "The powers that be wanted to make humans strong enough to fight the Orakh in short order, but they also didn't want them petitioning for full citizenship in the Empire. The Empire generally recruits anyone who is of high enough rank to actually risk overloading their classes, and when it happens, it usually only happens on the front line. The human soldiers and marines have some idea of what is going on, but the Empire hushes it up, so they really don't have anything more than rumors."

"That's horrible, though!" Dan frowned, setting the scrap of silver down in front of him. "All those people fighting and scraping to make something of themselves, and the only light at the end of the tunnel is their own self-immolation."

"It is terribly inefficient," Daeson agreed. "The Empire really needs to take the long view. Classes make humans powerful quickly, but this isn't a war that will be over in a decade. Already, we have been fighting the Orakh for almost four hundred years. Cannon fodder has its place, and I'm sure most human warriors won't amount to much more than that, but an allowance needs to be made for the truly talented. Take you, for example, Mr. Thrush. You're truly a credit to your race. None of the usual bestial instincts and lack of cleanliness that I've come to expect from humans. I see no reason why you shouldn't be allowed to join the Empire as a probationary citizen."

"Isn't there some way that you could let the humans know what they're signing up for when they take a class?" Dan asked the elf. "I'm sure plenty would still take a limited path to power like a class, but it just doesn't seem right to keep them completely uninformed."

"Of course, you would be a bleeding heart." Daeson huffed before taking another pull of wine. "What do you want us to do next? Let them know how bad the war is going? That despite us sacrificing entire worlds' worth of humans, the Orakh are still coming? No, there's a reason why more experienced heads are in charge of these things. You'd just cause a panic. The tributary worlds would just focus on their own survival and stop contributing to the Empire. Their eventual sacrifice would be meaningless."

Dan paused, fuzzy memories of his master's degree in electrical engineering bubbling to the surface. While runescripting wasn't exactly the same as the logic gates he'd studied early in his program, it was similar enough. He chewed on his lip briefly, wracking his brain for a solution to the crude class design.

"Couldn't there at least be some work done into stabilizing the classes?" Dan asked plaintively. "Put a hard cap into how much power someone could channel through the class to prevent them from overloading it. That way you can keep the class system without it being a death sentence. It's as simple as putting a fuse into each skill."

"What's a fuse?" Daeson questioned fuzzily.

"A portion of the rune that could safely overload and fizzle without destroying the rest of the rune," Dan supplied excitedly. "Probably in the stroke after the initial mana aperture stroke, you could use ink of a slightly worse quality and set it up to shunt off excess energy if that portion of the rune failed. Any time someone used too much power, only a small part of the rune would overload. They'd need to get the fuse tattooed on themselves again after blowing it out, but they would survive, and they could continue fighting. It lets us increase human survivability and combat potential at limited extra cost to the Tellask Empire. Everyone wins."

"Why would I want to make classes safer?" Daeson frowned as he took another pull from the wine bottle. "Classes were Jareth's infernal invention. If we improve them, that's tantamount to admitting that Jareth was right."

"Who cares if Jareth is right!" Dan continued. "You'll be a hero for helping the Empire and saving lives. You'll be back at the Academy in no time."

"Who cares if Jareth is right!?" Suddenly, Daeson was screaming, his wine bottle shattering next to Dan. "Jareth is the one who twisted society against me, just because of his petty jealousies. He didn't care that I had found the best way to use the Empire's resources in the oncoming war, no! Instead, he discredited me through libel and rumors! He told everyone that I wanted to teach humans magic because I was too close to them. Do you know what he said?"

Daeson grabbed Dan's collar and lifted him up with a surprising amount of strength before leaning forward and whispering in his ear. "He said I *fornicated* with them. That I tarnished my blood by laying with your kind. No! I will not be doing anything that makes Jareth look good. He owes me a debt of honor, and I'm not going to help him salvage his reputation when how poorly the human warriors are doing on the front is revealed. It can be his turn to fall from grace."

"But what about all of the people that will die?" Dan knew better than to ask the unstable elf, but he couldn't stop himself. "Surely there is something we can do for them?"

"Can do?" Daeson questioned rhetorically with a snort. "There's much I can do. Will do? Now, that is another question. This planet has done nothing but serve as a prison for me. If you think I'm going to help its inhabitants out of the goodness of my heart, I am sorry to disappoint you. That said, Daniel... unlike them, you have potential. You could turn this entire paradigm on its head and give your people a route forward."

Daeson pursed his lips, a brief flash of anger clouding his

golden eyes. "Perhaps I've been too easy on you. Your questions show that you've grown weak and soft. Twice a week, from now on, I will be sending you out into the wastes to bring back meat. As soon as we finish training you in the basics of runecrafting, you will inscript yourself, and you will spend a night outside."

Dan swallowed any further complaints. Daeson was drinking again, and that meant that Dan shouldn't push him. The elf was usually erratic, prone to fits of anger and flights of fancy. When he drank, however, Daeson became mean. He frequently drunkenly set dangerous or painful tasks for Dan to accomplish, often with very little purpose. Dan strongly suspected that, when the elf was feeling morose, he simply just wanted to watch Dan suffer. Arguing with him would only lead to more meritless and painful punishments.

The next morning, Dan journeyed out onto the wastes, a sullen and hungover Daeson in tow. Daeson provided no help whatsoever, instead grumbling the entire time about how slow Dan moved as they traversed the mountainside looking for prey. Eventually, they found the beast Dan was looking for, an armadillo-like monster that disguised itself as a boulder and whose blood was useful in gravity-based rune inscriptions. Dan quickly finished it off with a series of long-range Fireballs and Lightning Strokes before the ungainly creature could get close to him. Then, Daeson made Dan carry the beast's corpse back on his own after making some sort of statement about how "heavy lifting builds character."

Two months proceeded in this manner, with Dan hunting and killing for food, to accumulate mana, and to practice his spell and runes. Eventually, he gained enough mana to rank up, and for the first time, he experienced how much easier it was to clear his body of ambient mana once he started using the mana channels that Daeson had taught him about. As much as the elf's increased drinking and worsening sour moods troubled Dan, he really couldn't question that working with Daeson had been incredibly useful to him.

Finally, shortly after he reached rank 3, Daeson approached

him to inform him that it was time for him to runescript himself. Dan took a deep breath and followed the elf to a laboratory designed for such endeavors. He glanced at the tables covered in inscribing pens, whole orders of magnitude more ornate than anything Daeson had let him experiment with. Next to them was a cabinet filled with powdered silver, gold, and mythril as well as a wide assortment of monster blood and extracts.

"This is it, Daniel," Daeson stated with a level of formality that the mad elf usually couldn't muster. "Think of this as the most important exam you have ever taken. If you succeed in inscribing yourself and surviving a night, you will have proved me right, and I will be petitioning to make you a citizen of the Empire as part of my campaign to save my legacy. I never thought it would only take you ten months to reach this point, but you are the most talented individual I have ever encountered in my millennia as a professor."

Daeson shrugged. "Of course, if you fail, I will have wasted almost a year on fruitlessly training you. I will almost certainly murder you if you survive your failed inscription, but you probably won't survive such a failure, so... no pressure."

Dan took a second to review his status:

<USER> Status
Rank 3

Body 6
Agility 7
Mind 7
Perception 6
Spirit 22

Skills
Swords 7, Brawling 3, Archery 2, Runecrafting 4

Affinity

Space 11, Lightning 10, Fire 8, Gravity 5, Force 5

Runes+

Spells
Shocking Fist 8, Spark Field 2, Lightning Stroke 7, Spatial Shield 6,
Flame Jet 4, Gravitational Easing 5, Fireball 6, Force Bubble 5

He avoided expanding the list of known runes, content to simply let the plus sign hover next to it in his status. Over the last eight months, he had learned everything in the basic primer given to him by Daeson as well as a good number more. He already knew which runes he planned on chaining together into his personal inscription; it was just a matter of execution.

Dan closed the menu and picked up a pen. He was as ready as he was ever going to be. Now, it was just a matter of putting those hard months of training to the test.

CHAPTER THIRTY-SEVEN

Runeforged

Dan stepped in front of the room's mirror, an oval of polished silver contained within a gilt frame. Slowly, he removed his shirt and stared into the mirror while planning the runescript in his mind. Two years of constant exercise had done wonders for him. No one would be mistaking him for a professional athlete, but he finally had abs and noticeable muscle definition. Maybe, when he got back to Earth, he could update his profile on dating apps to something other than a formless winter jacket.

"Quit eyefucking yourself, Daniel," Daeson helpfully interjected. "There'll be plenty of time to take a gander at the goods once you finish the inscriptions. Or, you'll die and leave me with the final indignity of cleaning you off the laboratory's walls. Either or."

Dan chuckled nervously as he removed several small ingots of gold and monster blood before placing them next to a mortar and pestle. Daeson hovered over his shoulder the entire time, his keen elven vision taking in every one of Dan's movements. As Dan reached to pick up the pestle, Daeson put his hand on Dan's wrist to stop him.

"Mr. Thrush," the elf began, "crafting the initial runescript on yourself is a matter of utmost importance, so I've opened my stores fully to you. Still, before you waste materials that took me a century to gather, I would like you to go over your lessons with regard to runescripting flesh. We wouldn't want you to forget a step in the excitement of the moment and melt yourself along with a pile of valuable reagents now, would we?"

"The first and most important runes are the mana accumulation runes," Dan recited, his voice taking on an almost sing-song quality. "Usually drawn over the chest or the source of a being's mana, the accumulation runes allow the individual to control the amount and type of mana that flows into their script.

"Next after the accumulation runes are the regulation runes. Usually wreathing the accumulation runes, these runes serve the twofold purpose of balancing the accumulation runes while also giving the user an outlet for their mana. The regulation runes contain the connections on which other runes are inscribed, as well as the activation mechanism for those runes. Any mistake in the accumulation and regulation runes is almost certainly fatal. Later runes can be added or modified, but a failure there usually only results in severe injury and can be rectified with later scripting."

"Well it's good to know that you paid attention to my lessons, Daniel," Daeson handed him the pestle. "Now tell me, how is the quality of an inscription judged?"

"By the quality of the accumulation and regulation runes," Dan replied, beginning to powder the gold with the ichor from some deep sea beast to make the foundation for his crafting ink. "Notably, by the amount and types of mana that the accumulation rune can safely process as well as the number of open slots on the regulation rune where new runes can be added on."

"Good enough for me." Daeson shrugged, stepping back. "Remember, the scripting only needs to be good enough to handle a rank or two worth of mana and feed a strength and coordination rune. That's what you'll need to survive the night. but beyond that, it's not like you will be fighting. You are only a proof of concept and genetics; there's no need for you to risk yourself on something terribly complicated only to have it flare up and destroy you. Just keep it simple. Every extra pen stroke is another risk."

Dan didn't reply, the System already overlaying the predesigned runes onto his torso in the mirror. He might not be the world's first choice as an action hero or a magician, but he hadn't spent those years getting a master's degree in electrical engineering completely in vain, no matter what his mother might say. Individual runes were difficult and complicated to inscribe, but their true beauty was when they were scripted into chains. Runes that sensed the condition of the user's body could be conjoined via logic gates with other runes, allowing the inscription to tailor itself to the user. Without some sort of feed-back, the user would end up solely enhancing one muscle beyond the tolerance of their bones and tendons, causing their body to rip apart.

The runes weren't quite assembly code, but they were near enough for Dan to feel fairly comfortable with them. Of course, the System helped immeasurably. It allowed him to summon a model of himself and sketch the various runes on it. After the first month of practice, it even upgraded its understanding of the runes to the point that he could use the System to simulate the usage of the runes themselves.

Even the most complex runescripting Daeson had shown him paled in comparison to simple computer programs. For all of the Tellask Empire's splendor and glory, apparently no one had bothered to clue them in object-oriented programming. It took a little bit of doing, as the runes weren't exactly designed to run iterative loops or have a goto function, but between the System and Dan, he had managed to create what was theoreti-cally an accumulation rune that could handle seventeen ranks worth of mana of any type he had trained with, as well as a regulation rune that could safely supply twelve subsidiary runes. In theory.

Of course, it helped that he wouldn't have to repeat large

chunks of the runescripting ad nauseum. So much of traditional Elven runescripting was devoted to inefficient and drawn-out runes without much by way of safety mechanisms. Dan still couldn't figure out why the elves refused to use either a fuse or some sort of vent that would let off excess mana that would otherwise cause his runes to burn out and melt through his torso, but he decided to include both. It just seemed prudent.

Finally, the ink ground and mixed, Dan dipped his pen into it. Instantly, the first stroke of the runes superimposed on his reflection glowed green with a small orange mark above it notating the depth and width of the stroke. He touched the blade of the pen to his skin and hissed. The cut itself stung, but the mixture of monster blood, ichor, and powdered gold burned. He made the next incision. Somehow, the burning in both strokes increased infinitesimally. He made a third mark. Each time he completed a stroke, another glowed green in his vision.

Minute-by-minute for an hour, he kept marking his chest. By the time he was a quarter of the way done with the accumulation scripting, he realized he was in trouble. His eyes were bleary from their constant focus, his breath coming in short gasps, and his chest an incomprehensible mess of blood and ink. Still, he continued. The burning grew worse with each painstaking stroke, but he didn't dare stop. Each series of scripted runes must be completed as part of one continuous project. Stopping now would lead to the rune activating uncompleted and instantly killing him.

Gritting his teeth, Dan kept carving into his flesh. He was able to maintain his focus for another hour, but then he made his first mistake. Luckily, it was minor, a stroke slightly too shallow to accept the full load of mana that the rune was designed for. Without alteration, the rune would be limited to rank six or lower mana only. An ordinary runecrafter probably wouldn't have even noticed until years later when the user destroyed themselves by channeling too much mana. Dan, on the other hand, had the System. Instantly, the stroke he had completed flashed red and a series of yellow follow up strokes appeared in his vision. Each added another ten to twenty minutes onto the completion of the final runes, but they would allow the scripting to avoid the weakened rune and still operate at full capacity without overloading.

Over the next three hours, he screwed up two more times, the System saving him and recommending solutions on the fly each time. Finally, after five hours of crafting, he stopped for a break. His entire chest was a mess of blood and sweat that Dan was loath to clean lest he accidentally remove some of the ink from his runescripting. After a brief snack and a fair amount of hydration to replenish his lost blood, Dan began work on the regulation runes.

He was still in a mind-numbing amount of pain, something Daeson warned him would continue until he ran mana through his runes to activate them. Unfortunately, Daeson had forgotten to mention this little tidbit until Dan was almost crushed beneath the burning and itching pain of the runes. Maybe then, Dan would have thought to make the accumulation runes stable on their own without relying on the regulation runes, but as things stood, he would need to finish both in one sitting.

A sense of urgency settled over Dan as he made the first incision of the regulation inscription. He wasn't sure if he was more lightheaded from the loss of blood or the continuous pain, but it was definitely beginning to impede his focus, a major problem while engaging in such intricate work. For a second, he debated having the System shut off his pain receptors before rejecting the option as too risky. Really, his only option on that front would be to stop all tactile sensations, which would make judging the depth and the width of his strokes almost impossible. Holy hell did it burn, though. His entire body felt like it was buried in a pit of scorching sand. Every one of his motions was slow, weighed down by the weight of the scalding pain.

Quickly, he sank into a haze. His surroundings faded into a pain-wracked mist as the laboratory and Daeson's idle, caustic comments simply slipped from his attention. Each moment became nothing more than focusing on the glowing incision in the reflection. Dan became so consumed by his work that, before long, he lost all sense of self. His entire being was nothing but a glowing green light followed by a brief spike of pain as he cut through his flesh.

Then, abruptly, there was no more green light. Dan stared dumbly at the pen in his hand, covered in his own dried blood. The System blinked some notification or another at him, but he couldn't focus on anything but the burn. Daeson was saying something. Dan really didn't care. More than anything, he needed to run mana through runes to end the pain. It took him almost a full second to gather together enough of his conscious-ness to activate one of the balls of mana in his chest.

His body was doused in cool water as the pain stopped. Suddenly, his chest started glowing as the mana ran through each inscription, one-by-one. Concentric circles of tiny, intri-cately-crafted eldritch symbols burned with pink fire that quickly evaporated the blood from his skin.

Dan dropped to his knees, his mind white with pain. He could feel all of it. Every loop, swirl, cross, and curl of a rune. So long as mana ran through it, he could feel it. That fire wasn't a trick of the light or some sort of mystical illusion. Mana produced heat as a byproduct. A lot of heat. From somewhere, he could smell burning flesh as it seared his body. Dan knew that the runes could handle it, but it wasn't much comfort as he clenched his fists until his fingernails bit through the skin of his palms.

Then, the pain faded. It still echoed as Dan forced himself back to his feet and inspected his reflection once again. This time, he had a clear view of the tattoos as they glowed faintly pink. In response to his thoughts, the lattice of inscriptions that he had prepared for this day superimposed themselves on his body and glowed green with a few sporadic spots of warning amber.

"Let me take a look at you." Daeson woke Dan out of his stupor by turning him about by his shoulder. "Very good, Mr.

Thrush. I knew you had some talent in runecrafting, but this seems to be on another level. Almost a master's work. I'm very excited to see what enhancements you can add on to this. It seems robust enough to handle some fairly powerful modifications. With a little luck, you might be able to survive the night, after all."

CHAPTER THIRTY-EIGHT

Stalker in the Night

Daeson gave Dan a short period for rest and recovery, but all too soon Dan woke up to a hand on his shoulder as Daeson dragged him out of bed. Blearily, he returned to the inscription laboratory to continue his work. This time, the project was much more manageable. Rather than create the permanent runes that would be the foundation of his personal enhancements, Dan only had to inscribe the enchantments themselves. Unfortunately, manageable did not mean easy. Even if it would be possible to remove or overwrite the runes later, it was still painstaking work, with each rune taking almost two hours to craft, even with the aid of the System. Without the System, it flat out would have been impossible at Dan's level of skill.

The more he reflected on his initial crafting, the more Dan realized how lucky he had gotten. Apparently, most young elves being inscribed were put into magical comas for months to years while master runecrafters painstakingly crafted each glyph and double checked to ensure that there would be no negative reaction. Daeson flat out admitted that the only reason he let Dan inscribe himself was because he was "bored" and found the idea of the human "crippling himself in his hubris" rather funny. Only the greatest of elven heroes had successfully inscribed themselves, and even then, only in epic poems that had more an aura of myth than history about them.

Even with the System, there had been a thousand moments when the pain caused his pen to waver, and he stood a mere moment from absolute ruin. The worst of it was that he was in such a haze the entire time, he had never realized how bad his situation was. Without the System patiently correcting his errors even as they compounded, there was almost no chance whatsoever that he would have survived activating the runes.

This time, Dan only selected three runes to slot into the regulation inscriptions. The first was a defensive series of runes that worked by layering force mana just above his skin to cushion blows. The second was a utility rune that utilized both space and lightning mana to increase his reflexes and speed. The third was an offensive rune that used force and gravity mana to increase his brute strength. None of the runes were terribly simple, the runes to thin and layer the planes of force on the first runescript as well as the mana combination apertures on the second and third runescripts were particularly challenging. Still, given the more limited scope, the crafting went much smoother. After only about ten hours, with occasional multi-hour breaks to rest between runes, Dan finished the remaining scripting without any other major incident.

Feeling like a butterfly pinned in a book underneath Daeson's gaze, Dan clenched his jaw and ran mana through all three runes, one-by-one. For a couple seconds, Dan felt warmth and some tingling, but it was nowhere near as bad as his initial activation. With all of the runes operating at their basic level, each consumed about as much mana as a sphere produced. Dan relaxed slightly as his senses confirmed his and the System's predictions regarding the runes' mana draw. A large part of the reason he had stopped at three enhancement runes was simply a question of load management. His current rank couldn't sustainably support more runes, and he didn't want to find himself in a situation where he had to turn off runes mid-combat due to low mana.

That said, each of the three inscriptions also had a high output mode where they would operate at about 150% efficiency for 250% the cost in mana. It was hardly efficient, but Dan didn't want to be in a situation where a little bit of extra strength, speed, or durability would have been the factor that saved his life. Over the past couple of nights, he had already begun working on versions of the same runes with an overdrive 200% setting, but for the moment, he suspected that shunting that much power through his current body would probably rip it apart. An interesting idea for the future, but not something that would help him through his immediate problems.

Experimentally, Dan hopped into the air to try out his new muscles, only to bounce off of the metal ceiling with a dull thud. After having confirmed, at the cost of his dignity, that both the strength and armor runes worked, Dan stood up, rubbing the slightly sore spot on his head.

"Well, it worked, that's for certain." Daeson was laughing his ass off at Dan, his lips already stained red from the large mug of mulled wine in his hand. "Wait until Jareth gets a chance to see you. A full-fledged neophyte human battle mage with just a little under a year's worth of training. With a thousand of your children, I could change the face of this war, Daniel. Never mind the Orakh, the dwarves and the Myrruk Republic would fall before the Tellask as well. I would own a world and a House of my own."

"I trained on my own for a bit over a year before I met you." Dan shrugged. His head still hurt from smashing it into the roof of the room, but it was more like having a ball bounce off of your head while playing sports than the hammer blow it should have been.

"Psh," Daeson blew a raspberry and took another sip of the mulled wine. "That was rudderless training. Without a master or a direction. In the grand scheme of things, it means next to nothing. Rather than be a contrarian, let me enjoy a victory drink in peace. Go run the obstacle course a couple times to get used to your new body. We need you ready once night falls."

Dan sighed as he left Daeson behind in the laboratory. The elf was right; increased strength and speed hardly meant anything if he wasn't familiar with his new limits to actually use them. Overswinging in a fight could be just as dangerous as being too slow to avoid a blade or claw. Still, even though he should expect it by now, having Daeson completely ignore his achievements as anything but a reflection of the elf's teaching stung.

Both of them were just using each other, but over the last six months Daeson had transformed from a competent but distant tutor to a drunken braggart. Dan wasn't even sure that elven mental health worked anything like human psychology, but if he had to put money on a diagnosis, he would peg Daeson as a narcissist. Dan had lived with enough of those to know that the elf was a toxic factor in his life.

Worse, Daeson had lately been more and more willing to take sloppy risks with Dan's life. It really was only a matter of time before the elf got drunk reminiscing about the good old days and did something to him that even the System couldn't cure. Now that his runescript was active, maybe it was time to start looking for a way out. Not tonight, Daeson would be watching too closely, but sometime soon, an opportunity would present itself.

The obstacle course was a good idea. It helped acclimate Dan to his new strength and speed, and it helped him focus. After dealing with a round of agonizing "pranks" that had almost cost his life, only to be shoved into a dire combat situation for no real reason, Dan needed some way to blow off steam. He really only could suck up to Daeson for so long. One of these days, he would mouth off to the elf, and all hell would break loose.

After ten consecutive runs, each faster than the last, Dan stopped and stretched before running through a few basic sword forms. Finally, satisfied with his new mana-enhanced strength, Dan activated his status.

<USER> Status
Rank 3

Body 6(8)
Agility 7 (9)
Mind 7
Perception 6
Spirit 22

Skills
Swords 7, Brawling 3, Archery 2, Runecrafting 5

Affinity
Space 11, Lightning 10, Fire 8, Gravity 5, Force 5

Enhancements
Armor Rune V, Strength Rune +2, Agility Rune +2

Runes+

Spells
Shocking Fist 8, Spark Field 2, Lightning Stroke 7, Spatial Shield 6, Flame Jet 4, Gravitational Easing 5, Fireball 6, Force Bubble 5

Roughly a 20% increase to Body and Agility and a level up to Runecrafting. That all seemed about right. Even the Armor Rune was pretty straightforward. It consisted of five paper-thin sheets of force folded on top of each other, so it was named Armor Rune V. At least this time there wasn't some sort of forceful override from afar forcing him to name his abilities according to Henry Ibis' eclectic tastes.

Dan put on his torn chainmail and sharpened his sword on a nearby whetstone before settling into a meditative pose to focus himself for the upcoming night. He wasn't terribly sure why Daeson insisted that he meditate, but it was an effective way to pass the time. Finally, Daeson strode into the room and Dan stood up wordlessly. The elf was drunk as hell, and he already had another bottle in his hand. Maybe he wouldn't even need to escape the mansion. Unless Daeson had a potion of liver repair on hand, cirrhosis would do a better job of taking down the elven archmage than Dan ever would.

Dan stepped outside the mansion and glanced back at Daeson where he stood just inside the ornate runescripted pillars that provided the building with its defenses. The elf leered briefly at him before winking and activating the shield. With that, Dan exhaled and marched into the increasing gloom as the way back closed behind him.

The first twenty minutes passed without incident, outside of the eerie howling from what Dan suspected were the stalkers. He wracked his memory for the threats posed by a night outside. Between Nora's stories, Daeson's books, and his own brutal experience, he had a fairly decent picture of what he would be facing.

Stalkers, like the giant winged wolf he'd encountered earlier, would patrol the sky while gaunts prowled noiselessly, attacking the will and emotions of anyone unfortunate enough to be outside sanctuary. One could be fifty paces away, and he simply wouldn't know until it struck.

At least behemoths were straightforward. It was hard to confuse a couple tons of rampaging gorilla monster for anything else. If one were nearby, it would make its presence known via an immediate and straightforward attack.

Then, Dan heard the sound he was expecting. The soft, almost ghostly beat of muffled wings overhead. He closed his eyes and counted the beats as they grew infinitesimally louder until suddenly they stopped.

That meant that it was gliding, and gliding probably meant swooping. Dan kept his eyes closed and launched a fireball into the air above him, set to detonate at fifteen feet. A half second later, heat washed over him, singing his unruly hair before it dissipated. Dan's eyes flashed open as an unearthly screech filled the night. Quickly, he stepped to the side. The stalker, stunned by the sudden flash of light, slammed, still smoldering, into the ground where he had stood. Before it could recover, Dan stepped forward and activated the high-output mode on this strength rune. The same blade that had struggled to even wound a stalker almost a year ago cut the beast's right wing off in a single blow.

Dan danced back as the creature thrashed to and fro, its severed wing twitching spasmodically on the hard ground. Dan deactivated his armor and strength runes to conserve mana. Smiling slightly in the darkness, he raised his left hand and fired a Lightning Stroke from it into the stalker, causing the creature to twitch and spasm briefly. Then, he alternated to fire and detonated a fireball about six inches in front of it, placing his left arm in front of his head to shield his vision from the burst of light.

A second later, he was sprinting forward. His first blow took the beast in its wolflike head. Even with his enhanced strength, it wasn't enough to finish it, but the blow clearly concussed the monster, causing it to bonelessly drop to the ground for a split second. That moment was all it took for Dan to shove his sword through the side of the creature's neck and pull downward, severing its windpipe and arteries.

He stepped backward, almost casually letting a claw swing past his face. The stalker gasped fruitlessly as it tried in vain to breathe. Another claw thrust at Dan, but this time the blow was slow and clumsy as the stalker weakened. A third and final blow didn't even make it within feet of him as he stood still, watching the monster bleed out.

A smile split across his face. This had been his bogeyman. The creature that almost ripped him apart and forced him to run to Daeson with two crippled arms and barely a breath left in his body. Now? It was almost easy. Even before the mana rush hit him, Dan began laughing exultantly into the night air.

After two years of striving and practicing, it was finally paying off. He was more than some random bravo with a sword and a bad sense of hygiene telling strangers that he was an adventurer. He was *powerful*.

Then the stalker's last breath rattled out and the mana hit. It was delicious. Heat, ambrosia, and lust all rolled into one. Clouds of cotton-candy-flavored euphoria sprouted from the air around him. He had forgotten how much mana the first stalker had. They put all of the other monsters he had fought to shame.

As he stood, arms akimbo and his face to the night sky, beaming in the midst of the mana high, a chorus of howls erupted around him. Somehow, the other stalkers had sensed the death of their brother, and they were coming for him. This time, Dan didn't fear them. This time, they were just mana begging to be harvested.

CHAPTER THIRTY-NINE

The Third Night

The stalkers came for Dan, but even without using spells, his increased speed, strength, and durability were enough for him to fight them on equal footing. At least one-on-one they were. Three of the great flying wolves surrounded him, nipping and slashing at Dan while he used his new agility and Spatial Shield to keep himself whole.

Periodically, one of the stalkers moved a little too slow and he scored their muzzles or paws with his sword, but even through his mana-fueled courage, Dan knew that he was losing.

Eventually, he would slip up, and one of the stalkers would catch him. The armor rune might protect him from the worst of it, but even getting knocked to the ground would almost certainly lead to his death. Surrounded like he was, speed and strength on their own just weren't the solution. Internally, Dan shrugged. Maybe the mana rush was making him overly bold, but he was finally a wizard, and he'd be damned if he wasn't going to use magic to get out of this mess.

Without giving himself time to second-guess his decision, Dan threw a fireball into the air directly above himself, immediately following it with a force bubble. Almost immediately, the fireball detonated, and Dan clenched his jaw, praying that his hasty trigonometry was accurate. Fire washed over the clearing, but the force bubble directly under the epicenter projected a cone of calm over Dan as the burning gases originally propelled in his direction by the first spell were deflected by the second spell.

Around him, all three stalkers shrieked and pulled back, their heavy, matted fur smoldering. Dan lunged towards the nearest one, pushing his runes to their limit and burning mana at a dangerous rate. Despite being temporarily blinded by the flash from the fireball, the creature sensed his approach and tried to swipe at him with its paw. Dan slipped under the gleaming scimitars of its claws and stabbed upward into the monster's unprotected lower jaw. The beast's shudder vibrated his hand through the hilt of his sword as the blade sank through its tongue and the tip lodged in its brain.

Dan ripped the battered sword out of the dying animal and shuddered as its mana flowed into him. The pink clouds at the edge of his vision deepened as the pleasure intensified. At some point, his mouth had locked into a feral grin. He whipped around and charged another stalker, only to dodge backward at the last second to avoid its claws.

"You're not so tough, are you?" Dan's voice was slurred. His cheeks felt like they were stuffed with gauze and his tongue was swollen, heavy, and alien in his mouth. Still, he didn't care. His eyes didn't leave the two mana-filled stalkers that cautiously circled him. "For all your size and strength, you're ambush predators. You don't know how to properly fight something that fights back. All I hafta do is get you in the throat and it's all over. Just like anyone else wearing armor, I just hafta hit the weak spots."

One of the stalkers leapt at him, its wings flapping once as it tried to bury him beneath its claws and bulk. Madness flashed in Dan's eyes as he launched another fireball, this one set to detonate beneath the stalker. A moment later, the blast scorched the monster's vulnerable underside and knocked it further into the air, forcing it to sail over Dan's ducking form. The night filled with Dan's unhindered laughter as he darted forward, two quick slashes severing the off-balance stalker's rear hamstrings before its companion could come to its aid.

Dan spun away from the collapsing monster and faced down the sole remaining intact stalker. The final beast was cautious. Whether it learned from watching Dan maim and murder two of its brethren or some other sort of natural instinct, it refused to overextend itself. Dan took the initiative and moved the fight away from the injured animal. It may not be mobile, but he still didn't want to get within the reach of its jaws or front paws. After everything he had been through, dying to a crippled stalker would be a little too embarrassing.

For almost five minutes, they engaged in a game of cat and mouse, the injured stalker mewling pathetically as it tried to comprehend why its back legs no longer worked. Dan took the opportunity to turn off all but the agility rune to allow his depleted mana reserves to replenish. Finally, as the euphoria from absorbing the two dead stalkers' mana began to fade, Dan grew impatient. This fight should have already ended, but this animal refused to commit itself enough to a strike to allow a counterattack. If it would leave him alone for a second, he could finish off the wounded beast and take the edge off of the headache that was growing to fill the void left by the mana high.

He pretended to slip, falling to one knee with a pathetic yelp. The remaining stalker lunged at him, only for it to clip a stationary force bubble hovering in the air. The creature's momentum spun it to the side where a Lightning Stroke took it in the wing. It spasmed briefly before recovering from the attacks, but Dan was already there. Runes blazing, he stabbed his sword into the stalker's side. The blade cut through the creature's thick fur and deflected off of an iron-hard rib to sink into its lung. Dan jumped back before it could retaliate. Already, its breath came in a shallow wheeze.

"Just die already," he spat out through gritted teeth before raising both hands and unleashing a Lightning Stroke through each hand into the six to eight inches of his sword's blade that were still exposed. The stalker spasmed as the conductive material directed the electricity into its soft internal organs. Dan took a step forward and grimaced at the growing mana depletion headache before unleashing a Flame Jet from each hand into the twitching creature's face, erasing its eyes. Its mouth opened and closed mutely as it tried to respond with paralyzed lungs.

Dan walked around the creature and pulled his sword out of it. The stalker rolled over onto its side and pawed weakly at him, but he simply stepped to the side before returning to the creature's front and stabbing the sword into its empty eye socket. It stopped moving, and a second later, mana poured into him, easing his depletion headache immediately.

His smile restored, Dan slowly approached the hamstrung stalker. As it sensed his approach, it tried to paw at the ground and flap its wings to escape, only for a Lightning Stroke followed by a pair of sword blows to sever them. Almost indolently, he approached the mewling creature. Looking it in the eyes, Dan shook his head.

"Friend," he spoke to the crippled monster with faux sincerity, "almost a year ago I lay exactly where you were. Crippled from a fight that I had no business being in. I only survived due to tricks and luck. You, my friend, never had any tricks other than silence, and you are fresh out of luck."

He stepped past a desperate paw swipe and stabbed the sword into the creature's eye. A moment later, Dan shuddered as its mana poured into him. He removed the sword and wiped the gore from it on the side of the downed stalker. He looked up into the night sky, barely feeling the cold wind blow past him while his entire being was wrapped in the pink warmth of its mana.

The rest of the night passed in a blur. Stalkers challenged him in ones and twos, and he slew them. After his fifth kill of the night, the mana completely took Dan and he lost count.

Fights began to blur together. Dan's sword seemed to rise and fall on its own as he fired spell after spell from his rapidly-replenishing mana into the vague forms of monsters that plagued Twilight's perilous nights.

At some point, he ranked up, the change in his mana providing a brief moment of lucidity while he stood atop a gaunt's mutilated corpse. He shivered, the monster's rapidly-cooling blood covering his face and chest.

The creature had tried to warp his mind, its powers entirely useless against the pink fog of mana and pleasure that accompanied his rampage. Numerous System notifications blinked, awaiting his attention as they indicated that it had tried and failed to seize control of his emotions.

He glared down at its corpse, trying to piece together exactly what had happened as billowing clouds of pink smoke crowded at the corner of his vision, whispering at him to give in to the ecstasy of the moment.

Dan blinked to clear his vision, only for time to jump and skip again. He had no idea where he was, but his left arm held the bottom jaw of an unwilling stalker. He was riding the struggling creature, forcing its jaw shut while he sawed through its throat with his sword.

Distantly, Dan noted that his arms and legs should be tired to the point of exhaustion from the constant combat. Maybe it was the near constant mana high, but he felt fine. Better than fine.

Then, the stalkers stopped appearing. Dan searched, but nothing would approach. At least in this small corner of Twilight's night, he was the apex predator, and the locals recognized him as such. After no more prey appeared for almost twenty minutes and the mana high began to wear off, Dan noticed Tanloff beginning to peak over the horizon. For whatever it was worth, he had survived the night.

He sheathed his sword and began his hike back toward the mansion, his body still tingling with the flashes of mana from his long night. He had to look like a mess, a mass of drying blood and bits of monster meat. Still, Daeson had set an impossible task before him once again, and he returned triumphant.

After about ten minutes, Dan found himself approaching the mansion.

Daeson sat in a chair, an empty cup in his hand and wine staining his tunic. At his feet, five empty wine bottles cluttered the floor. The elf was asleep. Of course he was. While he sent Dan out to risk his life, Daeson threw himself a pity party and drank himself to sleep. Dan cleared his throat, taking some satisfaction in watching the startled elf stumble and fall out of his chair as he tried to stand up.

"Daniel," Daeson sputtered, clearly drunk, "whatever is the meaning of this? Sneaking up on me like that and forcing me to spill my drink."

"The drink was spilled when I got here Daeson," Dan replied, wiping some of the blood from his face. "You were drunk and asleep."

"I am not drunk!" Daeson shrieked, swinging his right hand, vambrace glinting in Tanloff's light. An invisible hand swatted Dan. His nose broke with a sickening crunch and spray of blood as he was sent flying.

"I am sick of Jareth's accusations that I'm a drunk!" the elf ranted, pacing back and forth. "I drink in moderation, but I am not an embarrassment to myself or this institution. Without me bringing in new students and grant money, where would this Academy be? Nothing but a collection of indolent second sons of merchants. No, without me we wouldn't be on the map to begin with, and now you cast me aside. You say that I'm a drunk. That I fornicate with humans!"

"*Ha!*" Daeson was shouting, insensible to the world around him. "This board of regents disgusts me almost as much as humans do. So you will take everything from me, exile me to a tributary world to finish my research. This is not the last of me. *Daeson Amberell will not be silenced by the likes of you!*"

Dan stood up, pain radiating from his face. The blood from his broken nose dripped warm against the cooling gore from the monsters he had spent the night killing. This was the last fucking straw. Daeson was insane, but for a time, he was actually teaching Dan. Now, he was just a ranting menace that would kill him sooner or later. Probably out of madness and boredom rather than malice.

Really, it was Daeson or him. Dan had known that for a while, but the elf had always seemed unassailable. Too powerful to challenge in a straight fight and too resourceful to successfully escape. Now, though? He was drunk. So drunk he was debating an imaginary chancellor. Just standing there defenseless and full of mana.

Sparkles of pleasure and energy floated through Dan's body as he thought of the prospect. Each stalker had been a banquet of pleasure, but they were candles compared to Daeson's bonfire. This was really his only chance to get the drop on the batty old elf, and Dan would be a fool not to take it.

Dan slowly walked toward Daeson as the elf ranted to himself, doing his best to not draw the erratic elf's attention. He licked his lips. The salt and iron from his blood mixed with the stalkers' caused him to shudder. Soon it would be over. He would no longer be at Daeson's mercy, and he would have all of the mana that the decadent elf hoarded for himself. Really, it was a service to Earth. Dan dismissed the voice in the back of his head that warned him he was about to make a mistake. Daeson was a threat to them all, and with his mana, Dan would be that much closer to reaching rank 5 and being able to return home.

He stopped ten feet behind the elf and raised his left hand. Plus, the idiot was just standing there defenseless. Dan would be an idiot not take the opportunity presented to him. He unleashed a Lightning Stroke at Daeson's unprotected back.

The electricity warped harmlessly around a shimmering bubble encasing the elf. Dan stared blankly at his empty left hand.

"Treachery!" Daeson hissed, his golden eyes burning as he whipped around with ghostly speed. "I should have pegged you for one of Jareth's agents from the beginning!"

CHAPTER FORTY

Two Weeks Notice

"Fuck." The blood drained from Dan's face as he realized the impact of his actions. Daeson had never revealed how old he was, but based on context clues, the elf was at least two thousand years old. He'd just picked a fight with an archmage who had been accumulating power and experience since before the fall of Rome.

"You arrogant monkey," Daeson snarled. "I spend my valuable time and resources training you, and this is how you repay me? You were nothing when I found you! A corpse that didn't know it was dead, abandoned to this awful planet's night. Now you have a little bit of mana in you, and you can't remember everything I've done for you."

"Done for me?" Dan's initial terror faded into anger. "You've trained me, but you've never respected me. You've taught me a couple tricks, but I was never a student to you. I was a pet that you would trot out at a party so I could shake hands and fetch before you locked me away so that you could get on with your life."

"Isn't that what you are, Daniel?" Daeson's needle-like teeth flashed as he sneered. "Humans aren't Imperial citizens for a reason. Your lives are short, violent, and ruled by emotion. I thought I could turn you into something more, but instead there you stand, flush with stolen mana puffing out your chest like your meager accomplishments are anything but a reflection of my skill as a teacher."

"If I wanted to make something of my life while avoiding a volatile drunk, I would just move back in with my dad," Dan replied, raising his sword to a guard position.

"Is that all you have?" Daeson rolled his golden eyes as he took a few steps towards Dan. "Pathetic repartee and amateur spells? You're higher on mana than any dockside dreamflower addict, and all you can think of is to insult my drinking. I gave you the tools to prevent the addiction! How many times did I tell you to meditate to temper your emotions and develop emotional self-control? But no, you were too impatient. You'd rather spend that time hunting more monsters and stealing their mana before you were fully in control of yourself."

"What the hell is that supposed to mean?" Dan questioned, a hint of confusion leaking into his voice.

"Look at yourself, Daniel!" Daeson shook his head. "Your eyes are glazed, your cheeks are flushed, and you're acting like an impulsive fool. That's mana addiction and a bad case. At this rate, you're going to throw away everything I taught you to become some back alley serial killer, hunting other sentients for another fix. Really, it's for the best that I cull you now before you can soil my reputation by hurting someone."

Dan's eyes only had a second to widen as an invisible fist closed around him, pinning his arms to his sides. His armor rune flickered as the layers of force surrounding him glowed visibly. Even through his euphoric haze, Dan realized Daeson was right. He wasn't acting logically. Rather than biding his time, he was lashing out aggressively when he wasn't ready. All he had to do was put a sleeping draught or poison in Daeson's wine and sneak away. It wasn't like the elf actually checked the stuff. Instead, he had challenged probably the most powerful individual on the planet to a one-on-one fight like an absolute idiot.

"How are you still alive?" Daeson asked him quizzically, cocking his head to the side as he kicked an empty wine bottle away. "I'm squeezing you hard enough to kill an ordinary man. At the very minimum, I should have broken bones right now, yet there you stand, more or less all right?"

The pressure surrounding Dan increased to the point where he struggled to breathe and his armor rune began to fail. Frantically, he activated its high-performance mode, causing the field around him to shimmer brighter. Almost instantly, the crushing force alleviated enough that he could draw in a breath, but the rune drained his mana at a rapid pace. Although he had bought himself some breathing room, it was far from a permanent solution.

"Your defensive rune is more impressive than I originally thought," Daeson remarked, a slight wine-induced hesitation in his voice as he inspected Dan. "At least killing you won't be a complete waste, if I can get a chance to look at the rune-scripting up close. I seem to recall it being fairly compact, and any rune that compact that can absorb this amount of damage will be worth something to the war effort. Maybe not enough to get me reinstated to my faculty committees, but at least enough to give me a class or two to teach. Probably something on rune-script theory. Nothing terribly interesting or fun, but at least I will be back at the Academy."

Dan struggled, helpless but at least not at risk from Daeson's attempt to crush the life out of him. The elf stared at his efforts to free himself for about ten seconds longer before shrugging. For one brief second, Dan was free from Daeson's grasp, then an invisible wall of force slammed into him, sending him careening into the wall of the mansion.

Dan was on his feet in a flash, launching a Lightning Stroke at Daeson. The elf barely registered the electricity as it was again absorbed by the spell shield surrounding him. Dan, on the other hand, immediately noticed the cracked rib from Daeson's most recent attack. Each breath felt like a shard of glass lodged under his left shoulder. Still, inaction meant death, so he charged Daeson, sword in hand.

The elf drunkenly waved his hand, and Dan was hit by a pillar of force at knee level, tripping him and sending him into a sprawl at Daeson's feet. He tried to pull himself up onto his hands and knees, only to discover invisible shackles binding his hands and feet to the floor. He yanked his arms several times, trying futilely to free himself, but only bruising his arms. Even if he had the strength to break whatever spell Daeson had cast, he just didn't have the leverage to effectively use it while pinned face-down.

One of the elf's soft-soled shoes pressed into the small of his back. A second later, a metallic scraping sound signalled that Daeson had picked up Dan's sword from where he had dropped it. A weary sigh escaped from above him.

"Look at you, Daniel." Daeson spoke softly, a mournful note in his voice. "You kill a couple monsters and convince yourself that you're a force of nature. As soon as you think that you don't need me, you try to take advantage of my kindness and a moment of weakness to murder me. Never mind that you are a millenia too young to stand in the dueling ring with me. Now, here you lay, broken and defeated at my feet. It really is a pity."

A sharp pain stabbed the back of his thigh as Daeson used Dan's own sword to hamstring him. The armor rune held for a second, but it fared much worse against a blade than a diffuse bludgeoning force. Dan screamed. He flung himself against his bonds, cursing incoherently as the blood drained from his right leg and pooled on the ground around him.

"Do you know what the real shame is, Daniel?" Daeson asked the question rhetorically as he stepped over his bleeding and writhing body. "Ultimately, this entire futile exercise proves Jareth right. I argued that humanity was worth training and nurturing, and he claimed that you were blunt instruments. Almost as brutish as the Orakh we are sending you to fight. He told us that, even if humanity could directly use magic, it would be a mistake to teach you. That you would betray us and try to tear us down. I fought him for years before I was eventually exiled, but at the end of this sad saga, here I am. Forced to execute my own student and ultimately concede the point to him. Humans are, by nature, prone to treachery and other base emotions."

A brief whistle sounded as Daeson swung his sword again. Then pain erupted in his other leg. His voice was hoarse from screaming as he thrashed, both legs useless. Dan's bindings disappeared, but he was too exhausted to take advantage of his brief moment of freedom. Invisible puppet strings pulled him up into the air and rotated his body until he hung, two feet in the air and staring at Daeson.

"Really, Daniel," the elf drunkenly giggled to himself, "if this was how things were going to turn out, the least you could have done was to die in the night. It would have been much more dignified for both of us."

Dan stared at the elf, pain dimming his vision. Something deep inside of him snapped. Daeson might kill him, but he wouldn't make it easy for the arrogant fuck. He might not win the fight, but he would be damned if he went through all of this and didn't even make the elf bleed.

Daeson left Dan hanging in the air and walked over to where he had left his last bottle of wine and removed the cork with his pointed teeth. The elf took a long pull from the bottle, his back still to Dan. Then Daeson turned around. Without thinking, Dan launched a pair of Fireballs at the elf, set to detonate right behind him. In the fraction of a second while the Fireballs were in the air, Dan struck the front of Daeson's shield with a pair of Lightning Strokes.

Immediately, his head hurt from the sudden massive mana expenditure. Daeson's eyes grew wide as he raised his hand, reinforcing the shield as lightning rippled over it. Then, the fireballs detonated behind the elf. Time seemed to slow down as the spheres of fire overlapped with Daeson at their center, panic on his face.

Daeson must have empowered the shield where the electricity struck it at the expense of areas he considered secure. For a second, the shield held, but then the combination of heat and concussive force overwhelmed Daeson's rear defenses. Cracks appeared in the force field for a brief moment before flames washed over Daeson's back.

The elf screamed and dropped to the ground, his expensive robes burning freely. Dan's restraints disappeared, and he joined the elf on the ground. Grunting, he hefted his body up with his right arm while unleashing a Lightning Stroke with his left. This time, there was no shield to stop the electricity. Daeson twitched and spasmed uncontrollably as the current flowed through him.

Frantically, Dan crawled over to the elf. He had a momentary advantage, but if Daeson recovered, there wouldn't be a second chance. Hell, he was surprised there was a first chance. He didn't know if his former mentor was too drunk to fight properly, didn't consider him a proper threat, or some combination of the two, but a proper shield spell would have stopped any attack he could throw. Only Daeson's casual and sloppy defense after he had grown confident in his win had given Dan an opening.

The seconds seemed to stretch into years as he pulled himself to Daeson, watching the elf's convulsions fade. Fear filled him. Fear that he would be just a half second late. That this moment right here on the mansion's porch would spell the end of Earth's freedom. He would die here and no one would come back to prepare Earth for the coming war. That he would die with so much left unfinished and undone. Then his hand closed on the elf's vambrace just as Daeson opened his eyes.

Dan ripped the gauntlet off of the elf and threw it across the porch, just as a wave of unfocused mana poured off of Daeson. Without an attunement stone to focus it, the archmage's wrath was as threatening as a spring breeze. Dan punched his arm into the elf's chest and began activating Shocking Fist in pulses, stunning Daeson once again. Then his left arm gave out, and he collapsed on top of the twitching elf.

Blindly, he fished around his blood-slicked belt for a second before he found his hunting knife. He stabbed it into Daeson's side once. Then again and again. He lost count of how many times he embedded the blade into his former mentor and only companion for almost a year. Finally, he rolled off of Daeson and onto his side and collapsed, breathing heavily, waiting for the mana to hit him.

After a couple of seconds, he frowned slightly and with some effort pulled himself up enough to look at Daeson. The elf's eyes were open and blood stained his lips.

"Well, I'll be," Daeson whispered, his voice coming out as a wet gurgle. "You got me. I gave a speech like a villain in some play rather than finishing you off, and I let down my guard."

Dan didn't reply, eyes focused on the blood steadily flowing from the elf's chest and sides.

"Oh, don't worry, Daniel," Daeson's speech was interrupted by a series of bloody coughs. "I can feel the blood in my lungs, and my potions are too far away. I'm dead, and I know it. It's just a matter of minutes."

"Still," Daeson spoke between clenched teeth. "Let me finish my role as your master by illustrating my final lesson. When you have someone weaker than you on the ropes, don't dither. Finish the job when you have the chance, or you'll end up like me."

Daeson's eyes went blank, and a tsunami of mana crashed into Dan.

CHAPTER FORTY-ONE

Freedom

Dan lay in the mansion's kitchen, exhausted while the nanites worked on repairing his damaged legs. After the fight, there had been a brief moment of panic when he realized that he was trapped alone on the mansion's porch without the materials he needed to fix his severed hamstrings. For a couple seconds, he even contemplated eating Daeson's corpse to get the nutrients. Then the panic subsided enough for him to remember the Gravitational Easing spell and the mansion's kitchen. The crawl through the hallways, dragging his useless and still-aching legs after him, was bad enough, but the staircase was a fresh brand of hell. He wasn't entirely sure he would have made it without the spell reducing his weight or the nanites shutting off the blood flow to the severed vessels in his legs, but eventually he reached the kitchen. There, he ate almost two entire haunches of monster meat raw, counting on the System to protect him from food poisoning and disease.

Finally, after collapsing against the wall, he took stock of his situation. It had taken him almost almost an hour after the fight to come down from the mana euphoria. Already, a rather insidious craving for more had blossomed in its wake. It wasn't all-consuming, but every time Dan found himself slightly distracted or lacking focus, it would creep back and whisper to him. Usually, it took the form of logical excuses: "You can better help Earth if you are more powerful." "Twilight is a dangerous world, and you need to protect yourself," and "Think of the spells and runes you will be able to develop if you have just a little more power." Sometimes, it was much simpler. A brief feeling of longing, a shudder down his spine when he thought of killing something.

Now that he knew what to look for, Dan could see a worrying pattern of behavior over the last year. He had always been quiet and reserved. Upon reflection, he was probably too reserved. That said, there had to be a better middle ground between not standing up for himself and actively seeking out fatal confrontations. He did need to grow as a mage, and mana was an essential part of that growth, but he was acting like an idiot. No one in their right mind would have attacked Daeson when Dan did, even if the elf was drunk. There were a hundred and one better ways he could have done the careless elf in, if he actually put his mind to it. Instead, he let his desire to acquire more mana get the better of him.

"No," Dan mumbled to himself, frowning slightly. "I should call it what it is. Addiction. I'm acting like a junkie. Throwing morality and reason out the window to get my next fix."

He paused. Morality. Up until now, he hadn't even thought about the "why" of killing Daeson, just the "how." For whatever reason, he'd never questioned that the elf needed to die, but really he couldn't determine how much of that was his addiction talking.

Daeson was a pompous asshole, but he'd saved Dan's life. If the elf hadn't rescued him from that first night, even a normal predator would have been enough to finish him off, let alone one of the many stalkers prowling the area.

Almost as importantly, Daeson had been his only companion and mentor for almost a year. He hesitated to call the elf a friend. The man was drunk, used Dan for his own ends, and put him at risk almost as often as he protected him from harm. Still, over their time together, they'd grown comfortable. Near the end, he was like a mostly pleasant, but occasionally erratic and violent roommate.

Dan's knowledge of magic and runecrafting he almost entirely owed to the elf's inebriated tutelage. As much as he might want to deny Daeson's words, almost everything that Dan had learned before was nothing more than skillful fumbling. Daeson actually taught him how to systematically develop, improve, and mix his spells.

Dan sighed. Almost worse, now that he actually thought of it, the elf had been something akin to a friend. True, his relationship with the elf wasn't anything that he would call healthy, but it was distressingly normal for him. His mother, ex-girlfriend, college friends, Sam, and Nora, all of them used him to some extent.

They had their reasons, but every real relationship he'd had seemed to involve the other side taking more than they gave. Any time he tried to speak up, they would just raise their voices and speak over him. Before too long, he learned to stop speaking up and became an emotional punching bag. At the time, he had convinced himself that conceding to stronger personalities was better than being alone, but as he sat in the kitchen covered in blood, he couldn't help but wonder why he had to settle.

Dan thought back to the resolve he'd felt when Nora had betrayed him. He deserved better than this. It didn't mean that he shouldn't feel down about killing Daeson. Their friendship was real despite all of its dysfunction, but in the future, he would avoid that kind of toxicity. Speaking up for himself didn't mean being an obnoxious boor, but if he just let people tell him what to do forever, nothing would change. One person after another would send him into danger for their own gain until eventually his luck gave out and he didn't make it back. Danger wasn't something to avoid either, but there needed to be a purpose for it.

He reached down and scratched the newly pink scar tissue on his thighs. The nanites were knitting his skin and muscle back together at a slow, but visible rate. He sighed and mentally indicated to the System that it should leave the scar behind. Let it be a reminder of his addictions, both physical and emotional. It's true that he never would have gotten injured without the mana impairing his judgement, but he also wouldn't be on Twilight risking himself without Sam and Henry pushing him. He wouldn't have met either of them if he hadn't been working a dead-end job in the army to get away from his mother, and he wouldn't have been in constant danger on Twilight without Nora pushing him beyond his limits.

Up until now, he hadn't really taken agency over his life. Everything was one excuse or another as to why he had to do something. He had to work for the government in a dead-end job to pay off student loans, he had to go to Twilight to save Earth, he had to cooperate with Nora because he needed a local guide, he had to cooperate with Daeson or the elf would leave him to die.

His mind strayed back to his undergraduate general education philosophy class. The teaching assistant would never shut up about a French philosopher named Jean-Paul Sartre. Sartre believed in something called radical freedom, the belief that you are never without a choice. You might dismiss some of those choices as unpalatable or impractical, but through everything, Dan had always had the power to say no. There were a thousand times when he should have told the people in his life "no." It would have upset them, but ultimately that was their problem, not his. He couldn't afford to live his life paralyzed by a fear of interpersonal conflict any more than he could afford to let himself be shackled by an addiction.

Dan closed his eyes to meditate. He was hardly in the proper lotus position, instead slumped against the wall with his useless legs splayed out in front of him. Still, he remembered that Daeson had always emphasized the importance of meditation. The elf had never explained why until minutes before his death, but it would make sense that emotional stability and equilibrium would be a useful tool against the sudden urges and intrusive thoughts that originated from the addiction.

All it would take is a sudden flash of temper for him to lose himself in his need to acquire more mana. Becoming a mage would be walking a tightrope of self control as he tried to gain enough mana to truly matter, without turning into an uncontrolled mass of bloodlust with super powers.

As his senses began to fade, Dan smiled to himself. It was worth it, though. Already, he could do things that he had only seen in movies. Soon, he would be able to return home, and this time he would have the leverage to stand up for himself. He still wanted to work with Sam and Henry, but this time it would be on his terms. With that thought, time became meaningless as he slipped fully into a meditative state.

Some time later, Dan blinked his eyes open. His thoughts had a clarity of purpose to them that they had been missing for years. He tested his legs briefly and then, noting that they were healed, stood up. Even his body felt more focused. Smiling, he called up his status to assess his gains from the previous night.

<USER> Status
Rank 5

Body 6(8)
Agility 7 (9)
Mind 8
Perception 7
Spirit 43

Skills
Swords 8, Brawling 4, Archery 2, Runecrafting 5

Affinity
Space 12, Lightning 10, Fire 10, Gravity 6, Force 6

Enhancements
Armor Rune V, Strength Rune +2, Agility Rune +2

Runes+

Spells
Shocking Fist 9, Spark Field 2, Lightning Stroke 9, Spatial Shield 7, Flame Jet 4, Gravitational Easing 6, Fireball 8, Force Bubble 6

Dan blinked. That was… that was a lot more than he had expected. He had even made gains in mind and perception, stats that had remained static for the last two years. Maybe it was his recent epiphany and focus on meditation, maybe it was making it past the rank 5 milestone. Either way, it bore further watching. Still, he had cleared rank 5, and it was time to return home.

Dan searched the mansion and found himself a much better sword made of tungsten/mythril and covered in runes, as well as a new backpack. Then, with a slight pang of guilt toward Daeson, he began looting the mansion in earnest. Before long, he identified his biggest problem. Weight. He found a map that pointed his way back to Morganville, the nearest village with a teleportation rune, but it would be at least a two-day hike to get there. That meant sanctuary runes and no multiple trips. He tried to focus on lightweight, but valuable materials. Over the course of a couple hours, he packed enough gold to bribe his way into the village, a small amount of food, a selection of Daeson's most valuable books/scrolls, and all of the runecrafting supplies he could find. He wasn't sure if Earth would be able to duplicate the complex inscription pens in the near future, and it certainly wouldn't have the monster essences he would need.

Finally, Dan exited the mansion. After walking for about ten minutes, he paused and looked back at it. A small wave of sadness and nostalgia washed over him. As awful as Daeson had been, the elf had been his only companion, and the mansion had been his only home for almost a year. It never would have worked out in the long run, the elf was too self-interested and his plans a bit too distressing for Dan to go along with them indefinitely, but a small, possibly Stockholm-Syndrome-affiliated portion of himself regretted how things had ended.

Shrugging, Dan adjusted the straps on his new backpack and resumed his march. Morganville was a long way away, and he wanted to make good time before nightfall.

CHAPTER FORTY-TWO

Triumphant Return

The hike back to Morganville was largely uneventful. Dan spotted several monsters, but after eyeing him up, most wisely avoided him. Briefly, Dan pondered chasing them down, giving in to his almost instinctive desire to collect more mana. Deep down, he knew that those impulses came from the darker side of himself. There wasn't anything to be gained from slaying something as weak as a blood bear. The monsters might have been a threat to him when he first came to Twilight, but now, unless there were large numbers, they didn't pose that much of a risk.

Finally, the whiteish walls of the village in sight, Dan set down his pack and pulled out a water flask while he considered his options. At this point, he was probably more powerful than anyone in town. Of course, probably didn't mean certainly, and after his run-in with Daeson, Dan wasn't all that keen to pick a fight that he wasn't sure of winning. Even if he was the strongest person around, that didn't mean a whole lot if enough people ganged up on him. Given that he could see four guards by the gate, two on the ground, and two leaning on bows in a guard tower, Dan didn't want to force the issue.

Worse, as Dan wracked his memory of entering the town from months ago, he recalled Nora always arranging entrance for him. He didn't know if getting in or out of the town required a pass, a toll, or nothing at all. He couldn't help but mentally kick himself. Yet another example of how she had led him to rely on her in an effort to keep him helpless. Even with her using magic on him, it was inexcusable that he had never bothered to question her dragging him into overly-dangerous dungeons and never letting him even look at a map or interact with any strangers. She hadn't given him a moment of down-time, and every resident of Morganville that he interacted with was carefully selected and vetted by her. It was entirely possible that everyone he knew inside the town was working for Nora's employers, and he was none the wiser the entire time.

Dan capped the water bottle and returned it to his hip. Picking up his pack, he slowly circumnavigated the town, looking for a way he could sneak in. He was doing his best to put his naive and dumb days behind him so there would be no cheerfully trying to walk in through the front. He sighed. That meant going over a wall fast enough that he didn't get caught by one of the guards. Luckily, they weren't very attentive, and they walked their circuits slowly, but by Dan's count, their circuit only left him about five to seven minutes to get over the wall. It would be close, but with his magic, he would be able to do it.

He sneaked as close as he dared before hunkering down and pulling a blanket over the reflective metal of his armor and weapons. Just barely peeking over the edge of the blanket, he waited until the bored guard walked past and bolted towards the wall, praying that the man didn't turn around. Dan activated the high performance mode of his strength rune at the same time as Gravitational Easing and jumped.

He hit the wall, his armor rune dulling the impact from the collision. He slammed the looted sword into the smooth stone wall, grimacing as the handle vibrated in his grip as if trying to buck him from the wall.

Frantically, he searched for a handhold with his right hand, only to find nothing but unmarked stone. Dan 's left hand slipped by a fraction. No matter how strong he was, his fingers only had so much surface area. There was no way they would be able to hold him indefinitely. In a panic, he drew Daeson's sword with his right hand and ran some mana into it. The blade had a sharpness rune along with a couple others in a sequence that he didn't recognize. Dan wasn't entirely sure what the sword did, but he suspected that the runescripting would make it more useful in combat. The sword glowed purple and vibrated slightly in Dan's hand. He jammed it into the stone wall and blinked in surprise when it sunk in halfway to the hilt.

Quickly, he carved out a generous handhold before clumsily sheathing the blade and pulling himself up a foot or so. He let go of the wall with his left hand and flexed his fingers in an effort to return feeling to them before drawing the sword with his left hand and repeating the performance. The blade sunk into the wall like it was made of clay. The stone still slowed the magical sword, but it was hardly a serious impediment to the humming weapon. With a grunt, he pulled himself up.

Slowly, he repeated the process, handhold by handhold, working his way up the wall. At one point he stopped, pulling himself as tight to the wall as possible when the guard's footfalls signalled that one was marching by overhead. He held his breath, but the patrolling guard had other concerns.

After all, who expects a threat to be flush to the wall a mere ten feet beneath them? Frankly, the guard would have had to pause in his rounds and put his head directly over the edge to catch Dan. So long as he didn't give the man any reason to do so, getting noticed was unlikely. Still, Dan breathed a sigh of relief when the guard finally passed him.

Dan pulled himself over the top of the battlements and looked both ways. The guard would be coming back shortly, but he had a moment. He let himself fall over the edge of the wall, jamming the magic sword into it with both hands to slow his descent before he hit the ground. He needed to move fast. The scar in the wall might not be noticed immediately, but it was only a matter of time before someone spotted it. Still, Dan didn't imagine himself staying in Morganville for a minute more than he needed to.

He walked into the town's streets and tried to blend in. It worked, to a certain extent. after almost a year away from the town, no one was looking for him. But people gave him a wide berth. It was like the monsters on his way back to the village, there was just something about higher-rank individuals that gave off a threatening aura. It didn't matter terribly much to him; he wasn't here to chitchat about the weather or a local sports team, he just needed to get to the teleportation array.

Finally, after wandering aimlessly for almost half an hour, Dan gave up on finding the array on his own. He stopped to purchase some fruit from a vendor and idly asked the old man for directions. The grandpa's eyes flashed with fear, but he hesitantly pointed out the directions to Dan. After tipping him heavily, Dan was back on his way.

After another twenty minutes of walking, he found the array. Really, it shouldn't have been that hard, given that the array itself was a giant set of runescripting around a towering quartz crystal that glowed faintly with yellow light in the center of a cobblestone plaza. Even from where he stood at the edge of the promenade, space mana poured off of the crystal in a palpable way. Unfortunately, the runes had a metal fence topped in spikes running around it and a guardpost with a toll booth erected at the only entrance. Unlike the guards at the walls, these men stared both at the crowd of citizens going about their day and the rune itself.

Realizing he wasn't going to be able to slip past these guards, Dan fingered the hilt of his new sword while striding forward. Even if they were alert, Dan had survived a night without runic protection. A handful of mundane-classed humans weren't going to slow him down from what he needed to do. Plus, a quick battle here would keep his skills sharp and give him a quick dose of--

A hand grabbed his forearm, interrupting his thoughts. Dan

stopped, still concealed from the guards by a crowd of milling citizens, and glanced to his side. There stood Nora, her face white, staring at him with her mouth slightly agape as she held onto his arm. Dan could have easily pulled away from her even before he had enhanced himself; her grip was fragile and her arm shook. Instead, he turned to her.

"Nora," he said smoothly, glancing her up and down and noticing that she was still armed with a dagger, bow, and leathers, much as she was when they first met. "It's hardly a pleasant one, but I have to say it is quite the surprise to see you again."

"How are you alive?" She asked, eyes wavering. "I saw your runes fail! I know what comes out after dark. I've seen it myself, when they came for my friends and family! How did you survive? How?"

"Luck, at first," Dan shrugged her hand off of his arm and turned to face her. "I killed a stalker one-on-one, but it crippled me. Someone saved me and helped me transform myself. I'm not the same pushover today that I was when you first scoped me out as a mark. Even now, everything you're saying is really about you. 'How did I survive when your family didn't.' You aren't even taking responsibility for what you did."

"I didn't do anything bad, Dan," she pleaded, her voice quivering. "The Alliance of Free Cities needs to have information on mages of your caliber that wander through their territory. I had to lie to you to see if you were a threat to Morgan or the Alliance. You have to believe me, I never had a choice."

"Never had a choice?" He questioned her, incredulously. "You could have just let me be when you saw me out on the moors. Hell, once you realized that I was ignorant of everything on Twilight and not a threat, you could have dropped things. I probably would have still worked with you while trying to rank up. I made it clear that I didn't particularly care what I was doing so long as I was getting stronger. Instead, you messed with my mind and pushed me to the brink of destruction and now, months after you thought you killed me, you actually have the gall to play the damsel in distress?" He could feel the rage building within him as he barely kept his voice in check.

"It doesn't work like that for someone like me, Dan," she whispered sadly. "I can understand why you hate me. I'd hate me too, but I have my own reasons for why I need to get stronger. Morgan found me as a refugee and an orphan, and she took me in when no one else would. She gave me my class. Without Morgan, I don't have the backing or support I'd need to be anything. I'd be a beggar or a whore until hunger or disease did me in."

"I owe her everything Dan," Nora was crying as she searched his face for pity. Finding none, she continued. "I can't betray Morgan or her vision, Dan. I'm sorry about what I did to you, but I would do it again in a second for her. I can see your anger and feel the mana coming off of you. I know there's no way that I could beat you in a fair fight right now, and I'm not sure that I want to. If you're so angry at me that you want to kill me right here and now, I just ask that you make it quick."

She closed her eyes, tears streaming down her cheeks and raised her head to Tanloff hanging in the sky above.

How dare she, Dan fumed. *How fucking dare she.* After everything she did to him when he trusted her, she pulled this stunt. She had almost killed him, almost enslaved him, and tried to mess with the framework of who he was as a person. All of this while claiming to be his friend. She didn't deserve his sympathy. Like everything else, her sob story was probably a ploy. In her upturned face, he saw both his mother and his ex-girlfriend. He saw their passive aggression, their emotional manipulation, their emotional brinkmanship. He saw the way they would turn every minor mistake of his into an all-consuming ordeal and turn him into the villian of every story.

Mana flowed into Daeson's sword, causing it to glow and vibrate in his hand. Around him, the crowd of civilians began screaming and running as he brought the blade back. Somewhere, the guards were screaming at him to drop his sword and charging him, but it didn't matter. He would kill Nora for what she had done to him and finally vent the anger that had been building up inside of him for the better part of two decades. Once she was done, he would harvest the guards' mana and be done with this treacherous planet.

Dan swung the blade, his arm a blur. Inside him, a traitorous voice whispered to him that she didn't deserve her mana. It would be his here and now.

Dan's eyes widened, and he cut the flow of mana to his sword. The blade was moving too fast to stop the blow entirely, but he rotated the blade at the last second. With a loud *crack* the flat of the blade impacted on the side of her head, and Nora dropped to the ground bonelessly, clearly concussed.

He swiveled back to the guards charging him. Without really thinking, he triggered Lightning Strokes into them, causing them to twitch and spasm as they fell to the ground. In the back of his mind, the voice screamed at him. To finish off Nora, to take the guards' mana. To give in to his anger and become a butcher, consumed by the ecstasy of the moment.

Instead, he ran past the insensible guards towards the platform. Maybe the voice was right; maybe he should kill the guards so that they couldn't stop him. Maybe he should kill Nora. She certainly would have done the same to him. Still, that decision was for him to make, not the ball of addiction, rage, and hunger that grew in his psyche like a cancer. If he ever returned to Twilight, he would make his decision at that time. Not now, when it wouldn't truly be him making the decision.

He reached the array and placed his hand on the giant quartz crystal. Instantly, he recognized it as a battery, like the ones he had charged to get him to Twilight in the first place. Activating the System, he instructed it to feed Earth's location into the runes.

For a second, nothing happened. He frowned, trying to activate System again.

Verifying heart rate.
Verifying surroundings.

<USER> has access to a teleportation array and is not under duress. Coordinates unlocked.

At the entrance to the plaza, a platoon of guards charged in. By their heavily-enchanted silver armor and their efficient and practiced movements, Dan could tell that they were a cut above the guards he had fought so far. Each one of them was at least a rank 3. On their own, they were not enough to kill him, but in numbers, they were a definite threat.

More elite guards poured in after the initial wave. Sweat prickled at the nape of his neck.

Then, the array sucked the mana from him, energy flowing into the battery as the magical artifact powered up.

He smiled and waved as the energy swelled around him, and the fabric of space itself seemed to reach down and pick him up. The world around him spun, then it went white. He couldn't see anything, but he felt a tremendous sense of acceleration. Then, he was spat out of the air and landed on his hands and knees on good, old-fashioned cement.

The System chimed.

Welcome back to Earth <USER>

Wifi detected

Synchronizing

CHAPTER FORTY-THREE

Epilogue

General William Finch carefully set down the report and shook his head. It would have been easier to read the report on a tablet or a computer, but after Malaysian hackers had crashed the economy out of boredom eight years ago, he just didn't trust them.

You knew where you stood with paper. Ink formed a word, and that word stayed the same. No need to enable cookies, change his firewall settings, and whatever else his grand-daughter did to his computer so she could play *World of Magic Online*.

He didn't really trust the game or the concept of e-sports. He had spent a lot of money and influence "talking" to the Dean of Admissions at Wenning University to ensure that she got into a top flight marketing program.

It didn't have the same cache as an Ivy League school, but Wenning was still an elite school heavily recruited by the Fortune 500. Then, after she graduated with high honors, instead of taking the job with a consulting firm that William had quietly lined up for her, she went "pro" in *World of Magic Online*. He still didn't understand how you could go "pro" in a sport that didn't involve moving from a chair, but evidently she was quite good at it. Hell, she was making almost a half million a year in endorsements alone, and there was talk of getting her a movie deal.

Still, William didn't trust it. After his son and daughter-in-law had died in a train accident, Jennifer became his responsibility. He wasn't sure he had been the best parent to her, but he tried. Deep in his heart, he knew the fame and money from being a professional gamer was fleeting. Sure, she might become famous, somehow, for a couple of years, but he was sure it wouldn't last. It wasn't something solid and enduring like a dependable office job.

He wasn't sure if it was fair, but he blamed Henry Ibis, the mastermind behind *World of Magic Online*. Without that game, his beautiful Jennifer would have been a vice president of communications or a lobbyist by now. Someone with weight and importance in the real world. Instead, thanks to the seductive thrill of virtual reality video games, she was some sort of half celebrity, known only to the nation's castoffs and malcontents.

Another man walked into the room and stood at attention before William. The new figure was six foot even and in great physical shape, despite his salt and pepper hair. It wasn't like he was bulging with muscles, focusing on strength tended to be counterproductive if you didn't have the agility or control to harness it. Instead, he was lean with a sort of whipcord intensity to him that promised an explosion of violence to anyone who crossed him.

"At ease, Major Bowman." William spoke evenly. "I don't suppose you've had a chance to review the report from the Thoth Foundation? Apparently, they found a way to send an explorer to one of the aliens' planets and he came back with a whole book's worth of advice and dire warnings."

"I've glanced over it, General," Hans Bowman nodded in response. "It sounds like they've found a way to level the playing field a bit against the elves."

"Aliens, Major," William growled back. "A bunch of fanciful kids with their heads in the clouds can name them elves, but that doesn't mean anything. All we know for sure is that they come from space, and that makes them aliens and a threat to our way of life."

"Aliens then, General," Bowman responded. "Still, despite their lack of modern technology, we haven't really been able to slow down their incursion into Brazil. We made some initial progress once they first landed about six months ago, but right now it's a stalemate. We can't bring heavy equipment into the jungle to fight them, and even with rifles, our infantry is struggling against theirs."

"Machine guns aren't the greatest tools against force fields." The Major grimaced. "Worse, there are some reports that the animals of the jungle are mutating. Getting larger and more aggressive. Some have even begun to display mag... anomalous powers similar to the invaders."

"What about anti-tank weapons?" William asked, brow furrowed. "I recall authorizing quite a few recoilless rifles and missile launchers to our contingent in the coalition forces. If bullets don't work well on a forcefield, how about an armor-penetrating round?"

"They pack a punch if we can hit them," Bowman replied. "But that's a tall order. Even the humans among the aliens move as fast as an olympic sprinter. The el... more alien aliens might as well be panthers. They're almost impossible to spot in the jungle, and our soldiers swear that they've seen the things moving at almost fifty to sixty miles per hour. The coalition forces have already taken enough losses that only us and the Brazilians are willing to actually send troops into the Amazon anymore. Everyone else is content to form a perimeter."

"Didn't I tell you to just bomb the aliens and be done with it?" William asked with a frown. "Even if we can't get tanks out there, that's no reason why we can't just level their hideouts."

"Unfortunately, the Brazilian Government didn't give us permission," Bowman demurred. "While everyone did see how

effective nuclear weapons were in defeating the Siberian land-
ing, their President would prefer that the Amazon not be irradi-
ated. Normal bombers are having a hard time targeting aliens
through the foliage, but gunships work. Unfortunately, any heli-
copters that linger too long are getting shot down by the aliens'
magi..."

Bowman wilted under William's withering glare.

"Anomalous abilities," he finished weakly. "Right now,
anything that leaves the jungle is spotted by a satellite and
destroyed by a rapid response force with air cover fairly quickly,
but we are struggling to make any headway within the jungle
itself."

"It figures," William muttered. "Europe and Asia are too
passive, and the locals are worried that we'll wreck up the place
and leave without paying for their drycleaning. Still, forming a
perimeter? Around the biggest rainforest in the goddang world?
I can't even begin to comprehend what kind of idiot would okay
that kind of strategy. It's only a matter of time before there are
aliens wandering out of the forest into Columbia or Peru where
no one has any assets. No, the only option is to keep pushing the
aliens until they get the hell off of our planet.

"I can't say I disagree," Bowman replied ruefully. "We just
need something that can tip the advantage back toward
humanity enough that we can justify a new offensive. The rest
of the coalition nations are content to let the situation fade from
the news cycle now that the shock of the alien invasion has
blown over. Already, most of the world's population is going
back to business as usual, confident that someone important is
dealing with it."

He paused for a second, gritting his teeth as he tried to
dismiss his anger. William had been a general for over forty
years. In that time, one commonality haunted him. He'd fought
in dozens of wars and police actions, and he could have won all
of them.

Except the suits back home forced them to fight with one
arm behind their backs. Limited rules of engagement he could

deal with. After all, it wasn't entirely sporting to carpet bomb every hamlet and village full of poor schmucks while they were out herding their sheep.

The real problem was the lack of political will. When he asked for ten thousand men, they gave him five. When he asked for tanks, they gave him infantry fighting vehicles. When he complained about the material he was given, someone in appropriations found him something worse that cost an exorbitant amount, always to the right political donor.

"What did you think of the report from the Thoth Foundation?" William calmed himself as he asked the younger man. There was no purpose biting Bowman's head off. The Major was just doing his job, and truth be told, pretty much everyone called the aliens elves and didn't treat them like a proper threat. William and the rest of high command were really the only holdouts.

"It certainly gives us more information than we had before." Bowman shrugged. "Up until now, the aliens would only stop fighting long enough to inform us that we were part of the 'Glorious Tellask Empire' and that we should 'lay down our arms so that House Amberell could incorporate us.' Obviously, I'm more interested in their plan. The man they sent, Daniel Thrush. I have his biometrics from his time in the army. Whatever happened to him in the last two years, he's almost a completely different person. If we could increase the strength and speed of actual soldiers rather than some technician, our infantry would be able to fight evenly with theirs. It would be a huge step forward."

"I agree completely." William leaned back in his chair. "I'm still not sure of this joint enterprise they've offered. They 'activate the mana' of a hundred of our soldiers in exchange for aid in training and developing a hundred of their own. I already tried to talk them into making it all soldiers, but that asshole Ibis refused to discuss it. Worse, he let me know that he planned on selecting their hundred from the upper ranks of one of his video games, *World of Magic Online*."

"That is certainly an interesting choice," Bowman responded slowly. "The cost to us for training the hundred soldiers is hardly a factor, barely even a rounding error in our current budget. We can do all of this without Congress even knowing a thing. Still, I would prefer it to be two hundred of our soldiers as well. The Thoth Foundation hasn't done anything untoward yet, but this almost feels like us sanctioning their development of a commando division or something, and I really don't know how to feel about that."

"I don't like it at all," William growled. "That's how I feel about that. I've already tried to talk to my contacts about strong-arming them or nationalizing the technology, but apparently Ibis has connections. Connections that stretch higher than our current president."

"So, you mean..." Bowman began.

"Don't say it," William shook his head in resignation. "We never know when they're listening, and I don't want to deal with waking up to some shrouded figure by the side of my bed telling me to stay out of their business. It interrupts sleep and proper digestion."

"Very good." Bowman gulped. "If I may ask, sir, why did you call me into your office?"

"I'm going to agree to Ibis' proposal." William stood up and handed a box to Bowman. "Effective immediately, you've been promoted to the rank of Lieutenant Colonel and put in charge of the Starshield initiative. You're going to be our interface with the Thoth Foundation and the commanding officer of the hundred soldiers that get trained as part of the initiative."

"I just have one order before you begin," William grumbled. "None of this new age nonsense. I don't want any of Ibis' quacks waving those crystals of theirs at your soldiers and telling them that their chakras are out of alignment."

"But the report says that individuals who try to harness the aliens' powers without meditation become unstable and violent!" Bowman frowned.

"You can teach meditation if you want," General Finch

grumbled. "I want you to be the one assessing it, though. I don't trust Ibis. The man's slimier than a frog in a rainstorm. I just don't trust the rest of what Thoth is selling.

"It stinks of pseudo-science and communism to me. My ex-wife's yoga instructor was big on all of that shit. He said it freed the mind and stabilized the soul and chakra. It sure didn't stop him from putting his chakra into her. Now she's out in California living in some commune, giving classes in guided astral projection to a bunch of drugged-out hippies. No, Bowman, we want our men to be raw, have a fighting edge. So what if it makes them a little aggressive? This is America. Men here are supposed to be a little unstable and violent. It's good for the soul."

Bowman smiled nervously. Orders were orders.

ABOUT CALE PLAMANN

A lifelong fan of Fantasy and Science Fiction, I usually spent my nerdy energy creating overly elaborate homebrew RPG campaigns. As it became harder and harder to juggle schedules for a half dozen players, I eventually made the logical choice and just cut them out of the picture entirely.

Now I write novels. They whine a lot less about critical failures.

If you enjoyed what you read, please make sure to visit my website or reach out to me on twitter (where I talk about writing amongst other things) or join my discord where I almost exclusively* talk about my existing books/what I'm currently writing.

*There are also memes. Lots of memes.

Connect with Cale:
CalePlamann-Author.com
Discord.gg/xzgycqtFNe
Twitter.com/WritesCoco
Patreon.com/CoCo_P

ABOUT MOUNTAINDALE PRESS

Dakota and Danielle Krout, a husband and wife team, strive to create as well as publish excellent fantasy and science fiction novels. Self-publishing *The Divine Dungeon: Dungeon Born* in 2016 transformed their careers from Dakota's military and programming background and Danielle's Ph.D. in pharmacology to President and CEO, respectively, of a small press. Their goal is to share their success with other authors and provide captivating fiction to readers with the purpose of solidifying Mountaindale Press as the place 'Where Fantasy Transforms Reality.'

Connect with Mountaindale Press:
MountaindalePress.com
Facebook.com/MountaindalePress
Twitter.com/_Mountaindale
Instagram.com/MountaindalePress

MOUNTAINDALE PRESS TITLES
GameLit and LitRPG

The Completionist Chronicles,
The Divine Dungeon, and
Full Murderhobo by Dakota Krout

Arcana Unlocked by Gregory Blackburn

A Touch of Power by Jay Boyce

Red Mage and
Farming Livia by Xander Boyce

Space Seasons by Dawn Chapman

Ether Collapse and
Ether Flows by Ryan DeBruyn

Bloodgames by Christian J. Gilliland

Threads of Fate by Michael Head

Lion's Lineage by Rohan Hublikar and Dakota Krout

Wolfman Warlock by James Hunter and Dakota Krout

Axe Druid,
Mephisto's Magic Online, and
High Table Hijinks by Christopher Johns

Skeleton in Space by Andries Louws

Chronicles of Ethan by John L. Monk

Pixel Dust and
Necrotic Apocalypse by David Petrie

Viceroy's Pride by Cale Plamann

Henchman by Carl Stubblefield

Artorian's Archives by Dennis Vanderkerken and Dakota Krout

APPENDIX

FINAL CHARACTER SHEET - MICAH

<USER> Status
Rank 5

Body 6 (8)
Agility 7 (9)
Mind 8
Perception 7
Spirit 43

Skills
Swords 8, Brawling 4, Archery 2, Runecrafting 5

Affinity
Space 12, Lightning 10, Fire 10, Gravity 6, Force 6

Enhancements
Armor Rune V, Strength Rune +2, Agility Rune +2

Runes+

Spells
Shocking Fist 9, Spark Field 2, Lightning Stroke 9, Spatial Shield 7, Flame Jet 4,
Gravitational Easing 6, Fireball 8, Force Bubble 6

GLOSSARY

Andrea Cragson
Emily and Andrea Cragson are sisters, recruited by Nora to
round out the combat team she founded in Dan's name. Neither
Emily nor Andrea trust Dan fully, and their behavior toward
him is more than a little off kilter, but a desperate man usually
doesn't have his pick of allies.

Behemoth
One of the three major subterranean horrors that come out
during the short periods of Twilight's 'nights.' Behemoths are
huge gorillas, capable of destroying walls and warriors with
equal disdainful ease. They are easily the largest, slowest, and
most dangerous of the threats that plague Twilight's nights.

Daeson Amberell
A high level elf, Daeson has been exiled to Twilight. Once a
professor, his theories on human development were too radical,
leading to him being exiled from the core of the Tellask Empire.
Now he spends his days, half in a wine bottle, trying to prove
that his proposals regarding human magical potential have
enough merit for him to return in Triumph.

Daniel Thrush
An electrical engineer that works as a subcontractor for the
United States Army. Originally assigned to work on the
Research and Development of priceless alien artifacts after he
happened to be present at the Tellask invasion, he was quickly
forgotten once the investigation into the alien magitech stalled
out. Now, he is the only Earthling capable of using magic, and
in order to keep Earth free, he has voluntarily entered a portal
to go to a Tellask colony world and gain the Spirit he will need
to awaken the rest of Earth's magical potential.

Emily Cragson

Emily and Andrea Cragson are sisters, recruited by Nora to round out the combat team she founded in Dan's name. Neither Emily nor Andrea trust Dan fully, and their behavior toward him is more than a little off kilter, but a desperate man usually doesn't have his pick of allies.

Fireball
A spell that shoots a ball of energy that explodes in a large, concussive blast of flame and heat.

Flame Jet
A spell that fires a burst of flame from the caster's hands. More distracting and painful than deadly, Flame Jet does have a potential to start its target on fire.

Force Bubble
A spell that creates a ball of invisible and immobile energy.

Gaunt
One of the three major subterranean horrors that come out during the short periods of Twilight's 'nights.' Gaunts resemble skeletal horses and use mind magic to feed on beings happiness and pleasant memories, often leaving the catatonic husks, unable to withstand the horror's follow up attacks. Their magic is muted by, but still can pass through a ward circle.

Gravitational Easing
A spell that lessons the weight of gravity on the caster, allowing Dan to move faster, jump higher and dodge quicker.

Henry Ibis
A reclusive and enigmatic old billionaire, larger than life and beyond Eccentric. Henry founded and runs the Thoth Foundation. According to him, he has some help from "the Illuminati," but that's probably a joke. Maybe. What is true is that Ibis has

connections, wealth and access to technology far beyond Dan's wildest dreams.

House Amberell
A noble house in the Tellask Empire, House Amberell defends much of the warfront with the Orakh. Although House Amberell is powerful, it has steadily been weakened by a lack of support from the Imperial Court while the Orakh Horde wore down its armies.

Ishlar
A brutal and not terribly intelligent warrior that wields a rune-scripted club.

Lightning Stroke
A spell that produces an arc of electricity, dealing some burn damage to its target. More importantly it locks up the muscles it runs through, causing spasms and freezing the caster's foes.

Nora Strasshill
Nora is a human, native to Twilight; she is forced to work as a scout by various unsavory forces. On meeting Dan she immediately notices his potential, clinging to him in an attempt to link their fate together.

Paltai Amberell
Paltai Amberell a scion of house Amberell. An elven warrior, he is fairly low in the order of inheritance for the noble house and is eager to raise his standing. Paltai commanded the Tellask/Amberell expedition that found Earth, and, underestimating humanity's numbers, tried to invade on his own.

Samantha Weathers
A researcher and Dan's closest mentor and friend on Earth.

Shocking Fist

A spell that allows Dan to deliver an electrical charge to his target via direct contact. Basically the magical equivalent of a cattle prod.

Spark Field
A spell that produces a highly charged electrical field. It doesn't deal much damage, but it is enough to distract and annoy a number of opponents inside its area of effect

Spatial Shield
A spell that shifts space slightly, curving attacks every so minutely around the caster. Although it won't stop a direct hit, it's enough to blunt and deflect glancing blows and turn them into near misses.

Stalker
One of the three major subterranean horrors that come out during the short periods of Twilight's 'nights.' Stalkers resemble huge winged wolves, and move with almost absolute silence both in the air and across the ground except when they voluntarily give their presence away via howling. Stalkers move very quickly and are able to run down almost any person foolish enough to spend their time outside of appropriate wards.

Tanloff
A gas giant orbiting Alpha Centauri B.

Tellask Empire
The Elven Empire, thousands and thousands of years old and spanning almost all of known space. There are some pockets of independent space occupied by smaller space kingdoms, but there is little that can truly threaten the entire Empire. Perhaps that is why the Tellask don't seem to be takin the Orakh threat seriously, instead resorting to power struggles and petty games rather than focusing their full power on the invaders.

Thoth Foundation
A philanthropic organization pursuing the 'betterment of the human race.' To many, it is nothing but a vanity project owned and run by Henry Ibis, but those in 'the know' are aware that Ibis had access to some truly cutting edge technology and research. Perhaps enough to make an actual difference.

Twilight
A moon, tidally locked and orbiting Tanloff, a gas giant that circles Alpha Centauri B. Twilight is the home to a Tellask tributary world. Technically independent, Twilight sends wealth and soldiers to the Tellask Empire and House Amberell in exchange for military protection.

Viceroy's Pride
The voidship, renamed by Paltai Amberell, that led the failed assault on Earth